Cover design and Photograph by the Author

ISBN: 978-1-300-63553-6

10 9 8 7 6 5 4 3

To Andrea,
Thanks very much!
I hope you enjoy
it!

CONVERGENCE

Jody Aberdeen

TABLE OF CONTENTS

ACKNOWLEDGEMENTS

Everything about *Convergence* has been one great big learning experience, and though I've now leveled up for my future projects, I'm confident none of them will feel the same as this, my first fiction baby.

Special thanks to my original band of reviewers: Nikki, Julius, Aaron, and Michael. You helped get what was then a rickety ship into the water and helped to plug some pretty big leaks, and I'm forever grateful.

To Lucianna, for taking the time out of a crazy schedule to read version two in its entirety, and helping to turn this rickety boat into a flagship. Thank you!

To my fellow Wordslingers, who as of this writing include Lucianna, Ashish, Katie, Amanda, and Janessa. Thanks for keeping me driven, focused, motivated, and sane. We're all gonna make it.

Thanks to Tamara for being an awesome editor on this first project with me.

To my family, friends, and everyone who has in some way helped to shape this book since I started scribbling in 2008, thank you. This is for you. I hope you enjoy it. And if not, well, I'll just write something else. Enjoy!

CONVERGENCE

DREAM GIRL

Max stood facing southwest, toward the garden.

Their backs were to each other, but each knew — without touching, without speaking — that the other was there.

The compass rose had been painted on, fresco-style, into the concrete of the walkway as the cement had dried. Both stood near the center, five feet away apart.

Leading up to the compass rose from the west was a grassy path lined with many little shrubs, poplars and flowers. The path ran out at a hedge wall, the windward side of a great maze. Just beyond the hedge wall, the top of a gazebo was just barely visible in the mist..

The eastern horizon bled into the stratus clouds that wrapped the wounded sky like a bandage, turning what would have otherwise been deep blood red into a coral pink not unlike the bricks of the walkway he had just trod upon to get here. The air was clear but cool, and little plumes of fog drifted over the sea like roving gangs of phantoms. His eyes stung in the strange light, and he squinted to see around him.

Max took it all in. The mildew scent in the air was very real: fresh and clean and natural. Everything seemed sharp, high-definition, and when Max looked down at the compass rose, he could see the flaws in the cement, the details of the etching and the spots where erosion had chipped away the paint of the fresco.

Max turned around to face her. He caught a glimpse of her in his peripheral vision, only to see her vanish. He didn't know what had happened, just that one minute he was looking at the path and fog, set aglow by the horizon behind her, and then he was staring at that horizon.

Max found himself now looking toward the garden, and he realized something: in this place, they could never look directly at each other. Not yet.

And yet, without looking, he imagined Lucy's full, red hair crumpling carelessly in long strings over her slender shoulders as she looked around from where she stood.

"This is a dream," said Lucy, and her voice echoed throughout the park, in the vacuum.

"What else could it be?" said Max, and his voice followed hers over the trees, rocks, playgrounds and grass.

"It feels pretty awake to me," he heard her say.

"But we're not awake, meaning this is—"

something in between."

The answer was as satisfying a solution as either one of them was able to accept as they looked around the dreamscape.

"Where are we?" asked Lucy.

"The ocean, a park," said Max. "I wonder if we can wake up..."

"Do you really want to?" he heard her ask.

Max smiled. "No, not really."

They stood together, backs to each other.

Poof!

Max found himself staring south-southeast. From behind and to the right, farther away than before, he heard a giggle.

"What are you—"

Poof! He vanished again. Now he faced north.

"We're sort of dreaming, after all," said Lucy. "Why not have some fun?"

Max took a heavy breath, but couldn't help a smile, which only frustrated him further. Here he was, baring his soul, and all she could do was—

Poof! West-southwest.

"Stop that!" he shouted. "That's it."

Max snapped his head around and glared at her.

"Ah!" said Lucy when she reappeared, now facing the path.

Max grinned as she vanished him again. They took turns, vanishing and reappearing the other at various spots throughout the compass rose. He found that twirling around helped him spot her faster.

Soon there they were, spinning around like kids on the playground, jumping in and out of existence like flashes of childhood memory, like stars born and swallowed up and reborn again into the firmament with the speed and light of fireflies.

"Stop now. I feel sick," she said as they stopped.

Poof! Max reappeared behind and to the left of her, and they began their game again.

At one point, they appeared facing each other directly, and for that split second of being, Max and Lucy saw each other. Max glimpsed Lucy's amazing red hair and beautiful smile.

Then they stopped, both of them exhausted and nauseous, their sides hurting from laughter. They stood back-to-back once more, at the center of the compass rose now. Max faced southeast. Lucy faced northwest.

And they knew it was about to end. The dreamscape had started to shimmer at the edges.

"Is this as close as we can get?" asked Lucy.

"Let's see," said Max, with equal parts desire and tenderness.

He reached his left hand behind him and found her right. They touched.

"We're waking up," she said.

"I know," he replied.

"And you don't need to worry about anything," she said.

"Why?"

"Because what's real isn't only what anyone else says it is. What's real is also what's right here."

"But it's a dream."

"But it's our dream."

"I—"

"Close your eyes."

And Max did. And despite no longer being able to see the dreamscape, he did not wake up right away, as had happened across the thousands of sleeps he had had over the course of his three decades on Earth. As real as waking life, he felt Lucy turn him around.

Max felt the tip of her nose touch his, cool and moist and delicate, felt her hot breath on his face, felt the soft contours of her body against his. And he knew that this was a beautiful place, and a moment that was beautiful no matter what. In his mind, he declared it real. And reality never seemed so joyous.

Then a sharp trill.

The cordless.

It was ringing next to his head.

***

Maxim Sinclair shot up in bed and picked up the receiver. The cordless phone had now rung four times, and the call had gone to voicemail. He looked at the display. The message light was off.

Tabbing through the call history, Max found the number. An 831 area code. He had no idea where that was, but it definitely wasn't local. Wrong number.

He checked the time. 2:10 am. Definitely a wrong number.

Then, he tabbed past the name. FITZGERALD L.

Max lay back in bed, his heart still racing.

Of all the names…

Not Fitzgerald, of course. That was a fairly common name to anyone of significant Irish-American ancestry. And especially not the initial L for the first name: hell, Ls were positively in vogue these days, with all

4

the Larrys, Lenas, Lauras, even Leroys now making their way into the pages of airport novels and through the airwaves on radio and TV.

But FITZGERALD L., no...to Max, that was something different.

She'd been there, of course. He'd dreamed of her before, and much like this time, he never saw her face.

This time, though, it felt more...concrete. The emotional charge wasn't that of a dream, but more of a memory, as if he and she had indeed been standing there at that compass, not long ago...

Max started to drift off, the afterimages of the call display still glowing on his retinas.

FITZGERALD L....

FITZGERALD L....

The letters faded into a memory only a few hours old as Max, sitting on the apartment balcony, laptop in hand, watched the sun set around eight thirty. When you're falling asleep, sensations that you missed when you were awake often return to your awareness, clearer than the first time they appeared. The air that evening had been humid, and the clouds at sunset were gorgeous, shapely splatters of gray on pink. A thunderstorm was forecast to arrive some time overnight.

Max had been sitting there for an hour by the time he looked down to the papers in his lap. He picked up the top page and read it over. It had two columns drawn in blue ink. The column on the right listed qualities that he didn't want in a potential mate, all written down in random order as he thought of them. Examples included "close-mindedness," "micromanagement of my daily affairs," "conservatism," "emotional dishonesty," "laziness," and "disloyalty".

On the left column, next to each entry, was the polar opposite of those negative qualities "Openness," "acceptance of who I am," "ambition," "loyalty," "someone who promotes my growth," and so on.

As you continue to drift to sleep, images become as tangible as the real thing. Max watched himself flip to the last page, which, according to the "Soul Mate" website that had given him the idea, was supposed to be reserved for "How We Would Meet." The expected response was to write it out. Instead Max drew a picture: A beach at sunset, the sharp orange light intensified by the elemental reality of the dreamscape. There were no clouds on the horizon, and Max knew he was looking at the Pacific, an ocean his waking eyes had never seen.

And she was there, a lonely silhouette sitting on the rocks, waiting for him.

In his mind's eye, the picture became real. Max was there, at that beach, looking for her. He approached her, and she turned and stood up. Max could see brilliant scarlet hair caught by a fast gust of wind, blazing in the dying sunlight. Lost in the glare, her face seemed to possess a light of its own, the light of a soul long lost to him that he had finally found.

As he walked to her, though, the image stopped moving, and Max found himself looking at a still image drawn in smudged ink on the page. He put the papers back in order, starting with the cover page, titled (appropriately) THE MATE LIST.

And there, on the last page, scrawled in capital letters almost as an afterthought, was her name. LUTHIEN FITZGERALD. An unusual name for a soul mate, taken from Tolkien's storytelling. Then again, Maxim was also an odd name. People called him Max. He figured, all things being equal, people would call her "Lucy."

Max kept the Mate List in the back pocket of his laptop bag, and carried it with him whenever he went to write or had other work to do. The exercise called for him to take the list out whenever he felt doubts about what he wanted out of life, or whenever the loneliness took him. That was probably the reason why Max had forgotten about it: though he'd felt lonely, it didn't make a lick of sense to him that thinking about what he didn't have would somehow make him feel better. Especially considering how damn near impossible it was for anyone to live up to what he had written. Until that afternoon, Max hadn't looked at it in months.

If dreams aren't the most stable creations, they're at their most flimsy in those few moments just before entering deep REM sleep — liable to snap, like a balloon tapped by a scalpel, at the slightest disturbance. However, the sound of the phone ringing anew was anything but "slight," and the dream-memory completely vanished as

Max's eyes flew open yet again. Still holding the cordless in his hand, Max checked the display. The same 831 number. And then, FITZGERALD L. He then looked at the time. 2:13 A.M.

The ringing continued. Two more and it would go to voicemail. Max had the feeling this person would just keep calling no matter how many times he let it go. Max pushed "Start."

"Hello?" he said.

Nothing at first. "Hello?"

"Um...hi there."

A woman's voice.

"Hi."

Dead air.

"Um...is this Maxim Sinclair?" she asked. Familiar voice.

"Speaking." Max caught a tickle as he spoke, and he cleared his throat.

"Who is this?"

"Um..." He heard her clear her throat. "This is Luthien Fitzgerald. But you can call me Lucy."

***

The dead air ensued for about a minute before anyone spoke.

"Hello? Still there?" she asked.

Max's tongue fumbled over his lips before finally gaining traction with his words.

"Yeah, umm...who is this?"

"I said, this is Lucy Fitzgerald."

"Lucy Fitzgerald," repeated Max.

"Mmhmm, Lucy Fitzgerald."

"But...you're not real."

Pause.

"It's funny you should say that, because I didn't think you were real either. When I started looking for you, I thought I was off my gourd, but, well, we're talking."

Pause. Outside Max's window, a car passed by the building, after which the night was absolutely mute.

"I am real, though," said Lucy. "And I've been looking for you."

"Where are you calling from?"

"Carmel, California," came the reply.

Dreaming. Still asleep. That's what's happening. New dream.

"This is Maxim Jeffrey Sinclair, right?"

"Uh...yeah, that's right," Max replied.

"And you're divorced from a Dinah Devonshire?"

"Now how do you know that?" asked Max, his brain snapping awake. "What, did you check my court records? You couldn't have Googled that about me."

"This is true. And that's the trick, because I didn't find any of this out from researching you. My source is more...reliable. In fact, that's why I'm calling now. Do you have a minute?"

He checked the clock again. "It's now 2:14 in the morning, eastern time, just FYI."

"Right...I'd forgotten the time difference, I'm sorry."

"It's okay," said Max.

"Um...I know you've been looking for me and, like I said, I've wanted to find you for a long time. There's a lot that we need to talk about. So why don't I call you back tomorrow?"

"Uh..."

"During better hours."

Max rubbed his eyes. The sleepy haze in his brain matter hadn't quite cleared out. "I'm working until five. That's, uh, 2:00 PM, Pacific Time."

Lucy's voice brightened, grew louder.

"Uh...great. That's cool. I'll give you a call around eight o'clock. Your time." She paused, and then, almost as an afterthought, ended the call. "Talk soon!"

Click.

Max didn't push "End" until he heard the "off the hook" signal. He put the phone back in its cradle and lay back in bed, staring up at the ceiling in the lamp-lit room.

Had that just happened? He picked up the phone and checked the message history. Yep, there was that 831 number. Monterey County, Max remembered now. It was on the rocky Pacific coastline, as California as one could get without the glitz of Hollywood or the sophisticated, hippie charm of San Francisco. Somewhere in between both. So whoever she was, she was real.

Could he have told someone about his list? Was this some kind of trick? No, that didn't make sense either. No one else knew about "Lucy Fitzgerald." None of his friends ever read the list, and up until ten minutes ago, the pages of the list were the only places where Lucy Fitzgerald existed.

The surrealism of the phone call took its toll. The human mind tends to shut down in strangeness. As Max found himself fading into the black, he concluded that this was especially true at 2:20 in the morning before a Monday workday.

Blackness.

And then, lightning.

Max's eyes flashed open. He got out of bed, gingerly avoiding the clothes and other items lying on the dark floor of his messy bedroom and went out to the living room for the list. Finding his laptop bag, he flicked on the lamp and found the page.

Scrawled on the next-to-last page, Max took a breath at the third-last line.

Luthien Fitzgerald will find me first.

***

"I call 'bullshit,' guy."

Nathan D sipped his Corona and stared out at the great lake as Max watched. Nathan D, a former fullback with trimmed curly blond hair, was taller than Max with a layer of fat over his once toned muscles, and a proclivity for wearing pink business shirts now that he was settled in at the consulting firm.

Beside him, the other members of their college crew who decided to meet for lunch beers and to hear about Max's latest crisis sat watching the exchange. Steven — short and skinny, with Travolta-like black hair and wearing a t shirt and ripped jeans — and Michael — a bit more portly with Latino features and wearing a golf shirt, slacks and glasses — had known Max for years. Max was pretty sure Nathan D had just said what was on their minds but that neither had wanted to say out loud. Only the most sporadic clusters of lunchtime clientele sat near enough to them at the Duke and Duchess, so their whole conversation could be a little more heated than normal without worrying about offending other patrons.

"What do you mean, you call 'bullshit'?" asked Max. The summer sun was bright on the lakeside patio, and their table had no umbrella.

Nathan D held up his arms as if Max had just asked him if the sky was blue.

"I call 'bullshit.' It's that simple," he said.

"I have the call record saved on the phone," said Max.

10

"It's got to be some kind of scam or a prank or some other thing like that."

"How?" asked Max, "Nobody else knew about the list until today. You guys are the first people I've told about that — and, by the way, I'd appreciate it if you could keep that under your hats."

Michael, Steven, and Nathan D all exchanged glances with that same knowing grin on their faces, and Max rolled his eyes.

"Fine, whatever, feel free to use it against me at next week's poker game," continued Max as they chuckled, "but the point is, there's no way she could have known about it. Unless, of course—"

She's the one?" said Steven. It was Nathan's turn to roll his eyes. Max looked Steven in the eye.

"Yes," he said. "Well, I mean, that's one possibility, anyway."

"Max," said Michael, leaning forward, "I get that you believe in this metaphysical New Age mumbo jumbo, but—"

"What mumbo jumbo? The list? It's just an exercise, I told you, that I—"

"Yeah, that you did after Dinah moved out. Fair enough," continued Michael. "But to hear you talking about that phone call, and the amazing coincidence with the names, you sound like you really believe this crap."

Max shook his head, sipped from his bottle, and gestured with his arms.

"What's not to believe, Mike?" asked Max. "It happened to me, and it all happened in sequence. Yesterday afternoon, not even twenty-four hours ago, I decide to take out the list and look at it. I go to sleep, then I get the phone call, and it's her. We talk, and she tells me she's gonna call me back tonight at eight. This isn't me making shit up, bro. It happened."

That silenced Michael, leaving the way open for Steven to enter the discussion.

"That's messed up, Max," he said.

"You think?"

"Are you going to call the cops?" asked Steven.

Max paused, thinking it over.

"No, not yet, anyway," he replied. "I mean, all it is so far is a phone call. I didn't get the impression she was crazy from how she sounded. It was just a normal phone call and I didn't feel I was in danger. It's what she said that's bat shit."

"But now the thing is, what do you think she's gonna ask you to do?" asked Steven.

Max looked at Steven for a few seconds. Good question...

"I really don't know," said Max, finally, "but I mean, what if this is for real? What if she's—"

"All right."

Nathan D stood up, scraping his chair back and stopping all conversation as the boys looked up at him. As long as Max had known him, he'd had a penchant for appearing like a bigger douche than he actually was. Most of the time, it was unintentional.

Nathan D downed his beer and took out his wallet, then paused after setting down a ten note, no doubt realizing he'd been louder than intended.

"Sorry, it's just my lunch hour's just about up", said Nathan, who then took a breath. "Still, though, Max, this is exactly the kind of thing I was worried would happen after your divorce."

Max flushed. He and Dinah had been over for well over a year now, but to have Nathan use the D word in this very public place still embarrassed him.

"And what kind of thing is that?" asked Max.

Nathan D hesitated at first, then spoke.

"Desperation."

Michael and Steven were bug-eyed. Max, though, wasn't as surprised that Nathan D had said it, as much as that he'd chosen now

12

to express what he'd so poorly hidden below the surface of all the Dinah chats they'd had since the split.

"That's right," continued Nathan D, "I said it, and I feel pretty fuckin' guilty saying it, but you know I'm your friend, and it's because of that that I don't want to see you becoming one of those guys. The ones who were with a girl for a long time and now have no idea how to live without them now that she's gone, so they run off to the first sexy shiny object they see that promises to give them exactly what they think they want."

"Is that what you think—"

"I'm not finished, Max," said Nathan, and now Max felt genuine irritation at his buddy's rant. "Look, I know you, guy. I was there when you proposed to Dinah. I was three feet to your left at the wedding, and I'm telling you, it's okay to feel desperate, and lonely, and like a failure…at first. But it's been over a year now, and you've dated how many girls?"

Max didn't budge, but watched as Nathan D made a goose egg with his thumb and forefinger.

"Zero," said Nathan D. "So I'm glad that you're showing a new interest in chicks, dude. It's a sign that you're all patched up from Dinah and ready to go. But not this chick. I've seen this happen all the time: she's gonna take you in, get you hooked on her, and then, when you're way too far in, ask you for something big. Credit card numbers, money, whatever, and once she gets what she wants, she's gonna leave. Either that, or she's one of these fucked-up emotional black holes who you'll never meet in person, but every time you try to leave, she'll tempt you over the phone with dirty talk or something else to keep you from finding someone new in real life."

"C'mon, Nathan," said Steven. "That's the kind of shit that only happens on the web. This is real life!"

Nathan D turned to Steven. "And how do you think she got his number, huh? Knew about the divorce being settled? Ever heard of

13

'social engineering scams'? There's so much information out there, it's not hard to find a phone number, even the other things, with the right connections. But—"

Nathan D turned back to Max. "I'll only ask this much. She's gonna call you again tonight, right?"

Max didn't budge at first, then he nodded.

"Ask her some smart questions," said Nathan D. "See if you can't trip her up on something. And whatever you do, if she asks you to do something for her, don't fuckin' do it. I will seriously slap you across the face if you do anything to hurt yourself."

Nathan D checked his watch. "Okay, gotta buzz," he said, then softened his tone as he extended handshakes to Michael, Steven, and then Max, who all stood up as he left. When he gripped Max's hand, Nathan D pulled him into a one-armed bro hug. "You know I love you, dude. Be careful. We'll talk later."

With that, Nathan D strode back to work, leaving Michael, Steven, and Max at the table. Max was still a little pissed, but it was fading with each second.

"The guy still thinks he's team captain," said Steven.

"No kidding," said Michael, who then turned back to Max. "You wanna know what I think?"

Max sipped the last out of his beer, tilting his head back to get every drop, and then plopped the empty down on the table.

"Sure," said Max, "I didn't play hooky just for the lunch beers."

"I think there's no harm in just getting more information, like what Nathan said," said Steven. "But I gotta ask, how's the other thing coming along?"

Max looked away to the lake. The other thing.

"It's…chugging along, I guess," he said. "Sometimes the ideas just don't flow, so the story just stays where it's at."

"So you haven't worked on it in a while, you've just been—"

"Yep, going to work and coming home and doing nothing," said Max. "Been like that for a few weeks now. Part of my new program to decompress."

"So work sucks donkey balls. I get it," said Michael. "But c'mon, Max, why work an office when you can make millions off of something that you made yourself? Isn't that the big reason why Dinah wanted out?"

Max sighed. "Dinah wanted out for a lot of reasons. The story wasn't one of them. She didn't know about it."

"No," said Michael, "but your being utterly miserable at work was the thing. Max, I'm going through the same thing as you. Difference is, I'm stuck doing what I'm doing because Leslie and I have a mortgage and two cars. And I don't have a thing. You've got a thing: it's writing."

"Mike, I don't even know if it's gonna be a book yet," said Max. "All I have are scrap sentences here and there."

"Still, it's a good hobby," said Steven. "Nathan's right, we're here for you, man, but we're getting a little tired of seeing you so lame. You're still just—"

"A shadow of my former self," said Max, finishing Steven's sentence, "Yeah, Mom still says that to me."

"And I know a broken life plan isn't something you fix overnight," said Michael, "but I don't want to see you just 'chugging along' five years from now. None of us do. You're as talented as the rest of us, and you know it. Or maybe you don't, and that's the real problem. So, you should write the book and get it published."

"Or, better yet," said Steven, "make use of that anthro degree somehow. Writing's not a real career option."

"Uh, Steve," said Michael, "I think if there was a way he could make money from anthro, he'd have found it by now."

"Not really," said Steven, "Do you know that something like sixty-three percent of anthro grads end up as CEOs?"

15

"Now you're just making shit up," said Michael.

"Actually..."

Max let the both of them talk at each other for a short while, not like he had much choice in the matter. He was grateful to have friends like these, especially this late into his twenties, when the closest people to you tended to be the ones who stuck with you from college, and the connections made with new friends at work didn't seem nearly as strong.

Still, this wasn't what Max had called them here to talk about.

"I appreciate that, I really do," said Max, finally cutting across the two, "and I'll do better to work on getting my shit together, but before I do, before I can, there's still the little matter of the phone call. What do you guys think?"

Michael and Steven, even though they were separated in age by at least four years, looked at each other with the same expression then looked back at Max.

"There could be something cool happening here," said Michael, "but if she's gonna call anyway, Max, just follow Nathan's advice. Don't give her money, don't agree to meet with her, and don't let her hang up without getting some more information about her."

"Yep, exactly that," seconded Steven, "I think you're only as vulnerable as you want to make yourself."

Steven checked his phone. "Okay, I gotta get back to the shop."

"Me too," said Michael.

They got up, settled their checks, and shook Max's hand.

"Be safe," said Michael. "Call us if you need us."

"Thanks," replied Max.

"And, dude," said Steven, "if you do decide to hook up with her, don't forget a rubber. Lots of diseases out in California. Just sayin'."

"Um....thanks, Steve," said Max, and watched them leave.

Sitting back down at the table, Max added his own cash to the bill and stared out over the lake. The sky was clear and the glints of

16

sunlight reflecting off the water stung him right in the back of his eyes. He looked away.

Michael, Steven, and Nathan D were all as different kinds of friends as you could have, and yet they somehow reached a consensus not seen since their fraternity days. The message was clear: whatever's happening here can't be good. Not at all. What could Max say to that?

Max checked his watch. Just after one o'clock.

Seven hours to go….

***

Returning home later that day for a quick microwave dinner before heading to the gym, Max checked the phone log again. No one else had called, and the 831 number was still there. Definitely for real.

After a quick workout, Max came back, showered, and put on his t shirt and shorts, typical summer home wear. Finally settling down to his living room chair, the phone right in front of him on the coffee table, he checked the time. 7:56 P.M. Not too shabby, considering all he'd gotten done.

And he waited.

Ten minutes passed. Nothing happened.

Outside, the street soccer kids fought over what seemed to be a disputed goal. Above him, someone was dragging a chair against the floor, unaware of how much noise they were making for the tenant below them. Cars drove past in the distance while the sun still shone at its summery high. It was a pleasant evening.

What if she wasn't going to call? Max asked himself. That would certainly make Nathan D feel better. Probably the others, too. Maybe this really was some kind of psychosis. Then again, if he'd invited any of his friends back to look at the call display on the phone, they'd see the exact same thing.

And, as always, there were the six words on his list that rose up to meet every feeling of doubt that came out of Max's reflections. Against those words, logic had no weapon.

Lucy Fitzgerald will find me first.

The phone rang.

Max's shoulders twitched at the sound, but he calmed down, took a breath. He checked the call display. 831 area code. Then, FITZGERALD L. He clicked the "Talk" button.

"Hello?"

"Hello Maxim Sinclair. It's Lucy."

Same voice, but much more upbeat and cheerful.

"So...you are real, then?"

Laughter.

"Yep, you bet! Don't worry, a big part of me can't believe that I'm talking to you, either. I was pacing for the last ten minutes wondering if last night had really happened. It's...well, it's just as crazy on this side of the phone, Maxim. Don't worry, you're not the only one."

Max had to smile. "You know, you can call me 'Max' if you want, unless you want me to start calling you 'Luthien' again."

More laughs. "Sure, no problem, Max."

"Listen, um…" Max thought what he wanted to say. "Did someone put you up to this? I mean, did Dominic or one of my other friends find you on Facebook or something and give you my number?"

"Uh, nope. I'm not on Facebook. Who's Dominic?"

There's my answer, I guess, thought Max.

"Oh...okay...then how did you find me? You told me last night that we'd met before."

Pause.

"We have...well, not so much me and you, but I met...well, it's complicated. I'm sorry, last night I was so happy to have you pick up the phone that I said more than what you're ready for. But you'll figure that out in a while. Listen."

18

Max heard her clear her throat. "I told you that I wanted to talk to you, and I'd like to meet you in person. You with me?"

"Not exactly," replied Max. "I have no idea who you are. What makes you think I'm going to drop everything to come out to see you in California? The only reason I'm even talking to you is because—"

"You have my name written down on a piece of paper that describes your ideal mate."

Max stopped, then pounced. "That's right! Seriously, who put you up to this?"

"No! No one! I know it's confusing, but no one put me up to this. I know about your list because…someone told me about it."

"Someone?" asked Max.

"I'm telling you, I'm real, and I'm for real. You want to know why?"

"Why?"

"Because I've had you written on some papers I've been keeping on my table for the past few months."

Pause.

"Okay…"

Neither of them said anything for about thirty seconds, until Lucy spoke up.

"Um, this is kind of a long distance call, one of us should say something." Nervous laugh.

"No, I'm sorry…no, you're right, um…" said Max. "So, you've been looking for me."

"I have…" said Lucy.

"How can this be possible?"

"I don't know. I didn't think it was."

Max heard her clear her throat before she continued.

"A few years back, I had dated a long string of boyfriends, but none of it went anywhere. My last breakup…it was pretty bad, so I took someone's advice and wrote down all the qualities I wanted in a soul mate. Then for some reason, I named this person 'Maxim Sinclair.' I'd always figured it was just something I'd made up that was just a pure exercise. But then, not long ago, I met...someone who told me you were real. It wasn't all that long ago. I was walking along the shore, and there was...this person. We talked. He told me who he was, that he was only here for a short time." She cleared her throat. "Max, he told me things about you — what you like, what you dislike, all of your favorite things in the entire world, what you are looking for in a life partner — and later, when I went back and checked my list, all of the things he mentioned were there. One of the other things he told me was that you also had a list of those qualities, and that if we compared them, they would be the same. That was because we really were connected to each other in life. Sooner or later, we would find each other."

"That's...that's incredible..." said Max.

"I know..." Another pause.

"You know something," said Max, "you sound so different today than last night."

"Ha, yeah, I guess I was nervous. Sorry, that was the dumb blond in me."

"You're a blonde?"

"Well, naturally. I dyed it red. Then people think you're crazy, they don't mess with you."

"Don't look now, but being a redhead is one of the items on my list."

Lucy giggled, and the sound was so pleasant, like healing waters...and Max had to shake it off.

"No, no, no...this...this still sounds crazy. Tell me more, what happened to this guy? He knew your name and mine. What was his name?"

"Well...I know it, but you'll have to trust me that as unbelievable as all of this is, this is the weirdest part of it, and I can't tell you about it

20

because you'll just dismiss the whole thing. Can I just leave this part out?"

"Luthien...Lucy, sorry," said Max. "You need to understand, and I think you do, where I'm sitting. I'm on the other end of the phone with a person who's got her name on a list I told nobody else about until today, who says that she's real, who's been looking for me, and who has the same list of soul mate qualities as mine. And somehow, even though this is the craziest shit I've heard pretty much ever, you've managed to keep me on the phone wanting to find out more. Trust me. At this point, if you told me you were the President, I'd listen."

"And if I told you that the person I met was you, would you still listen?"

"He was...what?" said Max.

He was you."

Pause.

"That's not possible," said Max. "I haven't left home for a year now. I was here last week."

"I know," said Lucy. "But I also know that that this person, also called Maxim Sinclair — but 'not the one on your list' was what he told me — knew a lot about you."

Max chose his next words carefully, his writer's mind searching for the most eloquent way to say what was exactly on his mind, so there was no misunderstanding.

"Bullshit."

A pause on the other end of the phone. "What?"

"I call 'bullshit.' I can't believe...no, I don't believe that."

On the other end of the phone, Max heard a sound that could have been a laugh, a scoff, static, or a combination of one or more of them.

"Get your list, Max."

"What?" said Max.

"Get your list."

Max looked over to the desk where he had left it this morning. He went and picked it up.

"Got it."

"Max," said Lucy, who then sighed before speaking. "I know how unreal all of this is, so I'm going to say this clearly, so that you know how serious I am. Look at your list. I'm the person you're describing. I don't even need you to read the qualities out loud to know that. And that's because right now, I'm holding a list in my hand that's all about you. Don't think there's not a part of me that thinks this is absolutely batshit crazy, because that's how I feel. But I follow my intuition, been doing it my whole life, and sure it's led me into the shit now and then, but can you deny the sheer coincidence?"

"No...it's incredible. But it's gotta be a trick or a dream or—"

"It's no dream, Max, and it is no coincidence. No trick. I'm just as awake as you are. I'm just as sane as you are. And I was just as skeptical as you are. I woke up, went to work today — I run a yoga studio — and came back to my place to call you, to give you a call because it was the only time you could talk, because I called you last night and you answered the phone. And if that's not real enough, the phone bill will be your wake-up call — well, it will be for me. We've been looking for each other for a long time, Maxim Jeffrey Sinclair, and I want to finally meet you."

Max heard Lucy take a breath.

"I'll let you go for now. Think about it. I'll wait for you, but not forever."

Max mulled. The air in the apartment felt heavy. Electric.

"Okay," he said.

"Good. Have a good night, Max."

The line went dead.

BAD TWIN

On the train, Tommy Thrones adjusted his duffel bag and looked up from his journal.

No one else sat in the car. When he'd last checked the time, it had been 10:33 P.M. Soon, the subway would reach the end of the line, and they'd force him off so they could shut down before curfew.

He flipped through the journal and caught the first two lines he'd written, a fragment of that crazy experience captured in ink:

> *"One decision can't change the world," I said.*
> *"This one did, in my world," he replied.*

Tommy closed the journal as the subway began its deceleration. Nothing more had happened since that encounter, and he'd begun to question whether or not it had been real. He had gone back to his routine: working the order picker with half a finger missing; getting high night after night with Michelle; spending his weekends running errands under close watch from the boots, cleaning up their bachelor apartment (in theory, anyway: there was always something on the floor).

This was life, the best he could hope for, not the one that his parents — well, his mother, anyway — had wanted for their son. So much in his world had gone to shit. It was a miracle that someone with his problems could even have a job and a place and food and a girl. There were people far worse off than he was, even though they stood on his level in this new society. And so Tommy Thrones went on with his life, such as it was.

Until six nights ago, when his weed man gotten capped and he had to find a new vendor. And he found him, along with something else that made his first find completely moot. No point in getting high when real life was presenting you with such opportunities.

The subway stopped and the doors opened. He stepped out into the night. The platform was dark. He kept a lookout for muggers and crack heads, hiding in the shadow where the boots couldn't find them at a glance.

Twenty minutes later, walking past the desolate streets, he came to the abandoned house. He put his hands in his pockets; his left fumbled around with a few dollars, twenties that he'd put aside for the past month, in the old green Pringles can.

The house was easily a hundred years old, but by the way it leaned north-by-northwest and how parts of the walls were literally peeling off the side, it would be lucky to last another hundred hours. The walls on this stretch of the pot-holed road were clear, mostly free of graffiti, but the bullet-riddled walls, rusted shell casings, and bloodied coke spoons hinted at the horrors that went on here from time to time.

Tonight, as he waited just in front of the porch, Tommy didn't sense anything was happening inside.

Suddenly, his man was there, stepping out from the black as though the shadow itself had become fruitful and spawned a child. He wore a black leather jacket and blue jeans, topped by one of those hats — Tommy never knew the real name — that reminded him of a Manchester factory worker from back in the last century.

"Not quite on time, Mr. Thrones," said the old man.

"I'm as on time as the subway lets me be, Mr. Weaver," Tommy replied coolly.

Weaver looked around.

"This really is a rough looking town," the old man observed.

"No shit," said Tommy. "But it's my home. What other choice do I have?"

24

"You know what choice you have. You can find him."

"That's not much of a choice."

Tommy looked down toward the end of the road. Once upon a time, police sirens would echo throughout the town. Nowadays, they didn't bother, not with the Army providing better coverage.

"What will happen to Michelle when I leave her?" Tommy could barely see Weaver's Cheshire smile against the blackness of the house.

"You take this trip, my friend, she won't even know you're gone. From what you say, she's always on a permanent vacation of a different kind."

Weaver stepped forward. "Son, don't make no mistake. There's nobility in what you're doin' by saying 'yes' to this, but when you really boil it down, you ain't got no choice. This is, true to the expression, the chance of a lifetime. Yours. You care about that, don't you?"

Tommy said nothing then started to walk away.

"Something else you should know," said Weaver, calling after him. Tommy stopped and turned around.

"When all this is done, if you haven't succeeded, you will just disappear, and no one and nothin' will be able to bring you back. We understand each other?"

Tommy stared at Weaver for a moment, then turned and continued walking down the street.

"Some incentive," he muttered to himself.

When Tommy came back to the steps of his apartment, Michelle was nowhere to be seen. Normally, she'd meet him out front. But tonight she simply wasn't there. In this town, at this time of day, in these times, that could only mean a handful of things, but his pounding heartbeat and the sinking feeling he got in his stomach told him which one it was.

There was no one else around. It was about half-past midnight. He took a moment to think of Michelle, honoring her as best he could. This was life now. Nothing you could do but keep living. Given how much he'd already lost, Tommy found it got easier to walk away from every new tragedy that decided to visit him.

Tommy dropped the weed on the steps and walked away, knowing someone would put it to use, eventually.

No one else lived on this street now, not really. If anyone had, they wouldn't have believed what happened, assuming they had been able to see it. Between the military curfew and the gangs, no one who still lived here came out much at night these days anyhow. Regardless of who may or may not have been around, or who may or may not have been looking had they been around, only Weaver saw Tommy, who now had nowhere else and thus no real choice in this "chance of a lifetime."

Before vanishing into the night, Tommy walked past a pile of trash and debris. The trash and debris piles were everywhere, a city within the city, but over time, you'd get to know them. Each one had something special about it. For this pile, it would be Tommy's journal, which he tossed, without ceremony, onto the pile.

It opened out to the last page of the last entry, and the words faced upwards into a sky, though no one lingered to read them.

There's an Alternate me. I'm in his dream world, and he's in mine. We might be one and the same. We might not. The question that still remains for both of us is that if this is still a dream, the flipside of some terrible nightmare, which one of us has got the stones to wake up first?

DOPPELGANGER

Two nights later, Max sat in the café near his apartment.

The dusk light was just starting to fade, letting the shadows take hold of the grounds not covered by the streetlights. His usual routine concluded, it was 8:00 when he walked into the place, found his usual spot by the window, and ordered a green tea.

Max still didn't know what to make of the whole thing. Frankly, anyone else would have been freaked out at this whole situation: a stranger, across the country, looking you up, finding out your basic details, and then calling you on the phone in the middle of the night and telling you that you're both meant to be together.

But Max noticed that he wasn't reacting as though he was in danger, didn't feel that calling the cops was the right move to make. That wasn't the feeling that came to mind. Instead, there was something familiar, like a relative or childhood friend who just found you on Facebook or who you bumped into at the bar last night after twenty years. You knew, on an intellectual level, that they may not be all that trustworthy — how many of your old friends turned out to be lowlifes or even psychotic murderers or rapists? — but you still decided to meet with them, if only to have the satisfaction of knowing how much better your life was than theirs. Such as it was, anyway.

"You see," said Samir Shaffir, "even this glass contains multitudes, the essence of Allah."

Max had written those words three days ago. The start of a new story — about what? He didn't yet know. They had just come to him, the same way they always did.

Probably something in Afghanistan: that was in these days. Maybe a topical political thriller about the rightness or wrongness of war; humanizing the "enemy." Maybe go the flipside and prove what barbarians those ungodly Islams were. Maybe somehow make it a vampire story. Cash in on the emo teenage girl crowd.
He didn't know yet. The story would present itself in time.

"Why even sweat it?" Max muttered out to no one in particular. "It's not like I'll get paid for it."

Even this glass contains multitudes...

Christ, he wasn't going to make any progress tonight. He'd go to sleep in a few hours, close his eyes, and see the afterimages of those words on the screen against the blackness of his eyelids.

Max took another sip. Looking out the window, the last of the dusk was now starting to seep away from the eastern sky, and the affluent people of the downtown were now making their nightly walks across the road to the lakeside park. Many of them were couples, holding hands as they crossed over. Every time he saw a couple pass by, Max missed being one of two. A sentiment which, of course, brought him right back to Lucy.

What bothered him most was that she was real. Odd, considering she was, on paper, everything he wanted. But Max hadn't realized how much Lucy Fitzgerald as simply an archetype worked for him until now. It was nice to think of an ideal soul mate, that perfect, cheesy New Age concept of a counterpoint of one's spirit. You never really think that person exists, and when you hear couples getting married suddenly tell their friends that they didn't think that their "soul mate" was real either, until they met them, you smile and nod and let them have their moment of self-delusion (unless, of course, you also thought that you had found yours).

So far, Lucy seemed to know everything else about him, but there was something about keeping his visual identity safe that seemed prudent. Then again, what made him think she didn't already know? He already had notes on her, a mental image of what she looked like. If he headed over to Carmel to meet her, odds are he would recognize her, same way that she would recognize him. Because she had notes on him.

Crazy. Just plain nuts.

At 9:49 P.M., Max was done for the night. He closed his computer, put it back in the bag, finished the last of his green tea, and slung the laptop over his shoulder as he left the now-vacant café. The sentence still hung at the top of the page.

The summer humidity hit him almost as soon as he stepped outside. The sky was now dark indigo, black to the east over the lake, and yet, it being a Sunday night, the streets along the posh lakeshore were empty of pedestrians. A few cars passing here and there, but that was it. The silence, combined with the dark and the muggy air, gave Max a creepy, seedy feeling as he made his way down the street back to his building.

Why am I on edge? Max asked himself. Must be the heat.

He reached the intersection and crossed over. An old French Catholic Church sat at the corner, easily a century old, and still in use. Beyond it was a graveyard, dating back to when settlers first lived here en masse, around 1850 or so. In subsequent decades, the houses and streets manifested into existence around it. Some of the graves were so old, they now sat at unnatural angles that gave them added menace, especially in the vomit orange of the dark night. Every now and then, especially in the spring and fall, Max would bike past to find that same fog patch hovering there, between the headstones.

Soon, Max found himself walking across the street from the cemetery. A car crept to the stop sign, then accelerated, creating the only human-made noise that Max could hear. The crickets and cicadas dominated the air waves.

Then Max heard his phone chirp. For text messages, he used the sonar noise that sounded like a submarine, but he didn't like bothering anyone at the café, so he always set it to vibrate. Maybe he'd forgotten this time. He took out his phone. There was no message.
He heard it again. Very loud. No vibration. No flashing red light indicating a message.

A third time, the sonar rang its little double ring, c-o-o-o-ng...c-o-o-o-ng.

Max looked to the house at his right. The windows were shuttered, the lights were off, and though there were two cars parked in the driveway, there didn't seem to be anyone around.

C-o-o-o-ng...c-o-o-o-ng...

Doppler effect. Max realized he was hearing the echo off the house. The actual sound was coming from across the street.

Max turned and saw it, clear even across the way in the haze. The burial grounds themselves weren't lit at night but sat in shadow. He'd heard that some of the more adventurous — and creepy — teens would go there to make out and drink during the summer. Sure enough, there was a flashing red light, coming from the near complete black that Max saw in the gap between two of the larger gravestones that lined the sidewalk. But where was the owner? Max couldn't make out any silhouette.

C-o-o-o-ng...c-o-o-o-ng...

I have no idea why I'm doing this, thought Max as he stepped off the sidewalk into the road, taking his time as he made his way to the light.

Growing closer, he still couldn't see anyone in there. A voice in his head screamed at him to stop and keep heading home. It was soon joined by an entire choir of voices from the rational part of his brain screaming at him that this was dangerous. Unfortunately for them, his gut moved him forward. This was important. Max made it across.

Three tall gravestones — one of them rectangular, maybe about forty years old — lined the sidewalk and acted as a visual barrier that marked the edge of the property. They were the only ones that caught the streetlight. Beyond them, the grass was soft and short, kept from growing by the century-old oaks and maples that towered about fifteen feet over them, keeping the grounds in perpetual shade even at the height of summer.

Smaller gravestones — about six or seven — lay in the middle of this dark area, which was now almost pitch black but for the red beacon of the phone that sat atop one of them. Max entered the dark zone and approached the phone. The gravestone upon which it sat was one of the older ones that had shifted over the decades, such that now it was almost completely horizontal, easily about forty degrees, and the phone was, in fact, sitting on what had been the side of the stone.

Max looked around. No one sat here, though he couldn't be sure there wasn't a mugger hiding behind the trees. Still, as bait went, sending an SMS to a phone set to loud was not the most effective way to mug someone, though it was creative. He turned back to the phone and picked it up.

It looked just like Max's own smartphone, surrounded by a thick black rubber skin. Looking around one more time — still nothing — he clicked a button. The screen sprang to life, and Max was so stunned he almost dropped the damned thing on the ground. The background was the standard wallpaper that came with the unit, but the display name read "Max Sinclair."

"It's yours," said a voice from behind him. Max started and turned around.

Later on, he would reflect on his reaction to seeing the face behind the voice, that after the initial surprise, everything seemed so natural when they spoke.

And why wouldn't it be natural, anyway? Why wouldn't you feel natural talking to yourself?

The two Maxim Jeffrey Sinclairs stood five feet apart in the middle of the graveyard. Max noted that the Alternate cast a much thinner shadow than he did, at least when he did step into the light. All he could recognize was the voice — sounding much like listening to yourself talk on a tape playback — and the face, which caught enough of the light to remove any doubt.

The Alternate looked to the sidewalk and then back at Max.

"Actually, I was just kidding. The phone's really mine. Hand it back?" He reached out his hand. Max looked down at the phone in his own hand, then handed it back to its true owner.

"Thanks." He nodded toward the sidewalk. "Think we can take this into the light? I hate not being able to see who I'm talking to, no matter who it is."

Max realized he was standing almost in complete darkness. Eyeing each other, both men sidestepped into the light.

The Alternate was wearing long ripped jeans, a gray T-shirt, and — surprisingly, considering the humidity — a faded brown leather jacket. Moreover, he wore boots and not the sandals that was standard summer dress code for Max. His face was gaunt and hadn't been shaved in day, which was alarming since Max's beard tended to grow very quickly.

Part of Max wanted to ask him who he was, what was happening, if this wasn't some joke, but his inner skeptic had taken a beating lately, and didn't get hold of the microphone connecting his brain to his mouth. Instead, Max went with the first thing that came to mind.

"Why didn't you just call out to me? Why the theatrics?"

32

The Alternate shrugged. "What fun would that be?" He looked around. "Nice place you got here. Better than where I come from."

"And where's that?" asked Max.

"The ass end of Detroit, which doesn't narrow it down much, I'll admit. World's a different place where I come from."

"So...you're from a different world?" asked Max. The Alternate looked at him, and smiled, but not with his eyes.

"Not really. I was talkin' metaphorically, guy. It's all the same world. Just that the different outcomes overlap each other in the same space."

Max had no idea what his doppelganger was talking about, but he kept quiet as the Alternate kept talking.

"My point is that the world's changing, so now more and more people are able to actually see how things would have turned out. Most of the worlds you can reach aren't terribly different from yours. You and me, we're among the 'lucky' ones." The way he said lucky was venomous.

"What do you mean?"

"I don't know the whole story. I just know that one day, I was minding my business, and then, I met myself. No drama, no flashes of light or sci-fi shit like that, though that other me...well, he knew more about it than what he told me, but I could tell that this guy, this other version of us, had it going on. He could see it in his eyes. He knew everything."

Max still had no idea what he was talking about. Still, he had to say something.

"And who was he?"

The Alternate scoffed. "Guy, he was you. He was me. Just...well, he's the version of us that did everything right. He said he was the 'Optimal,' whatever that means. And he told me that I had to get you to go to California to meet your Lucy. I didn't believe him at first, but then he gave me some information."

"Information?"

"Yeah, in a big yellow envelope. It had all the details I needed. After that, I had to come here to meet you. After I deliver the message he gave me, and run a couple more errands, I head back to my life."

The Alternate sighed, looked away. Max saw the regret in his face.

"How did you end up in Detroit?" he asked.

"Decided to move there with a girl I met, though we're broken up now," said the Alternate. "Met her three years after Lucy and I..." He trailed off then got his focus back. "Look, it doesn't matter. All that matters is that you gotta do what Lucy tells you. You gotta head out to California, and you've got to leave soon."

"How soon?"

"Like, yesterday."

"I can't just leave. I've got a job. I've got rent coming out. I've got—"

"Man, you ain't got shit!" The Alternate walked up to him. Max could now see the scars on his doppelganger's face, scars that spoke of other scrapes that he'd gotten into.

"Don't you get it? Everyone lives for themselves, that's fair, but some people have to share it with one other special person if they're going to make it big. They make that decision before their mommas even push them out. And I'm telling you, whatever you have going on in your life, whatever you think you can accomplish, the only way you're going to make it big, the only way you're going to make all the right choices, is to share it with Lucy Fitzgerald. You can mess around with other chicks all you want, you can stay alone, but you'll never be at your best without her. She's the only way you're going to live your life to the fullest. You with me?"

Max said nothing, taking all of it in. The Alternate backed down, stepped back the same number of feet he had taken only moments before.

"Lucy told me she wants to see me. That was two days ago."

"Yeah, that's what I figured," said the Alternate.

"How did you find out about Dinah? Lucy knew about her."

"Mr. 'Optimal' told me about her. He knows everything about all of us. It's time you got on your way. Leave tomorrow. Don't be late."

"But—" The Alternate threw his arms up.

"Call in sick, do whatever. There's limited time here."

"Time for what?" The Alternate sighed.

"For you to meet yourself."

"Isn't that what I'm doing right now?"

"Here's how this works, Max. You pack your shit up — not everything, just enough to last you a week — fill up your tank, and drive out to Detroit. I'll meet you there. I'll tell you my story. Then, you keep going from there, whatever the other directions say. Along the way, you'll meet another one of us. I have no idea which one, but then you sit and talk with him, find out his story. Then, in a week and a bit, you'll meet Lucy, and you two can live happily ever fucking after."

Max shook his head. "Why so bitter?"

"Because I'm pretty sure out of everyone, I'm what you would call your worst case scenario. Out of all of us, I seem to have the most fucked up life. But look, I'll save that for later. All of us are on this journey at the same time, but the only way everything and everyone is going to sync up is by following this exact route and leaving tomorrow. Got it?"

Max hesitated. "I think so. So...but...how does this work? I mean, why—"

The Alternate shook his head and held up his hands. "Look, I'm not the one you have to ask about that. I'm just the guy who's here to kick your ass and get it on the road."

The Alternate checked his phone. "Look, I gotta go," he said. "I'll meet you at the Doubletree in Detroit tomorrow night, okay?"

The Alternate stepped forward, took Max's hand. It felt weird, like grabbing your own left hand with your right.

"Trust me, all right? I'll tell you the rest tomorrow. Just do us both one more favor."

"What's that?"

"Believe that this shit is real. Believe that you'll want it. The sooner you do, the better off you'll be. The faster it'll happen."

With that, the Alternate released his hand and walked back into the graveyard. Max half expected him to vanish into the shadows again. Instead, he watched his doppelganger walk clear to the other side of the property to a parking lot bathed in orange light. Max watched the figure reach the little sidewalk that snaked its way between the houses to the next block, and then disappear around the corner, indistinguishable from any ordinary pedestrian out for a stroll on the humid night.

Max lingered another moment.

"Believe it," he said aloud, and then headed back to his apartment

Two hours later, Max would be lying in bed, his bags packed, waiting for sleep. But the turmoil of energy rolling and surging inside of him kept him awake for hours. When he did finally fall asleep, Max dreamed an imaginary itinerary of the next few days — a drive he'd always imagined, but had never taken. The route took him much of the next week, heading up and down across the plains — surreal and lurid in his dreamscape — into impossibly high Rocky Mountains, and then over into Oregon, before dropping down to California and Carmel and Lucy.

In his sleep, he passed over the plains into those cloud-shrouded peaks and valleys. And when he saw Lucy Fitzgerald, she was standing by the endless Pacific, at the edge of the ocean, waiting for him under an endless sunset in a salmon sky too perfect to be real, but good enough for a dream.

But before he could reach her, his alarm sounded and Max awoke from his spectral journey on the morning of his real one. The empty feeling in his chest felt far worse, needing to be filled by the presence of only one other human being on the planet who was far away to the west. All he could feel was the promise of a new love that was right, that would not fail like his marriage had, and that would bring him joy once again.

That, more than any convincing by an Alternate of himself or any mystical force, was what ultimately got him to want to go.

***

The sun rose over the water the next morning, as any other, and after loading up the car and fuelling up the tank, Max made a quick stop at the cafe for a coffee to go. Then he went to a different waterfront than the one in his dream, and for a time, watched the glittering orange and yellow flecks of the water, and the mix of cloud and blue in the sky that spoke of summer humidity here in The Great Lakes, and a beautiful June Monday.

That morning, Max called the virtual concierge where he worked and declared an emergency, that he'd be back in a few days. The call centre controller, the person looking after the schedule for the whole team, didn't seem too concerned: in the summertime, at least three people a day were having "emergencies" of some kind. Max sighed when he hung up on that call. As much as he was good at his day job, enjoyed it, he wasn't exactly indispensable. As for his friends, he left a voicemail on Steven's phone. Steven never picked up calls and very rarely answered text messages. By the time his friends noticed his absence, Max would be across the continent. He'd considered inventing some second cousin having a medical problem, or a great aunt who didn't exist before passing away in Seattle or Boulder, but his friends weren't stupid, and it was just easier telling the truth and running than having to lie.

There was another advantage to all of this, a peripheral target of opportunity that, if he hit it, it would help him in another area of his life. Max brought his laptop with him to ensure that whenever he met the others, he would be able to tell their stories in his story, the one he had started the year before.

Like doing the work for me, he thought.

No, Max didn't know how this worked or what it was all about, but he was rolling with it. And it was time to start rolling.

Max finished his coffee and tossed the cup in the trash as he inhaled the smell of the lake and the cool humid breeze. He stepped into his car, started the engine, and pulled out of the park, onto the highway ramp, westbound for Detroit, leaving behind the newborn sun as it shone upon the commuters on their way to their destinies, such as they were.

When he got to Detroit, Max parked in the hotel garage and made his way up to the brightly lit lobby, which was lovely, but not terribly remarkable with a ten-foot ceiling, two small ponds, and leafy green trees in pots lined up at intervals on the shale-colored floor".

With the reception desk immediately beside him, Max could see that the front doors—divided by a small museum section that had pictures and a few little trinkets from the city's history—let out into the street. Little railings— black iron ones, distinctly PoMo, but resembling the Victorian ones with those little accents at the end—crisscrossed the lobby"

Max looked ahead and saw his Alternate sitting on one of the chairs, reading USA Today, still wearing the same jacket and jeans he had on the day before, as if weather didn't happen around him.

The Alternate looked up from his paper as Max approached, and folded it unevenly on the table.

"You made it," he said. There was only the faintest hint of a smile. Other guests walking past saw them, did little double takes, but otherwise minded their business. Max caught their expressions.

"I guess people will just assume that we're twins," he said.

"True, true. Sit down." The Alternate motioned to the chair at the table nearby. Max pulled up and sat down.

"So, I guess you wanna know the whole story?"

Max nodded.

"Well, you can't," said the Alternate, "Not yet. For right now, all you get is what I have to tell you, and what I was told."

"Told by whom?" asked Max.

"I already told you about the guy who told me."

"Yeah, you called him 'the Optimal.'"

The Alternate sighed and leaned back in his seat. "Yeah, fuckin' guy...he literally is Mr. Perfect. I wouldn't be surprised if his shit actually had no discernible smell of its own, the way he presents himself. Nah, this guy is the only one who gets to visit everyone, all of other Max Sinclairs. You might even get to meet him somewhere along the line."

"And what did he tell you?"

"He did better than tell me," said The Alternate. "He gave me an entire envelope of information on you."

Max raised an eyebrow. What would have been written about him? "Can I see it?"

The Alternate laughed. "Sorry, bro. Left it in my other suit."

Max nodded, narrowed his eyes. "Exactly how many other Max Sinclairs are there?"

"Now that's a smart question," said the Alternate. "See, Mr. Perfect told me that the world's a lot bigger than we think it is, that when a person is born, they are born into more than one layer of the world."

"What do you mean 'layer'?"

"Like a cake, or one of those diner's spikes, you know, the ones that hold all of the checks from the customers at a diner? That kind of thing. Each layer is a different life, and each life sits on top of the other in the same world."

"So, like an alternate universe," said Max.

The Alternate winced, shook his head.

"Yeah...sort of, except it's all really the same place. What ends up happening is that every possible outcome you can have from the choices you've got ends up being a reality."

The Alternate must have seen the look on Max's face. "What? This doesn't excite you?"

"I guess," said Max. "I mean, it's classic sci-fi stuff. You know what I mean? Quantum physics, Schrödinger's Cat, Jet Lee movies from the 90s and all that. But it's not new. This is all stuff I've been reading about since high school. But to have it be real? I dunno. I mean, how do I know I'm not hallucinating all of this now? That this isn't some kind of weird ass dream?"

"Wait a minute, are you fuckin' kidding me?" The Alternate almost cracked a grin. "You still don't believe this is happening? Guy, you're talking to yourself *right now*."

The Alternate shook his head, looked around, and continued.

"Look, as I was sayin', everyone lives on each of these layers at once, but only a few get to be aware of it. Mr. Perfect didn't tell me why that is, or who gets to make that decision. He just said that Maxim Jeffrey Sinclair—" he pointed at Max. "You," pointed back at himself, "and me, and the others like us — Maxim Jeffrey Sinclair is one of those individuals. Those lucky few who get to go around and experience life in the different layers. And they can also help their Alternates out with whatever shit they're dealing with at the time. That's why you're here."

The Alternate stopped talking. A few other guests walked past, oblivious to their presence. Some kind of Latin music played overhead. Max mulled over what the Alternate had told him.

"What makes us lucky?" asked Max.

"He didn't tell me that part," said the Alternate. "Fact is, I wasn't exactly in a position to doubt myself, if you know what I mean."

"Okay," said Max, finally, "so if that's why I'm here, what does Lucy Fitzgerald have to do with anything?"

The Alternate cast his eyes down for an instant, then looked back up. "Luce... well, let's say she's your soul mate, and leave it at that."

"What? That simple?"

"Yep."

Max shook his head. "Oh, no way, I'm calling 'bullshit.' There's way more to her than that."

"Not really," said the Alternate. "Occam's Razor, guy. Sometimes the right answer is that simple."

"So she's my soul mate? What about all of the other 'us's'? How can she be a soul mate to all of us?"

"If she was one person, she couldn't, but there are as many Alternates of her as there are of us, of everyone else, except-"

"We're the lucky few who get to find out about it."

"Exactly."

"So what are—"

The Alternate waved him off. "Guy, just...shut up for a second, let me talk."

Max nodded, let the Alternate speak.

"Soul mates are real, though they're not always the people you'd think, and in a lot of lifespaces, they never meet."

"'Lifespaces'?" asked Max.

"Yeah, what we call each alternate universe or life or whatever."

"What is a soul mate, anyway? And why is Lucy Fitzgerald my soul mate?"

"Guy, you and I both know that you don't have to ask that question. You already know it, same way I do, same way that almost every single Max you're going to meet on this road trip knows it."

"Try me."

The Alternate looked away, toward the door, looking at something far beyond its glass windows. "A soul mate is your optimal match. Makes you one with life."

Max nodded, waiting for more, but the Alternate said nothing else.

"That's...very Zen, but what does that even mean?"

The Alternate kept looking away.

"It means that whatever great things you want out of life, Lucy Fitzgerald is the gal who's going to help you get it, as no other woman can or will. You'll never get to live fully on your own. All you'll be able to do is be okay. Maybe a little more. But you can't do it by giving everything you have to her, either, 'cause then you're going to be less than okay. She's got to add her power to yours, guy."

"It's tricky," continued the Alternate. "You can fall in love, spend the rest of your life with someone, and swear you two are soul mates, but be wrong. Half the time, it's just pure coincidence that you hooked up with that person in the first place. Changes in brain chemistry. But then you live your life, and you're about to die, and you realize you didn't get half the shit done that you wanted to. That's life for most people."

The Alternate leaned in, and Max couldn't help but think this guy would have made a hell of a personal coach, assuming he got beyond his own problems.

"But your soul mate," continued the Alternate, "she's like...adrenaline in your blood. She makes it easy for you to live to the fullest, to completely become the moments of your life instead of just the guy who watches them tick away, feeling like he didn't do anything with them. And you do the same for her. Then, when you die, you both can die satisfied you really did do it your way, like Sinatra. But half the time, either you don't meet, or you do, and it doesn't work out."

The Alternate paused. Max said nothing.

"I drove her away, man," continued the Alternate. "My Lucy. I used to live in Ann Arbor, and that's where we met. I thought we had it made, like nothing would happen to us."

"How did you end up in Ann Arbor?"

"Because I decided to travel the world before going to college. Remember when that had been an option for you?"

Max nodded. It had been a big argument with Mom and Dad, who both wanted him to go straight into college from high school. It had been one of his regrets, which came back again after college grad when he chose to stay and build a life with Dinah rather than strike out right after graduation.

"Yeah, I remember."

"Well, I took that trip, and I never ended up going to college, because when I was in England, I met this American dude in a hostel who offered me a job helping him start up his record label in Michigan. I would help with some of the songwriting. Anyway, I had a business trip to take to California, and that's where I met Lucy. We hit it off, and she moved back to Ann Arbor with me. We were together for two years. It was perfect. Shit...man, I still wonder what would have happened otherwise..."

"What did happen?" asked Max.

"My heroin habit." The Alternate glanced at Max, a lopsided grin on the right side of his grizzled mouth, then turned back to the door. "She got tired of trying. That's the thing about soul mates: they're not guaranteed to stay. You can break up with them, you can get divorced from them, they can die, you can die, or you'll wear them out and drive them away. They can drive you away. You can't take them for granted anymore than anyone else, otherwise you'll lose them, like I did. She left me, headed back to Carmel, but I've never seen her. I've been clean two years, but she won't look me up. Whatever feelings she had for me, I ground them down to the fucking nub until she had nothing left."

The Alternate stopped talking.

"I'm sorry," said Max.

The Alternate raised his eyebrows, sighed.

"Hey, whatever, right? That's why I'm here. I may have lost my Lucy, but I can help you get to yours."

"So the girl I'm looking for and yours...they're two different Lucys or the same one?"

The Alternate smiled. "You're looking for yours, but on your way to her, you need to set the other Maxes up with theirs."

"All of them?"

"No," said the Alternate. "There are three alternate Max Sinclairs you need to meet on your way to your dream girl. When you do, the way's gonna open where you'll have a chance to find the Lucy Fitzgeralds in their lifespaces, and get them to meet. Then the way will be clear for you to meet yours. Hell, if you even get one of them to meet, that would be amazing."

The Alternate fell silent, and amid the background sound of the hotel lobby, Max, too, said nothing as he pondered those words, and his next questions.

"What if I fail?" he finally asked.

The Alternate smiled. "You'll find a way."

"You sure about that?"

"When you see how amazing a woman that Luthien Fitzgerald really is, you'll literally move Heavens and Earth to make it happen."

"Why now?" asked Max. "How come I didn't get to do this years ago? Is it just destiny?"

The Alternate shook his head. "That's what I asked Mr. Perfect. He said that it wasn't destiny. It was the Convergence."

Max leaned forward. "What's the Convergence?"

The Alternate took a breath. "'Sometimes you get a solar system of eight, maybe nine, planets moving in their own orbits,' he said, 'and though they'll each move at different speeds, every now and then, they line up.' That's what this is. 'Destiny's a word for people who haven't done the math,' he said."

"How many others are there?"

"There can be as many Alternates as there are layers, meaning there could be hundreds, even thousands. But on this trip, you'll only get to meet three, maybe four others besides me, before Convergence ends."

"Why us? I mean, why me? How come I'm lucky enough to see how things would have turned out?"

The Alternate looked at him. "'Lucky'? Trust me, man, it's a mixed blessing at best. This is the type of trip where you find out what you would have gotten had you bought that lottery ticket, or if you'd just studied harder on that LSAT or taken that leap of faith with that dream job. On the flip side, you can find out just how much better you've got it than some of your other people. Don't tell me you're not feeling some of that last one with me right now. I know I fucked up.

"But now," he continued before Max could jump in. "Now you have the chance to do a little course correction. You wanna know why you? Mr. Perfect told me, and you'll hear it again when you meet the others along your way."

The Alternate leaned in and whispered in an almost melodramatic intensity. "No other Max Sinclair has been able to live a full life with Lucy Fitzgerald. We've all messed it up somehow."

"What about Mr. Perfect?" asked Max

The Alternate leaned back.

"Him too," he replied. "I guess, yeah, that means I shouldn't call him that, though his name for himself — the 'Optimal' — sounds so fuckin' arrogant, but it's true. Nobody bats a thousand forever. Even the best are still missing that small percent of life that they can't get. Mr. Perfect was only able to hook Lucy, but he couldn't land her. Not yet, anyway."

"Not yet?" asked Max.

The Alternate hesitated, not sure how to explain. "He...he said he was 'about to,' whatever that means. Who knows if he did? If the odds were that much in his favor, I don't think he'd be coming to a recovering junkie to help him get his shot."

"But...if she's supposed to be my soul mate...our collective soul mate...how come we can't get with her?" asked Max.

"Different reasons, everyone. Mine were drugs and co-dependency. Mr. Perfect didn't tell me his, and when you head out tonight, I'm guessing you'll find out the rest."

The phone rang at the reception desk, breaking the flow. Both Maxes started, looked over, then turned back to the conversation.

"Where are you sending me tonight? How long is this going to last?"

The Alternate leaned in. "It's very simple. All of us who get to make this trip have a checklist of Alternates they need to contact. You've got three, and the mission is simple: get one of them to meet their own Lucy Fitzgerald. Then you'll see the way to your own. Just do it before the Convergence." The Alternate paused. "What did you tell work?"

"I said there was an emergency—"

"Good, that'll buy you at least a couple of days before you have to call them again. Here,"

He reached into his pocket and took out a folded piece of faded paper, like one of those parchments out of the Old West. Max took it and opened it up. It was a hand-drawn map, a crude sketch of the highways Midwest, Great Plains, and West Coast. At the end was Carmel-by-the-Sea, and in between were three little meeting places that Max guessed were roughly a day's drive apart from each other.

"Your first meeting's at Weaver's Diner," said the Alternate, pointing down at the map as Max searched for it. "It's that place in Nebraska, see it? You should be able to get there by dark if you gas up now and keep moving. Hit the restroom first, though."

Max could see that his Alternate could see his hesitation, and why not? They had the same face.

"This is an opportunity you'll never get again," said the Alternate. "You gonna choose a job over that?"

"I can't get fired—"

"It won't matter anyway. When this is all over—"

"This is nuts. I can't do this, man, it's—"

The Alternate stood up. "Look!"

People around them turned and stared. The Alternate gave them a round of cut-eye, and they went back to their business.

"Do you think this is a coincidence? Mr. Perfect did his homework on you, you know. You have her on your list. Do you really think that all of that just came from your mind? It's deeper than that."

The Alternate took a wary look around, then sat back down, but leaned into Max's space.

"I'll tell you what I believe is true about this whole thing. Your life is messed up, my friend. You're numb. You're approaching the wrong side of thirty, you've reached the ceiling at your job and can't go any farther up, your ex-wife left you because you couldn't get your shit together, and you say you wanna write, but you haven't even gotten one book out of your system. And every day goes by, and you still don't see how things are shaping up, do you?"

The Alternate dropped his voice. "Do you think you and Dinah were fighting for nothing last year? Why did she leave you when everything else was starting to turn around in every other part of your life? Steady work? A great new apartment in a great neighborhood by the water? And why did it end up being so damned cordial? Most marriages like the one you had — where you and the girl were in so deep you could blink each other's eyes — end in a big explosion with half your guts ripped out. Could it be that something out there doesn't want you to feel bitter, wants your heart to stay open to something else, something better on the horizon?"

He took a breath. "I'll tell you something else, guy. I think that piece of paper that you and Lucy wrote about each other opened the door between you, and now you've got to act on it. That's why your life is in flux right now: whatever was in place before has to get torn down so that you can take the next step. That's why Mr. Perfect was so serious about getting me to kick your ass and get you moving. There's something happening here that's well on its way, Max, and you know that you can't walk away from this and never be curious for the rest of your life about what might have happened."

The Alternate took a breath and put his hand on Max's shoulder. He actually grinned.

"Tell me you're not excited to be doing this. I fucking dare you."

Max looked at him...then smiled. A big smile. It was true: he felt the excitement to his core. This was a big adventure. The biggest.

The Alternate clapped him on the shoulder.

"Good. Weaver's Diner. Get your ass moving. And good luck."

With that, the Alternate got up and started out of the lobby.

"Two questions," said Max, facing away from him.

The Alternate turned. "Yeah?"

Max stood up, turned to face his Alternate for the last time before heading back to his car. "Did Mr. Perfect tell you which lives I was going to see?"

The Alternate shrugged. "Nothing in detail."

"But he did say something?" asked Max.

"Yeah..." The Alternate sighed and closed his eyes as if squeezing the memory out of his brain. "A lifetime slightly better. A lifetime slightly worse. A lifetime unexpected."

Max let the words sink in. "Three, then?"

"Just go with it, Max. It'll all be okay. All right?"

They looked at each other once more and Max nodded. His Alternate started down the hall.

"Are we going to meet again?"

The Alternate didn't turn around. "That's four questions. And nope." He reached the door, and left the hotel, leaving Max to look down at the directions.

Max scanned them for a few minutes, then got up and headed to the elevator. Whatever was happening, this was going to make a hell of a story, and it was time to go.

Before pocketing the map, Max glanced down at the bottom left corner. As basic as the map was, the original author had seen fit to sketch a little compass rose, identical to the one in his dream of Lucy only a few nights ago. Tame though it was compared to meeting oneself, it sent a shot of excitement up Max's spine as he wondered about the road ahead. He would literally meet the woman of his dreams in a few short days.

Weaver's Diner. The first stop. Time to go.

THIRTY-TWO DAYS

Make Lucy cry.

That was the standing dare around the cafeteria, way back in high school and light years away from here.

It wasn't like they didn't know what had been happening at home — oh no, everyone knew — but whoever still expects propriety in the eleventh grade is either a hopeless dreamer or a trustee on the board. Either way...

Lucy had learned to keep still during the teasing. That stillness, stoniness, was effective. The reason for it all wasn't that much more logical: when is teasing ever logical, after all? Teased not because she was ugly (far from it) or a teacher's pet (a steady C average throughout her years except the last two) or a loner (she had a few close friends instead of a lot of acquaintances), but the perennial, distinctly 1990s reason: she was still a virgin and didn't seem all that interested in boys.

And why would she have been, anyhow? Lucy was no lesbian, but boys at this age were either complete fucking idiots or just plain unattractive. It wasn't even a case of the whole "jocks versus nerds" debate that occupied the attention of the more self-aware models of maleness in the school yard. No, to her, it was more like, "Get out of my face, you're gross, wait three or four years and I'll consider taking you out to coffee."

So while others in her class were messing around, getting knocked up, pining their hours away at home for boys who would never notice them, or just turning against the game and toward Jesus Christ and the "no sex before marriage" movement, Lucy stayed out altogether. Flat out refused to step into the arena in the first place. Focused all of her attention on that one vision that required bumping up her grade average and going to good colleges. Spending time at home with parents who loved her. No high school boyfriends. No parties.

For that, they teased her. Tried to make her cry.

And sometimes it worked, but only sometimes.

Lucy shifted and adjusted herself on the meditation circle. A rounded stone platform, not like one of the faerie circles of Ireland, but a round marble platform, positioned just before the fence line, leaving enough room for one average-sized human being to sit in the lotus position for as long as their legs could keep circulation and their knees could hold out. Lucy had added a weather-proof cushion to the medication site. She wondered why it hadn't been part of the setup to start. Not that it had helped much.

She opened her eyes. The backyard was a highly symmetrical affair, about a four hundred square feet and quite large by the area standards. The semi-circle shaped, white concrete deck spilled out onto the soft grass in three steps, shaded by the dense black pines and leafy trees that made Carmel-by-the-Sea seem so cozy and compact. Lucy had put in a small wading pool — unlike many of her pool-happy neighbors, she felt that the ocean, only twenty minutes away on foot, was better — just to cool one's heels when it was too hot to walk.

There's a practice in meditation in which you just let go and observe your own stream of consciousness, not trying to think about "nothing," but letting the volume gradually turn itself down, just by watching. And Lucy did that, disengaging from the process, and watching. And that's what she had done for the past twenty-nine mornings.
And this morning, those three words came back. Make Lucy cry.

Her phone rang. Bells. Wind chimes, to be exact, loud enough to get attention, harmonious enough to not disrupt the serenity of the surroundings. Contrary to what her teachers at the center advised their students and customers, Lucy brought her phone to meditation. She had no choice. At any minute, someone might call with a major crisis — a construction crew on Highway 1 broke the water mains leading to

51

the center again, some Hollywood big shot wanting a private hot yoga session during their stay in town — and she'd have to get moving.

Today, it was Kate.

Lucy answered.

"Hey," she said.

"How's it going today, Luce?" said Kate.

Lucy sighed.

"Meditation's a super bitch sometimes," said Lucy. "All I could think about was high school."

"High school?"

"Yeah. This really isn't my thing, Kate. I've never seen the use in quieting my mind."

"Give it some more time," said Kate. "You've still got a few days left to practice."

Lucy sighed.

"I know," she said. Then nothing. Kate waited a few seconds before speaking.

"This is the best choice," said Kate. Again, a few seconds.

"If you say so," said Lucy, finally. "Just have to get used to it."

"Right....so, what was it like, talking to him?"

"Max is...funny, sweet, sincere. I dunno, Kate, it wasn't exactly normal. I still don't understand why I was able to call him, given where he is, but not my own lifesp—"

"Nothing about the Convergence is normal, sweetie," said Kate.

"There's no getting used to anything until it's over. Anyway, I was just calling to check on you. See you in two days?"

"I want to ask you something."

"Sure thing," said Kate.

Lucy looked around.

"Why would Weaver have asked me to lie?" asked Lucy. "That's the one thing I can't accept about this."

Kate didn't respond at first, and Lucy used the opening to vent the issue's that had been dogging her."

"Thirty-two days, Kate," said Lucy. "Thirty-two days of calling numbers of friends and family back in Seattle only to find they don't know me, or don't exist. Thirty-two days to become an expert on yoga, meditation, Eastern healing practices, California business law, a whole new social network in Carmel-by-the-Sea who have apparently known me for years. Thirty-TWO days…"

Lucy realized how loud she was now talking into the phone, and dropped her tone somewhat. "Thirty-two days to get settled into a house that's not mine, and yet has my name splashed all over the mortgage paperwork, the power and phone bills, and the mailbox." She took a breath. "And…thirty-two days to track down Maxim Sinclair and convince him to come here to meet me. All because I took you and Weaver on faith that you guys knew what you were doing. But that lie just won't get out of my mind. It doesn't fit. How can I trust that what's happening is legit if you're telling me to lie?"

"Weaver said that it would only be a lie at first," said Kate. "From where we stand, it's the absolute truth."

"What? That another Alternate of Max Sinclair met with me and gave me that envelope?" said Lucy. "Kate, Weaver gave me that envelope. He knows that. You know that. How can that possibly be true from where you stand?"

"Because we can see just a lit—"

"Yeah, yeah, a little farther down the road," said Lucy, cutting Kate off. "You keep saying that, but it's getting frustrating trying to reason out your logic."

"Just…trust us, okay?" said Kate.

Did…did Lucy just hear that?

"What?"

"I said, 'just trust us,'" said Kate. There, that intonation again. Definitely not a bad connection or static.

Hesitation.

"This isn't only about using reason, Lucy," said Kate. "It's about having faith in higher mathematics. Don't you remember what that was like?"

Lucy said nothing, allowing Kate pressed the advantage of her silence. "Well, this is how you get it back. In a few days, Max Sinclair will be here, and you'll understand everything we've been saying is true. You're already where you need to be. Just stay there."
Kate paused. "I gotta go, Luce. Hang tight. I'll see you in a few days."

Then, the line went dead.

Lucy sat there, taking a breath. Around her, Carmel-by-the-Sea was just waking up. She could hear that hissing of cars in the distance, making their way down the hilly Ocean Avenue to the beach. She could hear renovation crews starting their work on rooftops and patios a few houses down. She checked the time on her phone. Lucy had at least ten minutes left to just sit here, and so she would sit.

Faith in higher math. That's what Weaver had said, just before telling her that he had trapped her here.

Lucy closed her eyes.

Breathe deep, in...and out...in...and out…

***

That Mr. Weaver had shown up again wasn't the most earth-shattering event. No, it was the news he brought with him that was the real stunner.

They had met, for the second time, on Carmel Beach. It was May, and the cold fogs and rough tides had kept most of the tourists off the white sand. Pebble Beach was still weeks away from the U.S. Open, so only a few golfers, off on the beach's north end, were carting around the links that afternoon. The gray was covering the horizon, so Lucy couldn't see the sunset at all over the Pacific.

She'd stopped in Carmel to stretch her legs. This had been one of the places she used to visit as a child with her parents before she'd left for Berkeley. It was right beside Highway 1, a quick pit stop on the way to Katarina Castillo's house down in Santa Barbara. Kate, her old friend who had suddenly come out of the woodwork and invited her down to meet her new husband, Richard, and take a break from everything that had happened in Seattle. How Kate had heard about Seattle didn't make sense: no direct contact info, no mutual friends. Lucy didn't do social media, and so how Kate had found her number and called her up, knowing in detail what had happened, was a mystery.

One that Mr. Herbert E. Weaver had solved on this, his second appearance in Lucy's life.

"You can't go home again," said Weaver. "This is your life now."

"What are you saying?" asked Lucy.

"I'm sayin' that you live here. You got in your car this morning and left Seattle. At the same time, yo'self from this world woke up and left Carmel. When your paths crossed, you switched places. She gets your life, you get hers."

He had walked in front of her, facing the sea.

"Why?" pressed Lucy. He shrugged.

"Part of the Convergence," he said. "The deal is that you get to live your Alternate's life for a while. She lives yours."

"And what is the main point?"

Weaver then turned back to face her.

"So you can meet Maxim Sinclair."

"He lives in Carmel?"

"No, not yet. You gotta invite him first." Weaver grinned. "One phone call. I'll give you the number. You call him when you're ready, and when you do, and only when you do, you get the choice. Till then, the way back is shut."

"That simple? Why stick me here instead of just taking me to where he lives?" asked Lucy.

"He lives in another lifespace," replied Weaver. Lucy scoffed at that.

"Then how am I supposed to call him?" she asked. Weaver grinned.

"We've worked out a special deal with the phone company. Don't you worry about it. Just do your part, child. It'll all work out."

"I can't do this now!" said Lucy, starting to panic. "My friend is expecting me tomorrow. I can't stay—"

"You're friend ain't gonna be expecting you no more. Don't worry."

"Why?" demanded Lucy, now in a panic.

Weaver smiled a Cheshire grin. "Because your friend is one of us."

***

The scene of that memory, now thirty-two days old, dissolved as a car honked its horn behind the fence at Lucy's back. She opened her eyes again, and here she was, in an Alternate universe, with no way back.

There was a wetness on her right cheek, and Lucy realized she'd been weeping now for some time. Make Lucy cry. Mission accomplished, even if it had been self-sabotage.

But Kate had hesitated. That was new.

For all of the hidden knowledge and "trust me, we know better" conversations they had shared since Lucy found herself here, that was the one thing she had not seen until now. Frankly, if Kate was one of them, and had her own doubts about all this, then she could very well be wrong about a lot of things, and Lucy could be right.

Kate could be wrong that Lucy would not have to wait for Max Sinclair to arrive in order to go home.

Her phone buzzed again. Lucy took a deep breath, wiped away the tear, and stood up, one leg at a time. If it was Kate calling back to apologize for being dismissive, she wasn't going to have anything of it.

Let it fucking go to voicemail, Lucy was done with her for a morning.

Only, this was a text message. Lucy flipped open the phone.

At first, she didn't understand what she was seeing. Her mind had been through so many shocks, it was slow to react to the unexpected, like a sore muscle.

After a few seconds, though, her mind fully grasped what she was seeing.

Lucy grinned.

No, she did more than that. Lucy laughed.

Two fences down, one of her neighbors, out of Lucy's sight, stopped to look across at the sound. She stepped up to the fence and called across to her.

"Good morning, Lucy!"

Lucy turned to face her.

"Morning!" she said in reply, her face all lit up and flush.

"What's got you in such a great mood?" asked her neighbor whose name Lucy never could remember.

"Nothing," said Lucy. "Just a funny text message."

"Oh," said the neighbor, who went back to her gardening.

Lucy then looked down at the phone with the greatest feeling of relief she'd felt in a long while. Her observations and reasoning had proven correct. On at least one very important issue, Kate Castillo had been wrong.

Lucy whispered to herself.

"I'm going home."

BLACK INDIGO

Tommy Thrones had three parts to this plan. And he was about to start the first.

Getting Weaver's confidence had been easier than he had thought it would be, considering the old man's involvement with the Convergence. Tommy had managed to keep Weaver convinced that he was going to stick to the plan he'd been given. He'd never met an easier mark.

Though only a day had passed so far to his knowledge, Tommy had already felt he had the power to change the trajectory of thousands of lives. Such power, unlike any he had ever known, was enough to make him rethink the second stage of the plan, but only for a few moments.

Then the feeling would return.

The black indigo...

He'd been to a club once while high, one of the first times he'd gotten high. Only a few years before everything had gone to shit, when there still were nightclubs and nightlife in the city, in the world. Out with friends with the usual fake ID's and older twenty-something siblings who had no qualms about sneaking high schoolers 8 balls and joints. The night out was a farewell bash before one of the older guys moved to the Caribbean for the next few years with his parents. They'd gone to a club, cover-free, and lingered for a bit in the bar of the three-level club before heading up.

Tommy had noticed the old man sitting at the end, stacking and restacking paper coasters. He was easily in his sixties, overweight with a full head of overgrown white hair, wearing a full three-piece suit and hunched over the bar. Tommy remembered that two cute girls with nice tits poking braless through neon green dresses over tanned legs were dancing and making out just behind him, oblivious. When patrons passed, they moved around him as though he didn't exist, as if he was just some inter dimensional disturbance that they could only sense by intuition, or if they were looking for him directly (which of course, they weren't).

Tommy was sky high by then, the path from his buddy's apartment to the bar a stretch of blurred images. The weed affected him differently, must have been laced with something extra. While most of his buddies tended to get overly excited or aggressive with the girls, Tommy became an observer, losing all interest in social interaction, wanting only to watch and see. He saw the gut feelings that most people instinctively get as colors in his mind, superimposed on the actual visible light coming through his corneas.

And what he saw surrounding the old man was black indigo. It spoke of a deep isolation, of being alone while surrounded by hundreds, of a life that had once been great and exciting, filled with passion and love and adventure, now reduced to a invisibility in a three-piece suit on a Saturday night. Tommy had visions of a dark apartment in the bad part of town, of a long lonely walk at closing time down empty streets, of a single blue light bulb over an empty kitchen table with two chairs, one of which was always empty. No one came to see him, not even at Christmas.

Tommy saw black indigo around the old man. And he couldn't look away.

Black indigo had been his color, too. He'd felt it, carried it with him ever since he was eleven, when something had changed between him and his father. He knew that Dad was always going to favor the other two. Many middle children feel that way, but what had happened to Tommy was quite different. The doctors had said that it was an imbalance, some trick of brain chemistry that had started with the onset of early puberty. They hadn't prescribed any drugs for him, so

Tommy started self-medicating with anything he could get his hands on.

The drugs had changed his life that night, and seeing the old man sitting there, surrounded by those energies.. They had shown him that not only was the black indigo something that others felt, but it had shown him the person he would become after having spent a life with it.

But this wasn't just about one life. This was about three.

And Tommy had to make sure that only one of them suffered.

To do that, though, he had to fulfill the conditions of Weaver's mission.

Weaver seemed intent on ensuring that the Primes were the only ones to connect, and Tommy didn't know why. Nor did he care, since it matched up with his own intentions. So he made sure to carry out Weaver's plan with great enthusiasm, at least to start. As he learned more about the dynamics of the Convergence, he would find his opportunity to act.

Until then, Tommy waited for them in Glastonbury.

WEAVER'S DINER

The impression on the left side of his forehead was superficial, but sore.

Max rubbed the place where he had fallen asleep and looked out the window. The truck stop parking lot was empty, but the sun had been up for at least a good hour, and already the cracked, faded asphalt had little wisps of steam rising up from it that betrayed the length of the day so far. Looking outside the driver's side window, toward the four filling stations, Max saw a big rig parked about thirty feet away. Suddenly, the truck's engine started as he looked at it and started down towards the rural road, out toward the Interstate.

The Interstate...

The realization struck that Max had no idea where he was. He had no memory of navigating his way here, how he managed to park himself perfectly between the lines of the space just in front of the truck stop's restaurant, no clue how far off course he was.

He got out of the car. The morning was fresh and crisp, but stirred by the heat of the asphalt. It was going to be a really hot drive today. Max took a quick look at the wear on the tires and found them to be in decent shape. His bladder complained to him again and he walked up to the restaurant door and pulled it. It didn't budge, and then he saw the hours. It didn't open until 8:00am.

Max checked his watch, 7:54 A.M. Not long to wait for food, but six minutes too late to pee. He ran behind the car, across the empty parking lot to the ditch, found some cover in the tall grass, and relieved himself before zipping up and walking back.

The sound of a lock turning drew his attention as the owner opened the door. He was an older gentleman, wearing suspenders on jeans

61

over a typical collared shirt you'd expect any farmer in the Midwest to own. From the way he walked and spoke, he reminded Max vaguely of Redd Foxx.

"Good morning. Come on in," he grumbled, holding open the door. Max hadn't seen anyone walk up to the building, nor did a truck or car drive up on the other side of the structure. Max checked his watch. 8:01 A.M.

Inside, the dining room was a little cluttered, but there was enough elbow room if you needed it. Five small booths lined the windows on the opposite side, while two large round tables sat in the middle of the room. Immediately to the right, three intimate tables, intended for couples, lined the wall where the door was. The kitchen and small bar, complete with four stools bolted to the floor, was off to the left.

The owner's assistant — Max wanted to say "sous-chef," but even the term seemed to outclass this place — was a younger kid, about sixteen or seventeen, with brown hair and a slim build. He didn't say anything to him as he entered, choosing to give all of his attention to the coffee pot. Max noticed the two predominant themes: UFOs and musical liner notes. An entire wallpaper border consisting of sheet music that ran around the length of the dining room just under the ceiling. A single ceiling fan in the center that had no dust, and was likely well used during these summer months here on the Great Plains.

Max turned around and looked up at the sheet music just above his head near the door. Mozart, by the look of it. Ironically, the radio was tuned to easy listening.

"Do you know where I can catch the I-80 West from here?" asked Max. The owner looked him in the eye. He didn't smile, but Max noticed a definite kindness there.

"Where you headed?" he asked.

"California. But first, I'm...meeting someone here soon," he lied. "Travel buddy."

"Not that hard to find," said the owner. "Just head back out where you came in, turn right. Keep going about five minutes, you'll see the sign. About ten minutes out after that, you'll come to the highway."

"Got it. Thanks."

The owner - Max now assumed he was the Mister Weaver of "Weaver's Diner" - nodded. "No problem. Have a seat, I'll bring out some coffee."

Minutes later, Max sipped his coffee — a dark brew, very rich, surprisingly tasty for a place like this. Some other travelers had come in — a heavyset gray-hair in a suit who looked like he was on business, and a young twenty-something couple who came in on two motorcycles — and were sitting on the other side of the dining room. The younger ones were signing to each other. The gray hair was writing in his notebook. Max wondered about their stories.

The young kid approached his table. "How's the coffee, sir?" Max noticed he didn't speak with a Midwestern accent, and was unusually articulate.

"Great," said Max, who decided making some conversation would help kill the time. "What kind is it?"

"Chilean," said the kid. "It's like a stronger Columbian."

"I'm surprised you got it all the way out here," said Max. How old are you, bud?"

The kid beamed. "Fifteen."

"Aren't you a little young to be working?"

The kid shrugged. "I don't mind. Mr. Weaver's a friend of my dad's, and I get money for the summer. It's pretty sweet. Um, anything else I can get you?"

"No thanks, I'm good for now."

"Okay, then."

As the server boy headed over to the other tables, the young couple got up to leave, the woman dropping some bills on the table. Max watched them walk out to their bikes, put on their helmets, and start them up.

As they kicked up dust in the parking lot on their way out, Max saw a new car pull up in front of his window, a grey Nissan Sentra that had seen some mileage, and a few dings here and there.

The car pulled up right beside his window. The headlights dimmed, then shut off. The driver's side door opened.

And out stepped Max Sinclair.

***

Their greeting had gone well — Max figured shaking hands with yourself wasn't something anyone could get used to — and they had at the table. Mr. Weaver and the kid, Justin, according to his name tag, had asked for their order, but neither wanted anything besides coffee, at least not just yet.

This Alternate wore a highly offensive pink polo shirt and khaki combination, with dirty white running shoes and a crew cut that seemed like something right out of Mayberry. Every forty seconds, he looked around the place with the clinical disgust of a food inspector at a cockroach-infested Chinese takeout joint. Max couldn't tell for sure until he had sat down, but, as his Alternate had approached the diner door, would have sworn he was the type of guy who would have gotten at least one manicure in the past month.

The only thing out of place was the bandage wrapping all the way around the Alternate's head.

"What happened to your head?" asked Max.

The Alternate winced before answering. "Fell off the roof. I was seeing if our shingles needed replacing, took a misstep."

"So, where are you from?" asked Max, figuring, well, what the hell else do you lead off with?

This new Alternate cleared his throat. "Glastonbury."

"Glastonbury?"

"Yep," replied the Alternate. "Glastonbury, Ohio."

Max blinked.

"I made that place up for one of my stories, years ago," said Max. "It doesn't exist."

His Alternate shrugged. "It's real enough to me."

"No, really, how is that possible?" Max repeated.

"Don't ask me," said the Alternate. "I'm just as caught up in this as you are."

"How caught up?" asked Max.

"I've met five others so far, and you're the last, and so far, I know I'm living the best life."

"Really?"

"Really. Dinah and I are soul mates."

"You know we're divorced, she and I, right? In my, uh, lifespace?" said Max.

The Alternate rolled his eyes and sighed.

"Why doesn't that surprise me?"

"Excuse me?" said Max.

"Most of you are," said the Alternate, "or otherwise not together."

"You're serious?" said Max. "Then how can you say that you and Dinah are soul mates?"

"Because we are," replied the Alternate. "The rest of you, at least the ones I've met so far, just found a way to screw it up royally."

The Alternate soured his face as he put down the cup.

"This is the worst latte I've ever had. But then again, I guess this isn't the house specialty."

Max found himself gnashing his teeth, and the reality of the situation dawned on him: he was actually pissed at himself.

"You're a dandy," said Max. The Alternate looked at him.

"I am not," he replied. "I just like things a certain way, that's all. That, by the way, is one thing you could learn from me. If you were clear on what you wanted in life, you wouldn't be where you are now."

"And where is that?"

"Completely lost. Always running damage control."

"I'm not running damage control," replied Max. "Dinah and I had an amicable split, decided it was best for both of us."

"And why did you split?" asked the Alternate.

"Actually," said Max, leaning in, "part of it was because near the end, I became an arrogant gasbag. Kind of like you."

The Alternate looked at him, gave him a lopsided grin.

"And the other part?" he asked.

Max paused, looked down at his cup. "Well…she simply fell out of love with me. When that happened, that was that. Nothing I could do to change her mind."

The Alternate's grin faded, but he tilted his head to the side, scrutinizing Max's words, chewing them up and spitting them back out in his mind, the way Max himself still did whenever presented with a complex problem.

"And why do you think that happened?"

Max sighed. It had been a long time since he'd really talked about his divorce out loud, and though the old emotional scar was gone, the underlying muscle still ached.

"Changes in brain chemistry," replied Max.

The Alternate's grin returned.

"C'mon, Max. Who do you think you're talking to?"

Max took a breath. "I dunno, Max, who am I talking to? Where do you rate on this whole scale of multidimensional awesomeness? Are you my optimal?"

"Ha!"

The Alternate laughed, loud enough to draw a glance from both Weaver and Justin across the hall.

"Oh no," said the Alternate. "I'm not the optimal, and I'm not like the others. Their life tangents split off from ours way back. From what I know about you, you and I are separated by maybe, oh, one or two major decisions."

Max thought about this for a moment.

"What makes for a major decision? Like, one that's enough to make another lifespace?"

Before the Alternate could answer, Weaver came over. Max waited for him to flinch or do a double-take when he saw the two identical men speaking to each other. He did neither.

"You want a refill?" he asked.

"Uh...sure, thanks," said Max. Weaver looked at the Alternate, who shook his head in mid sip, a wince still on his face, and walked away.

Max pointed at Weaver with his thumb. "How come he doesn't say anything? Not even a look."

"You don't know?" asked the Alternate. Max shook his head. "Weaver's in on this."

"He is?"

"Sure he is. You think you can just Google 'Weaver's Diner' and find it? No way, friend. This is a way station for others making this journey."

"So...so everyone who saunters in here—"

"is on the same trip."

Max rubbed his forehead. "Wow. How come none of them said anything? Made a scene? Came up to compare notes?"

"That's obvious, isn't it?"

The Alternate gulped down the last of the latte and pushed the cup away from him in disgust.

"Besides not wanting to look crazy, half of them probably don't even know they're on the journey. They'll run into their own Alternates after leaving here."

Max let that sink in, then remembered his mission. "So," said Max, "you, uh…you know I'm here to get you connect with your own Lucy Fitzgerald."

The Alternate smiled, but his eyes narrowed. "Yeah, good luck with that."

That was a non-starter, although Max wasn't sure yet how to work around it. His Alternate was clearly a stubborn asshole, and you don't succeed with stubborn assholes unless you soften them up first. He decided to circle back to that one later.

"Why do you think you have the best life?" asked Max, changing the subject.

"For starters," replied the Alternate, "I have a great, stable teaching job that brings in the cash. I have all of the toys that I could ever want or need, live in a great house, three weeks' vacation each year, and of course, I've got Dinah. We rent a cabin in the summer, head to Lauderdale in the winter, and let the third week carry over until next year. Dinah wants to take a wine tour of Tuscany for a month, so we're saving up for that. We have no debt, and we're making bi-weekly payments on the mortgage. We see our parents on Sundays for brunch, and you can see that I just got tinted windows done on the Sentra. Life is good."

Max said nothing. The Alternate waited for an answer, then held up his hands.

"So?"

"So what?" asked Max.

"I win. I have the best life."

"So…you think the reason why you have the best life is because you've got stuff?"

"Not just 'stuff,' as you put it," said the Alternate, "but the best. I have high standards, and I accept nothing but the best."

Max shook his head. "This is un-fucking believable."

"Jeez, mind the profanity. We're in public."

"Are you serious?"

"It's not just the toys, Max," continued the Alternate, "it's my relationship with Dinah. We're the most functional out of everyone that we know."

"Uh-huh," said Max. The Alternate folded his fingers together, and Max felt revulsion at the smugness.

"What else do we really want out of life, Max? I have everything. You want to know where I rank among all the Max Sinclairs? You and I are the two most closely-related out of our counterparts, separated maybe by only one major tangent. The difference is that back when Dinah and I were still in college, I didn't give up on teaching. I got in, did my year, got a job at the university within a month of graduating, and have been steady and stable ever since. Everything since has been different."

"That's not completely true," said Max. "We almost moved into 9800 Oak Knoll."

"But you didn't, did you? Because at the time, you were working at the virtual concierge and you were barely making ends meet for a rental. You were making next to minimum wage torturing yourself by working with the richest of the rich and realizing what you were missing. All you had to do was just re-apply, and you would have been teaching."

"I didn't want to teach!"

"Why not? It's stable, it's safe."

"It's boring!"

"Right, you want to live by taking chances. Be a writer. Get famous. How's that working out for you?"

Max wanted to punch him in the face, karma be damned.

"This is really the most you think you can get out of life?" asked Max."I can have more if I wanted to, but I choose not to. You've got to know when to walk away from the table. That's why the house always wins: more people choose to stay and try to beat the dealer. That's why they go bust, and those of us who played it smart have to pay for their mistakes. Life is a profitable casino for the universe."

Weaver cleared his throat as he approached with Max's new coffee.

"Thanks." Weaver nodded and walked away again as the Alternate continued.

"I'm the version of you — out of all of us — that decided to forego the BS and actually go out and get the life success that all of us said we wanted. That means making sacrifices, it means giving up this fantasy that I can become a novelist, that life is always going to be this time when you're living each moment like the last. It's romantic sentimentalist garbage. Life can be boring sometimes, but boredom's preferable to desperation, isn't it?"

The Alternate continued. "I don't know if you'll meet the same ones along the way, but like I said, I've met five other Alternates. Everyone of them is the very definition of 'risk-taker,' and though I admire them for that, when you meet them, you see the price they paid. Out of all of them, I'm the only one who's got a net profit out of life."

"So what about Mr. Perfect?" asked Max.

"Who?"

"Sorry, I mean the 'Optimal.' Why do you think he's not the best?"

"Because he's not with Dinah," replied the Alternate. "He's after that other one you guys all seem to be smitten with. Lucy Fitzgerald."

"And what's wrong with that?" asked Max.

"Dude!" Max was startled to find his Alternate reverting to slang. Everything he'd said so far had come out with perfect diction and class.

"What?"

"She's a fantasy! All of you guys have just dreamed her up. That she's a real flesh and blood person isn't in doubt, but you guys are all in love with this image of what you want her to stand for. It's just that, a freaking mirage that's gone as soon as you try to grab it with your hands. And compared to Dinah, who's real, and always was and will be very much herself, how can you still choose the mirage?"

70

Max was about to answer, then he stopped himself, acknowledging for the first time the fact in evidence that now bore mentioning: part of him really did miss life with Dinah. And just like that, his heart started to ache, and he lowered his guard.

"It's...well, it's nice to see you guys are still in love."

The Alternate was ready with another retort, but then the words registered and he smiled, looked down.

"Yeah, it's, um...well, it's very special being with her. I'm just sorry that almost every other Max Sinclair that I've met fell out of love with her, or never met her at all. We're still those two crazy kids who met in the lecture hall. That feeling never went away."

For the first time in the conversation, the Alternate looked at Max with the faintest trace of sympathy. "I'm sorry you had to go through that."

Max nodded. "There was a time when I would have never questioned that Dinah was my soul mate. But it was such a long time ago. How come you were able to make it work?"

"Sacrifice, Max," said the Alternate. "It's the key. It's how you grow up. It's one thing that all of the other guys — all of the other version of us, Max — haven't done. For all of their fortunes and tragedies, the bets with life that they've won and lost, they still haven't given up childish things. When you meet them, you'll see what it brought them. In the meantime, I can tell you about life with Dinah, at the house on Oak Knoll, and hopefully you can take something from that."

Max looked at him, then checked his watch. It had been about forty minutes since he'd arrived here, and he wanted to get started on the work he'd come here to do.

"So, how does this work" asked Max. "If I'm supposed to get you to connect with your Lucy, and you won't do it, what happens now?"

"Well, the way this works is that when we meet, the way opens between our two lifespaces. I'm already in yours, so now you get to enter mine."

"How?"

The Alternate shifted in his seat, cleared his throat. "Start writing."

This didn't make sense. "What do you mean?"

"That's your in," said the Alternate. "You went back to writing, didn't you?"

"Yeah, after Dinah left me," replied Max. "Helped me cope."

"And how long had it been since you'd put pen to paper?" asked the Alternate.

From the tone of his voice, it was clear now: this was one of Max's own interrogations, the kind he'd give to people before who he felt needed to be "educated" in some way, shape, or form.

"You mean fingers on keyboard. And it had been so long that half of my oldest friends thought I'd just discovered the whole concept in the past year," replied Max.

The Alternate leaned back, chin pointed toward Max. "Well, as I said, that's your 'in.' Everyone's got a slightly different one, though mine seems to be just showing up. Did you bring your laptop?"

"Yep."

"Then use that." He took a breath, then put his fingertips together.

"Although frankly, I figured you would have learned your lesson by now with writing."

Max felt his back muscles cramping up. This was how he had come across to others back when he and Dinah were together. It was that feeling that no matter what you did or said, you were somehow wrong and inadequate to the task. That was what his Alternate was doing to him now.

And like many of his family and friends at the time, and especially Dinah, Max wasn't going to have any of it.

"And what lesson would that be?" asked Max.

"Why even bother, Max? You know this is gonna be just like every other quote-unquote 'creative' thing you've tried and failed at. You just don't have the discipline."

"Like hell I don't!" Max straightened out his own posture and leaned away from the Alternate. "Out of everything I tried to make happen and fail, not making a living from writing was the biggest regret I had. Now I write at least 200 words a day."

"Really? And you care about it so much that your decision to bring your computer on this little trip was just a whim?"

"No, that's...that's not what I mean—"

"Why is the writing thing so important now, Max?" asked the Alternate. "You really think you're going to make it as an author? When millions of people around the world are sitting there with their 'calling' collecting dust on their desks? You want to be the next Stephen King?"

"It's not that simple, it's—"

"Tell me, Max, why is it so important?"

Max shot back. "Don't act like you don't already know, Mr. Safe Bet."

"Of course I do."

"Then why—?"

"I want you to say it out loud," said the Alternate, "and hear how ridiculous the words sound when they come out of your mouth."

"Ridiculous?...fine, whatever."

And there it was. The Alternate was using Max's own reverse psychology attack on him, and he had no choice but to bite. Max summoned all of his intention and concentration behind the words he was about to say. He didn't know at first what he was going to say.

Then, something opened up in his awareness, that familiar feeling of the words just rising up to meet him from the abyss just when he needed them.

"Legacy."

The Alternate frowned.

"Legacy?"

Max nodded.

"Legacy," said Max. "I want to be remembered, but differently than everyone else."

Max paused, waiting for the rest of the words to come streaming in. "You know, I've got so many ideas in here," he tapped his forehead, "and that's how I make them real. Pen to paper. Keyboard and screen. I don't give a shit about the house, the cash, even the fame, just the meaning in what I do. And if I can make a life from it, that's perfect. And if a story, or a poem, even a lousy article on the web is enough to change the lives of a lot of people for the better, then it's worth it. Does that sound ridiculous to you?"

The Alternate stared. Max waited for a retort, but didn't get—

"That's such utter bullshit, Max."

Max blinked. "How can you say th—"

"Because I was there, dude!" said the Alternate. "I remember all of that fear: staying up late at night when Dinah was asleep in the bedroom, not wanting to share this with her because she relied on me working like a dog. I remember that inability to take the leap, how goddamned frustrating it was to always work for someone else when this was right here, in front of me. Something I loved. But something was holding me back from the edge. Know what was? Two words: common sense. Same reflex that keeps you from splattering at the bottom of a cliff. When are you gonna start listening to your better nature?"

"I *am* listening—"

"Now that, I respect," said the Alternate, lowering his tone. "Then why not teach? You can change so many lives in person that way. That's why I do it."

"There's nothing wrong with a teacher's legacy," said Max, "it's just not the one I'm supposed to leave. Writing is—"

"Your destiny?" finished the Alternate.

Max blinked. "You make it sound ridiculous when you say it like that."

74

"Fine," replied the Alternate, "you say it."

Max took a breath. "Writing, changing lives through words, changing the world, is my legacy. Writing is my destiny. And I don't have to convince you of that."

"Just yourself? How unoriginal."

"Dinah was a big part of that doubt," continued Max. "I have no idea how it went down for you, but when she found out about writing, it was a disaster. She never brought in enough to sustain the lifestyle she wanted for us, so it was up to me. It was always up to me. And every time I thought of taking the chance, she'd say 'Sure, go for it!' in that empty voice. Then rent would be due the next week, or we'd need groceries, or whatever, and when that happened, she'd see me at the computer or out scribbling, and she'd give me that look. You know the one."

The Alternate blinked, and Max saw a crack in his defenses.

"So I just kept working," continued Max, "job after job until I found the virtual concierge, and even then, it wasn't working as well as it we — as she — needed it to. I couldn't win. But through it all, all I could think about was pen and paper, keyboard and screen, how simple it was, and just how much promise and potential it contained for the unthinkable: a life where the bills were paid doing something I loved. A life that you, apparently, wanted no part of."

The Alternate said nothing, and Max took a sip from the coffee, which suddenly tasted much more delicious.

"This was the other part of why we got divorced," said Max. "I couldn't stay employed anywhere long enough to give her security, and though she never said it, she expected me to give up on the one thing that I loved the most. There was no way that could last without one of us giving up, which, in your case, was you."

Ah, there! You only had to look into the Alternate's eyes to see the hot air leaking out. He had perched himself on his little finger arch, and the doubt was now tugging on every muscle in his face. Max had won.

"Well," said the Alternate, finally, "since you insist on jumping off the cliff in the vain and epic hope that you're gonna fly, I may as well help you grow some wings."

Max grinned. "You know, that's not too bad," but the Alternate would not laugh.

"Okay," he said simply, "go get your laptop, start jotting down notes. When the words come to you, you'll find yourself in my lifespace."

Max sat for a moment, taking stock of how he was feeling. Exhilarated. Proud. Certain. Feelings he hadn't had for such a long time, only absent of arrogance. No, there was none of that, not on either side of the table. The Alternate now stared off into space, in his own head.

And Max did feel some pity for him: given the fight he'd put up defending his lifestyle, there was no doubt the Alternate, too, still missed the feeling that came with putting pen to paper. But, frankly, that was the Alternate's problem. And Max had his own to deal with.

Moments later, Max had come back from his car with the laptop. As he set it up, he was frowning, and the Alternate saw.

"What's wrong?" he asked.

Max turned around. "What am I writing about, exactly?"

"You tell me, Mr. Hemingway."

"Even if it's made up?"

The Alternate shrugged.

"Whatever works for you, man." The Alternate saw Max still wasn't moving. "What else is bugging you?"

"Well," said Max, "if I made up Glastonbury, and it's real—"

"I get it," said the Alternate, waving him off. "It's …a little creepy to think about, I admit, but I can assure you, it's a real place, and I was living a whole separate lifespace before running into Weaver. Treat this as source material."

He paused. "You're not my maker."

"You sure about that?"

The Alternate only sipped his cup in response. Then, after a few moments, he got up. "Nice meeting you, Max."

"Wait, where are you going?"

The Alternate reached the door, and turned. "I've got to inspect the shingles on the house. Fall's gonna be here before you know it."

The Alternate shut the door behind him. Max watched as he strolled to his car. The engine started, and the Alternate left the parking lot.

Max took a breath. "Well…that went well, I guess," he said aloud to the room. He opened the word processor program and sat there, Mr. Weaver and Justin watching him in silence.

After a few minutes, a word appeared in his mind. Then two. Then more.

As Max typed, he suddenly felt vertigo take hold, light at first, a subtle swirling that flared into a hurricane faster than he expected. The soreness on his forehead suddenly erupted, and the last thing he saw was the screen, Weaver's Diner, and the Glastonbury Alternate all rotating to forty-five degrees as Max fell sideways out of the world and into another lifespace.

GLASTONBURY

A man in a suit with a resume in hand approached Max on the busy sidewalk, and gave him the most astonished look as they passed each other.

A couple of teen girls walking past laughed at Max as he stumbled around, regaining his footing. The tree was real, as were their laughs. He had to sit down. Looking over, he saw a bench and moved toward it, only to have an old couple intercept it when he was four feet away.

What am I doing here? What's happening?

Adrenaline started. Max had to find some place to sit down. He turned around to head back to the car when someone nearly bumped into him.

"Oh, there you are. I don't think I'm going to buy the dress after all, it looks hideous."

Dinah was carrying four shopping bags from just as many different boutique stores that operated out of the downtown. Her dark hair was long and well coiffed, and she wore a long black and white Dolce & Gabbana dress that revealed a slightly more enhanced waistline than Max had recalled in their last meeting. Her blue eyes were definitely brighter than he last remembered — happier and fuller. Her face was much the same.

Max said nothing, and Dinah took her attention away from her shopping, aware of his silence but not the shock.

"So, what do you think?" she asked, her eyebrows went up at the same time, a habit of hers that irritated Max to no end because they only did that when she knew Max hadn't been listening and wanted to embarrass him.

"I — I guess that's good," he managed to get out. Dinah's blue eyes briefly rolled in the back of her head.

"Of course it's a good thing. I wasn't going to pay full price for it when I could easily have bought the other one at Mayweather's, which I did!" She held up the other bag.

"Right," said Max, and Dinah held out her hand.

"Come on, I want to hit up the Atrium before we go home." Max took her hand, which she then slid around his arm as he escorted her — or rather, quite the other way around — down the street. It was that old feeling, something the two of them had done for years.

"So, when did you go back to the house to change?" asked Dinah.

"Uh, I didn't," he said, his voice more monotone than he intended.

"Really?" Really carried that tone, one familiar to deviant boyfriends and husbands everywhere.

"Yeah, I...didn't have time?"

"If you didn't like the golf shirt, you just had to say so, and I would have gotten you something else," said Dinah.

"No...it was fine, I—"

"Then where is it, honey?" Definitely a lot more vinegar in the way she said "honey" than its namesake nectar. Dinah, like most divas, would never get mad at you all at once. Instead, she would play this little game where her face would go all pouty, except for the fake smile that betrayed her true disappointment, and her sentences would be short and loaded.

"I...it's in the car."

Dinah stopped them both. By this time, she wasn't even pretending anymore.

"Look, don't be an asshole, okay? If you left the shirt at home, it's no big deal, but you should have told me so we don't have to head out again. All you had to do is say so."

Somehow, the prospect of getting into yet another fight with Dinah after so much acrimony snapped him out of his other-worldly trance, and Max fell into the moment.

"No, it's not that. Dinah...what the hell are we doing here?"

"Not shopping, that's for damned sure—"

"No, I mean, why are you here? You told me you didn't want to see me again, and now we're shopping together?"

Dinah frowned. "What the hell—" And then she stopped, and all of the anger washed away from her face. "Max, your forehead is blue! What happened to your bandages?"

"Bandages? Ow!" She reached up and touched the left side of his forehead, just below the hairline. Max felt a bruise that hadn't existed a second ago throb under her soft touch. Her hand dropped as Max reached up and probed the same spot.

"Max." He looked at her, and those blue eyes had lost all of their scorn. "I think we should go back to Dr. Maio."

"Who's Dr. Maio? It's just a bruise." The blue in those eyes now sparkled with genuine fear.

"If you don't remember who Dr. Maio is, then the accident was more serious than we thought. He said we have to go see him if there was any memory loss. What's the last thing you remember about last night?"

The last thing?

"Well, I was driving through Iowa, but I started falling asleep and so I had to get off the I-80, but..." Max stopped at the sound of shopping bags hitting the sidewalk. Dinah had brought her hands up over her mouth.

"Oh my God...Max, we have to go now. Give me the keys, you shouldn't be driving."

"What's going on?" he asked.

"Max, last night, you weren't on the Interstate."

"What? Where was I?"

"You were in bed, with me, at our house."

Max waited a moment. In fact, he waited for the dream to end. But it wasn't ending. Everything was already clear, the edges of the buildings and the staring faces walking past their little scene sharp and recognizable.

This was real, then, and then he smiled. Sometimes, when you're lost enough in strangeness, and you have no goddamned clue what's going on, all you can do is smile. Max's smile turned into a chuckle, then a laugh. Dinah took a step back as her (ex) husband laughed until he cried, reaching into his pocket as he did, and handing her the keys.

"I have no idea where I parked."

***

After the prelim exam and a second x-ray, Dr. Maio reached the same conclusion that the emergency room doctor had: no additional trauma had occurred, no sign of a hairline fracture or anything like that, but to be really sure, he would have to perform additional testing.

"I want to send him to a specialist," he said to Dinah in his strong Chinese-laden accent. "He's a psychologist who specializes in PTSD. Maybe Max has had some kind of psychological reaction to the injury. He can schedule you in for more brain scans, too."

"I don't understand it, Doctor," said Max. "How can I have all of these memories that don't exist, and not remember any of the ones that do? A bump on the head can't do that."

"Not a bump," said Maio, "but falling from the roof of your house hurts a lot more than that."

"You were inspecting the shingles," said Dinah. "You remember?"

Max shook his head.

"The scans didn't show any hairline fractures or a hematoma, nothing that should affect the nervous system physically," continued Maio. "But you'd be surprised, Mr. Sinclair, the brain is a very complex organ. You could have any number of subtle injuries that we can't see without scanning further. The mind, however...even stranger."

Dr. Maio turned back to Dinah.

"Did he ever have a fall like this when he was a child?" Max felt a little offended that Maio would ask Dinah about Max's childhood, as if she were his mother. Then again, even if Max could remember such an incident — and he couldn't — his memory wasn't exactly reliable at this point in time.

"I don't think he ever talked about it," said Dinah.

"I will let the specialist talk to you more about that whole thing. I'll call you when I can set up the appointment. You can go home for now, but get some rest, and for God's sake, don't go back on the roof!"

The doctor chuckled at his own joke, and Max couldn't help but smile a little bit. They parted company, and Max soon found himself headed back to his car with Dinah. It was now late afternoon, and the sun was starting to color the horizon.

"Let's get you home, honey," said Dinah, taking the driver's seat once again. "Maybe it'll help clear things up."

Max nodded and sat himself down in shotgun for the ride home, or rather, to the house.

***

9800 Oak Knoll sat in one of the more prominent neighborhoods in the county. Naturally, the residents tended to be higher up officials in the employ of the nearby college: professors, deans, administrators, some members of the Board of Governors. It wasn't so much for the neighbors and status that they had considered moving there as it was for the house itself.

Max hopped out of the car as Dinah pulled into the driveway. The house's three floors stood before him in the quiet neighborhood as the dusk set in. Four stairs led up to the porch and the wooden front door.

To the left, two large living room windows were partially covered by the growing brush of the small summer garden planted in front of them, and above, the second floor and its three smaller windows faced the road. Atop the house was the attic with a single half-moon window unencumbered by a curtain on the other side of the glass, providing an open view into that part of the house, which was probably the intent of the builders.

Dinah closed the door. "Remember anything?" she asked.

Max examined the house, shook his head. "Looks about the same as when we drove past it the first time," he said.

"That was months ago," she said. "Is that honestly the only memory that you have? You don't remember the showing, when we beat out the other guys for the offer? When I managed to get the new appliances in the kitchen?"

"Nope, nope, and nope," replied Max. "No memory of that at all."

"Well, come on in," said Dinah. "Even if it doesn't jog your memory today, then at least you can get some rest."

They wandered in. Max beheld a beautiful, quaint foyer adjacent to the equally lovely TV room with delightful white couches and Victorian decor: not his preference, but definitely Dinah's. Indeed, everything about this house — the kitchen and the new appliances that Dinah managed to hustle out of the other guys; the clean bathrooms with perfectly folded towels; and finally, the comfortable master bedroom upstairs with the empty companion rooms reserved for kids and guests — was beautiful, comfortable, and decorated par excellence by Dinah.

Only the third floor, the somewhat ill-named "attic," remained ceded to Max.

"That's where you do most of your own stuff," she said, heading up the last flight of stairs to the top of the house. "The study holds your computer desk, but upstairs is definitely your own. You can tell by the mess."

The staircase opened up right onto the floor of the attic. Dinah flicked a switch to turn on the main light, which came from a small chandelier fixture in the center of the ceiling. It was spacious, but clutter took up all of the room in the corners. Four semi-circle windows let light in from all four walls. The floor resembled a dance floor, but for the single easy chair in the center, presumably where Max sat and scribbled.

"Anything now?" asked Dinah.

"Still nothing. You know...I think I'd like to get to bed."

"Are you hungry? I can order a pizza or something if you'd like."

Max looked around. "No, I'm fine. Actually, I'll just hang around here for a few if I can."

"Sure thing, babe," said Dinah, and she kissed him on the cheek before descending the staircase. It felt good, so much like what they'd had before, their own special magic.

Max wandered around a bit, watching the twilight through the westernmost-facing window for a spell. The view outside was blocked by a big tree, but over the roofs of the houses, you could see the sky — crimson and violet — as night took over from the sun's long summer day.

He returned to the chair in the middle of the room and plunked himself down, trying to reason everything out.

Lucy Fitzgerald...

This was his house. Even if he didn't remember, the injury was real. He'd heard of a lot of victims of construction accidents, professional fighters, and assault victims who had suffered his type of injury. The stories of disorientation, memory loss, even phantom memories, were all characteristics....

I'm here to find Lucy Fitzgerald...but how do I do that?

If this was his life, then what about everything else? Had Lucy been real? She'd certainly felt real, but Dinah had no idea who she was.

She felt real, though, thought Max. No, this bump on my forehead is real. There are x-rays and veteran doctors to prove it. This attic in this house is real. Dinah is real. Lucy is not.

Max sat with these thoughts for some time until he heard a knock. The sky outside was now completely black, and Dinah had come up with some water. She was dressed in her robe and nightgown and was walking up the stairs in her slippers.

"You okay?" she said. "You've been up here for an hour."

"Yeah, I'm just — An hour?" Max didn't think he'd been here that long. Dinah must have known what was running through his mind at that moment.

"Dr. Maio said that injuries like yours cause you to lose your sense of time. Don't worry, I brought your meds." She handed him a tiny painkiller and the glass of water. Max hesitated for a second, then took the pill.

"Thanks," he said. "Good timing, too, I have a massive headache."

"Of course," replied Dinah. "You'd better get to bed, too. That pill always knocks you out cold."

Max took one last look around the attic and headed down.

Minutes later, he had undressed, in his sleeping clothes — a pajama top and bottom, courtesy of Dinah — and lay in bed. Dinah was reading some obscure romance novel next to him. The pill started taking effect, and as he grew drowsy, Dinah spoke.

"Babe, I'm curious," she said. "In the waiting room, you mentioned someone named Lucy. Who did you mean?"

Max didn't remember saying that. Much of the time between "waking up" downtown on the shopping trip and finding his way to Dr. Maio was a red haze.

Still, Lucy….

He remembered Lucy, from the other set of memories. Someone he'd spoken to on the phone. Someone he'd been waiting for, for a long time. Someone who wasn't Dinah.

"I don't remember asking you that," he said, and then closed his eyes. Dinah accepted it without question.

"That's okay. I'm sure it was nothing," said Dinah.

As he drifted into slumber, next to his caring wife, in their house, Max made a conscious decision to dismiss Lucy, and the drive out to the plains, as products of his injury. It was a beautiful adventure, and he was glad that it was coming to a close, and he could start his recovery back to normal life.

***

Max opened his eyes and reached for his head bandage.

The swelling had gone down, but there was still a subtle bump that would probably take longer than the three days it had taken to heal thus far. He reached around for Dinah, but she had long since gone off to work. He spread his body out, taking over the whole bed and continued to doze.

Max reflected on the past three days, the only three that he remembered in his supposed "real life." He was on extended leave from work, and would be for another couple of months. He'd spent most of the time in bed, an ache in his skull that throbbed, as if there was someone in there trying to hammer his way out.

The night before, the thought struck him: someone had given him a map. If he had indeed taken that trip, the map would be in the car. More than that, the fuel tank and the mileage in the Sunfire would reflect it. The thought elated him for a few seconds until he realized that, like most people, he never checked the mileage. Even if he'd added 500 miles to it, he'd never know the difference. Dinah wouldn't know, either: she drove her own car and had been up front with Max on that.

"I can't manage everything in your life and your oil change schedule, too, Max. You've got to do some things yourself."

The fuel meter, on the other hand, had been at three-quarter tank, and Max did have a memory of filling up at a Chevron somewhere near the state line with Illinois, but he never got a receipt from the pump, nor had he reset the trip ticker, so that was still inconclusive.

As for the map, he scavenged through the car to find it, coming up with nothing but a few wrappers, one or two dirty tissues, and some gas receipts. Nothing.

There was also the golf shirt. Dinah had said that he'd changed clothes since she'd last seen him. If he'd truly come in from the Interstate, there would have been no change of clothes sitting at home. Sure enough, Dinah had shown him the golf shirt, and he hadn't remembered a thing about it, but there it was, tags still on, and no way for it to have gotten back to the house on that day unless he had gone back there himself to drop it off.

In any case, Max figured that all of the remaining doubts would vanish after he had his session with the specialist that Dr. Maio had recommended. His own memories were in such doubt, he hoped that even if modern medicine didn't have all of the answers, at the very least it would give him back the certainty he needed to move on with his life.

Rising from his contemplative dozing, Max checked the clock. 7:55 A.M. Off to see the doc.

***

"It was so real," said Max. "The trip, the diner, Lucy...I feel no connection to this life. But it's obvious to me that this life is real. I'm sitting with you now, talking to you about this. I've never met you before at all..." Max paused, looked sharply at him. "Have I?"

Dr. Blake didn't smile. "No, you've never met me," he said. "It's totally understandable, though, to feel that way after an injury like

87

yours. But Dr. Maio said that there is nothing physiologically wrong with you."

"No, at least not without some deeper scans." said Max.

"Meaning that it's likely the injury's brought out a lot of other issues that might have been existent beforehand. You've mentioned a couple of things that stand out. First," Blake checked his notes. "Lucy Fitzgerald, who you remember falling in love with and heading out to see across the country."

"Yes?" said Max.

"What is life with Dinah like? Are you completely happy?"

A pause, then Max answered.

"Dinah loves me, and I love her, but she demands a lot from me to stay together, a lot of my own freedom. I feel like I have no identity with her, no breathing room to do my own thing."

"It's a common feeling with many husbands," said Blake.

"I know, but it's more than that. Our time is very...mediocre. With Lucy, I get the feeling everything would have been far more alive. I could feel more aware of everything — being in my own skin, noticing colors and smells and tastes more — and I felt so at home with her in a way I don't feel with Dinah"

"And yet, she never existed."

"No," said Max.

"Could it be that you needed this fantasy in order to feel release? Something that the injury may have unleashed from your subconscious?"

Max looked at Dr. Blake square in the eye. "Is it wrong to want more out of a marriage even when we have no problems?"

Dr. Blake replied, in an even tone. "Didn't you just say that you had no identity in the marriage? You don't consider that a problem?"

Max let that sink in for a bit. A few thought forms from that phantom tier of memory floated past his awareness. No images, just feelings. Exhilaration. Hope.

"It's possible it's a fantasy," continued Max, "but if it's all just a false memory, how could it have so much depth? I felt time passing."

"The mind is—"

"a lot stranger than the brain."

"It's not even a matter of strangeness," said Blake. "Our own sense of time is so fluid. Impulses that the brain fires off can create entire worlds that last only seconds — milliseconds — in our perception."

Blake leaned forward. "Max, one of my predecessors was one Dr. Maury. He was alive in France just after the Revolution. One night, he had a vivid dream in which he was on the run from Robespierre, during the Terror, when hundreds of suspected Royalists were rounded up and sent to the guillotine. He remembered everything clearly as if it were real — hiding in the streets, being caught by the Revolutionaries, being brought to a lengthy trial before Robespierre himself, and ultimately, being sent to be executed. He remembered, in vivid detail, being led to the killing machine, the smell of the blood on the streets, having his head forced into the machine and, finally, the blade coming down on his neck. At that point, he woke up, only to find that part of the bed frame had come down while he was sleeping, right on the same vertebrae where the guillotine would have struck.

"Now, that bed frame must have only taken a split second to fall and strike him, but he swore, in his writings afterward, that the dream seemed to last the span of days, possibly weeks. Nonetheless, in that split second, Dr. Maury's subconscious managed to produce a dream of cinematic proportions. The mind is strange that way, and even though it seems real, it's not. Eternity in an hour."

Max pondered this for a moment. "So, what happened to me?"

"Flashbacks related to PTSD can strike anytime, though most of the time, they require a specific stimulus: a small bump, a familiar flash of light or body movement." said Blake. "You're telling me that you had pulled into the parking lot downtown and started wandering."

"Yes, but I had been...well, I thought that I'd just come into town from the Interstate."

"And then you saw Dinah?"

"Yes, after stumbling around for a while, completely disoriented."

"And she then told you that your bruise had swollen up."

"Yeah, I hadn't noticed it, though. After she pointed it out, it started to hurt, just out of nowhere, like someone had just hit it with a baseball bat."

Dr. Blake paused, looking over his notes. "The episode could have happened within a few seconds of the flare-up," he said. "Can you think of anything else that happened that could have led to the flare-up?"

Try as he might, Max shook his head. Dr. Blake looked over his notes, took a breath.

"Well, I could prescribe a couple of treatment options, but until you have another episode, I don't really have much to go on. I think you should stay around town, take it easy, and try not to drive or operate machinery if you can after you go home. If you have more blackouts and hallucinations, call me right away." He took out a business card and wrote a number on the back. "That's my emergency line for patients. Call me any time of day you need to as soon as you have another attack. I'll want to get as many fresh details as I can as it happens."

Max took the card. "Thanks, doctor."

"No problem."

***

Max walked away from Dr. Blake's office and got back into the car. The sun had been hot, and the cab was sweltering. He cracked the window and checked the odometer. 85,342 miles. Not that it made a difference.

He sighed. Blake's prescription was no different than Maio's: sit tight, relax, and call if something else happens. Nothing in the way of definitive answers, except that it was a hallucination, and it might happen again, meaning he would have to live with this for a while longer.

He started the engine and started to drive. The roads were largely clear, and though he didn't check the clock, he figured it was sometime around lunch. On a whim, Max decided to steer himself back to the Atrium to have a coffee.

The drive was uneventful, but Max was vigilant and very aware of his body and surroundings, watchful for another attack. Pulling into the mall parking lot, he got out and walked toward the entrance, his mind entirely focused on sensations: the hot concrete underneath his feet, the humidity in the air that spoke of afternoon cloudbursts and thunderstorms, the smell of pizza from the Italian place just next to the mall entrance. Nothing strange, nothing new.

Like the town, the Atrium was clear and clean, and, Max observed, free of the construction crews and noise that had marked it for the past three months. Had he imagined even those small details? Indeed, the new wing was complete, with several more stores and a gorgeous crystalline skylight glass ceiling letting the sun fall on the newly-potted palm trees and benches. Everything truly seemed a little better off than what he could recall.

But as pretty as it all was, it was boring. Sedentary. Nothing was happening in here, and though he'd told himself he'd get used to it when they first moved here, Glastonbury PA seemed to be place you moved to when you had nothing left to do, when you'd already lived the adventure, and all you wanted was to settle down. There was no life here. Just existence.

Max approached the café, saw a free table and chair and sat down. There were few other customers inside the Atrium café, so Max settled in, flagged down the server, and ordered a green tea.

As the server walked away, a woman walked past. She was older, wearing a long sundress colored with the most vibrant shade of coral he had seen.

His forehead started to throb, and Max became vigilant for anything strange. If this was all in his head, something would happen soon. After a few minutes of agony, the pain dissipated and nothing had happened. The server had dropped off his tea and walked away without saying a word.

Frustrated, Max sipped at the tea. This was ridiculous. He couldn't live like this. Immediately, he reached into his pocket for his cell. He would call Dr. Blake back and demand one of those prescriptions he talked about. He started dialing.

"Excuse me, I hate to ask, but could I borrow your phone?"

Max looked up.

Lucy stood above him. He dropped the phone, and it clattered on the table.

"Lucy!"

She frowned.

"I'm sorry, have we met?" she asked.

The throbbing in his forehead returned. Max's vision suddenly grew blurry. He felt weightless, then saw the world turn ninety degrees, the floor suddenly drawing closer. The impact seemed distant, even as the pain subsided for an instant, interrupted by the sharper shock of the side of his head hitting the floor.

"Someone get a doctor!"

Max looked up into the green of Lucy's eyes as she leaned over him, put her hand on his forehead.

"It'll be okay," said Lucy, though to Max her voice was muffled, as if she was speaking to him across a chasm.

Everything dissolved by degrees, and the last thing he heard was her voice, familiar, calming, perfect as he faded into oblivion.

LEATHER GLADS

Lucy Fitzgerald was heading home in style.

She wasn't sure if the physics of the Convergence would allow her to take things back with her. And yes, she felt a little guilty taking back some of her Alternate's things, including a pretty set of earrings, three awesome pairs of pumps — illegal in Carmel due to their oddball by-laws — a few smaller outfits, even a bread maker — but then again, it was her name on it. Technically not stealing.

And why not, after all? Lucy hadn't exactly been living in the lap of luxury for most of her grown-up life. This may as well be her last chance to enjoy the feeling.

Plus, when her Alternate returned, she'd be coming back into money: the studio was one of the most lucrative businesses on Rio Drive, popular with locals as well as tourists. Lots and lots of green floating around Carmel-by-the-Sea. Where Lucy was going, that was the opposite of true.

All Lucy had to do now was book her flight back to Seattle. If the way was now open again, she wanted to get there as fast as humanly possible.

Lucy zipped up the suitcase and looked around the bedroom. She'd left most of it as resplendent as she had found it, and except for those "missing" items that her Alternate would easily replace, it was as if no one had stayed here. Of course, she'd be sleeping in the bed at least one more night. Her flight home was the next day.

Thirty-two days ago, Lucy had realized her relatives and friends from her life in Seattle were gone or didn't exist. But most devastating to her was when she tried to call Charles. The number was disconnected, and there was nothing in the Yellow Pages, Google, or

93

any other resource that showed where he was. Evidently, in this lifespace, he simply did not exist.

At first, she had experienced heartbreak all over again, far worse than what Charles had done to her. It was like losing a spouse, or as close as she had come — or would ever come— to becoming a widow, or watching her love waste away in a coma or vanish one random day, never to return, with no explanation. The void came back to say "hey," only it didn't stay beyond the first day, because she was so damned busy.

Lucy was suddenly running a business and a house, neither of which had been hers a few days ago, and her survival instinct kicked in, the same one that had gotten her through those rough days trying to find a job after high school, moving to Seattle, figuring out what she wanted to do with her life, living through her parents' divorce and all of that drama that only now was dissolving into the background of their relationships together, ancient history. Putting up with the daily dose of mediocrity and bullshit at work...no, Lucy was a survivor. And she would get through living in a world where Charles didn't exist. Thirty-two days later, she was surviving, prospering, in fact.

But now, Max was on his way, and she had to appreciate the irony that without him, there couldn't be Charles, either. A cruel irony, to be sure, but not for her. At least, that's what she told herself.

Lucy walked back to the closet to see if there was anything else she could take with her. Opening the door, she rifled through the shoe boxes until she noticed one that she hadn't opened. Taking it out, she pulled out a pair of brown leather gladiators.

This pair stood out. Lucy took a moment to look at them, noticing the details of the stitching, how worn they were at the heel. Brown leather glads weren't in and of themselves unusual, but for the significance they held in Lucy's mind.

The recent history that two simple shoes represented.

A history only six months old.

94

***

Flashback to early January. Seattle winter, and as if getting rain nine months out of twelve wasn't bad enough, add in unseasonable cold.

Add in the wind. Add in a hillside overlooking Seattle Central, the nexus where your love had started, grown, blossomed, and ended in a closed loop. Throw in the restaurants where you first got to feel safe with each other, the parks where you shared your picnics and kisses, the sidewalks where your hands never broke, the movie theaters and hotels where you made out, made love, and mix it together with the Space Needle as a ladle, the site of his proposal. Relationship pudding. Breakup pudding, really. Just add water. Serve cold.

How to describe the wretched emptiness? The rejection? Not originally, that was for sure.

Where had she read — many places, likely — of that feeling of wanting to claw into your chest to get at it? A bloodless wound that caused no bodily damage, but would kill you from the inside. And when you suffer enough, things like jumping off a building or putting a bullet in your brainpan seem like bright and shiny alternatives to the status quo.

A pain, an itch that just doesn't go away. You want to go to sleep and wake up and realize that it was just a nightmare. You don't of course. Instead, you have worse. You wake up into the nightmare.

There's no middle ground with the void: you're either dead to the world or you can't sit still. It forces you to choose. And when you're not tired, you just lay there in hell.

So you get up and walk, not giving two shits about putting concealer to hide the fact you've been crying for three days, that you haven't eaten a real meal or brushed your teeth, haven't showered or put a comb through your hair. You walk without an umbrella, but you wear a coat and cross your arms over your chest as the rain falls in torrents around you, and you see your breath. People stare at you.

Some mutter aloud rude musings about your homelessness. Your drug addiction. Your prostitution. And you pass by a window and catch your reflection and think, why wouldn't they? Look at you.

And you don't care. Because the void wants the whole world to know just how hurt you are. That someone did this to you, and you blame yourself anyway.

On top of everything, the void takes your modesty. You can cry openly in the rain, and the puffs of steam from your sobs are the only sign to passersby that something's wrong. A sick kind of freedom.

You walk for three miles, finding a hillside where you can sit alone on the yellowed grass and stare at Seattle Central, stare at the heart of it all, now broken. And the rain lets up. And there's no one else around, because it's 2:00 on a Wednesday in January. No one in their right mind would be out here. Good thing you're not one of them.

That's when you can sit and rest, because you're tired. The void eases when you're tired. And soon, it's just you and the city, and your mind can start to clear, waking sleepfulness.

When you're done, you head back home, a long march that ends in the early dark of the winter day. You go back to bed and drink yourself to sleep for a few hours, only to wake up and start the cycle all over again.

The first two days were much the same.

On the third, everything changed.

Lucy wasn't sure what had happened, or how she had gotten there. She remembered waking up in bed, with the feeling of utmost horror. She recalled no details, saw no leftover images in her mind's eye as she rose from slumber into wakefulness much like when you remember a vivid dream. All she remembered was the feeling. So strong. Thrilling in its impact and revelation.

Knowledge she had lived out an entire life away from this dark time — filled with notable moments and hours that dragged, routine biological processes and high sensory pursuits, entire groups of people

96

met, befriended, invited into one's home and heart and then released just as slowly, and all the bittersweet of growing older and living life…only to realize at the end that none of it had been real.

That she was still asleep.

And then she woke up.

The third day had been the worst one of them all.

Hours later, Lucy had found herself, once again, on that hillside, staring out at Seattle Central. That's what you do. You keep wandering the city. You keep walking. You stare at the city. You keep crying until you dry up, raw and wrinkled.

And that's when you hear him, shuffling up behind you.

You turn and see him, looking like the African-American version of the guy in those old American Express commercials: gray trench coat, hat, umbrella, walking up to you like there's nothing wrong in the world.

And you talk.

When she'd first encountered Herbert E. Weaver, the old man had been beyond vague. It was like he was pissing you off just to expand your mind through pressure, like he knew no other way to get you thinking, to bring your brain up to his heavyweight class.

The damndest thing about that whole encounter was that it was so strange. Lucy remembered very little about how it started, but she remembered what he had said to keep her attention.

Weaver had introduced himself, asked if she was all right, and then told her that she had to get herself ready to do her part.

"My part in what?" she had asked, her face still raw, staring off at the Seattle skyline, still holding Charles' wedding ring in the box he had sent it back in.

"'Fraid you'll have to figure that out in time, child," said Weaver in that Old South patois that sounded so archaic, and yet brimmed with authenticity, as if Weaver had been around during the antebellum times himself. "But if you want a starting place, write up a list."

"A list of what?"

"Of what you really want in love."

She looked him in the eye.

"I...*loved*...Charles."

At that point, Weaver had knelt down beside her.

"And why did it end, my child?" he asked.

Lucy sniffed.

"He found someone else," she said. "He was cheating on me." Lucy would remember that as being the first time she had said the words out loud to another human being, words she had been afraid to say, for fear she would lose all of her remaining dignity and fall apart again. But saying them to someone else relieved the pain, more than she thought possible. Even though it wouldn't last, when you're hurting this hurt, you do what you must to relieve the pain. You keep talking.

"I went to see him," continued Lucy. "He wasn't expecting me that early, but he'd left the door unlocked. He'd bought a new townhouse, the one we were supposed to move into. When I got there, the first thing I smelled was the perfume. Then, I saw the other pair of sandals: leather gladiators. For most girls, that would be enough, but I needed direct proof. I walked through the place, upstairs, and heard at least one person in the bedroom."

Weaver had listened, the best poker face Lucy had ever seen.

"Charles was there," said Lucy. "He was surprised to see me, deer-in-the-headlights surprised. I asked him about the sandals, and he confessed. Said it just didn't feel right between us, that it never had, not the way it felt with whoever had been in his bed that day. That's when..."

Lucy looked down to the box she had been fumbling with in her hand.

"That's when he gave me back the ring."

Lucy remembered — and would probably never forget — that Weaver never so much as handed her a tissue or put a comforting hand on her shoulder. Instead, all he'd given her was sympathy card consolation.

"If a door closes, a window opens," he said, standing up and taking a few steps behind her.

Then, Weaver said something not so typical.

"Before you can open the right window, though, you gotta know what it looks like. Sometimes they contain eternity in an hour."

Weaver walked away, letting the words have their impact. In the ten or so seconds it had taken Lucy to turn around and watch him go, he was gone.

Three days afterward, Lucy found herself writing her list of qualities possessed by her soul mate. When she had finished, for no reason, she went back to the top of the first page. Who was this perfect man?

And, just as randomly, she'd written in a name, the first one that came to mind, out of nowhere.

Big block letters. MAXIM SINCLAIR

Lucy had no idea what the name meant. But it sounded pleasant to her, like healing waters.

That was back in January. Getting over Charles wasn't the easiest process, but it went by quicker than the version of herself who had met Weaver could have imagined in her most optimistic dreams. Still, by the time May rolled around, Lucy hadn't figured out what that whole encounter had been about, not entirely.

That was when Kate had called her, and brought her into this supernatural trap that was Carmel-by-the-Sea.

***

The doorbell rang, drawing Lucy out of her reverie. She took a quick glance around the room, at the glads, and then strode down the stairs to the front door.

Opening it, she looked down to see the little girl, maybe about seven years old or so, with brown-red hair and a plump face with a pretty expression. Her jeans and plain black T-shirt, combined with the fact that she was an eight-year-old kid, all indicated she didn't live around here, given that Carmel seemed populated mostly by well-dressed retirees. She held a manila envelope in her hand.

The girl was grinning at her. What's so funny?

"Hi, I'm Mindy!" she said at a rapid fire pace. "I'm looking to get a summer job at the yoga studio. Here's my resume." She handed her the envelope, and Lucy had to smile.

"Well, hi, Mindy. I'm Lucy," she replied. "And I like your spunk, but you're a little younger than who we normally hire for the summer."

Mindy's expression dropped so dramatically into a frown that Lucy had to fight a laugh. "Awww! That's too bad! My neighbor said you had a lot of young people working there."

"That's very true," said Lucy, "but they're all teenagers. You have to be at least sixteen years old."

Mindy continued to frown. "That's not young."

"It's young to us," said Lucy. "You wanna know why?"

Mindy nodded, and Lucy knelt down to face her eye-to-eye. "Because we're all old!"

Hesitation, and then Mindy broke into a smile, and a laugh. Lucy laughed with her then stood back up. "Well, okay, then. Thanks anyway." She took off down the street.

"Wait!" called Lucy. Mindy turned around. Lucy waved the envelope. "Don't you want your resume back?"

"Naw," said Mindy, with a shrug. "You can keep it on file." She turned around, and Lucy laughed out loud as she watched her go.

When the girl turned a corner, Lucy looked down at the envelope. Opening it, she pulled out a full, uncreased 8 1/2 by 11 letter page. Mindy hadn't put her last name or address, but she left an email address and a phone number from a house off of Ninth, meaning she was indeed local.

The job qualifications, as one would have expected, were bare, but Mindy seemed to have made up for them by listing her door-to-door flower selling, Girl Scout cookies, and household chores in an oversized Sans Serif font. Lucy sighed: she'd definitely pass this off to her assistant before she left.

Flipping it over, Lucy saw that Mindy had written her qualifications on the back of a flyer.

"Delphi Airlines," Lucy read aloud. A start-up charter company, by the looks of it, with full routes to Denver, Vancouver, and Seattle. New website. Special rates, and flying out of Monterey Airport starting tomorrow.

If that wasn't serendipitous, Lucy didn't know what was.

Lucy returned to her bedroom. She was just about ready.

That's when she remembered Weaver's final instructions before he vanished again to wherever the hell he came from.

***

"How will it work? How long after we meet until I get to go home?" asked Lucy.

"Right away," Weaver had said when he met her on that beach, six months after Seattle, thirty-two days before this morning. "As soon as you get in touch with him, the way opens up again. After that, you're on your own, and you can choose how long or how short your time together will be."

"I don't understand..."

Lucy had paced in the cold sand at Carmel Beach as they were speaking.

"Why leave this to chance? I thought the whole point to this Convergence was that it was something natural. That it was like the planets turning or something. Now you're telling me it's my choice?"

"It has to be your choice to stay or not stay with him," said Weaver. "That's always the point, because no other Lucy Fitzgerald has ever succeeded with Maxim Sinclair," he'd said. "Even your Optimal managed to mess it up."

"And where is she?" asked Lucy.

"You ain't supposed to meet her," said Weaver. "Some get to meet each other, others only get to taste and touch the lives we would have led, and a few get both. But the mechanics are uneven for a reason, and this is just how the math works out for you."

"Why all the work? Why can't you just send him my way?"

"Because you are already looking for him," said Weaver. "He's on your list. You already want to meet him. You'll find the way."

"I only wrote that list because you told me to."

"But you named him on your own, didn't you?"

Lucy stopped. Weaver smiled, then continued.

"All I did was kick you in the behind to get you thinking authentically. That list is your heart on paper. And as for the business with Convergence, it's important you find him, because it's the only way Max is going to believe that destiny's at play. He's got a list, too. And he did that all on his own. What does that say, child?"

Lucy looked at him in silence for a few moments.

"I thought we were destined for each other," she finally said, "and now you're saying you've set almost everything up. It's a fix. So what gives? Are we soul mates or not? Do they even exist?"

Weaver smiled.

"What do you think?" he said.

Lucy didn't take the bait. It was a red herring. She stayed on the subject.

"And when I do find him," she continued, "how am I supposed to convince him to come this way?"

Weaver turned and smiled that Cheshire grin. "Tell Max that he told you where to find him."

"You mean....another Maxim Sinclair? An Alternate?"

Weaver nodded, winked. "That's right. That will be enough to get him curious."

Lucy blinked. "He'll think I'm crazy."

"Not our Max, honey-child," said Weaver. "He has his doubts, but he's still got that faint spark that gives him hope in the unexpected. That's all he needs. He'll be set on his course."

"It would be a lie."

"Only at first."

"How could I lie like that?" asked Lucy.

"Use your imagination. Then improvise. You'll come up with something."

With that, Weaver turned and started walking the other way down the beach. Lucy called after him.

"And what if I choose not to stay with him?" she asked. "What if I choose to go home?"

Weaver simply kept walking.

Lucy watched him head down the beach. Where the shoreline turned behind the tall grasses, behind a deposit of sea-softened rocks in the distance, he vanished.

***

Lucy turned her attention back to her room. The leather gladiators were in her hand. She was just about set.

As choices went, it seemed cruel at first. Hurt someone you didn't know, or let go of what you already had in this life, of everyone and everything else that you loved?

She could leave anytime. According to Weaver's rules, now that she made contact with Max, the way was open. She had already checked and found everyone was back, including Charles. Lucy could head home to her crappy little flat not far from Puget Sound, where the Central Line rumbled past only 400 feet away to wake her up each morning before going to her mediocre job. But she would get her family back, everyone she had known, who had been there for her when Charles had decided that "things weren't all right with this."

Only now, there could be more, would be more.

Lucy knew what was waiting for her in Seattle. Brushing past the physical rules of the whole Convergence business — would her friends and family notice she was gone? Would they believe that Carmel Lucy was, in fact, her, just as all of Carmel now thought she was her? — Lucy knew that she now had a choice that was more palatable when you really got into it, a true win–win from a selfish standpoint, though it was one that would be unimaginably unfair to Max if she went the one way over the other.

One thing she'd learned after things had ended with Charles was to think more selfishly. She'd given so much of herself to that relationship that she had lost her sense of authenticity, meaning she felt so guilty for doing what she knew she wanted and what was right for her, she spent most of her life in neutral.

Mediocre. Not bad, but not great, and never able to leave. No better definition of hell.

Because even through her guilt at what she was going to do to this poor stranger, who would have come all this way, she felt happy.

Goddammit, she deserved to be happy! Why the cosmic conspiracy to keep her miserable? To have her try again, and most likely fail, with a new stranger?

Because she had indeed a great choice, one that had presented itself just before she had left Seattle. One that the text message she had just received had guaranteed.

But how do you tell your supposed soul mate that your ex-fiancé and high school sweetheart Charles, whom you still love, who you had never stopped loving, has come to his senses and has asked you to come back?

How do you tell him that you are going to say yes to your ex? That no matter what other people think, you are always going to say "yes" to the one safe bet you'd had going for you all these last ten years?

How do you tell him that you've done the cost-benefits analysis and found that it made more sense for you to go home to Charles and get your life back, your "world" or "dimension" or whatever the hell it was called in the parlance of the Convergence, than take a chance with a stranger in a strange land?

How do you tell him? What do you tell him?

Do you tell him anything?

Lucy put the brown leather gladiators back in their box and looked at the flyer for Delphi Airlines. Flights starting out of Monterey Airport tomorrow.

Of course not.

STARDUST

Max found himself driving westward on the I-80 at 71 miles an hour.

The shock caused the car to shimmy as Max got his bearings, but he didn't lose control of the Sunfire. Recovering his composure, he took control of his attention and slowed down gradually, pulling to the shoulder right in front of a distance sign. He was now about a half hour outside of Omaha. Putting the car in park, but letting the engine idle, Max got out.

The sky was bigger out here, closer to the ground somehow, and every cloud on the horizon looked like he could touch it. Something about the effect of the prairie. If this had been just a pleasure trip, Max would have stopped, left the Interstate, pulled onto a side road or farmer's driveway, hopped out of the car, walked into the middle of those fields, and taken a picture. Not this time, though: this was no pleasure trip, and Dinah had taken the digital cameras in the divorce, which Max never bothered to replace.

His fingers hurt. The pain suddenly brought back little flashes of recent memory.

Coming to at Weaver's Diner, the Alternate from Glastonbury long gone.

His computer open in front of him. A document of over 6,000 words that he had no memory typing. Saving the file, closing it down, and moving toward the door in a trance. Barely noticing Mr. Weaver in his peripherals serving other customers, or the kid, Justin, beaming at him and wishing him a safe trip as he closed the door behind him.

And finally, before getting back into the car, realizing that there was no way Lucy Fitzgerald was going to connect with that version of Max Sinclair. He had failed in his first attempt.

And it had seemed like such a real place, Glastonbury. He had typed just about as quickly as his Alternate had been speaking, and the imagery of that other lifespace was vivid. There was no doubt: without leaving his table at the diner, Max had somehow gone there. And it had been real.

Max got back in his car.

At Des Moines, Max fuelled up yet again, checked the tires, and reviewed the map he'd been given. If he continued on the I-80, he'd travel all the way through Omaha, through Cheyenne and Salt Lake City. There, the map required him to head south. Junction 39B was the first stop on that new track. Vegas followed (Vegas!) and then, finally, California, where he would bypass Los Angeles altogether and head northwest to Highway 1 and Carmel-by-the-Sea.

If his interview with "Oak Knoll Max," as he called this Alternate, had taught him anything, it was how much more complicated Max actually was. Max still found himself unwilling to sell out, because that's what Oak Knoll Max had done on so many levels. He said he was fine with it, but so much of that life was so...sedentary. That was the word, sedentary. It was a life that didn't go any further than where it was, on any level. True, they had "stuff," but that's all they could look forward to: more stuff. A trip to Tuscany, not really Max's thing, but definitely Dinah's. Decorating the house, telling him what to wear, antiquing. Such a stereotype, almost embarrassing.

His Dinah had always had that capacity to evolve into the high maintenance bracket. How long, he wondered, would he have been happy playing second fiddle to his wife's lifestyle?

And yet, somehow, Oak Knoll really was happy, like a lobotomized mental patient. A lobotomy was the only way to get this Max to close himself off to the greater possibilities, but Oak Knoll Dinah had managed to do it for his Alternate without so much as scratching his scalp. It was such an old question: is ignorance really bliss, even willful ignorance?

More importantly, what did any of this have to do with cosmic events? What made him so special that forces beyond his perception, beyond what was supposed to be possible, were aligning to have him meet his soul mate? Why him?

The question lingered with Max throughout the rest of his drive, which spanned nearly 400 miles over that day, interrupted only by refueling and restroom breaks. The landscape changed as the sun moved across the ecliptic, the prairies sweeping a long, rising slope over the westward mileage into buttes and hilly rolls of land like baker's dough, until he found himself approaching Junction 39B.

At around 6:00, Max reached a tiny little place called Jefferson's Corners where Junction 39B lay. It was late afternoon now, and the landscape had shifted. It was as if the earth had grown bored with flat cornfields and empty prairie and had decided to start rolling deep curves and undulations, deposits of prehistoric rock and baby buttes thrown here and there for good measure, the first patches of high desert where only the simplest of grasses could grow.

As he approached the intersection, Max sighed. Jefferson's Corners had been abandoned not all that long ago, and he was longing for a shower and a soft bed. A few buildings — mechanics' garages, a motel, restaurant, gas station chain, and a bar, along with maybe five or six houses — all sat in a haphazard formation around the crossroads at the intersection. Max was facing west, and the sun sank right into his line of sight onto the road.

There were boards on nearly all of the windows of most of the buildings, except for a few where, Max figured, they left in a bigger hurry. One of them read "Lost to the Great Recession, 2009." Not a single car or truck sat in the empty lots, or in the gravel and dirt driveways of the houses. The traffic lights hung over the junction, serving out their functions even though there were no other cars to obey their signals.

According to the map, Max wouldn't have another place to stop for at least three hours. By then, it would be dark. And in any case, this was where his second "meetup" with an Alternate would take place. Why they picked here of all places, he couldn't even begin to guess.

Rather than chance camping out in his car on the barren plains approaching the foothills of the Rockies, Max decided this would be where he would rest for the night.

Max slowed down as he approached the lights, more out of habit than anything. The motel was just across the street. The Stardust Motel, according to the sign. The light turned green, and he crossed over and turned into the place. The owners hadn't been gone long: the place still looked clean, fairly well-kept. He parked the car and turned off the engine.

The silence when he got out frightened him at first. No sound but the wind, nothing indicating any human activity at all. He looked around. The five motel rooms sat perpendicular to the road, providing some shade from the sun that was just starting to sink behind them. The rental office was tucked away behind the fifth room, along with the small storage building where the cleaners kept their equipment. He looked over to the abandoned office and realized just how truly alone he was. The office was electrified. And there was no one around for miles.

An hour later, Max found himself relaxing in the lamp-lit comfort of Room Five at the Stardust Motel, showered and undressed, watching the snowy reception of some motivational speaker on the only channel that came through in the clear. The sheets were clean and it seemed the staff had washed them before the whole place went under. He hadn't had anything to eat, but at least he would get some decent rest before the next leg of his trip out to Carmel.

Not sure how you can abandon a business and still have the power and water running.

As he lay back, Max felt the room key in his hand, which he'd liberated from the rental office. He'd gone to break in, but had found the door open. A freebie, that was for sure.

The motivational speaker wasn't that much older than him. Latino or Indian, by his complexion, talking about the opportunities that lay before all of the younger people as they graduated college. At one point, he mentioned his own age, and Max scoffed. Twenty-three.

Twenty-three years old. Six years younger. And he was on fucking television giving lectures on how to be successful in life and take on opportunities.

That number felt like a punch in the gut. Max turned off the TV and tossed the remote onto the other bed. Flicking off the lamp, the room turned to inky black, lit only by the orange from the parking lot outside.

He'd once told his dad he was worried that he'd wasted his youth. Jeff Sinclair, of course, told his only son that he couldn't think that.

"Then again, I'm not reliable for this kind of advice," he'd told his son. "I joined the Air Force out of high school, and the fire hall when I was twenty-six."

Jeff, of course, had concluded with his usual closing statement. "Of course, the recruitment age limit in the Army is forty years old. You've still got time."

Max lay in the dark now, drifting to sleep, but not fast enough. All he could see when he closed his eyes were afterimages of turnpikes and stop signs, road dividers flicking past him and the mileage flicking west.

The question dogged him. Had he wasted his life?

If he had, then maybe there would be a little redemption if he could at least fulfill this particular mission. All he had to do was wait for his Alternate to show up and he would be all set. Until then, hed' chill.

As Max thought about sleep, he felt his breathing finally even out and deepen, his body relaxing into complete oblivion, his mind following soon thereafter.

***

No body. No form. When the dream started, those were the first two things Max observed about himself. No body, though he was there. No eyes, though he could see. The mountains were the third, visible through a haze that was as much a mental creation as a function of atmospheric pressure.

Looking below, he saw the golf course — massive, rolling, green, and largely empty of clientele, but for one spot. And as he took note of one particular cluster of people gathered around another player, Max suddenly found himself dropping into his Alternate, his thoughts enmeshed with those of his mark. He could see his Alternate's story, every step taken up to this point, every plan for the future, every secret ailment and hidden business plan.

And his Alternate sensed him.

IN-BETWEEN TASKS

Glastonbury had worn Tommy out, though Max had done most of the co-ordination work for him.

Tommy wasn't working on Max. No, Tommy's job for that first task had been to keep Lucy Fitzgerald away from Max at all times wherever he would be, even if that meant slashing the tires of her rental car or cutting the power to her motel room (both of which he'd done). It was gumshoe work, finding out her plans for the day, who she was meeting with, when and for how long, then being able to stay ahead of her plan.

Only at the end did Lucy run into Max, but Tommy had fixed that easily enough by calling in paramedics five minutes prior to the collapse that was no doubt going to happen as soon as he saw her. The injury was worse than they expected, and he could only assume they'd find that out after another ride on the ambulance.

And sure, maybe the others in that mall would notice the time discrepancy, wonder how someone could have known minutes before that their patient was going to seize, but it didn't matter. When they took him away, Lucy did not follow. That afternoon, her business in town concluded, she left, never to return.

Mission One: Accomplished.

Now Tommy, standing in the In-Between, contemplated his next task. Weaver had been clear that he do these in order, though if he'd had his way, he would have done this next one first. It was much, much easier, requiring far less actual work, and only two phone calls.

Now that Max was just settling in at the Junction, Mission Two would begin immediately.

HIGHER MATHEMATICS

"You don't know what you're doing."

The woman's voice came from right behind her, so close that Lucy jumped.

She turned and came face-to-face with Kate.

"Do you have any idea what a big mistake you're making?" asked Kate.

"W-what are you talking about, Kate?"

"You're going to head back to Seattle."

Lucy was mute.

They stood in the driveway of Lucy's house. It was dusk, and the narrow, rolling streets along 2nd were largely empty, except for the odd tourist or dog walker making their way downtown or to the beach with their pets. No one looked in their direction as Lucy confronted her friend in the flesh for the first time since this experience had started. Kate was different: blond highlights, a few extra lines under her eyes, she looked a good four or five years older than she should have, wearing long blue jeans and a white top.

"Oh yeah, I know," she continued, stepping toward Lucy and forcing her into a slow retreat back toward the house. "I know what you think is going to happen, but trust me, it's not what you think." Lucy was just awestruck, and let Kate continue.

"We can't accomplish what we have to do without your co-operation. You need to stick this out with Max, otherwise the whole plan falls apart. I know that you've got doubt and suspicion about Max, but both of those things go away with time when you realize that he is indeed the dream proven real."

"What about Charles? My love for him is very real."

At this, Kate blinked, and Lucy could see her working out what she'd just heard.

"Oh Christ..."

Kate put her hands on her hips and started pacing in front of Lucy. It's not going to work," she said.

"And how do you know that?" Lucy stepped up to her. "What? Is the 'me' in your world miserable and married to Charles Smith?"

"No," said Kate. "My 'you' is widowed and a successful restaurant owner in L.A."

"Widowed?" Kate nodded.

"Her husband was in a coma. Soldier, wounded in an explosion. They pulled the plug. Well, he would have been her husband."

Lucy took a moment to digest this disturbing vision.

"Then why are you here?" she asked Kate.

"I can't force you to do anything you don't want...well, technically, I can, but that goes against the spirit of what we're trying to do. It just won't work."

"Which is?"

Kate turned and smiled.

"The Convergence is an automatic process, a mathematical product of the sum total of interactions between all of the systems in existence. Picture a beam of sunlight at high noon. On its own, it's warm. Now, put a magnifying glass in front of it, and we can make fire from light. We're the glass, boosting the effects to the betterment of sentient life on Earth.

"But there's a catch," Kate went on. "You've got to choose to go that way. As I've said, we can't force you."

"Why is it so important that Max and I get together? What do you have planned for us?"

Kate's grin lasted a split second. "It's not our plan, and even if it was, if I told you everything, I would take away your free choice, because once you heard the reason, you'd feel obliged to stick around.

114

The irony of that would be that if you stuck around because you felt you had to, the plan would end up falling apart anyway. The only way this works is for you to create the reason for yourself. You'll just have to trust me, because trust is as much a part of this as anything else I could tell you."

"But you just told me to stay with him!"

"I can lobby, I can infer, I can do everything in my power to change your mind. I even have ways of physically making you go to him. But based on where we'd like to take this whole process, I know what the optimal solution would be. You have to be able to reach your own conclusion that what's best for us is also best for you."

"And if I decided that I belonged with Charles?" asked Lucy. Kate didn't speak right away, and Lucy saw the very hesitation she had heard on the phone not so long ago.

"Then as much as it works against our plans, we'd let it go."

"Why? If it's so important, why not force me?"

"Because you'd know it was forced, and whatever results we're looking for would be less than what's needed. This is about carrot, not stick."

"And out of all of these thousands of lifespaces, all these Alternates, no other one of mine has gotten with Max and given you your optimal solution?"

Kate shook her head, and Lucy sighed.

"That's not pressure, is it?"

"You seem to be standing up to it quite well."

Neither woman spoke, and Lucy wandered away a few steps.

"I don't know what to do with these feelings," said Lucy after a few moments, "but somehow...my gut's telling me that there's no future with Max Sinclair, and every bit of a future with Charles. If destiny's really behind Max and me being together, then there should be no barriers, it should just be easy, and it's not."

Kate shook her head.

115

"That's not your instinct, Luce," she said, "that's your survival mode."

Lucy stopped. "What?"

Kate looked down to the ground, then took slow, non-intimidating steps into Lucy's personal space.

"Listen," she said, and her tone was softer, the voice of Lucy's old friend. "You won't agree with me, and I'm not going to insult you by pretending I know how it feels, but I get it. You remember how I told you that all of the Katarina Castillos were working on the Convergence in all the lifespaces?"

Lucy nodded, and Kate went on.

"Well, here's something I know for sure that I didn't tell you before: we also have worked with all of the Lucy Fitzgeralds. You and I are friends across many lifespaces. And of all of them, I can tell you, you've had the most trouble. The most heartache. But you've got a chance at real happiness here, and you don't have to change anything about who you are, except for one thing."

Even as she listened to every word said, Lucy could not meet her friend's gaze. She focused intently on the car in the driveway.

"What's that?" asked Lucy.

Kate put her hand on Lucy's shoulder the way her mother used to when she was a child.

"I need you to be daring," she said. "I need you to have faith in higher mathematics."

Daring. Of all the things that Kate had said to her since first coming here, that word had scared Lucy the most. For this reason more than any words her friend had said, Lucy regained her control.

And yet, Lucy realized, for the first time, how curious she actually was about this. Who wouldn't be, after all, when such powerful, ethical forces were trying everything short of putting a gun to your head to get you to do something that they claimed was for the higher good?

Still, Lucy had seen too many dead cats by now to know where curiosity without guarantee tended to lead.

Still looking away from Kate, Lucy took a deep breath, pulled Kate's hand off her shoulder and turned her back to her. Opening the front door of this house — not my house! — Lucy turned and spoke with all the command she could muster.

"You want me to have faith in your numbers?" asked Lucy.

Kate nodded.

"Then show me your work. Otherwise, I've made my choice."

As the door closed on her, Kate got in the last three words.

"As you wish."

NEW YORK MINUTES

"What's wrong, dude?"

The putt was only five feet or so, something that even a beginner would be able to sink. Still, Max couldn't bring himself to move.

"I don't know," he said. "I feel...weird."

"Well, if you're not up for it, let me take the shot. If we don't sink this, we'll be in last place. Again."

Max looked up. Jake and the two Nathans were waiting. All had their sunglasses on in the bright August noon, and all of them were sweating pretty well this early in the day. Well, except Nathan D. On the fairway, he never broke a sweat. Ever.

Nathan D spoke again. "I can do it if you want, we could sure use the points." Max stood up, pulled the putter away from the ground and stepped aside. Nathan walked up and addressed the ball, leaving Max to look around.

The fairway was hazy today, and there were no other players on the green, meaning that the Brothers owned Oakwood Golf and Country Club today. In the distance, you were supposed to be able to see the Adirondacks, but with all of the haze in the atmosphere, there was nothing but shimmering white sky.

Nathan D sank the putt.

"Good job, buddy," said Liam, gathering up their clubs and walking back to the carts.

"I hope it doesn't rain out like it did last year," said Nate. Nathan D brought up the rear as they put their clubs away and hopped into the carts. Max found himself in the driver's seat.

"Yeah, that was balls," said Nathan D as they started up to Hole 10.

When they got there, some of the other alums were waiting to take their shots. These were the younger guys who had just graduated the previous spring.

"Look out, it's the bad swings!" said Liam.

Three of them looked up. Max didn't remember any of their names, but that was what the steak and beer afterward was for. He let Liam, Nathan D, and Nate taunt the newbies while he collected himself.

Something was different, he knew that much. The disorientation had come back. He'd started feeling it days ago. That waking dream...well, he had those on occasion: little glimpses of other places, daydreams in which he wasn't the junior partner in this virtual concierge firm they had started up. Daydreams when he was anywhere but here.

But this last one, catching him just when he was about to birdie that putt on Hole 9 to finally move Team Ramrod — as they were named — up in the top five of the standings of his eighth competition, what the hell had that been?

A full name came to him. Luthien Fitzgerald, called Lucy. She had red hair and green eyes, three years younger than him, gorgeous, adventurous, everything he could have wanted in a girlfriend, maybe a wife...

Max felt his heart lift up. She couldn't be real, of course. These waking dreams had a way of making you question your reality, second-guess yourself.

After all he had accomplished since graduating, the successful company he'd helped to build, the lives he'd changed during his time as the Fraternity's regional consultant for the Northeast, the one thing he couldn't achieve was a successful marriage. His brothers, partners in Celebrity Concierge Services, had all gotten married first, then decided to leave their jobs — as low level accountants, parents' businesses, teaching, the service — to start this up. Max had been the only one to settle his career ambitions first, then try to find a mate.

119

"Hey, your turn, dude."

Max looked. They had been waiting for him. He got out and set up the ball for the drive. Hole 10 was about 430 yards, but the terrain sloped downward for most of it, making for great visibility. The fairway sank away to the left behind a bunker before you could reach the green, but it was, nonetheless, a Par 4, so it wasn't as easy as it looked. Nate had already taken the first drive, and the ball had sliced just a bit in the crosswind, landing about a 150 yards away, according to the marker. The undergrads were on the fringe a little over halfway up the fairway, trying to dig out their ball.

Lucky for them this is best ball, otherwise...

"So, are you gonna take that drive or what, Max?"

Max turned to Nathan. "They're still on the fairway!"

"So? That's why they invented fore. They'll hear you. Besides, they're our little brothers. If we don't teach them the niceties of golf, who will?"

Max smiled, turned around and looked back. The undergrads were still there, and had managed to wedge the ball back onto the fairway, but only about five or so yards from where it had sat in the fringe. He shrugged, repositioned himself, wound up, and swung.

The driver connected with the ball with a perfect ting! Pure music to every golfer's ear. Max lost sight of the ball during his follow through and forgot to call out to the newbies, but his brothers covered him.

"Fore!" Nate and Liam shouted.

Ahead, he saw the undergrads turn around and duck, except one. The blur of white sped right at Steven and he went down.

"Oh shit!" said Liam, caught midway between genuine concern and amusement. Nate — the more experienced golfer who had taught Max the game — was already getting in his cart.

"Come on, let's go!"

Nathan, meanwhile, dropped to the ground in hysterics.

"Oh my God! That's awesome!" he said, his face red from laughter.

Max followed Nate to the cart and they sped over. As they drew closer, they saw Steven get up. Arriving at the side, they saw him grabbing his butt.

"You bastards tagged me in the ass!" shouted Steven as Nate and Max collapsed out of the cart.

"Looks like you got the million dollar wound, son," said Max when he'd stopped laughing enough to breathe. "You all right?"

"You know, when my girlfriend asks how I got this massive welt on my left cheek, I'm going to give her your number so you can explain it to her!"

"No thanks, I already have her on speed dial," said Max.

"At least it wasn't your head," said Nate, composing himself. "People can get killed by solid drives like that."

"So which one of you fuckers did it?" demanded Steven.

"That's no way to talk to your elders," Nate deadpanned. "Besides, you're also lucky it was Max who made the drive and not one of the older guys. One of them played at Pebble Beach and came in 16th place, pretty respectable for an amateur."

Steven took a breath and winced. "Point is, we got the ball out. C'mon Ewen, let's go find where yours went to."

"Where's mine?" asked Max. Steven nodded to the red streaked ball that sat in the grass not far from where they were. The undergrads got in their carts, and Steven got in the driver seat. Max noticed that Steven was sitting with one ass cheek hanging off the side. As they drove off, they broke into laughter, with Steven telling them to shut the fuck up.

Nathan D and Liam pulled up at the same time that Nate swung around to face Max and high fived him. "You are truly one lucky bastard! Plus the ball's on the fairway!"

"Yeah, not a bad angle at all.

"Definitely the best ball."

"Awesome. Tell you what, why don't you take the first shot and I'll sit this one out. I'm feeling pretty dangerous after that last one."

"You got it, Terminator."

Max retired to the cart as his brothers took over. He watched them set up their shots, measuring the angles, and picked up the thread where he'd left it.

Luthien "Lucy" Fitzgerald.

Was she a real person? In all of his online dating, he'd probably run past a listing for a dozen Lucy Fitzgeralds. But this one was specific: red hair, green eyes. Max felt she could have been. This dream didn't have that otherworldly feel that so many of his other episodes had had. He'd gone to a specialist to check for some underlying physical condition — brain cancer had been his big worry — but they'd found nothing wrong with him, and had suggested that his episodes were emotional in nature. There was no way he was going to see a shrink. Really, if all he needed was to find a mate, then that was going to be more effective — and less costly — than a couple of couch sessions.

Lucy Fitzgerald, Lucy Fitzgerald. The name seemed so familiar, like an old high school, maybe even elementary school, friend that you used to swing with at the playground at recess. Maybe he had met her briefly before, enough for the name and face to register in his subconscious.

Then it came back. Twenty fold.

From another vantage point altogether, Dreamer Max felt like a puppeteer. At once seeing out of this Alternate's eyes and viewing him at a distance, as you would a TV show or movie, Dreamer Max could feel the second set of thoughts flowing through his mind. All the knowledge and experiences of this Alternate flooded into his own awareness. He wondered if it worked both ways.

"Hey! Let's go, Max." Nathan D prodded him, snapping out of his reverie. Max started the cart and followed the others to where Liam's drive had taken them.

Around the bend where the fairway turned toward the green, the undergrads had somehow managed to make it to the putting green and were now sinking the putt. Ewan's shot couldn't have made it that far.

"Aw, come on! If they're going to cheat, they may as well make it look realistic," said Nathan D.

"We're playing with plebes, friend."

"True, but you have to remember: you guys were the plebes once."

"Very true. Actually, I was wondering if I could sit this next one out entirely. I dunno if it's the heat or what, but I want to wait until the beer girl comes around again, see if maybe she's carrying some Gatorade or something."

Nathan D looked at him. "Sure, I can do that. You sure there isn't anything else wrong with you?"

Yeah, I'm sure it'll pass, but we're doing good now, plus you've got Liam, so you won't need my help. Not for this hole, anyway."

"Sure, no worries, Max."

They found Nathan D's mark. Max stopped the cart and waited for the others to show up after looking for their shots. While Nathan explained to them why Max was sitting this one out, Max went back to his thoughts.

Maybe this vision of Lucy Fitzgerald was more than just a daydream. Maybe she was more than a person. Maybe she was his archetypal soul mate, an out product of his never ending quarter-life crisis, his mind's way of telling him where he had to look to settle this chapter of his life, and start the next.

Then again, maybe she was real.

She was real.

Nathan took a swing with the seven iron and lofted the ball a good distance, not quite reaching the green, but close enough for a chip-in.

"Good shot, dude," Nate said.

"Thanks! I don't know about you guys, but I say we go with that one." Liam and Nate nodded. The others took to their cart, and Nathan D hopped back in with Max.

As they drove up, Max made the decision.

"Hey Nathan, how are we doing with on the Carte Blanche deal?"

"So far, so good. They'll be coming up to tour the office on Tuesday, but at this point, I think it's more of a formality. We'll be part of their card benefits package in six months."

"So you don't really need me for that deal?" asked Max.

Nathan D didn't answer right away, but turned to him.

"Not really, but Max, I'm wondering if we should have needed you."

"What do you mean?"

"Lately, you're not as involved in the big decisions, and God forbid a recession hits and people stop wanting us to book their tables and buy their show tickets for them"

"What are you saying? You saying that I'm useless?"

"You're becoming useless, Max. The only reason I'm bringing this up now is because I'm guessing you're about to ask me for another LOA."

Max sighed. "Well...yeah, but this one will be short. It's just for a week, I promise I'll re-engage with the Product Team. I'll even pick up the slack on the Black Card Project, see if we can't lure them away from their current provider."

They drove in silence, reaching the edge of the green, the actives having moved on after their obvious cheat.

"All right, where are you going?" said Nathan D.

For a moment, Max saw Lucy Fitzgerald in his mind.

"To find a girl."

Nathan D. rolled his eyes and sighed.

"Glad to see you've got your priorities straight, Max."

Lucy Fitzgeralds were everywhere, but not the one he wanted. Night after night since Dreamer Max had persuaded his Alternate to take his leave from CCS, scanning the web, the singles sites, the individual homepages, and he could find nothing. He was about to give up on her, dismiss his vision as some kind of subconscious wish fulfillment, when it occurred to him that maybe she simply wasn't online. That's when he released the Alternate from his control and let him go for his walk.

Max stopped. He was on the sidewalk just outside his condo, unsure of how he'd gotten there. Around him, all of the affluence that this city seemed to attract was flowing past him. He saw it everywhere: in the boutique bags carried by the personal shoppers and rich housewives with nothing else to do with the day while their husbands divided and conquered at the stock exchange; the beautifully-inlaid stones along the sidewalk; the smell of bistro food and Chanel engaged in artful combat in the air; the passing of the occasional Town Car or limousine.

The blackout spells were growing worse. He was glad he'd taken the leave: if they did get to the point where he was losing massive portions of his day, Max would have the time to go back to Dr. Darshan, get that full MRI done that he'd been putting off since his last visit. He didn't want to black out on the road.

As he walked down the street, taking in the rain and food smells of his surroundings, Max did feel that something had changed. Suddenly, he was feeling more satisfied in ears. Indeed, he had done well by his life. Years of non-stop work, the sacrifice of his mid-twenties while most of his peers back in suburbia were out buying themselves modest-sized houses and working mediocre jobs, spending their meager wages and ample free time on beer and video games rather than directing their attention upward: all of it had paid off for Maxim Sinclair. People work their whole lives to achieve only a fraction of what Max had gotten in such a short time.

As he walked among the throngs of passers-by, he looked at each one of them. A blond lady in her fifties, clearly overdressed for a simple stroll down the street, walked past him with an anger in her eyes that she was sure to vent on the next unfortunate store clerk she encountered. A man, only a little older than Max, shoved a stroller while dressed in jeans and a raincoat, staring ahead with no discernible expression, except to get to the next place he had to go. Having children was even more of a seemingly unattainable concept for Max than finding a mate.

And yet, so much to be grateful for, thought Max. He turned the corner. More beautiful boutique shops and delis, tiny cafés with only one or two outdoor tables. The sky lightened, and Max could see patches of blue. Clean sidewalks, wet streets. This was home, and this was real.

The usual throngs of shoppers was thinner today, but the traffic was still thick and loud, drowning out the sound of the rain that had held such command over the airwaves back at Max's bedroom balcony.

And then—

Dreamer Max had no idea how he knew what was happening next, just that he did. He took back the reins. The Alternate was about to cross the street. Instead, he caused him to redirect to the left before releasing him again.

The fuck. It happened again!

The biggest sensation of déjà vu he'd ever felt in his entire life. He found himself staring down the sidewalk at the oncoming pedestrians.

But then…he knew. Somehow, it all made sense, why he had turned.

Max looked for her then, turning his head like a compass point to where she was, coming toward him. Lucy was now the beautiful woman fresh from the boutique hotspot, but she carried no bag, just an

126

umbrella. The traffic slowed down. The birds floated on the air as if it had turned to water.

Magnetism works both ways, and her gaze met his own eyes, and her pace slowed as the two drew closer, and closer...closer...

The heat rose in the narrowing air between them, Dreamer Max felt joy, true gratitude, that he'd found her this easily.

They stopped about a foot away from each other, nose to nose. She wore a white shirt and black skirt underneath a long flowing green jacket — *Dreamer Max couldn't read the look in her eyes* — but Max knew there was something more drawing them together that neither understood, but both accepted.

"I know you," she said to him, and her voice was the music of the café, throaty and passionate.

"I know you too," said Max. As the pedestrian river flowed around them, Max took her hand, and it felt warm and strong.

"You're Luthien Fitzgerald."

To Max's surprise, she wasn't surprised. Instead, she shook his hand.

"And you're Maxim Sinclair."

***

They walked, Max slightly behind her and to her right, trying to keep their umbrellas from hitting each other.

"Something had told me to take a stroll today," said Lucy, staring ahead as they walked. "I've been in town about two weeks now. That same intuition told me to come here."

Dreamer Lucy was still deceiving him, only now she was doing this through her puppet Alternate. She felt Max's presence as soon as she found herself here, but she knew it was pointless to resist. Even though she had no form to speak of, the only way to describe the feeling was that someone else — some creature or being far more powerful than she — was looking over her shoulder. And that creature would be angry if provoked, so she did as she was told, and kept moving the strings.

The sky over the city had taken on a pale gray-green, adding to the feeling of disbelief. Lucy's head, so loud only moments before with doubt and reason, had gone silent. Max Sinclair was here, he was real! And he'd been looking for her. There were no answers. Instead, Lucy seemed to be walking in question, and everything around him seemed like a blurry swirl of cars, clouds, and people.

"I had the same feeling a few days ago," replied Max. "It was just your name, and your face."

"It was the same with me," replied Lucy.

They'd reached Central Park, and the gloom that hung over the sky gave this sanctuary a sinister, ominous atmosphere. The humidity suddenly intensified. Small beads of sweat started to form on Lucy's forehead. Just above the skyline, a single dark cloud — black — was spreading out like ink spilling over the building and refusing to fade. The rain had stopped, and the two of them had put away their umbrellas and carried them across the street to the park.

Oooooh, this was going to be risky indeed. Dreamer Lucy could see and feel the whole picture. If the plan worked, it would ease the pressure to get them together in the waking world. If it didn't, things would get very confusing for her Alternate very quickly.

In the park now, they started walking toward the trees. The deep dark green atmosphere reminded Lucy of so many fairy-tale monsters lurking in gnarled roots, but they walked anyway, with no others in the park to disturb them.

"I don't know what's happening here," said Max.

"Neither do I," replied Lucy. "Everything's been surreal since I had the dream. Even now, I can't really focus...there's a bench up there."

They said nothing until they reached the bench, which sat just inside one of the forested paths under a couple of large oaks. It was wide enough that two people could share it and sit face-to-face, which is what they did.

"What was in the dream?" asked Max. Lucy shook her head, her eyes narrow.

"Something about water. I'd been on a boat, and had fallen overboard. All I felt was water everywhere, and then the dream changed. Random images. A wedding, kids, a hedge maze."

"Hedge maze?" asked Max.

"Yes, and your face. And your name."

Lucy felt the thrill surge from the pit of her stomach, up her spine, as she spoke the words. The dream had been real enough, but that didn't excuse what she was doing here. There was something divine here! Something beyond them — supernatural, spiritual — was orchestrating this meeting, bringing them together. All of it for real.

Still, how to tell him? What to tell him?

Simple, thought Dreamer Lucy. Lie. And lie well.

Lucy took a deep breath. "I've been having these dreams ever since Claude died."

"Who's Claude?" asked Max.

Here goes…

"My husband."

Dreamer Lucy's heart bobbed like a buoy hit by a stone.

"I'm sorry. How long has it been?"

Good question.

"A month tomorrow."

What a load of utter bullshit. Lucy Fitzgerald the widow, still wearing that black veil about her countenance long after the funeral. She hadn't come here to meet him out of some heartfelt errand. She had come here to help deal with her pain. Brilliant idea.

Why the hell am I lying in the first place? What's happening?

Lucy shook some of it off, looked up at Max.

"Two weeks ago, when I saw your face in that dream, when I couldn't forget your name even when I woke up, I thought to come to Manhattan. I thought it was crazy, but it made sense. My mentor agreed."

"Your mentor?"

"Yes. My mentor, Katarina, out in Ventura. She believes that attention to life is important to the soul. I started going there out of college, never stopped. Kat told me I had nothing to lose by coming here, if it helped with coping with Claude's death."

"Do you think it's helping?" asked Max. Lucy looked, and her smile was empty.

"Too soon to tell, but you're here, and you're real. At least now I know my tuition costs were worth it."

Lucy laughed then, just a small chuckle.

Dreamer Lucy felt guilty that she had now become the worst kind of liar in two lifespaces. She could sense her Alternate's apprehension at not being able to control her own words and actions. And at the same time, the Alternate was thrilled at the thought of being with another man. Dreamer Lucy could see from her story: life with Claude had long lost its zest, and she was looking to be close to someone again. The creature over her shoulder lingered, however. She had no choice but to obey orders.

***

"I think it's letting up," said Lucy. Max looked around. The skies had lightened, and the humidity had long since broken.

Dreamer Max had listened to her throughout, though he admitted some disappointment to himself midway through the conversation. Lucy wasn't all that interested in his Alternate, his life or achievements, or his wishes. The thought made him feel guilty; after all, you don't think of yourself when someone who's just lost their love is talking. You let them talk. You listen.

Something wasn't quite right. He let it play.

130

"Where would you like to go?" asked Max. Lucy looked at him.

"My hotel isn't far from here, at least I don't think. This city's bigger than it looks when you're walking."

"It's not that bad," Max said.

"I'd like to change, check my voicemail. I left my cell in my room. I don't know any good restaurants here. Can you recommend anything for a late lunch?"

Max grinned, and for the first time, Lucy's own smile was genuine. "Absolutely."

***

The rest of the day unfolded with that same surreal buzz that had started when Lucy and Max had first found each other.

Dreamer Max couldn't shake the feeling that something was off about this meeting. He began to be aware that there was some other presence in this Alternate space with him. Three more, in fact. But he couldn't quite identify them. It was like trying to hear a transmission in a rippling sea of static. He was starting to get the feeling he himself had been on autopilot when he set up this meeting. Still, things were going well. The more time the Alternate spent with Lucy, the less he felt he had to intervene.

They had headed back to the road and hailed a cab. Lucy was staying at a small place on 45th Street, not far from 4th Avenue. Neither of them spoke as the cabbie navigated through the streets.

Soon enough, they were at her hotel. She ran up and changed while Max held the cab and made a few phone calls to CCS to pull a few strings with some of the restaurant owners in town that were friendly to them. He always loved the reaction of some of his younger virtual concierges when they called up his profile on the computer and realized they were talking to one of the company's board members: he only hoped they gave that kind of service to every one of their clients.

131

Dreamer Lucy was not going to let go of the reins. There was no chance, because as soon as she did that, this would all be over, and the creature on her shoulder would be pissed. She had no intention of tugging the whiskers of a creature that was higher up on the food chain. She continued her marionette work and got her Alternate changed and freshened-up.

Lucy came back, still in her raincoat, but now wearing a black dress with long matching boots.

"I'm feeling ugly in this town," she said. "Thought I should step it up a bit."

They went back to the park and had an early dinner at Tavern, which Max was keen to explain wasn't really an authentic New York experience for the New Yorkers, but which every tourist seemed to think was the cat's meow. Max took the opportunity to talk about his life and experiences, and throughout the meal, Max had gotten that feeling of gratitude back. Here he was, eating with Lucy Fitzgerald in Manhattan, booked by his own company, with two more days to go before he would have to work again. And Lucy had listened to him with interest.

"So what do you make of all this?" asked Max after they'd finished dessert. "Us being together."

Lucy took her napkin away from her lips and folded it into a square onto the empty plate. "Just a cheesy movie line."

"Which is?"

"Do you believe in fate?"

"No...not really," replied Max.

Lucy nodded. "No, I don't either. I had thought that Claude and I were destined to be together. He was my first, but to be honest, before he died, we had been having problems. Nothing extreme — he wasn't beating me or anything — but even though I loved him, I'd fallen out of love with him. He changed over time, I changed...and really, everything changes, grows, rots. There's nothing you can do but change yourself in response."

"Still," Max said, "shouldn't there be some...order to life? Does it all have to be primordial sludge pools getting struck by stray bolts of lightning and monkeys somehow evolving into men? There's some higher power that brought us together, I know it. You can't just dismiss it as chance: what are the odds that you and I would have the same daydream about each other's name, and be walking down the same block at the same time in New York? It's a one in a million...one in a billion shot easy."

From above, Dreamer Lucy felt a new flush of guilt flow through her and into her Alternate. Dreamer Max felt a disruption in the space in front of where he found himself, but could see nothing.

Lucy shivered: an almost pathetic little shoulder bump. "I just got a chill," she said, then her cheeks went red. Max couldn't help but feel his pulse quicken.

"Sorry," she said. "This whole business freaks me out. I can't even believe I'm here, that you're real. I wonder if this happens a lot, people having these dreams."

"I'm sure more people have the dreams than actually follow them. Many more," said Max.

"So what do we do now?" asked Lucy, putting her fingers together and resting her chin on the arch they created.

"I don't know."

She sighed, and though he could see no trace of it in her expression, Max felt the air around him grow somber, like candles burning out.

"You still loved him, even though you weren't in love with him, I can see that," said Max, and taking a breath that he tried his best to hide from his dinner partner, reached his hand across the table. Lucy looked at his hand for a quick instant and took it in hers just as he was about to touch hers.

"I've been alone for a long time," said Max, "and to suddenly have you across the table from me is just as incredible as it must feel for you to be here. Everything I know about you, I learned from a single day, and even though I know that you are here because you're dealing with Claude's passing, I feel the connection between us, the energy. And I know you feel it, too."

For an instant, Max swore he saw an added glimmer in Lucy's eyes. But then, her hand pulled away from his and folded across her legs under the table. Max followed suit.

"I know it's really inappropriate to say now, but—"

"No," said Lucy, looking down at her hands. "You're right, I do feel the connection. There's such a mix of emotions right now, all I can do..."

She closed her eyes and started taking deep breaths. Max could see her inhale through her nose, exhale out of her mouth. The waiter came around with the bill, and Max quickly took out his charge card and sent him back the way he came.

"I don't mean to embarrass you," said Lucy, her eyes still closed.

"Not at all," said Max. "It's how you deal with it."

"I don't deal with the emotions as if they're separate from me. I let them flow through me, top to bottom, feeling them as much as I can for a few seconds in my physical body, then letting them go."

Lucy opened her eyes after breathing out one last time. "It's all about feeling more alive in the moment, like I said. Any emotion can make it happen — even fear and anger — but love and gratitude are the most energizing ones."

"You should meet some of my HR people. They're all about that."

"We're all about that, Max. Everyone's got something that wakes them up, summons joy."

"I know," said Max, and he wondered what it would be like to feel those lips on his own, what the scent of her body would be as they came closer together, what her skin would feel like against his own in the dark. Max felt the glow surge from the center of him, and as he looked at her and she at him, he knew the feeling was mutual, could feel that otherworldly feeling connecting the two of them, and he knew...

"Thank you, sir" said the server, returning with his platinum charge card sticking out from the bill. The energies fell away like a stone. Lucy looked down at her purse, started fiddling with it. Max signed for the charge and thanked the server.

When he was gone again, Max looked back at Lucy and broke into a laugh.

"So...I don't think I answered your question," he said. "But since we're finished eating, it's my turn to ask. What do we do now?"

"We should head back to my hotel," said Lucy.

***

She brought out her room key — Max thought it quaint that some places still hadn't gotten electronic cards — and unlocked the door. The room was surprisingly spacious, with a single queen sized bed against the right wall, the bathroom just to the right of the front door. Across from the bed was an old dresser that had probably been here since Eisenhower. A small card table sat parallel to the dresser in the center of the room, with two chairs facing each other. A TV sat atop the dresser.

Outside, lightning flashed here and there, and the thunder followed.

There were others in the room. Dreamer Lucy could almost make out an entity, another over mind occupying the three dimensional space just above the Alternate. For his part, Dreamer Max suddenly got a glimpse of...energies...flowing into the Alternate Lucy's mind from an amorphous source surrounding her from about three inches above her head. And something else...

Lucy turned to him and removed her raincoat. Max had observed at the restaurant just how much years in California had made their mark on her slender shoulders, yet they still seemed so natural, touchable, soft.

No sooner had Dreamer Lucy observed the other entity that the creature told her to refocus. The two Alternates had to get together, even if it was just one night. Lucy hesitated, but turned her full attention back.

A few feet away, Dreamer Max observed the third presence. It seemed angry.

To his surprise, Lucy took the lapels of his own jacket and started pulling them around his shoulders. Max reached up.

"This isn't right, Lucy," he said. She stopped.

"What isn't right?"

"We can't..." and, more dramatically than Max thought she'd intended, she brought her hands up to his mouth.

"I need this, Max. It's all right."

In one motion, she took away her fingers and replaced them with her own lips.

And that kiss was a maelstrom, wiping away whatever levies remained between them.

Max felt the blood surging throughout his entire body, felt the fire in the center of him, and let it carry him back to her lips. And he felt how smooth her shoulders were under his fingertips.

And Max needed it, too, needed her in the flesh, needed to manifest these energies between them into form. For Lucy, these were the healing waters in which she needed to wash away her grief and regret. For Max, they would give him the taste of what it was like, for just one night, to have it all together.

"Then let's do this right," said Max, taking her face in his hand, "slow, and aware of sensation. Alive."

And he kissed her, and her lips in his own were delicious rose petals in his mouth. Lucy kissed back, and pressed her body up against Max's chest. He felt her breasts, those soft, firm contradictions, against him and he felt himself hard against her.

This is incredibly wrong, thought Dreamer Lucy. The creature growled. Dreamer Max heard it. That's when he noticed a presence over his own amorphous shoulder....

At the window, still open to the buildings across the street, Max heard the quiet tap-tap-tap of the rain hitting the window in intermittent staccato. The storm was opening up, but not yet. More clouds needed to gather.

Lucy pulled out Max's shirt from his pants and lifted it over his head, then kissed his bare skin, starting at his chest and working lower, lower, and lower.

We can't do this to her, said Dreamer Lucy. Or to him.

Stay focused, hissed the creature.

Dreamer Max really wondered how he had gotten here.

Lucy kissed him again and again, pulled him toward the bed. She lay down and took his hand and passed it over her left breast.

Dreamer Max realized he couldn't retrace the origins of how this started.

They released, and Lucy flipped him around onto his back. In the dim light, Max watched her pull off her panties and toss them to the floor. She reached behind and pulled the halter strap over her head. He watched in slow motion as the fabric revealed the rest of those beautiful sun-kissed shoulders, and her breasts seemed to appear out from behind them like a twin sunrise. Lucy grabbed the waistline and pulled the rest of the outfit over her head, and there was Lucy Fitzgerald, naked in the dark glow of the Manhattan rainclouds letting down torrents over the window. She let Max's gaze devour her flesh for only a moment before she drew closer and kissed him hard, losing herself to the energies at last...

Dreamer Lucy saw a flicker, a brief manifestation of light in the air that had a certain essence, a taste, of a particular being. She also sensed above that being an emotional form. An image: a man in a trench coat and umbrella, walking up to her on a rainy day.

"If you release her now," said the creature, "I will destroy you."

"Relax, child," said the disembodied voice.

Dreamer Max turned left and sensed the presence of the old man, who wasn't talking to him, but the other two entities across from him.

She won't let go now, Katarina. She's too afraid of what would happen.

Dreamer Lucy heard him, and realized the dream as it was unfolding was no dream at all.

Dreamer Max realized the dream, and immediately vanished from the scene. So did the Weaver form.

Only Dreamer Lucy and the disembodied mind of Katarina Castillo, angry and violent after their last meeting, remained to see what happened between the two Alternates.

***

Hours later, sometime before dawn, Max awoke to passing thunder, finding himself naked and warm. The storm was on its way out to the Atlantic, out of the city. He was holding Lucy Fitzgerald in his arms, feeling her soft flesh against his own. Her hair smelled of herbal shampoo intertwined with her own scent.

She tossed away from him, and Max moved with her, spooning her. He kissed the nape of her neck, and she stirred, but didn't turn around for a new round of lovemaking. Instead, she burrowed backward, into the crook created by Max's body, and returned to sleep.

Dreamer Lucy could feel the Alternate Max's love for her, a supernova in his heart that filled the rest of his body, and he indeed felt fulfilled. She could see the other considerations: Would they stay together? Would his career and her ambitions be compatible? Would she be able to be with someone new so soon after Claude's death? But these were daylight questions, and there was plenty of nighttime still left.

For now, Max allowed himself to meditate on how Lucy's nakedness melted with his own, in this modest Manhattan hotel, as the thunder sent its parting shots over the city. As Max drifted away, he

138

followed the cloud paths in his mind's eye as they rumbled past New York and its suburbs, and finally out to the dark waters of the sea...

The poor bastard, thought Dreamer Lucy, as she watched them sleep.

***

The next morning, Max stood with Lucy outside the hotel. Unlike so many of his encounters, this one was missing something: that feeling of shame, awkwardness. Neither one of them had been embarrassed about what had happened. In fact, that night had healed Lucy, and she was almost ready to go home. Almost.

"Tavern was great, Maxim Sinclair," she said to him as they stood on the street, "but I'm interested to see what you can do with brunch."

"We could try a few options, but how about instead of all of that elite stuff, we just walk and see what we find. Jeans and T-shirt kind of places."

Lucy grinned and reached up to kiss him. "That sounds fantastic."

They began their walk down the sunny streets. Max was amazed at how everything stood out. The car horns and taunts that rang out like a discordant symphony, the smell of exhaust and food and the sight of airliners passing overhead in the rain-washed blue sky that seemed too clear to be real. Everyone around him seemed happier, taking their time down the street. This was still New York, wasn't it? And everything from the green on the trees to the feel of the summer heat on Max's face was as real and in the moment as it could be.

They stopped at Broadway and 50th, and waited for the traffic lights to change. Lucy had changed clothes, now wearing a gray tube top with black denim Capri pants and some kind of high-heeled sandals that would pass muster in any boutique. She looked at him and smiled, and despite his new awareness of everything around him, it all withdrew to the background of those shining green eyes.

Over Lucy's shoulders, a man was approaching. Older, balding, but very well established and definitely angry.

"Time to go," said the disembodied creature known as Katarina Castillo. "Release."

What? Thought Dreamer Lucy. Then she looked and saw him approaching. From Kat, she sensed confusion and shock. A self-contained world of bedazzlement.

"How does he know?" Asked Dreamer Lucy.

"I don't know," said Kat. "But you have to release now."

"Oh my God," said Lucy. Max turned around.

Before letting go, Dreamer Lucy saw the story of her Alternate again. How her husband had been away in Kuala Lumpur working for three weeks on a new contract that had been the last big obstacle to his retirement, and their moving away together to their dream home in San Francisco.

Then, memories Dreamer Lucy had always held but had been locked until this moment. Of appearing to her Alternate a few weeks ago in a dream, taking over her mind as she had now, and planting the idea in her head to go to Manhattan to meet a man named Max at a street corner. Of being told by Kate to maintain absolute control otherwise the lesson would fail. And yet, she'd done as she had been told. And they had failed.

"Release!"

Dreamer Lucy let go of her Alternate just as Claude entered their space and began shouting, but she could no longer hear the words, or the sounds of the city. She realized the dream. And the dream dissolved around her, and a new one appeared in its place....

DELPHI 442

Lucy woke up. The last time waking up in this house. Her flight was only hours away. Two dreams lingered in her memory.

As last night's went, this had been pretty ordinary. Dinner, then washing up. Taking out the garbage and recycling, cleaning and vacuuming to ensure that Carmel Lucy didn't have to walk into a smelly house. All told, Lucy was being a very considerate guest in this lifespace.

She thought about staying. After all, this had been the dream she'd given up on to pursue becoming a corporate executive. Not that it had led much beyond the customer service department where she worked, but it was a start of something bigger. Still, no matter how she swung it, this was not Lucy's life. And Charles was waiting. No way she could back out of the plan now.

Especially after the dreams she'd just had.

The first found her in Manhattan. She remembered little of it, only that it had ended badly. It hadn't felt like a vision conjured up by Weaver and his crew of conspirators, assuming they were his crew. Just an ordinary dream. At least she thought so. Hoped so.

In the second dream, Lucy had been in a waiting room, not really vivid. White walls with black leather chairs. A wooden table in the middle that didn't fit the remaining decor. Muzak playing in the air, and a single, Asian-styled ceiling fan that belonged more in colonial Siam than this presumably modern place. No one else but her. The receptionist window was closed, but the nurse behind it was looking down at her paperwork.

In that second dream, Lucy had felt sick. Flu-like, queasy stomach, mouth acidic as if she'd just vomited something up a few minutes

141

earlier and had rinsed with water, but there was no sign of any mess around the carpeted floor of the room. She was barefoot, though, and looking down, she realized that she was wearing the same chocolate-brown nightie she had worn to bed.

The door that suddenly existed where there was only a wall before opened up, and Kate walked up. And she said something, but Lucy couldn't understand her. Whatever she said, though, caused the mood in the room to electrify. The excitement of setting out on a trip that you've been looking forward to for ages.

Kate suddenly had a photo album in her hands. She opened it roughly in the middle, then presented it to Lucy. And Lucy saw animated images of children.

Her children. Two of them. A son and a daughter.

The ones she would have with Max.

And they were beautiful.

She could sense something about their spirits, shining through their smiles, reflected in the sunlight bouncing off the hair on their heads. They grew up before her eyes, running along the beach at three or four years old, parading through high school hallways, sitting at university lectures, and then...

Then there was something...wrong with it. Something about the children's movements on the page seemed...menacing, like watching a scene in a horror movie where you knew a character was about to get savagely killed by the monster, and all that was left was the suspense of waiting for the inevitable.

And Lucy looked up at Kate, and something about her countenance had changed. Her eyes. They were somehow dark despite their blue intensity, despite the otherwise beautiful smile she wore on her face. Menacing.

Just as the dream threatened to turn into a nightmare, someone knocked on the waiting room door. And the mood lifted.

Looking up, Lucy saw some non-descript figure, the ones that always appear in dreams. She knew who the figure was at the time, though — damned if she could figure it out now — and she followed him outside.

She found herself at Carmel Beach. It was sunset, clouds on the red horizon. An outcropping of rock, a tiny little peninsula that didn't exist on this beach in real life.

And a man was sitting there. A black silhouette against a glorious dusk. Lucy started to feel incredibly empowered, that going forward toward that silhouette meant liberty, the fulfillment of her own dreams, of ambitions she didn't even realize she'd had until that moment, not so much for material things, but the creation and sustenance of joy. Before she could take one step forward, she woke up and lay awake.

Dream interpretation was never her strong suit. Fucking hated it. But, here she was, stuck with a vivid dream that had to be relevant. No way it wasn't. Kate had said that the conspirators among the people working on the Convergence could send visions and dreams.

Lucy knew what she wanted it to mean. And she knew...felt, what it actually meant. What it actually meant was something so big, so overwhelming, she simply blocked it out.

The more she thought about it, the more tired she felt, and though only seconds earlier she was wide awake, Lucy now felt sleep taking her again.

As she drifted to sleep, Lucy revisited the last conversation she'd had with Kate at the front door, when she'd asked Kate to show her work. She heard Kate's words once more.

"As you wish."

The next thing she knew, Lucy was catching herself on the railing.

She was at the airport, boarding her plane. Delphi 442 from Monterey to Seattle had just opened their doors. She was in line at Gate 8.

"What the hell—?"

143

"You okay?" asked the man behind her. Lucy turned. He wore a suit and a crew cut. Large build, a cop face.

"Yeah...nodded off."

The man grunted. He sounded super annoyed.

Then the memory returned. She'd nodded off at the wheel on the way into the airport. Jumped the curb, almost hit a tree before she course corrected and steered herself back onto the road. Likely damaged the suspension on her Mercedes. Well, her Alternate's Mercedes, anyway.

Lucy had managed to park. Walked a good ten minutes to the Delphi counter, gotten her boarding pass. Lucy had brought a carry-on bag filled with the same clothes she'd brought with her when she'd left Seattle. At the last minute, Lucy had decided against taking anything of her Alternate's. She'd decided to herself that stealing was stealing, even if it was from your alter ego. God knows she'd felt enough guilt from lying to poor Max Sinclair, who would now be here any day.

Memory returned: a walk around the house that was almost hers, saying a mental goodbye to the meditation circle and her nice backyard — her Alternate's nice backyard — and savoring the last of what would have been the life that would hereafter exist only in dreams. One last check that the paperwork and next month's budget for the yoga studio had been drafted, all the bills paid, and everything otherwise hunky-dory for when her Alternate ended up returning.

That had been no guarantee, of course. She didn't know what her Alternate had been up to, where she had gone, what she thought of the whole mess of a life that Lucy had left behind when she'd headed down the coast to see her friend. Still, it didn't matter. Her Carmel-based counterpart could have set her apartment on fire and burned all of her meager possessions, gotten her fired from work, it wouldn't matter. She was going to make some serious changes when she got back.

Standing there in the airport, Lucy wondered why she had forgotten all of this.

What the hell. She'd slept fine...

Her turn came. Everyone in line scanned their tickets and paraded down the jet way to the plane. Row 15. Seat A.

She boarded, smiled at the attendant, and made her way down the cabin. Finding her row, Lucy reached up to put her bag in the overhead compartment. Just a short flight, but still —

Lucy was strapped in. Outside the window, the tarmac was blurring past beneath them. Tiny trees and semi-arid sand dissolved into a backward-moving blur, and cars on the Salinas Highway seemed to be standing still. The turbojets roared and the low vibration of the engines sang a deep baritone hum that rose ever so slightly up the scale. The plane was on its run-up.

When had she sat down? The seatbelt was fastened and everything. The plane tipped backward, and Lucy felt gravity as they rose into the air. Her stomach fought the forces working against it, and she felt even sicker. This never happened to her on flights. Rather than feeling gradual acceleration, it was as if the plane had just flung itself off the ground and into the sky without any warning.

Flight 442 gained altitude and banked to the left. Despite wanting to throw up the bagel and coffee she'd had for breakfast, Lucy had to look out the window. It was her MO.

The view shifted from south, southeast, east, east northeast. Lucy could see Carmel Valley, little glimmers of the Hollister Hills as the cars and trees and buildings below grew smaller and smaller. The plane breached a layer of stratocumulus, blocking the rest of the view, though she hoped they would fly along the coast, over the shallows of the Pacific.

Eventually, they'd fly over San Francisco, probably right below them and out of sight, though they'd probably be able to see the Inland Empire, Napa Valley. Then, the Cascades would appear, Mt. Rainier white-capped and swaddled in cloudy mist and glacial ice. Then, a descent, likely into mist and gray, and they'd land at SeaTac.

She noticed her nose was pressed to the window, leaving a little greasy spot. Gross. Lucy pulled back and eased her back into the contours of her chair. The girl next to her was staring straight ahead into the back of the seat in front of her, many other things on her mind besides the view from Row 15. Headphones on. No conversation. The plane leveled off, and after about twenty minutes, her stomach now reconciled to the G-forces around her, Lucy looked around. They were seated on the starboard side of the aisle, and the ratio of asses-to-seats was about 1 to 2. Families, little kids, a few business travelers, a couple of college-aged kids. Nothing really out of place.

Missing time. That's what she'd experienced. Blackouts. What the hell was happening? She'd had a decent night's sleep, remembered waking up, feeling rested and ready to go. She remembered packing their bags, looking around the house — was this the last time? Would she be coming back? — and heading out the door. She remembered the drive to Monterey Airport.

She didn't remember jumping the curb. And just now, she didn't remember closing the compartment after loading her bag, didn't remember sitting down, putting on her seatbelt...

Come to think of it, when had she checked in? Eaten breakfast? Stood in line? It was as if someone had taken the filmstrip of her memory of the past five hours and cut out the scenes that she now couldn't recall.

Now she wondered if this was mental illness. Maybe this whole thing had been in her head. Maybe she was still dreaming.

That feeling of a few days prior, waking up in her room — not my room! — in her house — not my house! — in Carmel. Disorientation. Anxiety in her stomach.

The flight attendant came by with the refreshment tray. A thin blond thing with perfectly manicured fingers.

146

"Would you like anything?" she asked.

The girl next to her shook her head.

"Water, please," said Lucy. The attendant smiled, took out the teeny translucent plastic cup, opened up a bottle of water with the Hellenic-styled Delphi Regional logo on it. The cup nearly full, the attendant handed it to Lucy.

She took it in her hand...

...and Lucy was back in the waiting room. The cup was still in her hand.

Kate and Weaver stood across from her. Kate wore a business power suit with a bright red shirt underneath the stylish brown jacket, a matching knee-length skirt, and red shoes. Weaver was dressed like the junior man on the accounting team: graph-patterned collared shirt and slacks, scuffed shoes.

"You wanted me to show my work. Here's a lesson in the intricacies of causal interconnectedness. I trust I have your attention?"

Kate held a professor's pointer stick. She pointed at a very large white marker board that sat atop a wooden easel. Lucy saw a rough drawing of an airplane at the bottom centre of the board. What looked to be navigational directions and trajectories — three dotted lines — led up from the nose of the airplane and diverged, one to the right, one straight up, connecting with the words "SEA TAC" printed in large black lettering at the center top, and one to the left.

"One airplane," said Kate. "Delphi Flight 442. Monterey to SeaTac. Three possible trajectories. One lands on schedule. One crashes into the ocean. One is diverted."

Lucy looked on as Weaver thumped the top of the marker board with his fingers. The drawings blurred and swirled, as if on a computer screen, and when they finished re-arranging themselves, she saw what looked to be several dots and more trajectory paths.

"Mercury is in Cancer. Mercury's in Libra. Mercury's in Aquarius. Retrograde, all three."

Thump. Blur. Swirl.

What looked to be a medical chart of an adult male.

"Flight 442 is piloted by one Captain Washburne," said Kate. "Heart rate at 97 BPM. Blood sugar is low. He hasn't slept in twenty hours, hasn't eaten in ten. He is breaking in a new co-pilot today. At his current metabolic rate, Captain Washburne will lose consciousness at 12:47 P.M., Pacific Standard Time." Kate checked her watch, which she didn't have a moment ago. "It is now 12:22 P.M. PST."

She looked back up at Lucy. "At 12:44 P.M., the co-pilot will leave the cockpit. He's not supposed to leave the cockpit, but he does it at the insistence of Captain Washburne. He will head to the tail section and meet with the flight attendant named Britt who is serving you water, who will have called him to investigate a disturbance involving a passenger toward the tail section. This leaves no one at the helm of the aircraft at the time that Washburne passes out."

Thump. Blur. Swirl. What looked to be a wanted poster. A balding white guy, maybe mid forties, with thick rimmed glasses and bland good looks. Lucy had no idea who he was.

"Thomas Mosley, forty-three years old. An anarchist, wanted by Homeland Security. At 11:15 A.M., he entered Terminal 2 at SeaTac Airport carrying a backpack with bricks of clay and wires. They're not real explosives, but they look convincing enough. He just wants to send a message . At 12:33 P.M., he'll leave the backpack in the men's restroom outside the United Airlines check-in booth."

Thump. Blur. Swirl. A security ID badge for a janitor at Sea-Tac.

"Sergio Diaz, thirty-three years old. Just got his green card two years ago. Migrated here from Oaxaca, Mexico with his wife Ana and their three children. He is scheduled to clean the restroom outside the United Airlines check-in at 12:40 P.M. But he is late for his lunch, and may decide to take a break, which would leave the backpack unattended for another half hour. He is deciding what he wants to do, right now."

Thump. Blur. Swirl. A tarot card. The Tower of Destruction.

"At 6:21 A.M., Hawaii Time Zone, Henry Maakawa'a sat this morning for his daily reading and drew this card. His daughter is on Delphi Flight 442."

Kate stepped toward Lucy, her eyes intense. "Mr. Maakawa'a knew immediately and exactly what one of the outcomes was going to be. Poor guy."

The board returned to the initial drawing, and Kate returned to it, calm and collected once more.

"At 12:47 P.M. PST, three divergent trajectories achieve manifestation potential." Kate swung her pointer with dramatic flourish.

"One lands on schedule. One crashes into the ocean. One is diverted."

Kate pointed the pointer at Lucy.

"You pick."

Then she fell silent. Lucy was upset.

"How? How can I pick?"

"You make the choice. That is, you create the options. You make them possible."

"How?"

"You wanted to know how it works. This is what we do, Lucy. We see a bit down the road to how it turns out, and identify the linchpins. Your choice has an 80 percent bearing on how everything turns out. That makes you the linchpin in this scenario. You set every possibility in motion."

Lucy looked back at the easel, then back at Kate.

"Then it's easy. I choose for the plane to land at Sea Tac, on time, as scheduled."

"That's not the choice you get to make," said Kate.

"What are you talking about? I thought you jus—"

149

"No one person gets to steer the ship, but when the call comes down to change course, each person has her own station to command. Your station is far simpler, but critical to how this goes."

"What station is that?"

"Water or no water."

"What?"

"Three trajectories."

"I..."

"Your choice."

"Ma'am?"

She blinked.

She was back in her seat. The attendant was standing in the aisle, looking polite and professional, but confused. The girl passenger stared at the back of the seat, rocking out to whatever tune was on her phones like she was the only one on the plane.

"Ma'am, do you want water or don't you?"

Lucy shook her head. "Um..."

She had nothing in her hand. Didn't she already take a glass?

Lucy looked at the attendant. She looked back, getting impatient. Everyone was in the same position they'd been only seconds before she evidently slipped out of this reality into that dream world.

Lucy looked at the water in the bottle on the trolley. And she hesitated. She agonized. She could feel sweat starting to form on her forehead, in her armpits, behind her knees.

"Um..."

How was this supposed to be key? Water or no water. A simple choice. Ridiculously simple.

"No problem, hon. I'll come back later."

The flight attendant moved on to the row behind them. The passenger girl turned, shot her a look, then went back to her music.

Lucy stared straight ahead, at the same spot in the seat in front of her, stressed out at the surrealism of what she'd just seen, where she'd been, what she'd been doing.

Pissed off that her whole life had gone off the rails for the past six months.

Really fucking pissed off that every single time something like this happened, she had no idea what was real afterward.

Tired from the lack of sleep.

Sad at the wedding that she never got to have, whose promise had meant more to her than she'd wanted to admit.

Afraid that everything that Weaver and Kate had told her about choice was all bogus, that no matter what she did or who she chose to stay with, where she chose to take this experience, there was no way out.

Terrified that she was down the rabbit hole, lost in Wonderland, lost in the Matrix, and she couldn't escape.

On that last thought, Lucy's eyelids dropped.

The surrealism of the vision took its toll. The human mind tends to shut down in strangeness. As Lucy found herself fading into the black, she concluded that this was especially true at 37,000 feet, flying north from Carmel to Seattle.

Blackness.

And then, a shout.

Lucy's eyes flew back open and she turned around.

"Don't you take my fuckin' magazine away from me!"

"Sir, calm down!"

"It's mine!"

The sound of a seat belt un-clicking nearby.

Lucy saw the back of the head of the passenger in front of her duck below the seat, then return to view. It was the guy she'd bumped into in line — maybe late forties, with silver crew-cut hair and about six foot-four — and wearing a plain blue collared shirt. As he stood up,

Lucy saw that he wore blue jeans with a black leather belt. And for a second, she saw the flash of black plastic and metal.

A sky marshal.

He made his way to the scene, every single passenger in the cabin now looking on, doing their best to avoid letting the terror migrate any further than the expression in their eyes and on their faces. Nobody ever wants to think that their plane might be the one making headlines.

"Sir, I need you to calm down," Lucy heard the marshal say.

"NO WAY!"

"He was reading a Hustler magazine with children around," said the stewardess. "I just told him to mind his surroundings."

"GET THE HELL AWAY FROM ME!"

"Sir! If you don't calm down, I'm going to have to subdue you."

"NO!"

"Sir—"

And that's when the passenger hauled off and punched the marshal in the face.

Lucy's heart jumped, passengers screamed as the pistol fell from his hands. Faster than she thought was possible for the hefty interloper, he reached down and grabbed it before the marshal could recover. The guy was easily 300 pounds and shouldn't have been able to land what was otherwise a lucky shot. But Lucy saw his eyes were bloodshot and his face was pale.

The marshal sat up. No sign of blood on his face, but Lucy could see the bruise. He put his hands in the air. Lucy was positive he had another gun on him somewhere. Didn't marshals carry two? But the interloper had the pistol he'd lost pointed at his head, and he couldn't make for it.

They were dead. This guy was going to hijack the plane, kill them all. Funny how sometimes, everyone around you thinks the same thing, and you all know it without having to ask. An obese mother held her young three-year-old son close. One man in a suit and a yarmulke was already in tears, doing his best to pray without completely freaking out, not even looking at what was unfolding behind them. Funny how some people only find such uniformity of thought when they are about to die.

Another attendant made her way to the cockpit, and now Lucy could see how it was going to go.

If I'd said yes to the water...

"Nobody move!" said the passenger. "I'm...I'm just gonna read my magazine...I just wanna see her! She's my girl! Leave me alone, okay?!"

The blond attendant stood behind him and was shaking as she whimpered, poor thing.

"Okay," said the marshal, still on the ground. "We'll leave you alone, okay? Just...just put the gun down."

The passenger — now a gunman — wrinkled his nose. He used the gun to scratch the itch, and for a split second, Lucy saw the barrel pointed right at her. Both she and the girl passenger ducked beneath their seats, waiting for the shot, but there was nothing.

"I'm just...I gotta back headache," she heard him say. "The titty mags make me feel better, okay? I need them. Let me read my mag, please."

Behind them, footsteps, quick at first, then slowing. A man in a white uniform stopped right at the row in front of them. Of all places.

The girl passenger grabbed her hand and both of them kept their heads down. Lucy heard the man and the gunman talking.

"Stay away!"

"I'm the co-pilot," said the man. "Are you Mr. Potts?"

"Yeah...Edgar."

"Edgar, I'm Paul. How are you doing?"

"She wants to take my magazine!"

"I know, but she won't do that, Edgar. None of us will take away your magazine."

Paul stepped forward. Three footsteps.

"Edgar, can I ask you a question?"

"Uhh...yeah?"

"Do you have pills you're supposed to take, Edgar?"

"Uh...yeah?"

"Where are they, Edgar?"

"Ummm...they're in my bag."

"When were you supposed to take them?"

No response.

"Do you need help taking them, Edgar?"

"Uh...yeah, Paul."

He sounds like he's five years old!, thought Lucy.

"Where are they?"

"In my backpack."

"And where's that?"

Lucy heard nothing, but she imagined him pointing to the overhead compartment.

"Okay, do you want me to help you take them?"

"Uh...sure."

The blond attendant whimpered.

"Do you believe me when I say that we won't take your magazine? I promise."

"Uh...yeah, I believe you."

"Okay then. I can't help you take the pills if you don't put down the gun. Can you do that for me?"

"Sure..."

No sound for a few seconds. Then...

"Here you go, mister, I'm sorry."

"Thanks, Edgar." It was the marshal.

Paul the co-pilot stepped forward, and it seemed that the freeze frame that had taken hold of Delphi Flight 442 released, and several passengers sighed audibly. Lucy and passenger girl both stood up and peeked over the backs of their chairs.

The marshal had the gun trained on Edgar and was now a few steps back, well out of range of Edgar's demonstrably effective left hook. Paul the co-pilot had opened the compartment and was speaking quietly to Edgar. Behind the scene, the blond attendant had fled to the tail section and was now being comforted by another of her coworkers. The other passengers were a hot mess of weeping, laughing, clapping, and praying.

"You okay?" she asked the girl. The girl nodded, but didn't speak. She didn't have to for Lucy to know how she felt.

And all she felt was gratitude.

Gratitude, and relief.

Lucy's head struck the overhead compartment as the plane suddenly dovetailed.

The world went upside down, then right-side up, then down again. Shouts of children and grownups from everywhere.

Weightlessness...

Weightlessness…

Lucy was weightless in the air. And then she felt heavy, weighted, pinned.

Someone's blood, not hers, a few drops on her hand (not hers? Maybe hers?).

Her own blood filled the inside of her skull, her ears popping over, muffling the screaming and the wail of the engines around her.

Lucy was in her seat now, she knew that, and the blood was definitely pouring down from a gash on her temple. It was hot and wet on the right side of her face. Dizziness (but from the gash or the plane?)...

The oxygen mask that swayed with the shifting gravitational forces curved in the air in front of her, moving with the changing trajectories of this falling aircraft.

How long did they have until the end?

No one else knew what had happened, of course. They'd figure it was some kind of attack, that Edgar had been part of some bigger plan to destroy the plane. Either that, or he had acted alone, done something out of the sight of the others to sabotage the engine. And why would they think otherwise? The probability of having one major event to disrupt the flight was slim enough, but two? Now we were talking pure fantasy.

Of all of the 108 passengers on Delphi Flight 442, only Lucy knew that Captain Washburne's low blood sugar had been the thing that had done them in. He knew about his condition, and he flew anyway.

That was the pilot's choice. His station on the ship. A choice that Lucy had made possible.

Something flew up against the ceiling, out of the corner of Lucy's left eye. She turned. It was a teddy bear. She never saw the little girl who owned it: Mommy was too busy holding her and screaming. Oh my, was she screaming...

Captain Washburne had chosen to save the airline money. And not long after that decision — maybe a few seconds, maybe two minutes — his low blood sugar had caught up with him. It would have had to have been quick: had he seen it coming, he would have put the plane back on autopilot, radioed a mayday. No, he would have just passed out, making him the only human being on Delphi Flight 442 who would not have to face his death awake.

And with the door to the cockpit closed to the outside, no one would have been able to get back in to stop the plane from its final plunge.

All because the co-pilot wasn't there to save them all.

All because Edgar Potts hadn't taken his happy pills and managed to disarm a federal air marshal by complete fluke.

All because Edgar had decided to read a porno magazine in full view of the cabin and hadn't had the time to put it away before getting caught.

156

All because a young, inexperienced flight attendant had asked him to put it away.

Because she'd had the time to wander over to his row.

Because Lucy had declined a cup of water that would have taken precisely enough seconds to pour to keep her from wandering over there too soon.

Lucy knew, because Lucy had seen. They'd shown it to her. Kate. Weaver. The Convergence workers. They had shown their work on this particular problem set.

How long did they have left?

Lucy looked out the window. She didn't understand what she was looking at. The horizon line ran from the bottom left of the window to the top right, a near-perfect 45 degree angle, dividing the rounded window into two triangles of two shades of blue. That, Lucy understood. What she didn't comprehend was why the top triangle was a darker blue, while the bottom was pale blue. It didn't make sense, until she felt subtle pressure in her sinuses, until she realized that her ears were still popping. Throbbing behind her eyes.

They were upside down. And the dark blue triangle was getting bigger. How much longer?

This was it. Everything in her life had led to this.

The water was getting closer. She could see flecks of sunlight appear on dark blue.

Soon.

Five seconds...

Her breath left her.

Four...

What about her supposed destiny?

No, this wasn't right.

Three...

The flecks of water grew larger.

Two...

This wasn't how it was supposed to be.
One...
The engines suddenly grew louder.
Shaking.
Black.

SEMA

Max's eyes flew open. The sun was in his face, and the heat was already building up in the air of the room. Where in the world...?

The motel. He was back at the motel.

He sat up in bed and shook off strangeness that had come in his sleep, dreams of Manhattan condos, of walking with Lucy in Central Park...

It had been so real, that other life. It was real.

Unlike other dreams, where you remember only blurry afterimages, sensations, feelings, Max remembered the imagery with great clarity. It was a memory of real experience, not phantasmal imaginings. And he really wondered.

"Manhattan" Max seemed to have it all, and now he seemed to have met Lucy Fitzgerald. Mission accomplished!

"At least one set of us will be together," Max said aloud to the room.

But that Lucy...she was so vulnerable, so different. There was damage there, and Max couldn't be sure now that his counterpart would be able to stay with her. Then again, they were off to a good start...

And the feeling he was left with was exquisite, and in that sense, the dream was like all those other dreams, the ones that you wake up from with a bittersweet gratitude for having had such a pleasant experience, but being unable to take it with you beyond the veil between sleep and wakefulness.

Max rubbed his eyes. The ambient temperature in the room was cold, but already, as the sun brightened in the desert outside, he could feel the change after only these few minutes. He was sure the AC worked, but he didn't really want to wait around to find out. He didn't have the time.

Because these other Alternates that he had seen had gotten together, was Max now off the hook?

As he showered and dressed, practicality returned to ground him. He'd told his bosses he needed a week, and it occurred to him: what if he needed longer? Was he willing to jeopardize his life back home for this?

It had been two days of travel now, and the third was just beginning. He was two days from California, and would need three days to come back. Including the weekend, he would only have really one, maybe two days to spend with Lucy, then the return trip. Truth be told, he could take longer, but he couldn't lose himself in this.

I'm not going to sacrifice what I already have for what I don't.

And how come I'm doing all of the work?

Max surprised himself at that thought. He stepped out of the shower, dried himself off, and went to change. There was now something...off about this whole experience. If his Detroit Alternate had been right about he and Lucy being linked by some kind of destiny, how come she wasn't meeting him halfway? Why was he the only one moving? The lack of symmetry in this aspect of it was not only disruptive, but it was costly. He'd spent over $300 in gas alone so far and was still a full two days away from Carmel

Maybe he really was crazy. But regardless, he was here now, and may as well keep going. The kicker had been the chat he'd had at Weaver's Diner. He would risk. He would not become his Alternate from Glastonbury, living in mediocrity in the house on Oak Knoll Road.

He got dressed, packed up his shit, and walked into the desert air. Oddly, the abandoned settlement at Junction 39B didn't seem as grim in the morning light, and the air was as clear as ever. He spent a few minutes looking around before getting into the Sunfire and continuing on his way, and saw what he needed to see.

The road to Las Vegas was empty.

***

Max arrived in Sin City later that afternoon. He had never seen desert before, and at his various stops along the way, he took the time to walk around the gritty stone and sand, notice there weren't as many cacti around as the movies would have you believe, stare at mountains that were both massive and distant, contemplate the thousand and one ways one could die out here. He also knew he would have to change the oil very soon in the car: he'd come along way, and though the car was performing smoothly, he didn't want to take any more chances. He would change it in Vegas.

Max's route took him right past the signature "Welcome to Las Vegas" sign just in front of the Mandalay, but the traffic on the Strip was choked. He turned right on a hunch, bypassing the Strip altogether, and before long, had found mom-and-pop motel with vacancies and reasonable rates. Checking in, he then made his way out, on foot, to explore famous Las Vegas, a city he had never seen except on TV.

After about an hour of being blown away by how big everything was — and developing a stiff neck from looking up and around all the time — Max stopped in front of MGM to take a few pictures with his phone. New York, New York was just across the street, and the sky had grayed over, making for quite the silhouette of the Statue of Liberty and the roller coaster rails.

He would have kept going, but for the creepy feeling that someone was following him.

"Must be tired," said Max aloud. He found an empty spot along the wall near the MGM and sat down. The feeling didn't go away, and

161

after watching the ebb and flow of the crowds for a time, Max got up. It was now dark — as dark as it gets in Vegas at night — and the crowds were now getting more intoxicated and younger. The mood should have been electric, but he couldn't shake the feeling. Someone was lurking close by, someone looking for him.

Max walked for the next hour back to where he had checked in, to the little two-level motel removed from the lights and crowds. His car was parked there, still safe and secure, now accompanied by four others. Max looked at the plates — Nevada, Arizona, New York, and Oregon — of his Sunfire's new neighbors as he took out his motel key.

That's when Max saw him. There, seated in the easy chair in front of his motel room door. And Max took a step back as his blood ran cold, for in the Alternate's hand was a gun.

Ten miles of bad road. That's how Dad would have described this Alternate had he been here to witness this. Dressed in military camouflage pants, combat boots, and a black T-shirt, the Alternate was slouched over the chair with a grizzled, sunburned face and sickly eyes. Though Max guessed they were the same age, the Alternate could have easily been five years older, by the look of him.

"You sightseeing, Max?" asked the Alternate. Max didn't break his stare. The gun was in the Alternate's hand, which rested in his lap. The Alternate followed Max's gaze and allowed a slight smile. "Sorry," he said, putting the weapon into his pants pocket and holding open his palms.

Max relaxed, exhaled the breath he didn't know he'd been holding. Guns and war were not his thing. "Never been to Vegas before," he managed to say.

The Alternate sighed. "Neither have I. Look…" The Alternate clasped his hands together. "I'll be quick about this. Your objective with my lifespace is to get me to write her a letter. Tell her I'm sorry."

"Who?" asked Max.

"Who do you think?"

162

"And why can't you do it?"

The Alternate smiled, a grim twisting of his gaunt face that never reached his eyes, and leaned his head up against the brick of the motel.

"You ever wonder what real death is, Max? It happens way before the end of the body. It happens when we see the one thing in our lives that's gonna guarantee life, but we're too chicken shit to step up. Either that, or we're too proud to beg for it back once we've lost it."

The Alternate leaned forward into a hunch. Max noticed a round, rusty stain on the wall where the Alternate's head had just been, and his stomach recoiled.

"I died a long time before I got here," continued the Alternate, "make no mistake."

"Are you…are you dead now?" asked Max.

The Alternate's grim smile never left his face. "I'm in the In-Between. Lost…until now. Not everyone gets to come here, but like Mr. Weaver says, we're special."

"The guy at the diner?" asked Max. The Alternate nodded.

Max finally mustered up enough courage to take a step toward him. "Who is he, really?" he asked. "Mr. Weaver?"

The Alternate shrugged. "Your guess is as good as mine about who or what he is, Max," he said, "but it's what he says that really counts. And what he told me about the real nature of death, life, and the love of our Lucy."

The Alternate stood up. Max saw that he was far more powerfully built than anything Max could muster at the gym. But the way he hunched told Max of a greater sadness, one that even a combat trooper couldn't defeat. The Alternate reached into his pants pocket — not the one with the gun — and took out a small black object, holding it out. Max hesitated for a moment, then stepped forward to take it.

It was a memory stick.

"My time here is up, Max," he said. "This should explain everything."

"What happened to you?" asked Max.

"I died two deaths in three years," said the Alternate, "and now I get to put an end to this nightmare I've been trapped in ever since the last one." He laughed bitterly. "I guess this one makes three."

Max's nearly jumped out of his skin when the Alternate grabbed his arm. "When you get into my lifespace, no matter what I'm doing or where you find me, when our minds become one, you've got to get me to write Lucy that letter. Resist the pride and the fear that comes with my reaction. Tell her that I'm sorry, that I want to make it work."

"But…"

"This is more important than Lucy, Max. Send her the letter, and you have a chance to save two lives, including your own."

"Are you sure that it'll work?" said Max. "Why would that be enough?"

The Alternate didn't say anything, and let go of his grip. "Read the file," he said after a moment, "and see the story for yourself. I have no idea at what point in my lifespace you'll find yourself, when the lifespace takes you, you've got to try anyway, for Lucy's sake, for my sake." The Alternate sighed. "And for Shaffir."

Max frowned. "Who's Shaf—?" but the Alternate had already started walking away. Max was about to follow after him when his heart skipped what felt like two beats.

There, at the back of the Alternate's head, near the top, was an exit wound. A bullet hole.

And it was still bleeding.

***

Max spent the next hour lying down in his room, letting the shock of what he had just seen dissipate. No thoughts, no movement. Just staring at the ceiling, fumbling with the memory stick in his fingers.

164

When it was over, his mind still quiet, but no longer traumatized by the experience, Max sat up. It was time to see the whole story behind the Alternate he had just met.

His laptop booted up on the table across from the bed, Max plugged in the USB stick and explored it. There was only one file. The file name was strange — "ARA 2432615184.PDF" — but Max opened it. Before reading it, he opened the MS for his story, and kept the two of them side-by-side.

When he was finished, about fifteen minutes later, Max opened up Word. His finger slipped along the touchpad and he opened an existing document.

The line he'd written days earlier appeared before him, and Max smiled. The moment had come to weave something out of that first thread he had spun.

"Shaffir," he said aloud. "Samir Shaffir."

The story of the third Alternate filled in Max's mind, and the computer, the motel room, and Las Vegas all dissolved away in a blur.

In his mind, Max carried with him the Alternate's instructions, his last mission on the way to his own soul mate.

Write her the letter. Tell her you're sorry.

***

"You see," said Samir Shaffir, "even this glass contains multitudes, the essence of Allah."

Sinclair opened his eyes, felt the lingering dizziness, but kept his cool. Shaffir hadn't been what he'd expected, but then again, that was no reason to lose face in front of him while he was learning this lesson. Still, the disorientation had been something fierce, like being woken up by thunder from a deep, deep sleep. He made a mental note to re-check the side effects on his medication when he got back.

165

This time, it felt different, something like déjà vu. The oddest feeling, like he was just in Las Vegas a moment ago...but that couldn't be right. Of course, that didn't stop him from wishing it were.

The Sufi's English was perfect, clear, with only the hint of a British accent that made him wonder if he wasn't descended from the former Ottoman ruling class itself.

"I see what you mean," said Sinclair, though he didn't, he really didn't. The canvas of the tent fluttered in the icy breeze. He couldn't believe it could get so cold here so quickly after the land baked in 120 degree heat. But this was the desert, after all, and temperatures in the plateau could sink quickly.

"Do you really see, Mr. Sinclair?" Shaffir continued. "For this is the greatest lesson I can teach you. Allah is in the light, and the light is everywhere, and we believe that we can reach that ecstasy while still in this life, without offence to Allah."

"Okay... How do you reach this ecstasy?" asked Max.

"The semazen follow the best path, and the ones I trained in Istanbul, among the best in the world," said Shaffir. "But there are other ways, and this flower — the poppy — is one such path. I do not use them to traffic, Mr. Sinclair, or to sell to others for profit. I use it for my disciples, and them alone."

"So why did some of the elders tell us that you had bought a large shipment from them?"

Shaffir leaned in. Though the rest of his face was shaved, Shaffir bore a well-coiffed Turkish mustache and a pillbox had that was completely out of place here in the plateau. His outfit was so gaudy — with bright gold and purple patterns — that Sinclair almost thought him a charlatan.

"They despise my presence here," said Shaffir. "But this is the birthplace of Rumi, the greatest mystic in my tradition. This man reached ecstasy well before he died. I have the right to lead my disciples here, to help them touch the hand of Allah in the land that gave birth to this great poet. The elders will not harm me, in the same way that they've fought each other. Instead, they will seek to destroy my reputation, and make you," he pointed a sharp finger at Sinclair, "do the work for me. If you must know, the small bushel that I purchased is sitting outside, in a crate marked "US Aid" at the entrance where you came in. You may look at it and assess for yourself whether or not I am in the service of lesser or greater demons."

"That seems a little out in the open, don't you think?"

"You only hide things when you have something to hide. I make no pretense about what it is I bought from the farmers."

Shaffir relaxed and sat back down. "Would you like me to ask my son to bring you some more tea?"

"No thank you, but it was delicious," replied Sinclair.

"Have you ever read Rumi's poetry?" asked Shaffir. Sinclair shook his head, and the Sufi elder laughed in obvious delight and clapped his hands together. He pointed to the two crates upon which Sinclair sat. "Underneath you are my books. I have an English version that I bought in Turkey just before coming here."

Sinclair got up and opened the crate that he'd been sitting on for the past hour. Inside were several new books, all in Arabic, except for the one. It was red, and written in clear English type. Sinclair took it out and showed it to Shaffir, who nodded.

"Keep it, Mr. Sinclair. It is a gift, for all of your kindness to me during our first meeting together."

"Thank you," replied Sinclair, who replaced the lid on the crate and sat back down. "I will be sure to read it as soon as my shift is over."

"So tell me, my new friend," said Shaffir. There was a glint in his eye that put Sinclair ill at ease, something in the way he said the word friend. "What do you intend to tell your people about the crop I bought?"

Sinclair sighed. "I will look at it, Shaffir," he said, "and if it is in too small quantities, I can tell my people that it is safe. However, if there is too much of it, I may have to return with more people to claim it as evidence of the sale. Still, I believe you are a man of honor, Shaffir, and I don't believe I will be back, except maybe to talk about Rumi."

Shaffir smiled a toothy grin, which Sinclair politely return, lips closed. The two men stood, and Shaffir reached out his hand. Max took it, and Shaffir reached around his other arm and shook his hand.

"Thank you, my friend. I hope to see you again soon." The Sufi shivered, and he rubbed his own shoulders with an almost dramatic enthusiasm. "Ah, you'll excuse me if I don't show you out. Please, feel free to wander our settlement and to see your way back. I believe I will be turning in for the evening."

Sinclair nodded, and stepped out of the canvas. His boots were waiting at the entrance, and he sat down to put them back on. As he laced up, he looked around. Seven or eight Sufi tents sat scattered around this little cul-de-sac in the mountains. The sky was gray, and there were traces of snow on the distant peaks. Someone had a fire going in the middle of the settlement and was boiling water for tea, but they were back in their tents, and no one was outside. Beyond, about a football field's length away, was Sinclair's ride, where his two travel buddies were waiting. He got up and started walking back, his boots crunching the gravel and stones like new-fallen snow back home.

Clutching the poetry book in hand, Sinclair indeed saw that there were many crates scattered here and there. Some were US Aid, others bore UN markings. One near the entrance, about halfway between him and his ride back, seemed more out of place than the others. That must be the one.

Walking up to it, Sinclair inspected it. No signs of wires or telltale signs that an IED or other booby trap lay beneath. Still, even if he wasn't trained to assess it, Sinclair felt that Samir Shaffir II was a man of his word, an outsider in the country of his ancestors. There was no harm here.

Satisfied that it was safe, Sinclair opened the crate. Inside were the dried poppy bushes, but only a few of them, not nearly enough to process for even a gram of heroine. Shaffir was a man of his word. Sinclair contemplated bringing it back, but he was still holding Shaffir's gift under his arm, and so he replaced the lid, and continued back to the Hummer.

As he approached the vehicle, one of the men, Corporal Doug Daniels, handed Sinclair his M-16.

"What's the word, El-Tee?" he asked.

"He checks out," said Sinclair. "Still, we'll come back in a few days, see how they're doing. We should bring some more supplies, too. They're running a little low on a few things. Remind me to tell the XO that some of the reports we're getting from the Pashtuns might not be entirely accurate, although...shit, I guess he could be lying."

The other man, Corporal Bill Sharpe, got in the driver's seat. "If we're going to head back, sir, we should probably get going. It's getting dark."

Daniels hopped around into shotgun. "I concur. Gettin' too fuckin' cold out here, El-Tee."

First Lieutenant Maxim Sinclair, U.S. Army, concurred.

"Let's get moving, gentlemen."

As the Hummer started and rolled to life, Sinclair noticed that the Afghan daylight was weakening quicker than he expected, and the air was getting just as cold. He put his rifle across his lap and flipped through the book of poetry. They were short stanzas, with the Persian on the left page and the English translation on the right. Normally, he liked to read the Persian so he could practice, but his patrol was over, and he had nothing left to do on the long ride back to base. He took a few moments to himself to lose himself in the ancient words of this Sufi mystic as they made their way back to Kandahar Airbase under the gray skies of this war-torn country.

＊＊

Sinclair put down Rumi's poetry and rubbed his eyes. He couldn't sleep. Not that he did much of that since before he came back to the Sandbox.

Sinclair never slept well at Kandahar Airbase, not on this last tour, not on this one.

The kicker had been the white scorpion. They'd briefed him on all of the major risks, but also on the surprising large number of little things that could kill you out here, aside from al Qaeda and the Taliban. Many varieties of snakes and poisonous creatures, of which the white scorpion was among the most deadly.

One morning, the sun bright and the air already as hot as jet blast, Sinclair awoke with a white scorpion sitting on his chest. Had he paid more attention to his briefings during his preparation to deploy, he would have recognized the serious danger he'd was in. Had he been more awake and lucid, he would have done something different.

Instead, his reflexes took over, and he brushed it away with the back of his bare hand onto the floor, where it scurried away. Only over breakfast when he was chatting with Doug Daniels did he realize his mistake. Doug didn't even have to say anything: the sheer look in his eyes was enough. One sting would have killed him, and the scorpion's stinger, as a rule, was quicker on the draw than a human hand. Sinclair never had a good night's sleep at Kandahar Airbase after that.

Tonight, his back and body sore from the armor and the patrols, Sinclair could only manage to get about fifteen or twenty minutes' worth of dozing. That was it. Thoughts of scorpions and all sorts of deadly creepy-crawlies occupied the back of his mind enough that he didn't want to chance getting stung while asleep. A soldier dies with his eyes open. A man faces death awake.

Outside the window, the pale blue dawn was just beginning to illuminate the bottom layer eastern sky. He had about forty minutes or so before reveille. Sinclair didn't want to think about that right now. All he could wonder about was her. Was Lucy okay? Had everything healed? Was she moving on now?

Tell her you're sorry.

Such a fucking waste, Sinclair thought, trying to make himself comfortable in his bunk, but then he cringed. All his fault. It had been all his fault.

Write to her. Tell her how you feel.

Sinclair had heard that voice before. As before, he ignored it, continuing with his reflection as the sky outside grew ever brighter. Joining the ROTC had been the first mistake. No, that wasn't true. Trying to prove something to Dad by giving up songwriting, that was the original sin, for it had led to everything that had unfolded to this point. If he'd wanted to prove something to the old man, the braver way would have been to make his songwriting profitable, find a way to spend the rest of his life doing something he loved instead of following in Daddy's much bigger footsteps. That was the irony: being a soldier in Max's case wasn't being courageous, but a coward, because it meant he didn't have the balls to carve his own path through the jungle.

It's not like he did it right, anyway. Dad was retired Air Force, not the Army.

Sinclair thought of the book that Samir Shaffir had given him. He'd heard of Rumi, of course, as many middle Americans had in passing, but never once did he think to pick up a book and read the man's poetry. He'd spent years of his life back in the States writing his own compositions; he had to come to Afghanistan to actually read some. The little red book that Shaffir had picked up for him in Istanbul lay on his desk. He a point to read it during his day off.

In fact, he'd been reading it last night before bed. The poem he flipped to saw Rumi setting the stage in one of his many gardens for his Beloved to arrive, and yet nobody showed up to this private party.

The desperation, the longing, in those words...how hard not to think of Lucy.

It wasn't always bad. Help her remember the good times. Write to her.

Their whole relationship had been an accident. He should have seen the symbolism that it began with a car wreck. She had t-boned his car while driving out in Ventura, when Max was on leave, and they both shared the ambulance ride to the hospital, and hours later, both of them were lucky to have walked out together with only the mildest cases of whiplash. Max's Sunfire, of course, bought the farm, but Lucy was very sweet to chauffeur him around for those two days before he bought his replacement car. The rest, as they say, was history from that point on.

Until the Taliban killed them.

Sinclair turned around to his side as the sky started to get brighter.

The first time he set foot in the sandbox, he was twenty years old. Lower Manhattan had stopped smoldering only a month prior, and the caves of Tora Bora had already felt the wrath of the Daisy Cutters. Everyone in his platoon was shocked, pissed off, and ready to kick some Taliban ass.

And they did, as fast as anyone savvy enough about the mightiest military force in the history of the species would have expected, although he himself saw no action, being relegated to rear guard during most of the operations.

Still, a victory for one was a victory for all, and when his six month tour was nearing an end, Sinclair volunteered to stay on for another rotation, and he ended up on the very critical billet of demining some of the local villages. It was satisfying work, getting to meet some of the locals, learn a bit of Urdu, Persian, and Arabic, and helping to remove that existential threat that had been maiming civilians since the Soviet invasion. The most heavily mined country in the world, and Sinclair

172

felt glad that he could help to chip away at that title in his own small way.

Then the suicide attacks started.

The first — and, to date, last — time Sinclair fired his weapon in anger, he'd shot to kill. His target hadn't even looked like a soldier. No uniform, no flags, no rank. He'd looked like he was sixteen years old — maybe a few days shy of seventeen — but the bomb belt was unmistakable. Worst yet, he came in from a part of town that Sinclair had had the chance to patrol only days ago, but had decided wasn't worth the extra time. After all, it was safe now, wasn't it? Hadn't they driven the Taliban into Pakistan? No point in wasting an hour on a patrol that would yield more old ladies and goat herders. Another mistake.

He remembered how warm the sun had been that day, how clear the sky and cheerful the surroundings. A wedding party had been taking place behind him in the village when the bomber approached, providing an unlikely soundtrack for the carnage to come.

Sinclair remembered his eyes — those eyes! — and how they weren't dead or black as he'd expected the eyes of a suicide bomber to be, but how utterly alive with awareness they were. This was someone living at peak experience, in the last few instants of life before killing and dying.

The cheers and shouts of the revelers and the music — songs that hadn't filled the airwaves since before the darkness of the Taliban rule — vanished, and all Sinclair could hear was his own voice. Each second slowed as he focused all of his awareness on the threat.
"Stop! Stay where you are!" he shouted in Urdu.

The boy continued his approach. Max raised his weapon and trained his sights.

And then Max saw the boy was carrying a dead man's trigger, and he knew they were all royally fucked.

Sinclair squeezed off a short burst. The rounds tore a hole through the middle of the boy, and he jerked and flailed backward in the blood spray. If he was far back enough, it would limit the blast radius, maybe save a few more lives.

Sinclair never saw the explosion as he turned around to warn the others, but he knew what would happen next. As the dead bomber fell to the ground, he would release the dead man's trigger — a detonator made of two parts that had to be held together by hand, and that, when separated, would allow the charge to travel through to the bombs strapped to the boy's chest.

The air expanded around them as the blast consumed that part of the village. Sinclair remembered flying, intense heat, remembered the sickening crunch and splatter of debris and bones and flesh and blood and brains against timeless stone walls and desert rocks, the smell of cooked meat that came from no animal, and the sick feeling and awareness of being cradled in so much death.

Lying on the ground, Sinclair wavered in and out of consciousness, but when he was lucid, the same thought repeated, over and over again.

I'm dead now, and I won't ever see her again after today.

Sinclair had been lucky to have survived with only a few fractures and shrapnel cuts, but his recovery took months, and the brass had decided to ship him back Stateside with the next rotation.

He remembered his parents meeting him at the airport, amidst the applause of hundreds of family members and grateful citizens welcoming their veterans home. And he remembered seeing Lucy, wearing a full yellow dress that hugged her body in pleasurable ways, weeping alongside his mother.

The next few months were a contrast between the pleasure of the daylight and the horror of the night. PTSD would manifest itself in a variety of symptoms, the doctors had said, and Max was under orders to go see a shrink every week just to keep things straight. But no amount of therapy could compete with Lucy's love and attention, and during those days of walking on the beach with Lucy, kissing her in the Pacific breezes, of Napa wine tastings and lovemaking in bed and breakfasts across the wine country, the daylight hours were magical.

At night, things would change.

Lucy never told him how many nights he woke up screaming only to fall back asleep, tossing around in a cold sweat fighting off invisible scorpions or reliving the trauma of the suicide attack. She never did because she respected his wish to face this like a man, though she was sure to inform his psychiatrist before his sessions. That much, Max didn't mind. Lucy demonstrated so much love and patience that Max felt he would never be safer anywhere else, not if he had an entire tank division at his command.

Then one night, while they were in San Diego to visit the zoo, they decided to stay the night. They'd enjoyed a lovely dinner in the Gaslamp, and checked into a Super 8. Max had been really tired and had dropped to sleep almost immediately, while Lucy went out to a local Internet café to check her mail.

Sometime around 11:30, she'd come back into the room. According to the official reports from the investigators, and her own statements, Lucy had turned off the lights so that Max could get some decent rest. She had tried not to make any noise during her entry, but, of course, no one was ever that quiet.

Max, for his part, only remembered waking in a dark, unfamiliar place to the sounds of someone creeping up beside him. He remembered grabbing the person in the black and throwing them to the ground and punching them five times in the head before hearing the voice behind the screams and realizing for the first horrible time who it was that had snuck up on him.

A week later, Lucy had dropped the charges, and Max hadn't heard from her since.

It's just a letter. Five minutes, paper and pen. One page. All it takes to save a better life.

Not long after that, Sinclair got the opportunity to return to Kandahar. The insurgency had picked up, and the American people had elected a new president who placed a priority on reaching out a friendly hand to those who were willing to unclench their fists. The new tour would last a year and would come with a promotion to full Lieutenant. Lt. Sinclair now returned as liaison officer to the local elders, and he would act as the friendly face of the U.S. military outside Kandahar, building a strong relationship with the community to help dissuade them away from the opium trade and the Taliban.

It was a good position, and best of all, it would take him away from California, away from Lucy, and what he — what they — had done to her.

Mistakes. We all make them. In the line of errors since his decision to join the Army, it was clear to him that it wasn't the choice not to patrol that part of the village where the bomber had come from, but rather the decision to come back for another tour in the first place. That bombing had been fated to happen no matter what, but he didn't have to have been a part of it. And look what it cost him, in the end.

Rumi's words returned to him. Here was someone else who had lost someone he could never get back, and he spent the rest of his life in anguish. The only difference is that Rumi wasn't in any way at fault for the loss of his beloved. But what wisdom this man would have acquired in the course of that lifetime of pain...

Shaffir had said that his people sought the light and ecstasy of God while still in this life. Something about that stirred something in Sinclair's heart, thrilled him as he hadn't been thrilled since he was younger. A childlike excitement at Christmas. Sinclair would return to the Sufi. Just as he was here to help the people heal, maybe so this one person could heal him, in turn.

He noticed the ray of light shining on the ceiling. The sun was up, and shining in early streaks of silver through the shale of stratus on the horizon. Lt. Maxim Sinclair stirred, checking for white scorpions on his belly before heading out to start his day.

You're meant to be together. You know this. You feel it. Even now, all she needs is to see your vulnerability again, and you'll be hers again.

Write the letter. Tell her how sorry you are. Let her heal you.

***

"You see them, don't you?"

Shaffir handed Sinclair the tea while he awaited an answer. Sinclair shook his head.

"I don't know what you mean."

"The regrets, the visions of how your life could have been otherwise, you remember something about them, even now."

Sinclair froze. How had he known about that? It was something that he'd kept to himself. The spells were coming on stronger now, more frequent, these blackouts and hallucinations of other lives, places, peoples. Only Lucy remained the constant factor in all of this, and so did her absence from his life.

"Some of it," said Sinclair, keeping his composure. "I even had a spell when we were speaking last, when you held up the glass." Shaffir smiled. "I felt it," said the Sufi. "For those moments, and ever after I showed you the glass, you were not the same. Your eyes changed, seemed less certain and far more bright than they were before. A darkness left you."

"What does it all mean?" asked Sinclair.

"I do not know, Mr. Sinclair," replied Shaffir. "I am no more a fortune teller than you are a glassmaker. But I have seen it before, those eyes, in the faces of other men like yourself. America seems to be full of them. There are many of your countrymen, especially at your age, who have a lifetime of regrets already, and not just soldiers, either."

Shaffir leaned forward. "What is your given name?"

"Maxim, though you can call me Max."

"Oh, I prefer Maxim, it seems more timeless, ancient. A Roman name. And your family, Sinclair, descended no doubt from the legendary Templar, Henry Sinclair."

The soldier smiled wanly and nodded. "Not something I like to mention as a Western soldier in a Muslim country."

Shaffir smiled. "Ah...no, that would not be prudent," Sinclair sipped his tea while Shaffir continued.

"I know what your mission here is, Maxim, to build friendship with those who live here so that your President can continue his war. I know you have protocol to follow, but as I am neither an Afghan or a local, we can speak as men."

Sinclair said nothing, and Shaffir stood up, began to pace around the room like a professor at lecture hall.

"I do believe that Allah gave us as much freedom to choose the lives that we want, meaning that Allah also had to give us those possibilities; possibilities which I think you are seeing now when your eyes go distant. But what's done is done, and you can spend a lifetime thinking about what you could have done. You'll never reach ecstasy in this life by so living. Ecstasy depends on the lightness of being, a lightness that you cannot have if you weigh yourself down with all of these regrets. If I may tell you as a friend and an elder, Maxim, you must leave these regrets behind, starting now."

Sinclair hesitated, then decided to press ahead with what was on his mind.

"Did Rumi ever get his beloved back?" he asked.

"No," replied Shaffir, and the atmosphere in the room shifted, subtle, like distant thunder.

"That loss defined his life, as it has defined mine, and the thousands like me who follow in his ways," continued Shaffir. "I chose to be on this path, I gave up the chance at a family, at children, at love with my own wife, to be on this path. My wife waits for me back in Bursa with my family, and only one of my sons joined me on this journey."

Sinclair smiled. "I haven't met your son," he said.

Shaffir met his gaze, smiled back. "Yes you have, though briefly. He brought you tea yesterday."

"Yes, that's true, my mistake."

"He does chores for me, looks after the other followers," said Shaffir. "He's gone with a group who are getting new food supplies. When they return tonight, we will be roasting some lamb and having *sema*. If you would like, you can attend."

Sinclair sipped the last of his tea: in these tiny cups, there was only so much. *Sema* was the Sufi ritual that Westerners associated with whirling dervishes. A once-in-a-lifetime experience, to be sure.

"I would be honored. Thank you. But I have to know, how do you cope? Don't you wish that you stayed with her? Could have her back?"

"What would be the point?" asked Shaffir. "If I'd wanted her as badly as I wanted ecstasy, I would never have left her. No, the pleasures that I enjoy extend far beyond flesh, beyond companionship with a woman. That part of my heart is dead, destroyed a long time ago by the heat and the light of Allah in this life. Better to keep it that way."

"I can't...how do you deaden your heart? Doesn't that make you less...human?"

"Not at all, Maxim Sinclair. It helps you leave behind the weight of this Earth behind, and become a channel for the glory of God in this body. You cannot find light where there are shadows. Better to abandon regret altogether."

The two men sat on the words for some time. Outside, the morning air picked up a breeze, throwing gusts of sand against the canvas of the tent.

"I had a love back home," said Sinclair, finally. Shaffir looked at his guest and listened. "I hurt her badly, and now she's gone, and I can't stop thinking about her, and I can't stop thinking about how everything else would have turned out in my life. But you're saying that I should kill that part of my heart that cares about such things?"

"No, not kill. That would make you inhuman. That is what the Wahabbists have done. It is what the Taliban have done, or anyone who would pervert faith to kill and die needlessly. Only Allah can help you to deaden that part of yourself that casts doubt on your life. That is where my semazen look, that is why they spin. They find him in the light. He is the one and all. You may look for him in the places of light. The light deadens your doubts, but only if you choose to follow."

Shaffir stood up, walked over to the flap of the door. He called out something in Turkish before sitting back down. A few seconds later, another one of his semazen had come in with more tea.

"You are a soldier now, Maxim Sinclair," said Shaffir, pouring his guest a new cup and handing it to him. "You are no longer the person you were before you became one. Yours is a volunteer army, I know that much, meaning you chose this path. Why would you contemplate other paths having traveled half a world away on the one you now walk?"

Sinclair sipped. He was about to share the story of the suicide bombing, but his training kicked in. Never give our more information than you have to. Ironically, he could share more intimate details about his private life than matters of record. He tried to let the question pass, but Shaffir said nothing, and was awaiting a response.

"Many reasons," said Sinclair, "but I think mostly because I want to know what would have brought me the greatest happiness, satisfaction."

Shaffir frowned. Sinclair could swear he had never seen more incredulity in a face than in that moment.

"And why would you want to know that? That knowledge would make you absolutely miserable, unless you were already living the best possibility. In any case, it is redundant. I do not know your beliefs, Maxim Sinclair, but Allah has already laid out all of our lives as they should be. There is no choice but what you have chosen."

Sinclair sighed. "I suppose so," he said, and he checked his watch. Time to head back.

"I'd like to accept your invitation, Shaffir," said Sinclair, standing up to leave.

Shaffir nodded, and rose to see him off. "Of course. But bring no weapons."

"I don't know if I can agree—" Sinclair stopped as Shaffir waved him off.

"That is my only requirement," he said, "no harm will come to you during your stay with us. Remember, we are telling your people where the Taliban are. We would not ourselves be anywhere unsafe."

The Sufi said nothing. Sinclair knew the other man was sizing him up. The tactical risk was significant: without weapons, he would be leaving himself exposed without defense. Sinclair had been on the outside of those hostage situations, the ones that made headlines back home and that didn't end well, even if they got their man back. He had no intention of seeing the inside of one.

Still, that feeling returned, and with it, Max's old sense of adventure, long since buried by the training, the routine, and the blood and mud he had seen so far on this other side of the world. He had a duty to perform, that was true, but he had to honor that part of himself, that kid-at-Christmas thrill that he hadn't felt since he'd penned his last song, just before beginning his time in ROTC.

"Fair enough," he said, finally. "I will attend, alone, and unarmed. In the name of trust."

"Agreed," said the Sufi, and extended his hand outwards. Sinclair shook it, and at once felt the guilt, knowing that, per standing protocol, he would have his sidearm tucked away on his person during the dance.

***

Lieutenant Sinclair returned later that evening for the *sema*. The air had gotten very cold, and he saw his breath steam away from him in the chill as he approached Samir Shaffir's campsite. He parked the Hummer just at the bottom of the rise and turned off the engine.

Beside him in the passenger seat was a small box of tea from a maker in California. A supply clerk back at Kandahar owed him a favor and had a number of these teas stacked away for the officers. He picked it up, got out, and walked the hundred yards or so to the cul-de-sac where the Sufis were camped.

Two of the Sufis had been waiting for Sinclair's arrival and had held up hands for him to stop. They wore black robes and pillbox hats. Sinclair's heart jumped when he saw that they carried weapons, two AK-47s at their sides.

Sure, I can't bring weapons, but you "peaceful" mystics can be absolutely bristling with assault rifles...

Sinclair's pistol was tucked inside his uniform, far enough that unless they stripped him down, they wouldn't find it, but convenient enough that he could reach it with minimal effort if he had to. The Sufi to the right motioned for him to step forward. Sinclair slowly put the box of tea down and held up his hands. He approached, one step after the other, until his face caught the light from the two bonfires. The one on the left said something in Turkish: Max recognized him as the man who had brought them the second pot of tea that morning. The one on the right smiled, ran inside while his new friend patted him on the shoulder.

"Welcome," he said to the Lieutenant. Sinclair smiled and nodded, but adrenaline continued to sear through his bloodstream.

"I brought a gift for Shaffir," he said, nodding toward the box he had left. "May I get it?"

"Yes," said the Sufi. Max collected his gift and was soon escorted into the site.

He found that the Sufis had changed the layout of the camp for the *sema*, having spaced most of their tents out to leave a large space between them all. Five of them formed a five-pointed star like a pentacle that the Lieutenant wasn't sure was intentional or not, while the others sat in the background. Two large bonfires marked the entrance into the pentacle, forming a gateway, while two other fires opposite the entrance surrounding Shaffir's tent. A single object that Sinclair saw was a log in between them marked the spot — presumably — where Sinclair would sit, and just before that, the space between him and Shaffir's tent was clear, and the Sufis had raked it clean of all debris that could trip their dancers.

Shaffir himself emerged. He, too, was dressed in black ceremonial robes, but Sinclair could see the skirt of the flowing white robes worn by the dervishes. He presented the Sufi with the tea.

"A gift, in return for your hospitality," he said as Shaffir took the box.

"Thank you," he said, looking it over. Sinclair saw the glint in his eye, and the man sighed. "You know, by tradition, I cannot take any of this for myself, but must share it with others on this path."

Sinclair smiled. "That's fine, of course. It's yours to do with as you please."

"Once again, thank you." Shaffir nodded over to Max's new friend, who promptly took the tea over to one of the tents.

"So, thank you again for inviting me. I'm not sure what to do."

"Sit, please," said Shaffir, and showed him to the log. Sinclair sat down while Shaffir knelt to the ground in front of him. The Lieutenant noticed, with dismay, that he couldn't see into the blackness beyond the bonfires in front and behind him.

"Aren't you worried about attack?" asked Sinclair.

"What?" said Shaffir.

"The bonfires. They tell too many people that you're here."

"I see," said Shaffir. "We have not encountered any trouble during our time here. If the Taliban are aware we are here, they will dismiss us as lowly villagers and nothing more. Besides, as you saw from my men when you entered, we can protect ourselves."

"Why did you ask me to come unarmed if your men have so many guns?" asked Max.

"Because my men are here to protect you, and in my sect, we believe that the one experiencing Divinity must approach it with pure intention. Otherwise, we insult Allah. Are you still comfortable?"

Max nodded. The pistol was chafing his ribs. He tried to ignore it.

Shaffir cleared his throat and continued.

"This ritual is called *sema*, what you in the West would consider 'dervish dancing,' though we call ourselves semazen. I have shown this to a few Westerners back in Turkey, so take no insult when I say, please do not clap. It is disrespectful in this context: this is for us a sacred ritual, not a performance."

Sinclair listened as Shaffir outlined the three stages of the ceremony itself, of the nature of all things in the universe to rotate — even proven scientifically by the motions of molecules and atoms in all matter — and that, while many semazen do reach ecstasy, the overall goal is, in fact, harmony with both Creator and Creation, something that the semazen achieve by the whirling dance.

As they spoke, Sinclair observed a number of observers gathering between the tents around the site. Some were women, which caught him by surprise, as Sinclair had not seen any women at all during his visits here, and a number of children.

"We will be starting without my son's presence," said Shaffir, after seeing Sinclair's gaze reach the surroundings of the camp. "A runner came just an hour ago to tell me that one of their horses died on the way back and they had to add to the burden of the other animals, slowing them down. They aren't far from here, but I'm afraid they won't be coming back until morning. The terrain is too dangerous at night without a vehicle."

Sinclair nodded.

"Are you ready?" Shaffir smiled again with that familiar twinkle. Sinclair returned his smile.

"Absolutely," said the Lieutenant.

"Then let's begin."

Shaffir walked over to just in front of his tent. Turning his head to his right, he nodded to someone in the darkness, and the music began.

A drumming, echoing off the stone of these Afghan mountains, throbbing in the center of Sinclair's brain. They had to be big, where had they kept them? How could they carry them over the distances they have traveled?

One, two, three, four, then five semazen, each wearing black robes and tall pillbox hats, emerged from the tents, lining up just to Shaffir's left, Sinclair's right. They removed their black robes, revealing beautiful white gowns with billowing skirts that caught the light of the bonfires and reflected them over the rocky ground, brightening up the scene. They crossed their arms over their chests, and when they were all ready, they walked over to Shaffir, who remained in his black shroud, and bowed to him. As Shaffir returned their bow, each man began to rotate, counter-clockwise, arms still folded, turning on his left foot as he circled around the empty space in a semi-circle in front of Sinclair.

Two, three, four, then all five semazen made their way, and took up their positions, forming a five-sided star that interlocked with the pentacle layout of the camp.

All five men spread their arms out and tilted their heads in the direction of the turn, the palms of their left hands facing down to the earth, while the palms of their right hands turned upward, toward the stars.

They whirled and whirled, and the drumbeats echoed off the mountainsides and up into the sky. Sinclair's situational awareness started to dim. Whirling, whirling for only minutes, and yet those minutes were full.

Words filled Max's mind as they hadn't done in ages. The songwriter and poet, so quieted in his heart, reawakened, the door to that chamber unlocked by the dance of the dervishes.

Look at their faces...their faces!

So serious, eyes open, unmoving, like masks caught in a whirlwind. No smiles, not even a grin. Just focus, meditation, loss...

Rotating like stars, like the sun, like the moon, like the molecules in my body. How their robes billow like fast-moving clouds in the stormy breeze.

The bonfires flickered as a small gust of wind rode the canyon walls over the camp.

The flickering lights caused some of the semazen to vanish for a few instants into the black of the dark night behind them, and Max watched them blink in and out of existence.

They flicker like torches, they are the fire! We are!

Max abandoned his peripheral observation of the fringes beyond the fire. What evil could enter this sacred space? Death had no monopoly here!

The wheeling of the semazen, the turning feet and throbbing drumbeats and heartbreaking chanting of the Sufi were masters here, and yet only servants of the true One, to whom we must all surrender at life's end.

Situational awareness vanished. Sinclair gave himself to the billowing robes and the voice and the flickering lights of the bonfires and the thump-THUMP, thump-THUMP, thump-THUMP...

Pop! Like a dislocated shoulder, like a cracked knuckle, and something was free in the air.

Max watched the dancers descend below him, watched himself sitting before them, surrendered, catching the spray of ecstasy, and then it vanished but the drums...

Thump-thump, thump-thump, thump-thump, the rapid beating heart of the faithful, of all of them in harmony with the stars.

And he saw his heart for what it was, a thundercloud of conflict, the whirlwinds taking his mood this way and that without direction, without mercy, without satisfaction or any ending but violence and injury. A short lifetime of hurts and passions, childhood fears of the night and comfort at the safety of nightlights; gifts on Christmas morning; prepubescent victories in the outfield, the catch that saved the game; riding a BMX full tilt under the meteor showers of August and letting the handles go and whooping like wild Indians at the falling stars; his first kiss with Luthien Fitzgerald, call her Lucy, as the sun set over the Pacific.

And then Lucy was whirling among the dervishes, her white robes speckled with coral and crimson, like droplets of blood from the heart of Rumi himself.

And Max was turning with her as the drums continued their thump-thump, thump-thump, thump-thump, thump-thump, and it was the heartbeat of their love and their lives and their hurts.

And Max saw her green eyes sparkle with the nuclear energy of ten thousand distant suns and he wondered, Why did you leave me? Why did we end?

Thump-THUMP, thump-THUMP, thump-THUMP...

And then he was beating her.

The smell of motel room at the Super 8. The soft mattress giving comfort to his knees while his fists collided with Lucy's face and body to the beat of the drums, which still filled the dark room.

Thump-THUMP, thump-THUMP, thump-THUMP.

He stopped, and in the darkness, could see her blood, could feel her blood like warm oil on his knuckles, and the shock tore him in half, slicing through him like cold, wet steel.

They did it! They killed us!

Who's they? He asked himself.

thump-THUMP, thump-THUMP...

The sun shone down in anger over the wedding. If only they'd known how angry.

Sinclair had just met the young groom and congratulated his family. They asked if they had secured the village, and he had assured them it was safe.

Only it wasn't.

The dancing and the music went on, and Sinclair knew the danger. He looked to the west. A few houses and a well-worn road led out to a part of town that Sinclair had decided not to patrol. Nothing but goat herders and old women. No point, no danger.

Only there was.

Even now, he could see the boy approach. Sixteen or seventeen, but much farther away. He was a killer, this child. The Taliban had gotten to him, promised him glories in the afterlife, maybe even using poppy money — poppies to process heroine, heroine to sell back home so that junkies from Seattle to Miami could pay Islamic terrorists to kill their brothers and sisters serving overseas — to compensate his family, who would live a little better for the next few years until they ran out or had their payment stolen from them, and had to provide another of their children for martyrdom.

Sinclair looked back. The revelers were dancing, carrying on, laughing. The flash of teeth and the blaring of formerly-outlawed

Persian pop music and traditional songs on decades' old speakers. They didn't see. They weren't supposed to. That was Sinclair's job.

Only his M-16 was gone. Where was it? No rifle. Had someone grabbed it?

The boy drew closer, entered an empty path where only two or three Afghans lingered. Two or three dead, in exchange for dozens. The lethal range was thirty feet.

Sinclair felt his sidearm inside his vest, tucked away so no one would find it. He reached in...

The boy was fifty feet away.

He could save them all.

Forty-five feet...

The button wouldn't undo. Sinclair tore at it and felt for the butt of the pistol.

Forty feet...

His hand gripped the gun. He pulled it out.

Thirty-five feet.

Sinclair pointed and released the safety.

Thirty-two feet.

Crack! Crack Crack!

And the boy fell away, and Sinclair braced himself for the blast, only to look again and see that he held no trigger...

He doesn't have a trigger! No trigger, no bomb! No trigger, no bomb!!

A woman cried out. The sun blinked out, and it was dark in the mountain pass, save for the flickering of the bonfires around the Sufi camp. And the semazen stopped in their tracks. The drums stopped.

Sinclair was standing up, his gun in his hand, the barrel still steaming in the cold night.

Men screamed and shouted. Someone tackled him from behind. His training responded for him, as Sinclair turned him around in the direction of his motion and threw him off. In his left peripherals, he saw two men with AK-47s trained on him.

He darted into the crowd where they wouldn't dare fire, pushing past them as they tried to make a hole, to get away from this crazy infidel who had just killed...

Who had he killed? Who?

Sinclair chanced a look back to see the boy's body on the ground, and Shaffir wailing over him. His cries were the worst of all. A hole opened up inside Sinclair's chest, though no bullets pierced him. He couldn't breathe. And words came to him again, words that have special meaning to all those who find themselves holding the smoking gun after an atrocity, the same words that came to him the night he beat up Lucy in San Diego.

What have I done? My God, what have I done?

The armed semazen aimed their weapons again, and Sinclair ran along the cave wall, ducking the sparks and ricochets off the rocks. The black ate away at his heart like a parasite, and he ran into the outer darkness just as the inner one consumed the last of him, and all he knew was fear and guilt and regret.

Sinclair was fifty feet away when he stopped running. He could make it to his Hummer, but what awaited him? A court martial. Who would support him? Not his father. Not his family, not after what he had just done. Not his country, not his countrymen. A baby killer.

You killed a boy.

They were coming for him. Sinclair could hear their footfalls in the brush and sand. His career was over, Lucy was gone, and there was nothing left. You killed a boy.

The semazen would make his death long and painful. Fortunately — or unfortunately — Sinclair had a solution for that. As the men approached, he put the gun in his mouth.

He pulled the trigger.

Black.

OFF THE GRID

Then there was Afghanistan.

Afghanistan was where it had gotten complicated for Tommy.

Tommy didn't like Max very much. Not really. But nor did he want to see him dead. And yet, for this to work, trauma was essential.

Weaver had already given him the solution, it was just a matter of him using it. It was also easier for someone his age to convince the mark in question to do as he was told.

The Afghan kid was actually American-born and spoke English. His imam had done the appropriate brainwashing at mosque, and his parents were ready for their son's impending martyrdom. Hafiz had been his name. Tommy could relate to him: middle of three children, the least happy, parents weren't terribly impressed by him, seemed too enthusiastic to sacrifice him to the will of Allah. No real talents or special skills that set him apart from everyone else. No appeal to the other girls, though in Afghan culture, Tommy wondered how that kind of thing ever manifested itself out in the open. They'd given him the target — the wedding — and the date and time. That was all done.

All Tommy had to do was give Hafiz the explosives and teach him how to use the dead man's trigger.

Weaver had assured him that Lt. Sinclair would survive the attack, and he did. Despite the all-access pass Weaver had supposedly given him, Tommy could not go forward to see what his actions would do to the lifespace, or how it affected the overall plan, short of enabling senseless slaughter. All he knew was that as he sent Hafiz away, he had felt kinship, the shared fate of self-annihilation, even if it meant death for innocent people having nothing to do with the mission at hand. Collateral damage. Such a neutral way to justify a massacre, stripped of

191

sentimentality. Tommy had read Dickens and never understood why anyone would have a problem with "decreasing the surplus population."

Mission Three: Accomplished.

Weaver's plan was done. The easy part.

Now Tommy was ready to start his plan, the one that Weaver didn't know existed. And this plan was much, much simpler.

After finishing in Afghanistan, Tommy turned his attention to Lucy. Tommy liked her better, but the fact remained, her fate was tied to that of Max, which made her a target of equal importance in all of this.

Tommy believed in covering all of his bases, especially given that he only had one shot at making this happen. He knew that Weaver had gone to Carmel to warn Lucy of Max's importance, and to advise her of the choice she had to take. He also knew that Lucy was very much in love with another man in her home lifespace, that Weaver wanted to challenge her with a difficult choice to ensure she committed to their work, 100 percent.

He also knew that the drive time to California from the great lakes required at least three days. That gave Tommy enough time to head up to Seattle, and send a number of false replies from Charles Smith who was now very busy with Lucy's Alternate in Carmel.

Convergence wasn't far away now. Things wouldn't be making a helluva lot more sense from here on in. The deal was for Tommy to head back to his life, where Weaver would be waiting with some more drugs and dollars for him.

As if Tommy could be so easily bought.

As if Tommy wanted to go back to a world of privation and playing around inside the bleached ribcage of a fallen superpower.

As if Tommy was too stupid to see that the creative power of Convergence had a dark side, that just as it could result in the start of new life, it could be used to abort one in utero.

192

After she ran into her Alternate and realized the true plan, Tommy followed Lucy from the restaurant to the old street she used to walk, unsure what to do next. He was running out of time and had to figure it out.

That's when he saw Justin Sinclair appear through the junction at the hillside. That simplified things.

Tommy waited for the train.

BLUE HEATHER

Black.

Shaking.

No, someone was shaking her.

Wake up.

This wasn't right.

Wake up.

This wasn't how it was supposed to go.

"Ma'am, wake up. We've landed at SeaTac."

Lucy opened her eyes.

The young blond attendant was prodding her on the shoulder.
The air was cool and humid in the cabin. Everyone was standing up in the aisle, some getting their carry-ons out of the compartments, others ready to leave, just standing around until the queue started moving.

Lucy looked at the window. They were at SeaTac. It was sunny out, with a few puffy clouds here and there. Beautiful. More beautiful than she would have thought possible.

She unbuckled her seatbelt and slowly got to her feet. She felt the right side of her cheek. No blood. Felt her temple. No gash.

The line started to move, and she joined the queue of people leaving the airplane.

Lucy saw Edgar in front of them, and her heart skipped a beat. In his right hand he carried a magazine, folded up so that the ad-laden back cover was all you could see on the outside. She imagined there was very little offensive content to be found in a du Maurier ad.

194

Lucy also saw the sky marshal, whistling as he walked out, chatting to an older lady in front of him. She couldn't hear about what.

They got to the front. Captain Washburne, Paul the co-pilot, and the blond attendant stood. Blondie was all smiles as they thanked everyone for flying Delphi Airlines. "Have a great day!" Captain Washburne looked like he was in good shape, wide awake, and she smiled wanly at him as she stepped onto the jet way.

They had lived.

Lucy saw in her mind — not a vision, but memory — the marker board from the waiting room. The airplane at the bottom — their airplane — and the dotted lines leading straight to Seattle-Tacoma Airport. One of the three outcomes.

They had landed safely at Sea-Tac. That was the only one that mattered. And she remembered: she had said yes to the water.

Lucy wandered like one of the undead to the baggage claim. She stood waiting, with the other passengers, taking little notice of her surroundings as the luggage started to come down the conveyer.

She'd vaguely overheard some mutterings about a lock down they'd just had at the airport that had lasted about an hour. Was on the news and everything. CNN had been around, interviewing passengers, taking footage of the emergency vehicles, airport security, TSA officials and FBI agents investigating a suspicious package found in the restroom near the United Airlines counter. Lucy heard the name Mosley a few times, something about him being apprehended outside the airport within twenty minutes of the discovery. They'd done some searches, delayed a few flights, diverted a few, but Delphi Regional 442 had been just far out enough that the authorities had had enough time to decide everything else was secure, and to resume normal operations. Someone else's decision to make.

Her bag appeared. She took it.

Due to the heightened security, they had to go through an extra checkpoint, where guards wanded them, swabbed their fingerprints to show telltale signs if they had been handling explosive materials within the past 24 hours. Through it all, Lucy went through the motions, muttered responses to the inquiries of the security guards and U.S. Army personnel, and then they were in the spacious, crystalline glass lobby of the terminal.

Lucy took no further notice of her surroundings, however, because she looked over and saw the two of them standing there. They were off in the distance, talking to each other, unaware that Lucy had stopped in her tracks with her suitcase and carry-on and was staring at them. They started to walk away. Without another word, Lucy took off toward them. Passengers crisscrossed in front of her in long rows, but she weaved and bobbed through them, navigating the busy invisible thoroughfares of the terminal lobby until she closed in on her marks.

"Hey!" she called.

Weaver and Kate turned around. Lucy saw, they were wearing the same outfits that she had seen in the vision, and she knew without having to ask, she knew...

"What the hell was the point, huh?"

Kate turned and faced her directly. She commanded a power, subtle, that Lucy had never seen before.

"You told me to show you our work. I did as you wished."

"I thought I was dead, that we were all dead. How...how could you do that to me?"

"So you'd finally see how lucky you are!" Kate shot back. A few heads turned at the scene they were making, but Lucy didn't shout back. That gave Kate cause to continue.

"For Christ's sake, Lucy, of all your Alternates I've met, you're the toughest nut to crack. You struggle for so long to get an amazing life, and even when it's handed to you on a silver platter, you don't know what to do with it. You're still clamoring for your safe place. Are you completely off your gourd?"

"You think I don't already know that my choices have consequences?" said Lucy. "I step on a bug, and three million years from now, the planet explodes because that bug was the ancestor of some new intelligent species that was going to figure out that the fucking planet was going to blow up. I park my car far away from the entrance instead of looking for something close to the door, and I'm safe, but the guy who takes the closer space gets jacked."

Lucy and Kate faced off, less than two feet of air between them. Weaver stood off to the side, as demure and deferential as he was during the vision of the waiting room.

"I get it! I get that all possibilities are in every moment. I get that it's a never-ending chain of events. What I don't get, even after all this time, is what the hell all of this has to do with me? Huh? I want my life back, Kate! As shitty and as full of scars and old injuries as it is, my old life has one guaranteed bit of happiness. He's going to take me back, Kate."

"He's not your gateway to happiness, Lucy, Max Sincl—"

"Is a fantasy!"

That stopped Kate, and now it was Lucy's turn to circle around.

"Is he a great guy? Sure. Do I have his name on my list? Yes. But…"

She pointed a finger at Kate, and dropped her voice. "How do I know you didn't plant his name in my head? Huh? You guys control everything else about the Convergence, and you've said you've got these amazing powers to control me. I saw them in action in that dream or whatever it was. I was your puppeteer puppet. I could still be now, if I listen to you."

Lucy stepped back and took a deep breath. "But Charles…Charles is sweet. Charles is successful. And Charles is real. I know this from evidence, not from faith. He's as real as the earth under my feet, and I know that's where I belong. Why won't you let me go home?"

Her voice had cracked on that last word. Kate sighed.

"I... it's not that simple, Luce," she said. Lucy wiped a tear, born more of sheer frustration than sadness. and paced in front of her (non)friend.

"The Convergence. We're close now, and not all of the pieces are in place for what we need to do. So very close, though."

"Right, here we go again. Look, just let me go back, okay? Leave me alone."

"It's not up to me, it's up to you."

"Then why—"

"You have to know the consequences of your choices."

"I heard you."

"You weren't listening. Knowing the consequences of your choices means recognizing your power. It's not just you, sweet cheeks, it's everyone else after you. It's the harmony of all human choices, all human voices."

Kate now closed in on Lucy, and they stood nose-to-nose. "You want to know why you and Max are so important? You'll make key decisions that change everything for the better. You can only make them as a couple in love. By choice. You won't know when they're upon you, you won't make them all at once, and you'll never live to see the ramifications of your choices for the rest of the species."

Kate stopped. A beat passed.

"So what, now you can see the future on top of everything?"

"There is no seeing the future," replied Kate. "There's only mathematical probability and immanent human experience."

"Okay, what the hell does that even mean?"

"It means that we've done the math. It means we can see, along the chain of possible events, five key choices that you and Max are going to make down the road that have ramifications for the entire species. The Convergence is the first cause of it all. It enables the experiences and event chains that makes the choices possible."

"Just for us?"

"No, not just for you. You're part of the chain, and other people have their roles. But you two are the lynchpins. You enable the bigger choices that others make, the same way that you made it possible for the stewardess on the Delphi flight to catch or not catch Edgar Potts with the magazine."

"What are these choices?" Then she saw the look on Kate's face and rolled her eyes. "Oh, right, you can't tell me."

"You're not in the right place. You need to be with Max."

"I'm going back to Charles, Kate, back to my life. I'm done with this. I'm hailing a cab." She stepped into Kate's face. "Where is he? I know that you know. You guys seem to know everything."

"He's at a restaurant called Blue Heather," said Weaver suddenly. "He's havin' a late lunch there in about a half hour. If this is your move, child, you'd better make it fast."

Kate looked back at her companion, who simply met her gaze and didn't waver. She turned back to Lucy.

"I...we can fix this. I wish I could tell you —"

"Tell me what, Kate?"

Kate stopped talking, and Lucy shook her head and sighed.

"No, you can't tell me anything to change my mind, Kate. You keep saying it's up to me to choose. This is it. I'm done."

Lucy and Kate stood for a moment, and then Kate extended her arms and wrapped Lucy in a hug. Lucy hadn't expected that, but it felt like old times, the old Kate, not involved in anything beyond the next night out or a big party with the girls.

Lucy lingered a moment before stepping out of the hug, and then walked away from Kate and Weaver. She didn't turn back to see them leave, but about fifteen feet away, she knew they were gone.

Lucy took a few deep breaths then turned her back on the terminal, starting for the exit, leaving behind this episode in her life and hopefully entering a new one without anymore tears, only smiles and laughter, peace.

Outside, she hailed a taxi and threw her luggage in the trunk. She got in.

"Can you take me to the Blue Heather Restaurant, please?"

"Sure thing," said the driver.

And Lucy left Seattle Tacoma Airport, and left Max Sinclair and the Convergence behind. Ahead of her was Charles, and her old apartment, the threads of her old life that she was now ready to pick up after Charles' hesitation and anxiety had cut them.

She was grateful for the experience. Sometimes it's good to take a break from life and see what else would have been possible for you. There will always be something that's better or worse about the choices you could have made. Maybe that was the real thing that she had to learn about "the consequences of her choices," as Kate had said to her: that you should be happy where you are, and things could always be better, but they could always be worse.

And as for those key choices that she and Max had to make, well...maybe that was another mistake in the math. Lucy believed that. She wanted to.

The Blue Heather wasn't that far away.

***

The restaurant itself was typical postmodern, with stainless steel, wood, and shades of slate and cobalt, tall beams and cozy booths. You could see the piping and the metal rafters in the ceiling, that same industrial look that nonetheless attracts the type of clientele who have never worked in warehouses, but probably own them.

It was that intermediate period between lunch and dinner, the window for business deals between potential clients and partners, for illicit lunches between married men and their mistresses — after all, what suspicious housewife would think to check on their husbands around the same time you had to pick the kids up from school or get

200

your hair done? — and for tourists and visitors, likely accompanied by a wealthy host.

Lucy stood at the entrance.

She hadn't had time to visit her apartment. Weaver had said this was where Charles was, and so this was where she had to be. The cab had dropped her luggage off with her, and she put her carry-on on the ground next to her suitcase.

The maître d' approached, a younger balding man with dark eyebrows, about two inches taller than Lucy, who was still looking over the tables as he approached.

"Hello again, ma'am. Are you looking for something?"

"Yes, hi," Lucy looked him in the eye and noticed he was staring at her luggage. "I'm looking for Charles Smith. I was told he'd be here."

The maître d' frowned. "Um...okay, I...could take you back to where he is."

"Thank you! I hope you don't mind the luggage."

"Uh, no, that's fine." His dark eyebrows rose sky-high as he said that, taking another long look at her suitcase and carry-on, which Lucy slung over her shoulder as he led her.

This is it! Everything starts over from here! From now!

Lucy allowed herself a moment of vulnerability, lowering the shields and removing the armor that years of survival mode had fixed around her body and soul. Her mind was her only offensive weapon, highly tuned, sharp as the tip of a spear, highly disciplined and militarized...and she allowed some shore leave in those seconds before she arrived at the table. She allowed it to drift toward renewed love, the reclamation of years, the reactivation of energies by the same man who had shut them down so ruthlessly and suddenly.

Schoolgirl visions of wedding bells and white picket fences, of beautiful houses and summer picnics. Maybe even children. All the stereotypes and magazine bluster she'd publicly dismissed over the years, that Kate had said were just images planted in her mind by the consumer culture, but that she'd secretly held near to her heavily-armored heart and longed to have. A life absent of the problems she'd faced ever since she'd left home. Nothing but the relief of houses, spouses, and kids, where the problems seem a little less real, and thus more manageable. A safe happiness, for a change.

They walked past the aisle of booths. Overhead, she caught the words of the song playing on the speakers, just at that volume that creates atmosphere while also letting you talk. A Spanish guitar piece, sung by a woman with a sultry, serious voice.

No no no, it ain't me you're lookin' for, babe.

Huh, Bob Dylan. Bob Dylan had written that song first.

They turned a corner and stopped.

"Here is your table, madam," he said, then walked away. Had Lucy turned, she would have seen him pass his hands over the shiny sheen reflecting the ceiling lights over his bald scalp, then shake his head twice.

The table was unoccupied, but she could see Charles's watch sitting there. That meant he'd gone to the bathroom. Charles was always prissy that way with his watches, even willing to risk leaving it on the table for some unscrupulous customer or even waiter to steal.

Then, Lucy noticed three details.

First, on the table, there were two plates with half-eaten food, across from each other.

Then, she saw two wine glasses, one with coral lipstick on the side of the rim facing her direction.

And last, a shadow, the presence of someone standing right behind her.

Lucy turned around and felt her heart stop for a full second.

"What are you doing here?" hissed the woman.

Carmel Lucy was a sight. Too much of one, in fact, to maintain discretion. At least six pairs of eyes had fixed on her as she had followed her shabbier, luggage toting doppelganger down the aisle of booths to the table.

Carmel Lucy wore a beautiful coral halter dress that showed off her California tan, well-defined shoulders, outstanding figure, a shade of coral that matched her fingernails exactly.

Carmel Lucy's breasts were so firm that you had to wonder if they were implants (which they probably weren't, of course, making them seem even more dreamlike and perfect).

Carmel Lucy wore glasses, no rim, Dolce and Gabana, and somehow she made the look work.

Carmel Lucy had a stance that looked like she could kick your ass on a whim. Maybe some martial arts training?

In short, Carmel Lucy was a knockout, worthy of any man.

And she was having a late lunch with Charles. Her Charles.

That's when Lucy looked down and noticed she was wearing a pair of brown leather gladiators.

"It...it was you?"

"We can't talk here, come on!"

Her Alternate took Real Lucy's arm in a tight grip, tighter than she would have expected from this seemingly fragile figure. She practically dragged her, baggage and all, toward the back of the restaurant.

Had Lucy been more lucid and less stunned, she would have noticed that her coral-clad Carmel counterpart had avoided the restroom area, just in case Charles walked out and saw his not-so-secret twin sister fantasy come to life in front of him.

The two Lucys went out the restaurant's employee entrance. Outside, next to the dumpster, two line cooks were having a smoke break. They glanced at her Alternate — bright neon coral being something of an attention-grabbing color on a sunny day — and then went back to their smoke. They hadn't noticed Lucy at all.

Carmel Lucy was pissed.

"What are you doing back? This isn't how this goes."

"I...I thought...Charles—"

"You were supposed to stay, that was the idea of my coming up here! Don't you get it?"

Lucy had to breathe. Why couldn't she breathe?

"Didn't you talk to Kate?"

"I did! Kate told me to come down. I stopped in Carmel, I stayed at your house."

"It's not my house anymore, honey. It's all yours. That was the deal."

"What deal?" asked Lucy.

Carmel sighed. "Our switch was permanent. I'm supposed to be partnered up with Charles. You're supposed to inherit my business, my life in Carmel, and be with Max Sinclair."

Cold blood again.

"It was you he was sleeping with back in January."

Carmel Lucy's eyes brightened — was the bitch actually smiling? — and then refocused on her with steely seriousness. "You...you were early. I heard the knock and barely had time to get out of there before you came barging into the bedroom."

Lucy's whole world was pitching and yawing, much as it had when she'd found out about her mom and dad splitting up, as it had when she had first walked into Charles' place and found he'd been sneaking around.

She took a breath. "When the blockage fell, didn't you call Mom and Dad? Your Mom and Dad?"

"No...I only thought—"

"to send Charles a text message, see if he'd answer you back. Not to mention the twelve emails he got from you that somehow all ended up in his inbox at once when the block came down. Good thing I was able to delete them all before he could read them. That's a conversation I would have no way of knowing how to even start. Wiggling out of the text message fiasco was bad enough, especially after he answered it."

Lucy couldn't believe this. Mostly, she blamed herself (typical) for not considering that in addition to taking her apartment, her job, her credit card debt, her Alternate could also take her man.

"How could you take him from me?" asked Lucy. "He'd realized he'd made a mistake."

"And he had," replied her Alternate. "He wasn't getting back with you, he was getting together with me."

"How?"

"Did you remember what he said when you caught him?"

Lucy didn't hesitate. You don't forget something like that.

"He said it didn't feel right," said Lucy.

"The reason why it didn't feel right was because he's not supposed to be with you, honey. He's supposed to be with me."

Her Carmel counterpart took a breath, walked past her. Despite the armor, Lucy was devastated as she followed her Alternate like a missile lock.

"For so long, I had everything all together," said the Alternate. "Got the studio running, profitable. Got myself in the best shape I've ever been in, the finest things. Had any guy I wanted, but nothing stuck. The studio lost its luster. I got sick of teaching yuppie California housewives the lotus position, how to meditate, quotes from Lao Tzu and Ram Dass on the walls. It didn't feel real to me. For all the supposed depth and spirituality, there was nothing of substance, nothing real, at least not near the end. At least not for me. I stopped feeling authentic, and that's all that mattered. It was my shop."

"Then I ran into Weaver. He told me about the Convergence, said there was only one chance, and I agreed to take the leap. He told me everything, told me where my place was, and it's here. He told me about Charles, and I fell in love almost immediately, as hard as that is for you to hear."

The Alternate looked right at Lucy. "And he told me about you. Everything you've just left behind to come back here is everything you ever wanted."

She turned around. "Where's Maxim Sinclair? What happened to him?"

"I...he's on his way."

Now it was Lucy's turn to pace. "You know...how do I go back? Huh? What am I going back to? On so many levels, I want your life, and from what you're saying, I've got it now. But what next? I'm so heartbroken, Luce."

The tears started, and her Alternate sighed, took her shoulder. It felt weird, like holding your own left shoulder with your right hand.

"My whole life, I've never been happy," said Lucy, "always been just surviving, and when Charles showed up, I thought it was all fixed. Then it was over, and suddenly it was like I couldn't survive anymore, couldn't function. Then I learned about Max and how we have this supposed destiny, and you know...as much as it made some sense, I didn't want to believe it. Charles said he wanted me back, and that much I could believe. When does it stop, Lucy? When do I get everything figured out?"

Her Alternate shook her head.

"You never do, honey. I still haven't. This is just the next step of where I've got to be. There are always more steps afterward. And yeah, clinging to Charles makes sense. He's the only dose of real happiness you've had in a long while. You know for a fact that you were happy with him. You don't know if you'll be happy with any other person, in any other place, in any other lifetime."

She took Lucy's hand, and it was the strangest thing, like holding your own left hand with your right.

"When I started the studio, I did a lot of mentoring. One of my teachers told me that if you're always looking to the old, you'll never let in the new. And what you could have with Max Sinclair — the one

206

that the Convergence workers need you to be with, the one that deep down, you know you need to be with — is so incredibly new that you'll never feel old again. You'll never have to just survive. You'll truly live. And even if you don't believe me now, the only way to find out is to take the leap."

Carmel Lucy stepped back. They stood two feet away.

"I fit in the life that you have. Charles is an essential step to something else around the corner that's authentically where I'm supposed to be, even if I have no clue what it is yet. The small apartment, the crappy job, it's where I'm supposed to be, because it's something real to me. Sure it's got its own set of stresses, but along with everything else, it's also how I get to combine my powers with Charles. That's how I find my power again. I'd forgotten how much a simple life is the very thing that most of us are looking for but never get. And I owe it to you. And you know you belong in that house, running that studio, walking that beach, because that's how you get to be truly happy. That's your dharma. And that's how you get to be with Max.

"And understand something," she went on. "No person completes another. But they add their power to yours. They open up the possibilities that we could never have on our own, and the specific possibilities that you and Max open up are important, not just to you."

"What are they?"

Carmel Lucy grinned. She was guarding a great, wonderful secret, and Lucy could see she was doing all in her power not to give it away, to keep her lips sealed tight.

"Just trust me," she said. "You're not going to feel better about this right away, I understand that. But you'll see what I mean soon enough. In fact, you should know..." she took a breath,. "that despite knowing what the right next step is for me, I actually envy you, for what you have to look forward to, for what you will be able to set in motion."

Lucy looked around. The two line cooks who had been out there when they came out of the restaurant had gone back to work. The day was cool, but pretty.

"Now what?" asked Lucy.

"Go back," said Carmel Lucy.

"And what about my things that are here? The lingering workload that I've got at the office? My debts?"

"I inherit your debts, and your workload, and your old things. If there's anything you really want, you can stop by your old place and get them. I didn't change the locks or anything."

"No, there's nothing I really want. And my own family? My friends?"

Carmel Lucy shrugged, took a breath.

"They're mostly similar between lifespaces," said the Alternate. "Mom and Dad seem to be unchanged between our two, but really, they're not the same person. There will be times you'll miss them, even though they're on the other end of the phone, because as similar as they are, they're not the same people. The good part is, you're the only one missing them. They'll think I'm you, and you're me. You might have to pretend to remember things you never did. You may have a few new friends and relatives you didn't know before, and you might find that the people you thought you knew never existed." She sighed, and Lucy imagined she was thinking of those who were gone. "It's not supposed to be easy, but it does serve a higher joy. You just have to trust in that. Besides, after Convergence has come and gone, the workers say you won't know the difference."

"Are they right?"

The Alternate looked away for a moment, then back at her. "I hope so," she said.

Lucy nodded. They lingered for a couple of minutes in silence. Then her Carmel — now Seattle — counterpart broke the spell.

"I have to go back in. He's waiting for me."

"I know."

"It doesn't feel this way now, but you've got some exciting times ahead of you."

"Right. I just...I just need to walk this off, clear my head."

At that, Carmel Lucy smiled. "If you fancy a walk, you should head back to your old neighborhood. To the place where you met Weaver. You remember that?"

Lucy scoffed. "How could I forget?"

"This time it'll be different. Go there first before you do anything else."

A last look. "Good luck, Lucy. I mean it."

Lucy's doppelganger in a coral dress turned back toward the restaurant, and for a second, Lucy felt the compulsion to duck in, take one last look at Charles. She didn't, of course. No need to draw more attention to themselves, and plus, she couldn't yet bear the sight. Still, she felt...relieved. And empty, which wasn't altogether bad.

Just before her Alternate walked in, Lucy called after her.

"How do I find him? What should I do?'

The figure in coral didn't turn around.

"Let it happen."

The door closed behind her.

***

Full circle.

The hillside looked so much better in July than December. Lucy hadn't been back since that difficult day. Seattle Central looked beautiful under the blue sky, and this time, there were many people around, just milling about, enjoying the same day.

She sat in the same spot where Weaver had found her, the same place where her face had been raw with tears. Where she'd held Charles' ring.

Only there was no void in the middle of her chest this time. No emptiness. Just a heartbeat.

And a brewing cloud of urgency.

It had started out when the cab had dropped her off. The numbness of the surrealism of the past few hours wore off, and she was getting feeling back. A thrill.

She had died. Lucy and everyone aboard that plane had died in a horrific, unexplainable plane crash only hours ago. It was all over the Web, on the airwaves, on the lips of workers around water coolers and phone chatter. Right now, all of her relatives were watching the coverage, her parents weeping at the loss of their child. It had all happened, was happening now, just beside this lifespace.

How strange, then, that though still breathing, still walking, her plane having landed safely without incident hours ago — and at the intended destination, having never diverted, either, which had been the other possibility — that Lucy still felt that calm that acceptance of death brings to those facing it.

At this very moment, across a thousand lifespaces, Lucy was dead or dying. She was also being born, and re-born, to life. And she could say the same for every human being, except that in her case, and a select few of others, she was able to take a peek at what was happening in the house next door, and in this case, to move into that space and make it her life.

Lucy didn't bother going back to the apartment. The stuff inside didn't matter. That goodbye had happened well over a month ago. And home was now hundreds of miles to the south of her.

Indeed, this city no longer felt like her home, her lifespace. There were subtleties about this Convergence: a chill in the air isn't simply a chill in the air anymore. It's a sign of far more fundamental changes in the underlying dynamics of the space. And the air had changed in Seattle.

Like the knowledge the first choice that she and Max Sinclair had to make, the first of the five key ones, was to be together, to find each other. Kate could say what she wanted: that was the lynchpin choice, the only one that mattered. It made the other ones possible.

And she knew what had to happen next. What was happening right now.

"Uh, hello there," said a voice from behind, and this time, it didn't surprise Lucy to hear it. She didn't know who would show up here, but she knew that the only way to move forward was to come back to the beginning. The hillside was some kind of crossroads. Lucy felt it, even if she couldn't explain it all.

The person who owned that young-sounding voice sat down next to her. A teenaged kid, brown hair, tan skin, a few freckles, taller than Lucy by about an inch, lanky, walking with a hunch. He wore a white, short-sleeved collared shirt and blue jeans, white sneakers that looked about five years old.

"Hi," said Lucy, turning back to the horizon. The boy hugged his knees, mimicking her pose.

"I'm Justin," he said. "You're Lucy."

Lucy nodded. A helicopter — Med Evac, by the looks of it — was flying over the downtown.

"Nice to meet you," she said.

"Sure," replied Justin.

They stared at the city for a while, feeling the gentle breezes and smelling the scent of the little coral wildflowers that grew at their feet.

"I'm here to help you with the last part of your trip," said the boy, breaking the reverie. "Do you know where you have to go?"

"Back to Carmel," said Lucy. "But let me guess, it won't be that easy."

Justin stared alongside her. "You're figuring this out fast."

"I am," said Lucy, who grew silent again. Another thirty seconds passed with no words.

"The tricky part to all this is accepting what's weird," said Justin. "But it gets easier, and faster, as you let the workers do their work. Quit slowin' 'em down by looking for proof and reasons. Answers. They've already done the math for you."

"That's not going to be a problem anymore. I...get that it's going to work out," said Lucy. "I can feel it. I just have to get moving."

Justin turned to her.

"Well...that much is true," he said. "But don't be so sure that you won't mess it up this late in the game. Stranger things have happened."

"I doubt it."

Justin smiled — beautiful teeth on this young man — and looked down.

"I'm guessing that's also why you're here," Lucy said. Justin didn't look up right away. A shy kid on top of everything.

"Mmmhmm."

Justin got up, and Lucy followed suit. The two turned their backs on Seattle Central and started walking away from the hill. Lucy didn't have to be told she'd never see it again, or at least, not this Seattle.

"So, what's the big task or mission I have to do for you guys now to get to my Max?"

"What makes you think it's like that?" asked Justin.

"It's the only thing that can happen," said Lucy.

"Kate told you to be aware of the power of your choices. She did tell you that, right?"

"And then some."

"And are you?"

Lucy reflected on the experience on the plane. Three entire branches of reality had come out of a simple choice to take or not to take a glass of water from the stewardess. That was a power typically assigned to God, and she'd exercised it.

"I'd say so."

212

"Max is what we call a first mover," said Justin. "His words have power. He can connect the lifespaces with the stroke of a key."

"Why him? How is he able to do that?"

"Because that's his medium, the way that he projects the power of his choices. He just doesn't know it yet, or if he does, is only vaguely aware of how much of an influence over the events he actually has. On top of that, you've got to use yours."

Justin paused, then went on.

"You're at the beginning of the end. So is he. The difference is, you know it. Do everything right, and you'll both be together before Convergence happens."

Lucy turned and faced the boy directly.

"How does that work?"

"It's simpler than you think," replied Justin. "Right now, the veils between the lifespaces are thin, and getting thinner, so they're more easily navigable. When we reach the instant of Convergence, they'll drop entirely."

Justin took a breath. "I'll explain more about all of that later. For now, you've got to find it on your way back to Carmel. Lucky for you, you've got help."

"Well that's a relief. Who from? You?"

"Do you remember the waiting room?"

"Of course."

"You remember your kids?"

She remembered the waiting room, of Kate showing her the picture books. Two beautiful kids, spirits on Earth.

Lucy smiled. "Yes."

"Maybe not."

"What do you mean?"

Justin stopped. Lucy turned around to face this shy, intelligent, well-spoken kid, this unlikely guide to the last leg of this journey home.

He met her gaze, and with some effort, smiling ever so slightly, extended his hand.

"Hi, Mom."

NO RETURN

Max stopped writing.

The time in the corner of his screen read 3:42 A.M. He had been up all night, and given the time difference between Eastern time and Mountain, it was now morning, as far as his creb cycles were concerned.

The U.S. Army report in the memory stick was substantial about his Alternate's mission in Afghanistan, but when it came to why he had suddenly gone rogue and killed the boy, nobody had any explanation, and no one would get one. Lt. Sinclair's comatose was described as a "permanent vegetative state," the bullet having failed to kill him outright, but had left him in a state of living death: a concept that scared the shit out of Max almost as much as the idea of battle, the whole notion of going to war altogether.

And at the point where he had entered the lifespace, there was no way that Max could have gotten his Alternate to have written that letter to Lucy. Not after what had happened between them. Not with the stubbornness and pride of the Lieutenant. The letter was a desperate plea from a dead man, nothing more, who must have known Max was destined to fail in this lifespace, no matter what he tried.

And what of that comatose? A dream is a dream, Max supposed, and for some reason, the Convergence thrived on dreams as much as it worked in reality.

Max yawned and stretched. It would be daylight soon, and he would have to get moving again. He felt some slight guilt that he didn't get to explore more of Las Vegas: maybe he and Lucy, if they had time, would be able to come back here, maybe play the giant slot machine at New York, New York he'd come across in his brief walk, maybe take in a Cirque show or eat at a Michelin-starred steakhouse. They would check into the Bellagio or the Wynn and get room service. They would fly over the Grand Canyon—

"and become a couple's cliché," said Max aloud, to the room.

He closed the laptop and rubbed his eyes.

Max was still questioning his actions this late in the game, when he was practically hours away — about two-thirds of a day's drive — from his destination, well past the point of no return, and that bothered him. If he could still be questioning this thing now, then something was still off.

And I don't think it's entirely on my end.

Something about Lucy bothered him, something that he couldn't identify, like that word that barely escapes your tongue's ability to pronounce it, but it hangs in the air that fills out the roof of your mouth and doesn't go away until you figure out how to fucking say it. Aside from the obvious strangeness of the situation which, he had to admit to himself, he had gotten used to over time, it all seemed too good to be true.

They were supposed to be soul mates, twin flames, whatever, two people whose destinies were so important that it wasn't enough that one universe conspired in their favor, but several different realities were now re-arranging themselves to get them together.

Why? What was so vital that the two of them had to get together? Would the world, the fate of civilization, of humanity, of existence itself, hang in the balance like some cheesy epic movie plot, if they didn't meet? Max highly doubted it. He'd seen nothing in his experiences so far that demonstrated that this served any other purpose short of his own personal development and—

Max stopped.

He thought about what he'd written, most of which were details he had to fill in that were missing in the report. In fact...

216

Max reopened the laptop and re-read everything he'd said about Lieutenant Sinclair. He skimmed, then read in depth, every single detail that he'd been forced to invent.

It occurred to him that he'd been relying solely on his own creative license to piece together a convincing vision of this particular Alternate. The real Lieutenant Sinclair could be nothing like what he portrayed. In fact, the one that ended up in the MS could easily be a complete fabrication.

Then a crazy thought, which was saying something: None of this existed until I just wrote it, but I actually met Lieutenant Sinclair, who gave me this report. Does that mean…did I create him? Does the Convergence let me do that?

Then, another crazy thought. Scarier: And if I'm just making them up, could some other Alternate be doing the same with me?

Then, Manhattan returned to his thoughts. And Max remembered his role in it, not as player, but as puppeteer.

"Yeaahhhh…" he muttered to the room.

The weirdest feeling sank in. Primal, like how our ancestors, wandering the jungles, used to anticipate a boa constrictor about to land on our shoulders.

Someone could be in the room now, just as he had been in New York, watching, possibly controlling what he did. There was the sensation of life as architecture, unfolding strictly by the blueprint, paint-by-numbers…

The idea that Max himself could be the invention of some other reality wasn't new to him — it had been done to death in several of his favorite novels and TV shows — but given the manifest evidence of the Convergence, given the three Alternate selves he had met in the flesh, given the sheer feeling that was enveloping him, suddenly this fanciful sci-fi concept was becoming less and less a concept and very real.

Too real.

The probability itself scared the shit out of him. He felt his heart pounding. His palms were sweaty. Too real, too real…

Before, Max's sense of reality had shifted to accommodate the adventure he was on. Now it felt as though his very existence could be frozen in time, be tossed left and right and up and down, even shuffled out of existence altogether, on the whim of some other, far more powerful version of himself in some other reality.

Maybe you should head back before you find out just how much of a Daffy Duck cartoon you really are.

And there it was. There it was….

Max sat with the idea for a while, thinking nothing, instead meditating on the feeling of a return. And he felt relieved…relieved!

Abandon the adventure, very much the definition of a fool's errand that had already cost him time, money, some of his reputation at work, and very likely his own sanity.

More than that, reject becoming Daffy Duck in that one Looney Tunes sketch where he broke the fourth wall and fought with the cartoonist. In any war between cartoonist and toon, the cartoonist always wins

Max listened to the noises in that motel room. The music had long since stopped thumping in from his neighbors, and while he half-expected to hear the moans of two (or more) of his neighbors having sex, there was silence, which he enjoyed.

He was clear. Everything made sense again.

Go east, young man. Head home and get back to your life.

Give a big middle finger to the metaphysical conductor orchestrating this whole Convergence business, and get back to paying off your debts, working on your book, and maybe meet someone who was going to be realistic. Maybe Dinah was right.

Find someone local, someone who wasn't perfection made manifest in the world, but who was good enough.

Lose weight, get rich, get married, buy a house somewhere, have those 2.5 kids, and settle down. Raise kids, send them to whatever college they want to go to, take the wife and travel across the world while arthritis and diabetes and climate change haven't claimed your ability do so. Stay at three-star hotels. Steal the little soaps. Let kids take care of you when you can't walk anymore, and hope to die before your wife does so you're not the one who's left waiting and alone.

It would be Oak Knoll Max, except this one would be less of a dandy. He'd buy his underwear at Wal-Mart like everyone else. Really, it was the sanest choice available to him.

Max was tired. He set the alarm to give him a little over a half-hour before check-out, and then tomorrow, after some breakfast, he would explore Vegas a little bit more, get the oil changed in the Sunfire, and then head back the way he came.

The thought gave him comfort as he closed the laptop again, turned off the lamp, kicked off his socks and pants and just threw himself under the covers of the motel bed, and went to sleep. And thankfully, this time, he didn't dream a damned thing.

***

The next morning, Max took the car in for its oil change at the garage near the motel. The service was friendly, fast, and within about twenty minutes of him getting there, the clerk was coming out with his keys.

"Oil change is all done, sir," said the clerk. "We threw in a wash, too. Just sign here."

"Thanks."

Max settled the bill at the desk. All the while, the clerk was staring at him, smiling, and not in the fakey customer service style, either. Max tried to ignore it as he went through the paperwork. It was intense to the point of menace, as if they'd just been talking about him behind his back. Finished, he handed everything back to the clerk.

"All right. Our guy's just going to bring it around for you."

"Thanks," said Max, and he turned and walked out the door.

Outside, the temperature had grown hotter and drier, but to the west, there were clouds. Max didn't know how often it rained in Las Vegas, but it was going to get here fast.

The familiar sound of a Sunfire engine came from behind the garage, and the mechanic pulled up in front of him.

Max saw Mr. Weaver get out from behind the driver's seat.

"How are you here?" asked Max. "I thought I left you in Iowa." Weaver said nothing.

"Am I making all of this up?"

Weaver looked at him, looked back down to his hands, chuckled toothily.

"What's your part in all of this?" asked Max. "Aren't you running this whole Convergence?"

"Oh no, child, not a chance. I ain't nearly as high up to be able to control nature. This ain't destiny: destiny's just a word for people who can't do math."

"Right."

"Uh-huh," continued the old man. "Same way the stars line up sometimes, same way the seasons change."

"So if it all happens naturally, why does someone like you have to be around?" asked Max.

"You ever seen a windmill?" asked Weaver.

"Yeah."

The old man finished wiping his hands.

"The mill don't make the wind, it just uses it. Wind changes now and then, always does, can't control that. But when it blows your way, you can use it. Grind wheat. Make 'lectricity."

"That's what you're doing, then? Using the Convergence to make something?"

"It's an enhancer of human power, son," said Weaver, "and there's a lotta good we can do with it. But the wind doesn't blow this way all the time, maybe once in a while. When it does, we do with it what we can."

"Who's 'we'?" asked Max.

"Don't matter."

"Of course it does! How else—"

"I got a warning for you, son," said Weaver.

Max stopped. "What?"

"You sure you wanna do this?"

Max blinked. "Are...are you serious? What — You got me into this, mister! Now it's my choice?"

"It was always your choice, Max," replied Weaver calmly, "and it's your choice now to keep going or come back. I'm telling you this because everything changes when you meet Lucy Fitzgerald. You'll be the first to make it work."

"What changes?"

"Everything. That's why we call it a 'convergence.' Gettin' everyone back in line. But there's no goin' back, son. You cross that line and you know what they say: you can't go home again."

"Who are you?"

"It's complicated—"

"Look! I've done what both you and the Alternate from Detroit told me to do, and I want some answers now. Why am I 'special'? What is so important about getting the Maxim Sinclairs and the Lucy Fitzgeralds of the universe together?"

Weaver wasn't daunted, Max could see that. If anything, the old man could see right through the act: he knew everything else about him, anyway, why wouldn't he? And yet, Weaver backed off as Max continued.

"And what about Mr. Perfect — I mean, the Optimal Me? I thought I was supposed to meet him."

Weaver squinted at him. "You can't meet him, but you met the guy who was second best."

"Where?"

"Junction 39B. That's why I sent you there. That dream you had."

For a moment, Max thought of his "home" in the Upper West, of rain and skyscrapers and Central Park and the Lucy whose ex-husband had...

"So that was real then?"

"There's more than one Junction at 39B."

"But they ended up together! I saw it."

"No, son. You woke up before you saw how it ended. Turned out that Lucy was lying. Her husband Claude was still very much alive. They'd been havin' issues. The morning after what you saw, he showed up in New York. They had it out, and then, they reconciled. Yo'self in Manhattan was devastated."

Max blinked. Manhattan Lucy had been lying the whole time.

"What happened to him?"

"Not gonna say, son."

"Why not?" Weaver sighed, held up his hand.

"Son, just...relax. Listen to me."

"I'm listening!"

"You ain't never gonna meet your Optimal, 'cause he still ain't got what you gonna get. What...did yo'self from Detroit tell you you would?"

Max nodded. Weaver looked at him for a few seconds, then sucked his teeth. "Man, that boy doesn't know his asshole from a sinkhole. You ain't never gonna meet that one."

"Why not?"

"Max, there ain't no Mr. Perfect or Miss Perfect. There's only what you got and what you ain't got. Nobody has everything, and that's what you're learnin' on this path, if you want to keep doin' this."

"Tell me why we're both so important and I'll be able to decide," said Max.

"Son, if I tell you, that takes away your choice. That ain't the best way for us to do what we do. That was the lesson of the dream at 39B. When we force it, it doesn't work."

"But what choice? You guys have all made it sound like I 'have' to do this. You must be great salesmen, then, but I'm officially done with this, right now, if you don't tell me the truth.

"This is your point of no return, Max," said Weaver, suddenly speaking with such authority that Max took a step back, and Weaver stepped in to fill the space. "That's why I'm here now. You've come all this way, son, and this is your last chance to turn back. You've sensed it, I know you have, that's why I made it so that you would see them."

"See who?"

"See the slightly better lifespace where you got it made, 'cept for her. See the slightly worse world where you went to the sandbox as a soldier and came back in a coma. You wonder if you made that all up, I know it, but it was real, too. But now that you have seen, you gotta choose, 'cause once you leave Las Vegas, there's no goin' back. It's almost time. You head east, you get to go home. But you head west, there ain't no way to have things be the same."

"What do you mean?"

"Convergence is just about here, Max. Today's the 4th of July. You got only a few more hours to get in place. Lucy and you are a force of nature. Once you two meet, you won't want to leave each other. And if I tell you why you two are important, whatever choice you still feel you have is gone."

"Why is having the choice important?"

Weaver stood his ground. "You really need to ask that?"

223

Max didn't budge, either. He stared the old man down. Three questions came to mind.

"What happens if I go back?" he asked. "What happens if I move forward? And why are she and I so important?"
And Weaver hesitated, the first real sign of uncertainty Max had seen from the old man. He pressed his advantage.

"I know it's a choice. My whole life right now is one big compass, anyway, but I'm not going anywhere, west or east, north or south, until you tell me, what happens if I go back? What happens if I move forward? And why are Lucy and I so important? That—" Max stopped, leaned into Weaver's personal space, "is my choice." Then he backed off, standing three feet away.

The two men eyed each other for several minutes, like two Twenty-first Century cowboys in the high noon Nevada sun. Neither budged. Neither spoke. But Max did not intend to cave. He crossed his arms like a small child, innocent of larger grown-up realities around him, but not caring, not until he got what he wanted.

And Weaver, true to form, saw what he was up against. He saw it all.

And called Max's bluff.

"Head for the water," said the old man. "You know where to go. You'll know her on sight. And if you can't find her, stop looking. She'll find you when it's time."

The old man backed off, tipped his grease monkey cap to Max, tossing him the keys to the Sunfire on his way.

And Max stood for a time, keys in hand, feeling the heat of the Nevada sun on the back and top of his head, taking in the soreness of his feet from walking and standing, the blood flowing from his heart to his feet and hands and head and back again.

And then he was getting into his car, feeling the key in his hand, the soft-hardness of the black key handle as he put it into the ignition. The deep ranging sound of the engine turning. The grip of the gearshift in his right hand and the shifting of the transmission as he put it in drive.

He pulled out of the driveway onto the road. Finding the I-15 wouldn't be hard from here. Max made his way through town, noticing that he was catching every single green light, and the traffic was light. Finding an on-ramp, he noticed that he was just past a construction zone, missing the snarl that was engulfing the other drivers.

A clear road ahead, and Weaver waving at him in the rearview mirror.

Max could have gone back, as he had threatened to do. He could have stayed there until Weaver turned right around and gave him his answers. But he'd come this far, and the promise of what could be was too much to resist. The workers had him, and there was nothing he could do about it.

None of the other Max Sinclairs were going to meet their soul mates. It was on him to get to Lucy Fitzgerald, and get there before the Convergence.

No time to spare.

BEHIND THE CURTAIN

"It's kind of like a singularity, but not the kind in space. You know what that is?"

Lucy and Justin sat on the train. She would have bought a plane ticket back, but she now shared a fear with Justin: aviophobia. In any case, they still had time. The train ride would get them back to Carmel with time to spare. Dusk was approaching, though, and Lucy was tired.

Mother and Son sat across from each other, both of them fully accepting the strangeness that they would be here like this, particularly Mother. She had adapted. She had no choice but to adapt, or completely lose her remaining marbles, such as they were.
"No, what's that?"

"It's a point in space and time when all points in space and time merge into one. That's the closest image I can use to describe Convergence: a point when all the numbers in the universe reach the infinite. Like a black hole, only it lasts for an instant. As we get closer to that instant, boundaries start to vanish. Numbers and natural cycles start lining up. Everything in space and time start to converge."

"Which is how you're able to meet me, right?" said Lucy. "You came here from the future."

Justin started to speak, then stopped himself, glanced down as he tried to find the words. Lucy saw a touch of arrogance to this kid, the smugness of someone used to being the smartest person in the room.

"Sort of," said Justin. "There's no 'future' or 'past' as far as Convergence is concerned. It's always happening now. I mean, really, that's all that there is anyway. Humans just perceive time in those three terms, in a straight line, left to center to right. But with the

Convergence, there's a physical boundary that drops that keeps us from experiencing them all now. We can see the future, the past, and the other lifespaces. And we can travel freely to them."

"Who's 'we'?"

"Workers," he said. "I'm kind of like a special agent."

"And how do you travel?"

Justin frowned at this. "I'm not really sure, to be honest. Kate and Mr. Weaver taught me. There are just places...I guess points of connection, that are already in convergence where the boundaries are already gone. But they're not places, either, they're also points in time. I...It's hard to explain, I don't know how it works, just that it does. You crossed one when you first set out, remember?"

She didn't know what he meant at first. Then, she thought of her way to the airport, the blackouts and—

"My missing time," she said. "Those were all—"

"The result of passing through the connection points as they appeared," finished Justin.

Lucy had been on the literal edge of her seat listening to Justin speak, and now she leaned back into the soft cushion of her chair.

"And how do you know when you're at one of those points?"

"You just learn to feel it, that's all," said Justin. "Same way you can get a 'feel' for throwing darts on target or doing acrobatics. Just takes time."

"So how did we meet?" asked Lucy

"Excuse me?"

"Well, you're our son, right? Max and me. Why not make this whole thing simple and explain to me where he and I first met? Then all we have to do is go there."

"It is simple. In my memory, you and Dad met on the beach at home in Carmel. That's why we're headed back."

Lucy blinked. "That simple?"

Justin nodded. "That simple."

Lucy mulled for about ten seconds before—

"Bullshit,"

Justin frowned. "What?"

"I call bullshit," said Lucy. Justin winced.

"That's...that's weird hearing you curse. Especially considering your 'no cursing' rule."

Lucy shrugged. "I'm not your mother yet. If the rest is so simple, then why are you here to — your words — 'help me' with the rest of the trip?"

Justin looked down and smiled with an awkward sigh. "Uh...well, see, Convergence is only about a day away, and as we get closer, things are going to get a little weird with the boundaries falling. It's the unpredictable, uncontrollable part of this event that even the workers can't do anything about. I'm here to keep you stable in this lifespace in case something happens."

"Like what?"

"Unexpected falls into other lifespaces, encounters with Alternates who may try to switch with you, things like that."

"Huh," said Lucy. "And how can you do that?"

"Just by being here."

Lucy nodded. "Uh-huh...all right, I think I can wrap my brain around that. And what about the visions I've been having? The dreams?"

Justin smiled. "That's another cool part about this. Everything's connected, like I said. Every human experience is a real lifespace. Dreams included, many of them."

"And the waiting room, what's that?"

"What's the waiting room?"

"A place that I've been to."

Justin leaned in. "Who brought you there?"

Lucy thought back. "The last time I was there, I saw Kate and Weaver together. You're telling me it's a real place?"

Justin shrugged, walked over to the window. "I guess it could be," he said, then glanced back at her. "You wanna know what's really tricky about all of this?"

Lucy smiled. "You mean, aside from everything?" Justin grinned back for a second, then looked back out at the landscape rushing by them.

"The Convergence sometimes connects you to places that are in between real and fantasy," he continued. "They're like little fragments of lifespaces — a waiting room, like yours, or maybe a park or a monument — that somehow break off from whole and end up in their own little universes."

"So that's where half my socks have been vanishing, then?" said Lucy. "Here I thought it was just the dryer eating them."

Justin grinned, then started drawing a line in the air between them both. "You wanna know about Dad?" he asked. Lucy nodded, and Justin continued to draw little imaginary lines. "Picture real life — past-present-future — as one line, left to right." He traced one line. "Now, picture the other lifespaces, like where you came from, as existing above and below our real life." He traced two lines, one above, one below.

"For most people, the only lifespaces that exist are the ones that are parallel. They're born into them, live them, die in them. But Dad has a special talent. He's kind of like a transmitter. Or, more like a receiver, something like that. He's got the ability to see beyond the boundaries. Whenever someone does that with enough power, they link to a separate lifespace. They open a new portal. It's usually weaker, but as Convergence approaches, you can actually move into it."

He finished, sat back in his chair. "Dad's pretty special. Those stories he's telling aren't just scribbles, they're drawn from real lifespaces."

"So, even something like Little Red Riding Hood or—"

Justin held up a hand. "No, it's not like that. Dad's not writing anything completely original or fake: he's picking up impressions from the other lifespaces. From his perspective, he's just writing a story about another version of himself that he can sorta see in his mind, but doing that strengthens his connection to a real Alternate lifespace that was already there before he wrote about it."

"And how is he able to do that?" asked Lucy.

Justin cringed a little. "It's never something he likes talking about with us, but...well...yeah, it was his divorce."

Lucy raised an eyebrow. "Divorce?"

Justin nodded. "Yeah," he said. "The girl he was married to before he met you. Dinah Devonshire." Justin chuckled awkwardly. "I'd find an old picture of them, or something that she left that he didn't throw out, and I'd ask him about it. All he'd ever say was that the divorce 'tore him a new one.'"

"But how does—?"

"Trauma, Mom," said Justin, cutting her off. "The trauma of the divorce opened him up to that power. That was his racket. Some people have drug addictions, others go to war, some people just bump their heads, but no matter what it is, it's the trauma that gets them going somehow. The workers never figured out why. It just does that." Justin smiled. "But Dad's a fighter. That kind of trauma wipes people out for life, but he decided to do something about it, to get better. People like that are prime. They can become the greatest version of themselves."

Justin then sighed, sat back down. "But yeah, 'tore me a new one.' That's how Dad describes his first marriage. It must have really sucked to be him back then."

Lucy didn't move as Justin finished talking, but she couldn't help but feel some sympathy for Max. She'd had her heart in the ringer with Charles at least twice in the past month. She was on the train headed south away from the 'sure bet" she'd come to believe was all that was ever possible for her. Though she'd felt an intellectual connection to the man before, Lucy felt something warming inside the middle of her for

Max Sinclair, who, too, had experienced heartbreak.

Justin started pacing back and forth in front of her, like a professor, hands clasped behind his back. "Normally, his writing would stay on the page. But with Convergence getting closer, his Alternate is fair game to have more of an impact in the other lifespaces than the others. He can literally take over their minds and lives, make decisions for them, take actions."

"So you're saying that he's...creating himself?"

"Don't we all do that?" said Justin.

Lucy was aware that Justin didn't answer the question at all, but let it pass. She was starting to feel the strain of the past few days take its toll on her stamina.

The train car shifted slightly as the locomotive continued to follow the tracks into the night.

Despite her fatigue, Lucy had so many questions. What to ask next?

"How many other lifespaces are there? Millions?" asked Lucy, after a few minutes of silence. Justin had gone to sit back down across from her and shook his head.

"Not as many as you think," he said. "There are only ever a few set circumstances that have to happen for a human being to be born. You, for example, have ninety-two other lifespaces. Dad, on the other hand, has ninety-four."

"That's all? That doesn't seem like much, for either of us."

"It's about average. How many things could have gotten in the way of your parents meeting? Their parents? And so on."

"But wouldn't a whole other universe open up for each choice I make?" asked Lucy.

"Not really. Only the choices that have the greatest impact on the greatest number of people...those are the ones that have enough power to make new lifespaces."

"Can I visit worlds where I don't exist? Where I was never born?"

Justin smiled. "Ah...the short answer's no. The long answer is, not normally, unless you — like me — are given that ability by the workers. The junctions between the experiences open, but there's something about the mind that affects it."

"What do you mean?"

Justin cleared his throat. "Well, Mr. Weaver explained it to me like this. Each mind is like its own personal universe. Even though Convergence brings all things together, there's a boundary that the mind makes that keeps you from going where you can't exist. This boundary is the last to dissolve, and it only goes away in that last instant before Convergence happens. The workers don't know for sure why that is, but they don't have any choice but to go with it."

Lucy let that soak for a few minutes. "What do the workers do between Convergences?"

"Between Convergences?" Justin furrowed his brows. "No...from their perspective, there's only ever one Convergence. The rest of us mere mortals caught in the time stream see it as several recurring events. From outside the regular flow of time, all moments are one. Convergence will happen. It is happening. It's already happened, all at once."

Finally, the big question.

"So why are you here?" asked Lucy. The boy looked at her as if she'd asked him what color the sky was.

"I told you, to keep you grounded."

"If that's the case, why wouldn't they have sent someone else, an actual worker who's not just a 'guest star' in all of this?"

"Isn't that obvious?" asked Justin.

"No..."

Then Lucy thought about it some more. And it was obvious.

"You're here to ensure you're born."

Justin nodded. "I don't trust anyone else to do the job for me."

"But...I thought you said you were from the future?"

"No...well, yes, and no."

Lucy stared at him. "Now you're just being cryptic on purpose."

The boy laughed. "Yeah, a little." Then he leaned forward. "Mom, obviously I won't be here if you and Dad don't get together. What'll really bake your noodle, though, is that I can still cease to exist if you don't meet him, even though I'm in front of you right now."

"Why?"

"Because after the Convergence, the timeline's more or less permanent. No more changes are possible, so that means that if there was ever anything you wanted to change in your life — choices you could make or un-make, lives you wanted to lead, people you wanted to be with — this is the time to do it. The cement dries, and if you're stuck, you're stuck."

"Uh-huh...so if in twenty-four hours, we don't get our act together, you'll just disappear? Like Marty McFly"

Justin raised an eyebrow, then looked away for a moment before meeting her gaze again, smiling a little smile.

"I don't know who that is, but...yep, that's the basic idea."

"But if there are so many alternate lifespaces, then—"

"Remember: there's only one lifespace where you and Dad actually get together. That means there's only one lifespace where I can exist. That's this one."

Justin checked his watch — some no-name brand that looked like a Timex or Casio — and took a breath. "And we don't have much time left. Time stops being normal the closer we get to the point of singularity."

"Meaning what?"

"Meaning we have to get you to the beach as soon as possible, and keep you there."

Lucy nodded toward the watch. "If you're from the future, how come your watch doesn't look more...futuristic?"

Justin laughed, then looked away. "Um…we've had a few setbacks."

""We,' as in—"

"Civilization." He said nothing after that, and Lucy didn't push. If she'd learned anything from the movies, the guy doing the time traveling was never going to tell you too much about where he came from.

"And what about your father? How are you going to help him get to where he needs to be?"

"Don't worry, he's already on his way. And as a back-up plan, someone else is on that. A true expert player."

"Who?"

Justin only grinned.

***

"You lost, kid?"

Max had seen the silhouette on the horizon. A shorter person, but definitely a person, walking along the side of the road. He'd just crossed into California, and she was maybe a mile back from the sign. Max looked at the figure next to the Sunfire: a tom-boyish, awkward looking girl, no more than maybe seven or eight, brownish red hair, in a T-shirt, jeans, and clean runners, carrying a knapsack.

The girl grinned at him. "Nope," she said, and nothing more but that grin.

"Um...how did you get all the way out here?" asked Max.

"I'm going to my friend's house," she said.

"And where's that?"

"How much is it worth to you?"

Max blinked.

"What?" he asked.

"I said, how much is it worth to you?"

234

"Um...are you asking me for a bribe?"

The girl grinned. Braces. "It's la mortee-tah."

Max raised an eyebrow, but couldn't fight the smile forming at the corner of his mouth.

"I think you mean, *la mordida*, with two 'd's."

"You heard me."

Max looked around. It was late morning and the desert was blazing hot. Looking at the girl, she wasn't even sweating, almost as if she'd been in the air conditioned car with him the whole time.

"I don't think you're in a position to be asking for bribes, here, kiddo," said Max.

"Don't call me 'kiddo,' please and thanks." She crossed her arms.

"Uh, sorry, didn't mean to offend you." Her arms uncrossed.

"You didn't, I just don't like being called kid. I'm eight years old. Kids are, like, five."

"You'd be surprised. I know a lot of grown-up kids."

The girl suddenly adopted a more coquettish air about her. "Well, I'm very mature for my age."

"Uh-huh..."

She extended a hand. "I'm Mindy."

Max hesitated, then shook it. "I'm Max."

Mindy giggled. "Nice to meet you!"

Max wasn't sure what to make of this, just that he had his own bigger destiny to meet, and he wasn't comfortable leaving her out here.

"Well, I'm headed to Carmel in a hurry. If you don't want to tell me where your friend lives—"

"Oh!" She suddenly perked up. "That's exactly where my friend lives!"

Max blinked. "What happened to *la mordida*?"

"Don't be silly. This isn't Mexico."

"Huh." Cute kid.

Max took a look around. This route, from what he'd heard, was normally busy with traffic between Vegas and LA, but today, for some reason, there was no one else.

He contemplated the prospect of kidnapping and pedophilia charges if a state trooper were to pull him over and find an unrelated kid in his midst, likely someone who's missing.

"Do your parents know you're gone?" he asked.

"Of course they do," said Mindy. "They sent me out there."

"On your own? Hitchhiking? Are you serious?"

"Yep, yep, and yep."

Max shook his head. "That's horrible."

Mindy giggled. "Not really," she said.

"What do you mean, not really?" Max said. "I'm going drop you off at the first sheriff's station I find, make sure you get to your friend's place safely."

Mindy now simply smiled, lips closed.

"No, you're not."

The certainty of how she said the words stopped that line of thought in its tracks, and he knew there was something more here.

"Do you know about Convergence?"

"Is that, like, a rock band?" asked Mindy.

"Uh...no." Max coughed. The air was too dry here and his throat was scratchy. The air conditioning of the car called to him. "Look, do you want a ride or not? You can put your stuff in the trunk."

"Waiting on you."

With that, Max walked around and opened the trunk. Mindy put her knapsack inside and headed back around to the passenger side as Max closed the trunk and got into the car.

"I still say your dad should be ashamed of himself for letting you all the way out here," said Max, starting the engine.

"My dad knows what he's doing," she said, "most of the time," and left it at that.

As they pulled back onto the Interstate, Max glanced over at his new passenger. As he did, he saw Mindy's smile, and really wondered what the heck she was grinning at.

DISRUPTION

"The dilation is starting to get worse," said Justin as the train pulled in at Salinas.

Lucy had only been half awake, but stirred when she felt the great engine slowing to a halt.

By train, it was a twenty-eight hour trip, requiring a quick transfer onto another train to get to Carmel that would take another two hours. From Salinas, however, it was only a half hour drive, so the plan was to get her car at the Monterey Airport and go from there. Until then, all they could do was bide their time.

Lucy and Justin hadn't spoken much during that time. Instead, she had drifted in and out of sleep, interrupted only by the occasional meal service and trips to the restroom. Idle time had been rare along this whole experience, and there was so much to take in that Lucy's mind had decided to shut down and rest.

Justin left her alone, for the most part, spending much of his time staring out the window at the wine country as it blew past them, adjusting his watch from time to time, or just taking the odd nap for himself. A normal, ordinary kid in every way. The only weird thing he did was time his bathroom breaks with hers, but she chalked it up to his "grounding" duties and his obvious distrust of other peoples' inefficiency, even the workers. It was almost cute in its way.

A son. A mother. As much weird as it all made sense. Over their time together, Lucy felt the truth of the teenager sitting across from her, right in her chest, in the whole of her being, that this kid was her flesh and blood. She couldn't explain it, had never understood it when her other friends and relatives, after giving birth to their own children, tried in vain to explain it to her. Now she got it — she got it! — and

238

knew that this was one of those feelings, those human experiences, that defied total capture in words.

Lucy hadn't dreamed at all. She hadn't expected that, given the enhanced power of dreaming as Convergence — now only hours away — seemed to have, but given how tired she was, REM sleep probably wasn't physically possible anyway.

As she opened her eyes, Justin was sitting in front of her, turning his watch.

"What did you say?" she asked, sitting up and stretching. Justin frowned as he fiddled with the buttons.

"There's a part of a black hole called the 'event horizon' where the gravitational effects start to take hold," he said. "Technically, we passed the Convergence's equivalent a while ago, but it's getting stronger. The flow of time is starting to change."

Lucy yawned, felt the dryness in her mouth as she rubbed some sleep away from her eyes. "In what way?"

"Speeding up, slowing down. It'll get worse the closer we get to Convergence."

"And how to you know that?"

Justin held up his watch. "It's now 6:34 A.M. according to this watch. I've been staring at the time non-stop since it was 6:33. It took a full fourteen seconds longer to change over to 6:34 than it should have."

"That doesn't seem like much," said Lucy.

"Oh, it's a lot. Quite a lot."

"If we can't measure time accurately anymore, how do we even know when Convergence will happen?"

Justin took off the watch. "We use the only measures that matter." He tapped his forehead. "One thing we kids got from you and Dad was a hyper accurate sense of timing."

Lucy frowned. "That can't be true," she said. "Do you know how many meetings I'm late for in any given month?"

239

"Trust me on this one. My sense of time is one major reason the workers let me do this. It keeps me grounded where I am."

Lucy rubbed her eyes. Still too early for this. "I guess some skill sets are more attractive than others?"

Justin nodded. "It's true. Then again, becoming a worker isn't strictly a volunteer thing. You have to be born with the predisposition to be able to move your consciousness, and yourself, out of time. After that, there are some preferences."

"And what are some of the preferred skills that they look for?"

Justin cleared his throat. "A certain genetic profile, first of all. Nothing anyone can do about that if you don't meet it. After that hurdle…high intelligence. Decent physical strength. Good inner ear. Average blood pressure. Timing—" Justin tapped his forehead again. "Imagination, strong organizational skills, and inner calm."

"Doesn't sound like much of a candidate pool," said Lucy.

"There are more than you think."

Lucy had a ton of unanswered questions, but she was still waking up.

"All right... wait."

"What?"

Suddenly awake, Lucy stood up, staring him right in the eye. "You said 'we kids.' How many kids do we end up having, Max and I?"

"Two," he said, standing up.

Lucy remembered the vision in the waiting room. Still, that memory wasn't enough: she wanted to hear the words.

"Two sons or a daughter?"

"Didn't you already find out in the waiting room?"

Lucy smiled. "Indulge me."

Justin smiled without looking up.

"Come on, Mom. I can't spoil all the surprises for you."

"Isn't your telling me about this already changing things?" asked Lucy.

240

Justin shrugged.

"The best kinds of prophecies are the bad ones that don't come true, and the good ones that do. You guys taught us kids to cover all our bases. I'm just being a good son."

Justin dropped his watch onto the seat and left it there as they disembarked.

***

"You're not wearing your seatbelt," said Mindy.

Max looked down. Sure enough, he'd forgotten to fasten it after he'd picked her up just after crossing into California. They were approaching Junction 15, but it seemed like the drive was taking longer than it should have. And yet, as he checked the time — 1:41 P.M. — he was right on schedule. He pulled the seatbelt across his chest and clicked it in the fastener.

"Thanks," he said, and returned his gaze to the road.

"It's important that you wear your seatbelt," said Mindy. "The highway's gonna get pretty wonky in the next little bit."

"Really? How many times have you made this trip?" asked Max.

"A bunch of times," she said. "But it's really important you wear your seatbelt, anywhere you go."

Max looked over. Mindy had one of the most expressive faces he'd ever seen. She was staring him in the eye with a look of such seriousness that it triggered that old feeling of being scolded for chewing gum in the middle of math class.

"Do you know something I don't?" asked Max.

Mindy just looked at him for a few seconds. Suddenly, she burst out laughing and turned her attention back to the passenger window. Something about that laugh unsettled Max more than most of the strangeness he'd encountered along the way.

241

1:42 P.M. That minute had felt like five. Probably just my imagination, thought Max. He looked ahead.

***

At first, neither person was sure what the sound was.

The airport parking garage in Monterey had been surprisingly empty when they'd arrived, though there were many cars. Finding the zone, Lucy and Justin had been making their way to the pay machine so she could validate the ticket and leave. They found the machine near the now vacant kiosk on the first level.

Lucy had just finished validating the ticket when they heard it. It was a sharp ping! followed by a thump! that seemed to come from the far wall of the rental office.

Justin and Lucy looked at each other.

"Did you hear—"

The glass window near her suddenly shattered as another ping! echoed out, and it was obvious: someone was shooting at them.

"This way!" shouted Justin. The boy ran for the cover of the rental cars as three more shots — ping! ping! ping! — rang out. Lucy ran the other way.

"No, Mom! Stay close! This wa—"

The world winked out of existence.

***

1:13 P.M.

No...no, that wasn't possible.

Max took his hand off the wheel to rub his eyes, make sure what he was seeing was real.

"Both hands," said Mindy. Max looked over. She couldn't have had a more disinterested look on her face as she watched the road.

242

"What?" Mindy continued to stare.

"Eyes forward."

"Huh?"

Max turned to face the road.

The world winked out of existence...

...and reappeared in front of him a full second later.

At least it seemed like it.

"Uh..."

Max took his foot off the gas and coasted for a few seconds. He checked his blind spots, rear view mirror. The road was still in front of him, sloping nicely to the northwest toward Bakersfield. Everything seemed normal. He accelerated again to just over the speed limit.

What the hell? His mind was still processing the data he'd just taken in, but at the outset, it looked as though the world outside the Sunfire had just vanished for an instant, replaced by pure...whiteness...and then back to the Interstate, now surrounded by green farmlands and filling up with traffic.

And the clock read 1:54 P.M.

"What just happened?" he asked. "Did you see that?"

"Mmhmm..." said Mindy. He turned to her.

"That's all you can say?" he said.

Mindy turned and looked him in the eye.

"Yep, Alaska plates. Wonder how long it took him to get down here."

"What?"

Mindy regarded her chauffeur like he'd just gotten out of remedial. She nodded her head back.

"The truck."

Max looked over. Sure enough, some beat up old Chevy with Alaska plates was passing them to the right.

"That's not what I meant. Did you see the flash?"

Mindy shook her head and turned away to stare out the passenger side window.

His question unanswered, Max returned his attention to the road, wary that it would happen again and he'd end up rolling in a ditch with someone else's kid under his car.

The clock now read 1:42 P.M.

***

Tommy Thrones hadn't expected Justin Sinclair to get the drop on him

It took only a few seconds for Justin — not that much older than he was — to tackle him, disarm him, and punch him squarely in the face three times. Tommy concluded he'd just gotten sloppy. That he should have watched his back as he ran up to the kiosk to finish the job. That he had run past an SUV that had easily concealed his quarry, giving him the advantage.

Tommy had been sloppy. There was no way around it. And it didn't matter, anyway. Not anymore.

Tommy felt Justin's hands grabbing his shirt, but there wasn't enough power in his grip to do anything more than make him uncomfortable. No, Justin Sinclair hadn't yet buffed up in this lifespace.

"Why are you trying to kill us?!" asked Justin. He glared right back at his ineffective torturer.

"Kill you? What do—"

Justin released his throat and, realizing his lack of arm strength, stood up and kicked Tommy in the ribcage. His legs clearly had more power.

"Ah!" Tommy cried out at the sharp pain from Justin's shoes on his sides.

"The workers did the math," said Justin, "and the formulas are perfect. Perfect. There is no reason why we shouldn't all be where

244

we're supposed to be with time to spare. Weaver and Kate, the work of thousands, even my own baby sister, all getting them into place. Hell, they almost got two of their Alternates together as a backup, which up to this point they said was impossible. And each time, there was a wildcard, a variable that just completely threw things out of whack. Something that shouldn't have been, but they just assumed it was because the Primes made for the optimal match."

Justin got back down on the ground and grabbed Tommy's collar.

"You know that without them together I'll never exist. Keeping them apart is the same as murder. It's birth control. It's abortion. Why are you trying to kill us? Me and my sister. Why?"

Tommy admired and despised Justin's sudden display of intellectual and physical *cojones*. Admired because for a nerdy kid like the boy now holding him by the collar, it was a tough quality to summon as needed. Despised because, over time, after you get used to thinking and acting with your balls, it changes you, eats away at whatever innocent qualities you had before. Worse yet, it doesn't solve your insecurities, and before too long, you're beating people up in back alleys because you don't know any other way to feel safe in your own skin.

Tommy smiled in his face.

"I took tenth grade physics once," said Tommy. "At a really shitty school in a really shitty city in what has turned out to be a really shitty world for all those involved. Nothing works the way it should. Nobody's doing well."

Tommy saw that he had Justin's rapt attention. "But my physics teacher, Mr. Bell, he had his shit together. He never took money, stayed clean and sober, and knew his trade. And the rest of us respected him for it, even the bangers who ran the protection rackets over the faculty after hours, they left him alone. The eye of the storm.

"One day, he asked us a question. 'Suppose you could go back and kill your grandparents. Would you be able to succeed? Because if you did, you'd never be born to go back and kill your grandparents, which would mean you would, of course, be born to go back and do it, and so on.' I thought about it for a long time, not so much to figure out the paradox, but to really ask myself, if I could kill my grandparents, would I do it?"

"And you know what, the answer was no. I could never do that. I liked my grandparents. They had been very kind and generous to me. They were long gone, though, moved away before everything went to shit, before they knew it would be impossible for them to come home without travelling for years on end, like pilgrims."

Tommy glared at Justin. "But my father..."

Neither of them broke their gaze, but Tommy could see, behind the wheels turning inside Justin's eyes, a glimmer of understanding shining through the gears and pulleys.

"I couldn't kill him, either. And I'd killed before — people I hated, people who'd otherwise tried to fuck with me, steal from me, hurt me. Killing someone wasn't the problem, not after all that had happened. But I could never do that to my own blood, to someone who'd given me life, no matter how much I despised him."

Justin leaned back, sat his ass down on the ground, arms across his knees, the glimmer of realization slowly turning into a full dawn across his face. Tommy, too, felt some relief telling this to someone, though the hatred was still bubbling, never far below.

"The school systems were broken, like everything else. The new guys in charge, they only kept it going to maintain the illusion that things were all right. So I dropped out, left my father's house, got a job, an apartment, a girl. I went through the routine.

"And then, a month and a bit ago, something weird happened. I was getting on a bus, and there he was. An Alternate me. A better me. Like a dream...I'm still not sure if it wasn't. And he told me how much better life was where he lived. And I knew he was my better, my best, and I was never going to be that guy. Not that he existed — it was just a fucking dream. Then Weaver showed up, telling me that I had a chance to help contribute to making not just this world better, but the big picture, that I could save my own life."

Tommy paused for the effect, and saw he still had Justin's rapt attention.

"And I saw my chance. He thinks I've been helping him, Weaver. And I have been. I did my part...but now it's done. At least, it will be. Because though I can't kill my grandfather, I can make sure that he never meets my grandmother. Convergence gave me that chance."

Tommy stopped talking. His tongue was dry, his throat raw, his ribs still smarting from being kicked.

Justin sat dumbstruck, staring at him.

"You missed us on purpose," said Justin.

"No shit."

"But if you weren't going to kill me, why did you chase me back here?"

Tommy grinned. "I didn't say I wasn't above wounding you."

He watched his young father's expression soften; go inward. "Why...why do you hate me so much? How did I become that kind of person?"

Tommy hadn't expected that one. He felt his blood slow down.

"I've never known you any other way," he replied.

"What happens?" asked Justin. Tommy shook his head.

"War...economic collapse. Environmental disaster. Your generation may have had some setbacks, but that's nothing compared to what you left us. At least, in my lifespace. Now? I'm not so sure. I might have made everything better. Thing is, I won't be around to see it for myself."

"And my sister...your aunt..."

At that, Tommy looked down. He remembered.

"Aunt Min...she was very sweet for all the time she was alive."

Justin's eyes widened. "What do you mean 'was' —"

"She was murdered, Dad," said Tommy. "Seven years ago, if that's even going to happen anymore, either. But I remember it...it wasn't quick. She didn't deserve to die, especially not so horribly."

Tommy gave Justin the chance to take that in. Then the anger reasserted itself.

"I still hate you," he growled. "Even now, even though you haven't done what you did to me yet, even though you might never, that's not going away. The reason I haven't skipped out of here is because the last thing I want to see when Convergence happens is my grandmother on her own, without my grandfather. It means they will be okay on their own, that you won't live to become who I know you to be, and it means Aunt Min will never live to suffer what she suffered."

Justin simply sat. Tommy imagined what was happening behind the gears of his young father's mind, all the bits of data he'd just presented being sorted and put into little pre-assigned category boxes that Justin used to make sense of his world. He knew that because he, too, thought much the same way, until recently, until he had decided to abort his own life. When facing death, even if it's what you want, you can't help but think in bigger terms.

"You're lying," said Justin, his eyes tearing.

Tommy turned his attention back. "What?"

"You're a liar!"

Justin got up, and Tommy felt the adrenaline shoot through his veins.

"I'm telling you the truth!" he shouted back.

Justin kicked him in the stomach. Tommy felt his organs contract, felt the air leaving his lungs in a wave of nauseous pain.

"It's not true! It can't be!"

Tommy looked up in time for Justin to grab his collar with his left hand and hit him again with his fists, which were suddenly more effective. He clenched his teeth as Justin hit him, again and again and

248

again. He felt his lip burst, saw blood dripping down on his shirt and his pants as he took his father's pummeling.

When Justin stopped, Tommy watched in disgust as he sat down and bawled like a baby. Tommy grinned a bloody grin.

"You see, Dad? Nothing's changed about you. What you're doing here, you'll be doing years from now. You'll do this to me every time I come home with a bad report card. You'll do this when you've stopped beating up Mom, and after she leaves, you'll do it twice as much. You'll even do this to me even after the Collapse, when there are troops and cops and gangs shooting each other in the streets for a week before they put things back together."

Tommy leaned himself forward. "This is who you really are, Dad. It would be better if you just never were." Tommy slumped back, turned his head to let the blood drip down onto his shoulder. He spit a red wad onto the ground. "Doesn't matter now anyway," he said. "Lucy's unstuck. She'll never find her way back in time for the Convergence."

Justin stopped his sobbing. He stood up on one knee, then the other, then on both feet. Tommy wiped the blood from his nose and his lip, his whole body pounding from the beating he'd just received from his young father, and looked up.

He watched Justin clasp the raw knuckles of his right hand in his left, then stand, wipe his face and run back the way he came. Though he couldn't see it, he knew that he was running toward the junction that had just opened up after the shooting, when Justin had run for cover one way, and Lucy had gone the other. She'd run straight into it, outside the anchoring effect that Justin's presence had, the one that protected her from shifting between the lifespaces as the singularity approached.

Tommy lay there for a good few minutes until he heard the police sirens wailing. Not that the cops would be able to keep him long before another portal opened up to give him escape.

He got up and looked around...then smiled. In his haste to chase after Lucy, Justin had forgotten to grab the gun.

LOOSE THREADS

Max suddenly found himself at Paso Robles with absolutely no sense of the passage of time between there and Bakersfield.

According to the clock on the dash, however, it was now 4:02 P.M. The fuel gauge also read just under half tank.

He wanted to believe it was an effect of the Convergence. It probably was, but the feeling of being unhinged was still unsettling. Max hated the lack of control over what was happening, but he battled through the fear and the lack of sense in his world as he was now experiencing it.

A sign directing him to the police station passed behind him. He looked to Mindy. She was sleeping soundly.

That she was connected to Convergence was not in question. Why she chose not to talk about it was baffling and irritating. And yet, Max was still a grown man travelling with an unrelated minor, and in the mounting number of anomalous phenomena around him, Max clung to this one conventional bit of common sense that still applied to him. Go to the police. Make a report. Let them take her the rest of the way.

The exit to the station came up. Max signaled and changed lanes.

Mindy stirred.

***

Lucy could perceive the different doorways from here. They weren't visible, but she could sense them nonetheless, the same way you can't see a thought in your mind's eye, but when you hear or read the word "doorway," you think of a doorway, disembodied, immaterial.

They blinked in and out of existence in front of her. Some lingered, others were there and gone before you could register their presence, like the sighting of shooting stars in one's peripheral vision. Still others found themselves manifesting and dissolving at some middle pace, and yet somehow choreographed to the patterns of their faster and slower cousins in a rhythmic dance.

The background to this space was white...only it wasn't. It was the absence of color altogether. Close your eyes and you see black, but after a while, black itself loses all meaning. This was the opposite: lose yourself in white, and white becomes meaningless, not the unity of all colors, but a fluid acknowledgement of their absence. And the portals, doorways, gateways, or whatever you wanted to call them that connected the lifespaces, that the Convergence was bringing together: this was where they intersected.

She had run so far away from the gunshots, thinking Justin was right behind her. When she realized they had gone in opposite directions, she stopped, but she had already reached the threshold.

Now, with one foot completely across, but the other foot still touching the edge of the lifespace she'd just left behind, she looked back to see the action frozen. Justin's back was toward her, his frame caught in mid-motion as he fled toward the cars. Shards of glass stood in midair like captured snowflakes from where the bullets had caught the window. She tried turning to the right to see the shooter, but the vision dissolved where the doorway stood.

If this was the space between spaces, then there was nothing she could do here for her son. And the helplessness was overwhelming. Lucy tried going back, but almost as soon as she had the thought, the way closed, like curtains being pulled across window. As soon as it happened, a subtle force nudged the lingering foot out of the threshold and backward, out of one doorway, through another, into a new world.

***

"You're not gonna turn me in."

Max had parked outside the police station. A few patrol officers walked into the station and shot him a glance as they chatted, but paid him no mind otherwise as he opened the passenger side door to get Mindy out. Mindy had crossed her arms, seatbelt still fastened.

"I don't have a choice, kiddo," said Max. "I'm probably in for a lot of questioning as to how I ended up finding you at the side of the road, so it's not like it's something I'm doing for shits and giggles." Mindy's eyes widened. "You said the 's' word!"

Max blushed. "Right...sorry. I mean, it's not like it's something I'm doing for fun." Mindy's gaze was made of steel.

"You always said we should never say the 's' word."

Max knelt down in front of her. "What do you mean?" Mindy said nothing, and Max pressed. "Oh no, now I know you're connected to Convergence. I've never met you before, so how could I have 'always said' to never use the 's' word? Are you working with Mr. Weaver, Mindy? Did he send you here?"

Mindy hadn't broken her gaze, and she remained silent. And yet, she took off her seatbelt.

"Do me a favor, *Max*," she said.

"What's that?"

Max stood up and backed away to give Mindy room as she got out of the car and stood straight up.

"I want you to walk backward. Look at me, and take six steps back, but only six. Okay?"

Max raised an eyebrow. "Oh-kaaay..." he said, glancing behind him. The parking lot was mostly empty, and he would easily cross two parking spaces walking six feet.

He looked Mindy in the eye and obliged. One step. Then two. Three...four...

On the fifth step, Max felt queasy in his stomach, like airsickness. He hadn't eaten in hours. He ignored the sensation and kept going.

Six steps. Now his vision started going wonky, as if a translucent white film, like tissue paper, had covered everything. Mindy, however, remained sharp and clear.

At six feet, Max noticed passing cars slowing down, then stopping in the middle of the road. Vulture's he'd observed circling in the distance froze in midair. A police officer leaving the station had paused in the doorway of the station and seemed content to stare at the door handle.

"Take one more step, then turn around," said Mindy, suddenly with an authority in her voice that belied her youth, "but don't move after that."

Max found it difficult to refuse her. He stepped forward — seven feet away — and he saw the cars, the vultures, and the officer start to move in slow motion. Turning around, Max was stunned to see another scene altogether in front of him. There was no boundary, and the transition from the California desert to a dark alley in a big city was seamless.

Then, just as it had appeared, by subtle degrees, the scene vanished. The normal motion of objects in space and time resumed.

Max turned back and found Mindy standing right next to him. She smiled, the most peculiar blend of childish delight and smug satisfaction he'd ever seen.

"I'm not gonna turn you in."

"Told you so."

***

How long had Lucy really been here?

Somehow along the way, she had forgotten that Convergence was only a few real hours away. But what was real anymore?

Lucy walked the Irish coast. The jagged, toothy edge of the cliff ran for miles and miles, lit by a western sun at mid afternoon in the summer. The spray from the water below didn't reach this height, but she could feel the presence of the waves and churning tidal movements.

She knew it wasn't real, that the sunlight here was just too bright and too orange to be natural. She retained that much grounding in her reality. But it was beautiful, alive, fresh...the smell of salt and flower and grass...

How was she here, so far away from home? What had happened in this lifespace to bring her across the sea? Lucy didn't know, nor could she find out. There wasn't another soul in sight, and yet she was here.

Fifteen of these Alternate lifespaces she had wandered now. Fifteen. Never once did she feel a hunger pang or a need to find a restroom. Nor had she slept: she never grew tired. Her muscles didn't ache. Lucy felt like she could walk forever and this was good, because that was the most likely scenario she faced.

Fifteen. All around the world as she knew it. What had Lucy seen? A village in Algeria where her Alternate worked for UNICEF. A warehouse near the airport in Toronto where she had worked a full shift picking cigarette cartons from shelves along an assembly line. A mansion in Phuket. Another airplane flight over Chicago (which scared her greatly, but mercifully, another portal had opened up within five minutes). Lucy remembered them all.

It seemed like a trek of days had passed, but that was just for now. Right now, here in Ireland, Lucy felt like she'd been wandering for days. Back in Africa, her Alternate had been assigned for five years, and she felt the years. In Toronto, it had been her first day on the job, and she'd felt the hours pass as though they were real.

In every case, a portal opened when it was meant to, and as she stepped through, each time she would stop at the threshold between lifespaces and stay there for as long as she could. In that space between the spaces, Lucy would find her inner clock reset to quote-unquote "real time." The only time she really knew how much time she had before Convergence came and went. The only time she could sense that new portals were appearing in and out of existence with faster and faster frequency as the moment of singularity approached.

But within seconds, the door behind would close, and push her forward into another reality. Then Lucy would find herself adjusting to the life and times of the new world, and "real time" would fade, as quickly as it had appeared.

Here in Ireland, Lucy had been wandering for days. But that was all right. She wasn't hungry, she wasn't tired, and it was pretty here. What else could she do but wait until the way home appeared?

Lucy walked the coast. It was all she could do.

***

"So you're like an insurance policy?" asked Max.

They were back on the road. Carmel was not far, but the time differences were getting more erratic, and he wanted to hurry.

"I don't know what that is," said Mindy. "I'm only eight."

Max raised an eyebrow and looked over at the child. "I thought you said you were very mature for your age?"

Mindy rolled her eyes.

"That doesn't mean I know *everything*," she scoffed.

Max sighed. "Okay, let's try again. You're here to make sure that I get there okay, right?"

"Mmhmm."

"That somehow, some random effect of the Convergence doesn't throw me off track and into limbo or some kind of rift."

"Mmhmm."

"But — and I mean this with all respect for your maturity — why would they send a child? What's the reason behind that?"

Mindy giggled.

"What's so funny?" asked Max.

"I can't tell you, it would ruin the joke."

"What joke?"

"I'll tell you later."

"What can you tell me now? What was that that I saw?"

"The In-Between," said Mindy.

"The what?"

Mindy said nothing, and Max didn't feel like waiting for an answer, so he pressed on.

"And you...I have to stay close to you otherwise I'd end up falling into that place, or others like it."

"That's right," said Mindy. "Seven feet's as far as you can get from me before you get unstuck."

"Why seven?"

"I don't know. Just 'cause."

"Fair enough...and do you know how much time we have?"

Mindy rolled her eyes upward as she counted, nodding and mumbling out the numbers. "Three hours."

"I've watched the clock change thirteen times now," said Max. "What are you using to measure time? How do you know it's right?"

Mindy said nothing, but tapped her forehead several times with her finger.

"Huh," said Max. "Well the last distance marker said Carmel was an hour away. Why the big hurry?"

"Because once you're there," said Mindy, "you have two very important things to do first. They'll take up some of that time. Plus, it's the Fourth of July, and Carmel's gonna be crowded."

"What 'things' would those be?"

Mindy looked forward. Max followed her gaze back to the road. The landscape was now becoming more green and forested. Hilly. Not long now. It was 3:43 P.M. A few minutes ago, it was 3:58 P.M.

"I'll tell you more when we get to the beach," said Mindy.

"What beach?"

"Carmel Beach. That's where we're going."

"But what if I want to know sooner?" said Max.

"Then you'd better drive faster."

"I don't want to get a ticket. Or get into an accident."

Mindy smiled — again, that silent command and authority.

"You won't."

Max hesitated, then pushed the accelerator to 75 mph. The Sunfire responded beautifully.

Before Max could press, Mindy closed her eyes and leaned her head away. Within thirty seconds, he could hear subtle snoring.

What a weird kid.

And yet, she was right. Along the road, there were no cops, and no accidents.

***

Tommy had stopped the bleeding, but his ribs and most of the rest of his goddamned body was still sore from the beating he'd received.

Nonetheless, he followed Justin through the worlds, navigating the portals, leaping from one to the other like an acrobat, all the skill that his ability and cover as a Convergence worker gave him.

Like his young father, Tommy had seen so many worlds — so many possibilities. Each one made him sick. So many others had done better, so many lifespaces had been more prosperous and peaceful and filled with light than where he had come from, it drove him to fire. Drove him to want to set alight all of the goodness in which he could not share and watch the conflagration burn from the In-Between.

So few lifespaces had been as bad, or worse, than his own, and he knew why. The work of Weaver and Kate and the five hundred thousand or so people who harnessed the power of this singularity and brought it into the service of optimal creation was bearing fruit. And he was only a loose thread, deserving to be snipped off.

Now he hid in the cover of the moonless night in the Chilean Andes in his own year, almost in his own lifespace, but far away from the shell of his home. He watched Justin approach his mother, and waited for his chance.

***

Eighty-nine years. Thirty-two thousand, four-hundred and eighty-five days.

As she lay here, looking up into the night, Lucy wondered if there were that many stars in front of her now.

The Andean air was frigid, but there were precious few souls here. Just as in Ireland...Ireland...five years ago? But it was only yesterday?

No...no, it was only a minute ago. Seconds...

Lucy held onto...something. Some reminder that told her, this was not her world, but...how could it be?

Eighty-nine years. The world had changed so much, and she remembered most of it. Great, great grandchildren. A mass exodus from home to other countries. A general falling of global temperatures, mass starvations and war. Fighting like rats over what was left in the first world, only rats don't use missiles and guns.

Coming here alone, becoming fluent in Chilean Spanish. Marrying a farmer, bearing his children. Raising them in thin air, in a new world that was smaller, much more basic, bereft of the ambitions of previous centuries, but maintaining its knowledge. Surviving, and feeling joy at the simple act of waking up, each and every new day a gift of providence. A joy that was not complete. There was always that sense of loss. This was not the best it could be, not for anyone, but it was what humanity had left.

But the passage of time, somehow, had not aged her. Her breasts were firm, her skin supple, her vision sharp. What of that inconsistency in reality? Her mind couldn't address it. No, her mind itself was wrinkled, soft, blurry. She had always been here, and yet she'd only been here moments. Only moments...

Now, Lucy lay back on the roof of her modest stone house, on her mountain farm outside Calama, looking up. The only light came from the gibbous moon, now rising in the east, and from thirty thousand stars that filled the dark heavens.

No, there weren't thirty thousand stars. There were more, many more.

"There you are," whispered a voice next to her. English. A language she hadn't spoken in so long. The language of better days, of civilizations passed, of polluted skies and television, chicken wings and porn. It sounded young.

Lucy wasn't startled by the voice. After eighty-nine years, though her body felt no entropy, her mind was loosened, dazed. The voice wasn't enough to scare her.

"I was lucky that I found you in time," said the voice again. Did the language always seem so appropriate as when it was spoken by a child? Lucy knew who it was.

"It's...it's been so long..." she responded, in English, acutely aware of an accent she didn't have before, and yet...no...she'd had it for years.

"No...only an hour," said Justin. The boy lay down next to her, stared up at the sky.

"Do you know what happened here? Where and when we are?"

"I don't," said the boy. "Like you, I wandered the lifespaces looking for you. Once unstuck from your home, you can wander the possibilities for a lifetime. Parallels in the past...the future...anywhere, anytime. It really is all one."

Lucy nodded, even though neither of them were looking at each other. "The world I've known, prepared for, is gone."

260

The boy didn't move. "What happened?"

"War. Economic collapse. Environmental disaster. You name it, it happened. But here, I survived...I'm eighty-nine years old and don't look a day over twenty-eight. Why?"

"Your physical body moves through the lifespaces as is, and the freedom to move forward and backward in time doesn't happen except when Convergence is very close. I remember so much about what I've seen. The horrors. The losses. The goodbyes. They seem at once ages ago and minutes, like some waking dream in which you find yourself in a lifetime that isn't your own, but you play the part anyway."

A sniffle. Lucy looked over. He was weeping.

"Why are you crying?" she asked. Justin didn't respond right away. Around them, the silence of the mountains was near absolute, and the stars looked back at them, just as wordlessly.

"I'm not a bad person," said Justin, finally.

"Why would you be a bad person, kiddo?" The slang was returning.

"We're all bad people in some ways, aren't we? We do horrible things, don't we? No matter how smart or good we are. Sometimes?"

"Yes...sometimes we do," said Lucy.

Justin turned, wiped the tears from his face. "So...so good people do bad things?"

Lucy looked at him. Such sadness. She reached over and held his cheek, cold from the air.

"Every now and then. All you can do is remember not to do it again. Not to let the badness take over."

The boy looked at his mother, who could see a resolve of steel, of diamonds, forming behind his gaze.

"Future's unfrozen," he said.

"Lives and times and spaces can change there as well as now, as well as in the past," said Lucy.

"All I can do is remember..." he said. "Then...then that's what I'll do, when it comes back around. When it does, it'll be different" He sighed. "I'll be different."

In the dim rising moonlight, Lucy saw him grip the knuckles of his right hand.

"You're here to take me back?"

Justin sighed a puff of steam into the heavens. "No, I'm here to say goodbye. Convergence has only thirty minutes left in real time, and soon, all too soon, I'll be going back to my own lifespace, before I become unstuck from my home."

Lucy remembered: the beach, the fourth of July, so long ago...but only minutes from now. Minutes! Her whole countenance flared to life. She sat up on the roof of (not) her house.

"Then what do I do? I'm far from where I need to be."

Justin looked at her and smiled. He stood up, helping her to her feet.

Climbing down the ladder that led down from the roof, they stood in the gravel road leading away from the farmhouse to the main road. The moonlight was spreading over the darkness, stealing the night away.

"Face me, Mom," said Justin. Lucy obliged. Justin sighed.

"When I say so, take seven steps backward. Then turn around. No matter what you see, don't move."

"What are you doing?" asked Lucy.

"My being here keeps you grounded in whatever lifespace we're in. It's why I came here, to make sure you get to where you need to be okay. It's how you got lost when we got off the train at Salinas."

"What happened there? Who was that?"

"It's a long story, but it doesn't matter now, I've found you, and you're all right. I was supposed to take you straight to Carmel, but now we're out of time. All I can do is help you find the way on your own."

"How?"

"I'll tell you."

BY-THE-SEA

Rio Road was jam packed with cars. Having cruised for most of the day, and having had the apparent time dilations of the Convergence working his favor to get there on time, Max found the sudden delay frustrating as hell.

It was a left turn from the Cabrillo toward Carmel-by-the-Sea, and he'd barely passed the old mission when suddenly Rio Road turned into a parking lot. He sighed out loud. The Convergence could happen any time, and he was stuck in gridlock. He had to get to the beach.

Mindy watched him. "You look ugly when you're angry."

Max looked down at her, and had to grin. Mindy was more expressive than most, and the clinical seriousness with which she was regarding him now was so over the top, Max thought she was making a face, and waited for her to laugh. She did not.

"Uh...thanks, my ex-wife used to say the same thing."

"Do you miss her?" asked Mindy. Again, the seriousness.

Max took another breath. For once, focusing on past problems would help him feel better about present pains in his ass.

"Sometimes," he said.

Mindy leaned in, frowned.

"You sure you over her?"

That caught him off guard.

"What?"

Mindy didn't flinch, said nothing. In front of him, the cars were creeping along.

"Am I over her? Kid, why do you think I'm out here?"

"I dunno, why are you out here?"

"To find the girl of my dreams, don't you know? Who's definitely not my ex wife."

"Oh...and what's her name?" asked Mindy. Suddenly, she was neutral, though there were hints of a smile at the corner of her mouth.

"Lucy. Lucy Fitzgerald."

Mindy grinned, a prolonged, toothy grin. Max saw, not for the first time on the trip, that she was missing a baby tooth here and there.

"Okay, that works for me," she said.

"Um...thank you?"

A small break in the traffic allowed Max to turn onto Junipero. The roads here were wavy and hilly, and Max felt a little claustrophobic after all those miles of wide spaces and big skies that had led him here.

"So, where am I dropping you off?" asked Max.

"What?" asked Mindy.

"This is where I was taking you, right? So where am I dropping you off?"

"Um..." For the first time since he'd agreed to take her on, Max's young passenger seemed unsure of herself. "I don't think it's a good idea to drop me off right at the house."

"Why not?"

"Mom and Dad told me never show other people where we live."

Max had to laugh at that one. "Are you serious? But they told you it was okay to hitchhike? Jeez. Mindy, you really are an odd duck."

"I'm not a duck, I'm a girl," said Mindy, without missing a beat.

"Wow...okay, then, where should we stop?"

"Anywhere. Walking's faster than driving," said Mindy.

"You're telling me."

By this time, Max had reached 11th Avenue and the cars were still creeping along. Moreover, there were now legions of pedestrians making their way downtown in a steady flow. The sun was still high enough in the sky and the car was getting warm. Max checked the engine temperature and saw it was creeping up on the danger zone.

"How far is the beach from here?" asked Max.

"About twenty minutes."

"Works for me."

Max saw a spot immediately to his right, right at the bottom of a small muddy hill topped with black pines and leafy bushes. He pulled to the right and parked.

Max turned off the ignition and popped the trunk. Both he and Mindy opened the doors and gingerly stepped out. Walking around to the back, he collected Mindy's backpack.

He hadn't taken a good look at it the first time he'd seen it. A coral and chocolate brown color scheme, one large pocket, two smaller zippered pockets on the back. The whole thing seemed very new, as if she'd just bought it a few days ago.

Max looked up. Mindy was tying her shoes. This was his chance to do some snooping. A small slip of paper was sticking out of the slightly-opened zipper of the main pocket. If tugged, he'd be able to yank it out easily without tearing it. So Max did.

It was a receipt. Wal-Mart, no less, but it outlined the purchase of this one backpack on June 28th, 20—

No. No, that couldn't be right.

And yet... no...it all made sense.

She's...

"Hey!"

Max looked up. Mindy stood before him, arms crossed, head shaking.

"It's not polite to go through someone else's property. My Dad taught me that, you know."

"I'm sure he taught you a lot of things," said Max, putting the receipt back and handing the knapsack to its owner.

"Thank you."

"You're welcome." Max looked around. "So...we're here," he said.

Mindy had set the backpack on the ground. "We're here."

"And there are two errands I have to run before Convergence."

Mindy unzipped the main compartment. "This is true," she replied.

Max looked sharply into the girl's eyes. "And you're from the future."

Mindy wasn't expecting him to say that. She broke her gaze, looked down at the inside of the bag. She reached in.

"Maybe...I'm not supposed to tell you. It's part of the secret, and the joke."

"But that's how you knew where to find me?"

"Not only," said Mindy, taking out two large manila envelopes. "You're important for a bunch of reasons."

"I know I am," said Max. "Weaver told me."

Mindy stopped what she was doing, looked up, her eyes bright and wide

"He did?"

"Yes"

"He can't spoil it like that! It's not allowed," said Mindy.

"Well, I forced him. Told him I wasn't going to go any further unless he told me why."

Mindy frowned and stood up, still holding the two envelopes. She took one step forward, and kicked Max in the shin. A few passers-by took notice, but kept walking.

"Ow!" he shouted. "What did you do that for?"

"Because it's supposed to be your choice! You can't make choices for people. You told me that! Oops!"

Mindy covered her mouth with the envelopes, and Max grinned through his wince. The girl had quite the kick.

"First of all, Weaver didn't actually tell me any details, just that I had to go. My choice, so he's off the hook. And second...I told you? Like I told you not to say the S word? I never met you before today. That means we know each other in the future quite a bit, we have to have!" He stepped toward the girl, knelt before her on the unkicked leg.

"So tell me, who are we to each other? Who—"

It was then that Max looked at her. Really looked at her. Noticed the shape of her face. The brown of her eyes. The way that she walked with her left foot turned slightly inward, same as him.

The feeling of protectiveness and connection Max had felt almost immediately after meeting her.

And he started to understand...

Mindy smiled, no doubt seeing the look on his face.

"You get it now?" she asked.

Max nodded. The girl giggled.

"Take these," said Mindy, handing him the two manila envelopes.

"What's inside?"

Mindy now leaned in, and she put her arms around Max's neck and pulled him into a hug. And Max found himself hugging her back, and it was the most natural feeling in the world, that everything was going to be okay.

Mindy whispered.

"It's your whole life, Daddy."

***

"I stand here, I keep the doorway open," said Justin. "You stand on the threshold and watch for your gateway to Carmel Beach, on the 4th of July, where Dad's waiting."

Lucy stood in the dark, back toward her son. The moon was now lighting the entire hilltop. She could see the land sweeping away from the house, the other peaks in the distance where the high ground dropped off, thousands of feet below the cloud line.

"How will I know which one?" asked Lucy. "There are too many."

"You have ninety-two lifespaces. This is one of them. The way back to Carmel will show up sooner or later. You'll just have to be fast."

"We could be here for a long time," said Lucy. "I've already wasted so much time."

"I found you, it's all right. You'll stop shifting as long as I'm here. When the time comes, tell me to step back, and you step forward."

Lucy felt a lump in her throat. "And what happens to you?"

"I go home."

"Just like that?"

"Just like that."

Lucy tried to smile through her fear. "No bullshit?"

Justin smiled back. "No, no bullshit."

7TH AND JUNIPERO

"So what are these 'errands' I have to run?"

The intersection at 7th and Junipero was crowded with people, many of them decked out in Fourth of July attire. Carmel was a contradiction, a tiny little down with the atmosphere of a busy downtown square. But Mindy had taken his hand and was leading him through the masses toward where they needed to go.

"They're really simple," said Mindy, her voice barely registering over the din. "You just have to mail something."

"Okay, but isn't the post office going to be closed today? Where is it?"

"Across town near Hog's Breath," said Mindy, "but you won't need them for this."

"Why?"

"These have to be hand delivered."

"And why do I have to do it? Who are they going to?"

They crossed Junipero to the other side of 7th. A small pedestrian shopping plaza, built on three levels Latin American style, was brimming with American flags and children running to and fro with big balloons as their parents watched, lay right in front of them. As soon as they crossed, Mindy gripped Max's hand and they ran through the center courtyard where there were games, vendors, and what seemed to be a Mexican children's pop band performing on a small stage.

Mindy dragged them both to the other side of the plaza and stopped them. Before them was a small doorway leading out to the next intersection. Max could see the sign: Ocean Avenue.

Mindy removed her backpack and took out one of the manila envelopes. Handing it to Max, she pointed to the doorway.

"Here, your first errand's right there," she said.

Max looked toward the doorway, and had no idea what she was talking about.

"Start walking," she said. "We're running out of time."

Max looked at Mindy. Her face was neutral, but her eyes belied a sense of command that was absolute.

He started walking.

Three feet.

Four.

At five feet, he saw his surroundings slow down. The mass of people blurred around him in a swirl of flesh and cloth and plastic. Max felt the queasiness again, but kept going.

Six feet.

Then, seven.

He found himself in the In-Between again. He looked ahead, seeing a dark alley in a snow-speckled city under a gray sky. He turned back to Mindy, just in time to watch her take one step back.

The cold air hit him like a slap in the face. Max's summer wear gave him absolutely no protection here. It was dark, and snow was falling from above. That disgusting orange hue of streetlights illuminated a largely empty alley, save for a few garbage cans that sat beside the evenly spaced doors backing onto the space.

Max turned around and found he could no longer see Carmel Beach, but he knew, he felt that Mindy was still there. Taking one step back toward where he came, the doorway reopened, and he could see her. She waved. He waved back. He was all right.

No cars passed in front, but Max could hear the constant background whooshing of the living city, off in the distance. Above, the sky was maroon gray, the color of winter night, and though most of the buildings he could see had windows, very few of them were lit. Must have been late at night.

Just ahead, about twenty feet away, a figure stumbled into view, wandering his way with all the dignity he could muster. He wore dark ripped jeans and a torn leather jacket, black boots. The figure stopped, drew out something from his coat pocket. A little bag, by the looks of it. Max watched him shake the contents onto his bare palms and lick it, swallowing it down.

He stopped when he turned and saw Max standing there.

"Who are you?" he shouted. "Leave me alone, will ya? Get lost!"

Familiar voice. Too familiar, almost awkward to hear spoken out loud. Max held his ground.

The figure stormed toward him now, all traces of clumsiness gone, but Max still didn't move. He knew who it was.

"Hey, asswipe, I said mo—"

Max...Detroit Max, the Alternate who had sent Max on this adventure, stood before him. Only gone was the certainty in his eyes, the cocksure attitude of success and the need to do what was right.

Max had a hunch.

"What's the date today, pal?" he asked. The Alternate, unsure of what was happening, hesitated before answering.

"March 4th, 2009... you look just like me. Who are you?"

Max smiled. Mindy was right: he knew exactly what do say. He knew what was in the envelopes. And he knew why there were two of them.

"I'm you're optimal."

The Alternate's bloodshot eyes narrowed.

"What?" Then he saw how Max was dressed.

"Mister, you are fucked up."

"No...no way, guy, that's not possible."

"Dude? Are you kidding me? You are talking to yourself right now!"

The Detroit Alternate was being the same type of stubborn asshole he'd accused Max of being. Only Max was persistent. And why not? This had already happened before. Anything he said now would make this work.

Still, Max was grateful that the Alternate had loaned him his coat.

Max took a breath as he looked around, turned to the Alternate, and handed him the envelope.
"Take this," he said.

"What is it?' asked the Alternate.

"It's everything you need to know, outside of what I've told you. Convergence is coming, my friend. Just ask Mr. Weaver."

"Yeah, and who the hell's that?" asked the Alternate.

"You'll see."

Turning around, Max could still sense Mindy and Carmel-by-the-Sea, shimmering behind him through the portal, seemingly invisible to the Alternate, who would have most likely said something had he seen an interdimensional doorway.

"If you haven't met him yet," said Max, turning back to face his Alternate, "you will, all in good time." He pointed to the envelope. "Read that, and if you have any more questions, save them for Weaver. I've got to go."

Max took off the coat, tossed it back to his Alternate. He turned around, and acting more on instinct than any solid theory of interdimensional travel, headed back toward where he had come. The Alternate's voice behind him stopped him.

"Two questions." Max looked back at the Alternate.

"Yeah?"

The Alternate stepped forward.

"So...if you're the Optimal, you've already snagged Lucy, right?"

"Um...no...not yet."

"Then how can you consider yourself the best of us?"

Max thought about his response.

"Because I'm about to be," he said.

The Alternate looked at him, then grinned.

"Huh."

"Huh, indeed," replied Max.

"We ever going to meet again?"

Max turned to leave, then turned back.

"That's three questions. And nope."

Max vanished from the alley…

…and reappeared in the plaza, and the warm sunny air of Carmel. Someone — a fat woman with rosascia, bumped into him, turned and gave him a dirty look before continuing on. Mindy was right there.

"How did no one see me?" asked Max.

"No one can see anything in this crowd," said Mindy. "How did you do?"

"Great," said Max. "How did you not lose me?"

"This gateway's solid," said Mindy, who handed him the second envelope.

"C'mon, next stop is the Beach! Hurry!"

***

Tommy recognized what Justin was doing.

He also knew that it had a better than average chance of working. Given that all the veils between lifespaces were falling, that the frequency of the appearance of the portals was increasing, and given that she only had ninety-two Alternate lifespaces to choose from while so many others had hundreds, even thousands...the odds were good that Lucy would find her way back to Max.

Tommy and Justin stood twenty feet apart. A few minutes ago, Tommy could have sneaked across the black, but the moon was now shining. He'd have to approach, slow and soft, and get the jump on them.

This one would be easier. This time, he'd do it right, and make sure that the beating he'd just sustained from his father was the last one either one would ever experience.

***

"How long do I have?" asked the Alternate.

"Not as long as you'd think," said Max.

They stood on the streets of Glastonbury, Pennsylvania. It was raining — warm, late spring rain that contained all hope and excitement for a new summer, much better than Detroit in winter — and the sidewalks along Oak Knoll Road were empty. Century-old trees hung their branches low over the sidewalk, bearing adolescent leaves that Max was careful to avoid as they talked about Convergence.

Despite the dark gray, the Alternate wore dark sunglasses and carried his umbrella low over his face. Despite the surprising openness that he had shown to the concept and reality of the Convergence, he didn't feel comfortable revealing his likeness to the new guest in this place. The neighbors might talk. That talk might reach the wife. And once the wife started asking questions, she wouldn't stop.

"And this Mr....Weaver, will find me at some point to explain the rest?" asked the Alternate.

"That he will," said Max. "In the meantime, the contents of the envelope will get you started."

"I see."

The two men stood in silence for a minute or so.

"So...you really are the optimal version of me? Of us?" asked the Alternate.

"I am," replied Max, with absolutely no hesitation.

"But you're not a teacher. You're still a phone concierge. You and Dinah divorced."

"Nope, and yep," said Max.

"Huh," said the Alternate. "Doesn't sound like it's the best life to me."

"You know what I've come to appreciate from this whole experience, Max?"

"What's that?"

"That every risk I've taken has paid off. It's paying off right now. It will pay off in the future. That it's all going to be okay, even if I haven't yet gotten what I'm looking for. That I never settled."

"Are you saying that's what I'm doing?" said the Alternate. Max looked him in the face. He could only slightly see his Alternate's eyes staring back at him from under the sunshades.

"I'm not saying anything," said Max. "You made your set of choices, and I made mine."

"But you think yours were better," replied the Alternate. "Because you're on the verge of getting the bigger, better things you were willing to risk everything for? Am I right?"

Max didn't answer. His Alternate nodded.

"Oh, I get it...well, let me tell you something, friend. I'm perfectly happy with what I've chosen, and what I've got. Great job, great house, great wife, great life. You can go look down your nose at some other Alternate."

Max frowned. "I'm not saying anything of the sort, Max—"

"Oh, like hell!" The Alternate tipped his umbrella back, tucked the manila envelope in his armpit and removed the sunglasses with the other.

"You can stand there and judge me all you want, Max, but I'm perfectly happy with the choices I've made. I have no regrets. Absolutely none."

Max raised an eyebrow and stepped into his Alternate's personal space. "Who do you think you're talking to, Max? You think you can fool me with your bullshit just because you say it with that faux Ivy League diction of yours? Of course you have regrets. You've got ten years' worth of them. You used to dream big, bud, but you got used to playing the sure bets. That's what marriage to Dinah does to you. Just that you're too much of an arrogant gasbag to admit it to anyone, not even yourself."

The Alternate flushed, couldn't meet his gaze. Max continued.

"But you know what? I'm actually not judging you on anything, because for all of your risk aversion, you've got things in your life that I wish I had years ago. You have your pride and your energy. It's who you are, but I'm looking for more. And so are you, if you're honest with yourself."

Max pointed to the envelope, tucked under Oak Knoll Max's arm. "Convergence is going to happen, whether you want it to or not. And you've got a part to play to help make things better for everyone. You think you're the optimal and not me? Not any other Alternate? Here's your chance to find out."

He took a breath. Max could see the jaw muscles grinding behind the Alternate's face. None of the pretentious foppery he'd shown, and would show, at Weaver's Diner. This was the real deal.

Sure, the Alternate had no regrets. No regrets whatsoever.

"That's all I have for you," said Max. "Weaver will find you when he finds you. Then you'll understand. Good luck."

Max took a step back and turned around, walking back the way he'd come, back to the beach.

"Take another step," a voice said as he returned to Carmel.

***

Lucy watched in silent awe at the manifest realizations of all the possibilities of her life from the In-Between.

Such riches and adventures beyond what she had seen before. And such tragedies. And yet, even the best ones she had seen could not equal what she had in this one.

So it was that Lucy realized that she was the optimal version of all Lucy Fitzgeralds in all of space and time. And she had to find her way back.

Justin stayed within range, shifting back and forth on his heels if it seemed his mother was going to get pulled into the In-Between and be lost again. He had been staring at her with such focus that he did not hear Tommy sneaking up on him until it was too late.

"Take another step," a voice said.

Lucy looked back.

A figure — a kid, maybe a little younger than Justin — holding the gun, aiming at her son.

She turned to see Justin, staring at the new arrival with a curious mix of fear, defiance, and guilt on his face. He dug his heels into the ground.

"Mom, it's okay," he said. "Turn back and keep looking for the doorway."

But Lucy stood still. Behind her, the shimmering whiteness of the space between the spaces sat, seamlessly opening the way to the other lifespaces. She couldn't see, but she knew that the gateways to all of her ninety-two Alternate lives were opening and closing at a speed just beyond the ability of her mind's perception. Behind her was the way home, and she had to muster whatever speed she could.

But how do you turn your back to someone aiming a gun at your child? How do you do that?

Lucy heard a click. The figure was now standing still. "Take a step, Lucy. I don't want to kill you, but you know how this goes. Do what I'm telling you."

"He won't do it, Mom," said Justin. "Don't move until you feel ready."

Tommy lifted the gun and fired it. In the vast openness of the high Andes, it may as well have been an atom bomb. Lucy's shoulders leaped in surprise, but her feet remained where they were.

"I'm serious!" shouted the gunman. "I've stopped you every other chance I've gotten, and I'm not going to lose this close to the end."

"If you were going to kill us, you would have done it at the airport," said Justin.

"Seems the universe believes in second chances."

Justin put his hands up and began walking toward the figure. Lucy saw her surroundings shimmering, and she saw that he was walking on a curve, at the very edges of where he could walk for her to remain here.

"Do you really believe that?" asked Justin. "That you can have a second chance?"

The figure did not move, but shifted his aim toward her son as he drew to within five feet of the intruder.

"Because if you do, then you need to believe that I can change, too. That what you went through doesn't have to happen."

"Stop where you are," said the figure. Justin stopped. Four feet separated them, but it was just far enough to push Lucy into the threshold between worlds.

"I'm sorry for what you went through," said Justin.

"No you're not," said the figure.

"Yes, I am. And I know sorry isn't enough. But I can promise you this much: I won't forget you, and I'll remember that when the moment comes where I start down this path, I'll choose differently. I promise." The figure said nothing, and the stalemate remained.

Lucy wondered what the hell this was all about. Who was this kid? What had he gone through? These questions were muted, however. Someone was holding a gun to her child. That hadn't changed.

"Justin," called Lucy. "What's going on?"

"Mom, keep looking, keep—"

The figure swung around and aimed the gun at Lucy.

"No!" shouted Justin.

The figure fired.

By pure reflex, Lucy jumped back through the doorway, entering the In-Between, and leaving behind her son and the gunman on that Andean plain to whatever fate awaited them in that distant future.

***

Tommy was dying.

The cold was almost as crippling as the bullet wound in his stomach that was bleeding out in hot, surging gushes. Only seconds now. Seconds to live.

He'd gotten his wish. Tommy would not live. But that didn't necessarily mean that he would never be born. And Justin Sinclair was gone, but that didn't necessarily mean that he was no longer alive. Both of them had grappled with the gun in the last few moments before Justin had vanished, and the gun had gone off twice. Whether or not Tommy had hit Justin was immaterial. Justin had gotten the weapon and pulled the trigger at the right moment. After that, nothing else mattered.

Crawling to the edge of the grassy cliff, Tommy could feel his systems shutting down, death encroaching on all sides, cold. In the little time he had left, he thought of his pathetic life, all the hurt he had sustained, the wasteland of a home and way of life that had succumbed to disaster before he was able to enjoy the fruits of that dead civilization. He thought of Michelle, the closest thing to love he'd ever felt, except for poor Aunt Mindy, who had cared for him like her own baby.

"What a fucking waste," he muttered as he reached the edge and peered over. Before him, a field of stratus clouds, impossibly low, stretched across lands he could not see. A few dark peaks rose above, silhouetted in the moonlight. On the horizon, stars glittered by the thousands.

Then…it all went fuzzy. This is it. This is death.

Only…

No…he was unstuck.

By degrees, another scene began to appear.

Grass underneath him. Cold grass…

No, not grass.

Sand.

Tommy found himself in sand. Pain from the wound still stabbed at him, but his midsection was starting to numb, allowing him to look around.

The beach was busy, but the crowds were scattered, and no one seemed to be within earshot, or notice the wounded teenager in a heap only feet away from the parking lot.

All except one, a little girl of about seven or eight with reddish-brown hair, a black shirt, and jeans. The girl was looking at him. And smiling.

"Hi," she said. Tommy managed to get to a dignified sitting position.

"Hi," he said back. No point in asking for help: he could already feel the life draining away from his torso. The girl noticed his wound, and alarm briefly crossed her face, only to be washed away by what Tommy could only describe as sad compassion.

"Mr. Weaver said I'd meet you here, too," said the girl. "He wanted me to tell you that if you made it this far, then you did everything you were supposed to, and it worked."

Where had he seen her before? The girl's face was so familiar.

"He sent me to die," said Tommy. "And I didn't do a damn thing right."

The girl was about three feet away and didn't budge. A worker, most definitely. She was anchoring someone here. But who?

"No, Thomas," said the girl, "you did okay. It's all gonna work out now."

The way she'd said Thomas…the voice was far younger, but the way she'd said it…

"Min?"

The girl nodded. "Yep. Min. Short for Mindy."

She smiled, and for the first time in a long time, Tommy remembered that he was loved once. Through bloodied teeth, he smiled back.

A wave of queasiness appeared, and Tommy's head swam and swooned as he saw the beach, the sand, and Mindy, his Aunt Min, the younger version of the only relative who'd ever loved him, all dissolve away.

Cold mountain air replaced the sun, and he was back in the Andes, on the patch of grass at the edge of the valley.

Tommy shifted his weight onto his back, feeling blood running up his throat and spilling out the side of his mouth.

Looking up now at a clear night sky, Tommy realized what he had done. He hadn't any proof, but when you only have seconds to live, your mind achieves one last gasp of insight, leaping beyond strings of mere logic or eye-witness evidence, to immanent knowledge of what is. Your awareness starts to detach itself from the dying mass of flesh and sees everything it had missed while being body-bound.

What Tommy saw in those few seconds was that Lucy had made it to the one place she needed to be for this to work. That Max was there with her, and that Mindy was no doubt keeping him grounded. That both would wake up together in the right space, in the right time, for the Convergence.

Tommy saw that all would be as it was going to be.

And yet, that it would be different. Better.

Tommy saw that he'd been more of a part of Weaver's plans than he had given the old man credit for.

Staring up at the stars, Tommy started counting them all. Ten...no, thirteen...fourteen...fifteen...

Thirty-thousand stars. Somewhere, he had heard that number. That on any given night, there were thirty thousand stars in the sky.

That was the last thought that passed through his mind as Tommy rose into death.

***

"Take another step," said Mindy. "You're still in the doorway."

"Sorry."

Max stepped out of the men's restroom just overlooking Carmel Beach.

Immediately he saw that the lighting had changed: the sun was lower in the sky, setting the clouds hovering over the land to the east in pink and orange. The light from around stung the eyes at the corners, and Max squinted as he turned around to see how many people were now gathering at the beach.

The restroom building stood atop the last small hill, about fifteen feet above the beach itself. To get to the water, all he had to do was descend through the cool, white sand. Weaver had said, "head for the water." Max was there now.

Considering how crowded the rest of the town was, he was shocked to see so few people on the beach itself, especially on a day like this.

"How come all of these other people don't feel anything? Oh wait, don't tell me. They're not the special ones."

Mindy smiled.

"Mmhmm!" She looked at him with a big smile. "They won't know a thing. Did you meet the others?"

Max saw this little girl — his little girl — beaming at him.

"Mmhmm!" he replied.

Mindy clapped. "Yay! Now I can go home."

She ran up to him and hugged him. A quick hug, but tight. Before he could hug her back, Mindy broke away and started running in the opposite direction.

"Wait! Wait a second!"

Mindy stopped, about three feet away. Max held his hands open in question.

"That's it?" he asked. "We're done? How long until Convergence?"

Mindy looked up and away. "Um...about ten minutes."

"Ten minutes? And you're leaving?"

"Mmhmm!"

Max walked closer. "How am I supposed to stay put for that long?"

"It'll be fine now," said Mindy.

"Uh-huh," said Max. "And what about the whole thing about me being your dad?" He smiled. The thought made him feel so happy, happier than he would have thought he would be.

"What about it?"

"C'mon, kid — I'm sorry. I mean c'mon, Mindy. How could you tell me that and not expect me to be curious about it? There's so much I want to ask you."

Mindy looked right at him, and that power and authority returned one last time.

"Ask me the only question that really matters. You know the one."

He suddenly felt very heavy hearted. Max took a deep breath, for it had been in the back of his mind. A feeling he couldn't identify when he'd first met this little girl, hours ago it seemed, though time being what it was, he could no longer be sure it wasn't a whole lifetime. It felt like he'd known this girl forever. And as that time had demonstrated, she knew all too well what was on his mind.

"Am I a good dad?"

Mindy walked up to him, tugged his shirt. Max knelt down until he was eye level with her. Without a word, Mindy leaned in, and Max found himself rubbing his nose against hers, side to side. Mindy giggled, and so did Max, who found his heart lighter. In that moment, he felt like he could do anything he wanted, and he'd be willing to give this soul the best of everything he could muster.

Mindy kissed him on the cheek.

"The best."

She pulled away, then waved at him. As Mindy turned and ran toward the parking lot, Max felt a suddenly sense of alarm. The question returned: wouldn't he become unstuck?

But Mindy soon ran past the eight foot mark, and nothing happened. He watched her turn around the corner and vanish.

"You've got one more thing to do, son," a man's voice said behind him.

Weaver stood where the doorway had been, standing in front of the sun, making it hard for Max to make out his face. He could see Weaver was wearing an old-fashioned gray and black suit, much like the ones worn in Dickensian times by wealthy merchants. He was missing the top hat, but he did have the cane.

"Who are you, Mr. Weaver?"

Weaver smiled, looked down.

"Someone who used to be like you," he said. "Don't 'member much about where I came from, don't really care anymore. But I know this much: I am the only one of my kind. Only one space where my momma and daddy were able to get together."

Weaver started to pace, and Max was mindful to follow him, keeping close to avoid slipping out of this place.

284

"They's extra special, you know? The children of those who only exist in one lifespace in the 'verse. Gifted with powers that nobody expects them to have. Talents."

"And what was your talent, Mr. Weaver?" asked Max.

Weaver stopped, looked up. "Threading gold into the tapestry. Starting at the end, and moving back to the beginning, then back again. Looping a thread here, cutting one there, until it's all done. I've done it once. Doin' it now. And I'm gonna do it again. Always and everywhere. World without end. Amen."

Weaver pointed at Max with his cane. "And you know you an' Lucy ain't the only golden threads. There are many. Together, all will bring light and gold to history and the future."

Max stood at rapt attention. "Then why didn't you just move us together directly? Why the adventure?"

"Because most of you don't choose it at first," said Weaver. "Threads that don't want to stay will fray, ruin the tapestry. Ain't for no mythical reason why we make sure that you gotta choose, son: it's practical. People have to grow up on they own before they grow old together. They gotta realize that it's worth the risk to want the best outcome. You gotta choose joy, son, 'cause it don't choose you by accident. Joy is conscious energy. It's alive, has a mind of its own. You gotta want it. That's the only way that what we weave stays in place. The whole tapestry shines brighter for it."

Max thought back to all those years, unsure of himself, what he wanted, tolerating mediocrity because it was better than what some people had, because he was "lucky." How much he'd learned in that time, and in this small time, less than a week since he'd left everything behind.

"It's going to be all right, then?" asked Max.

Weaver smiled. "Almost time," he said.

"She...Lucy's really on her way?"

"Almost," said Weaver. "Are you ready, then, to wake up, Max?"

"What do you mean?"

"You've been asleep for a long time," said Weaver. "The dream isn't something you wake up from. You awake into it. You've created so much of this moment, but somehow you're still sleeping, and that can't work. Not when all hours are about to become one instant."

An old feeling suddenly appeared on the periphery of Max's experience. A sensation, like someone calling your name from a great distance. A subtle shaking of the shoulder by small hands. And, he saw, a shimmering on the edges of sky and ocean. It was the feeling he'd felt at the compass rose, way back in the beginning, before Lucy had called.

"This…is a dream?" he asked.

"Not literally, child," said Weaver. "This is real, and that's the beauty of it all. And yet, in only three minutes and one second in absolute time, will you be able to look back and tell the difference? Will it matter?"

Weaver put his hand on Max's shoulder. "You are special, Maxim Sinclair. And so is young Lucy. Both of you have opened up to your great powers — her faith in higher mathematics, your great creativity — and have made many new worlds possible. You've already done it, are doing it, and will do it again."

Max smiled. "Always and everywhere."

Weaver grinned and clapped him on the shoulder, the first time he had smiled so openly in the time Max had known him.

"World without end."

Max looked down. "Amen."

"Look over there." Weaver turned and pointed to the ocean. Max didn't see anything.

"What am I looking at?"

Suddenly, there was no longer a hand on his shoulder. Max turned. Weaver was gone.

DREAM GUY

Lucy stood facing northeast, to the sea.

Their backs were to each other, but each knew, without touching, without speaking, that the other was there.

The compass rose had been painted on, fresco-style, into the concrete of the walkway as the cement had dried. Both stood near the center, five feet away from each other.

Leading up to the compass rose from the east was a path that led through the grass lined with many little shrubs, poplars, and flowers. The path ran out along the shore, into the fog, and out of sight.

Lucy noticed the tree lined boardwalk at the water's edge, emerging out of the thick cloud of fog hanging at the edge of the cul-de-sac where they stood on the compass, opened up from a narrow pink and coral brick work into the concrete enclosure, then narrowed beyond it and continued on into another patch of thick fog.

There was anticipation, nervous electricity in the pit of her stomach, in the middle of her heart. Was this their fateful meeting?

In her thoughts, Lucy saw Max: dark brown hair, simple T-shirt and jeans, standing right behind her, looking away.

"This is a dream," said Lucy, and her voice echoed throughout the park, in the vacuum.

"What else could it be?" said Max, and his voice followed hers over the trees, rocks, playgrounds, and grass.

"It feels pretty awake to me," she said.

"But we're not awake," she heard Max say, "meaning this is—"

"something in between."

The answer was satisfying, as satisfying a solution as either one of them was able to accept as they looked around the dreamscape.

"Where are we?" asked Lucy.

"The ocean, a park," said Max. "I wonder if we can wake up..."

"Do you really want to?" she asked.

Lucy heard Max speak. "No, not really."

She turned around and felt Max right beside her. She tried to look at him, only to see him dissolve into nothing before her eyes. She realized, without knowing why, that in this place, they could never look directly at each other. Not here.

Lucy giggled.

"What are you—" said Max.

Poof!

"We're in a dream, after all," said Lucy. "Why not have some fun?"

Poof!

"Stop that!" he shouted. And Lucy had to stop herself from doubling over from laughter.

"That's it."

Poof! West-southwest. She felt sick to her stomach at the same time, enjoyed the dizzy playing around in the dreamscape. She found that twirling around helped her spot him faster.

They turned, vanishing and reappearing the other at various spots throughout the compass rose.

Soon, there they were, spinning around like kids on the playground, jumping in and out of existence like flashes of childhood memory, like stars born and swallowed up and reborn again into the firmament with the speed and light of fireflies.

"Stop now, I feel sick," she said, holding her stomach as she recovered her balance.

Poof! Lucy reappeared behind and to the right of her, and they began their game again.

At one point, they appeared directly facing each other, and for that split second of being, they saw each other. Lucy saw Max's hazel eyes and the goofiest look on his face that melted her heart and made her laugh even more.

More importantly was the perception of the other's soul, the equal and complementary energy that at once completed and added to the completeness of each of them and both of them. They were Prime. And this was their first time truly together.

Then they stopped, both of them exhausted and nauseous, their sides hurting from laughter. They stood back-to-back once more, at the center of the compass rose now. Lucy faced northwest. Max faced southeast.

And they knew it was about to end. The dreamscape had started to shimmer at the edges.

"Is this is as close as we can get?" asked Lucy, the tenderness in her voice revealing the intensity of the soul's desire now palpable in the dream space.

"Let's see," said Max, with equal desire and tenderness.

She felt his hand reach hers. They touched.

"We're waking up," she said.

"I know," he replied.

"And you don't need to worry about anything," she said.

"Why?"

"Because what's real isn't what anyone else says it is. What's real is what's right here."

"But this is a dream."

"But it's our dream."

"I—"

"Close your eyes."

Lucy felt the tip of his nose touch hers, cool and moist and delicate, felt his hot breath on her face as she knew it was time, felt the firmness of his body against hers. And she knew that this was a beautiful place, and a moment that was beautiful no matter what. In her mind, she declared it real. And reality never seemed so joyous.

And Lucy suddenly found the way home. Transformed by this (non)dream, she could feel Max's essence, and knew and felt the doorway open up to where she needed to be. All she had to do was carry that feeling and leave this place. This was the junction to the end of the adventure...

Lucy found herself at Carmel Beach, sitting at the end of the little isthmus that jutted out into the sea. And she remembered. It was the Fourth of July.

CONVERGENCE

And Max found himself staring at the ocean.

The Pacific, as deep and surreal as any dream of man or beast. And the beach was mostly empty, though off in the distance, a few hundred feet away, a group of teens were huddled around one particular spot, probably up to no good. And though Max was free to walk, unobstructed and unencumbered, he also knew he was stuck, grounded in this place, in this time, by the energy of the dream of the compass rose. It would be soon, any second now.

***

Lucy felt the spray of the sea against her legs. One minute, the compass rose had been there, the next it was gone, and she was here, sitting on rock, the narrow tidal isthmus extending out into the swirling ocean sunset.

She was grounded, because another soul — one with the power to keep her here — was nearby. Justin was gone, and a millisecond of terror flashed through her system before calm settled over. A sensation that told her everything was all right. Despite all that she had witnessed, Lucy took a breath and embraced the faith that those who had done the math would keep her son safe in this critical time.

The dream of the compass rose had given her direction and a sense of space, and she was right where she needed to be. Her mind fluttered with the wings of thousands of little thoughts and worries, but the noise turned to static, then background noise, then silence as she became aware of the familiar smell of her surroundings and the feeling of sand under her feet.

Any second now. It would be any second now.

Someone else was here. Someone familiar, and yet new all at once.

***

Turning to the true west, the sun was blinding orange and gold, and Max was forced to look just to the left of it to be able to see.

A small outcropping of primordial stone jutted out into the water, seven feet away. Max noticed it was partly covered in patches of beach sand, and it had been disturbed recently, sandal prints made hours ago by some stranger, almost obliterated by the wind.

There stood a young lady with red hair that caught slivers of sunlight here and there and gleamed with dusk. She stood with her back turned, looking to the horizon.

Max watched her turn.

***

Lucy got to her feet and turned toward the shore. The small isthmus ran seven feet back to the beach. She felt the heat of the sunset on her back as she glanced a group of people on the beach, little ants in the sandbox. Before her stood a man with familiar posture, facing her.

Lucy started moving toward Maxim Sinclair ("Call me Max").

***

Max could see brilliant scarlet hair caught by a fast gust of wind, blazing in the dying sunlight. Lost in the glare, her face seemed to possess a light of its own, the light of a soul long lost to him that he had finally found.

A warmth started in Max's solar plexus. A nova that exploded into new heat and life, his heart leaping, his awareness reaching a dizzy zenith

Max started walking toward Luthien Fitzgerald ("but you can call me Lucy").

***

Whether it was some effect of the imminent Convergence, Lucy didn't know. Probably not, as walking feet had never carried her faster in her life as they did that day. It was the Fourth of July.

***

Max found the space around him blurring. But this was no dream. Seven feet never seemed so far away, and yet they passed behind him quickly.

He vaguely heard someone shout to his far left. The group of teens was scattering.

***

They met halfway and froze.

The seconds that passed between them seemed so, so much longer, the lifetime of civilizations rising and falling in the spaces between heartbeats, but Maxim Sinclair and Luthien Fitzgerald didn't take note of these millisecond histories as they elapsed into oblivion. Only now mattered. Now...

Now...

A whistling noise. Off to Max's left, Lucy's right, a single firework crackled and launched. It rose a few hundred feet in the air, and then exploded. A supernova. A new star.

Lucy broke the spell first and laughed. Max laughed back.

The energies around them, that connected them, that brought them here from different coasts and lifetimes, flared like light of a thousand supernovas in dozens more brilliant galaxies in a dark universe.

They hugged, and it was like coming home, like being three years old and laughing with the purest delight at Santa's bounty under the tree. Like the first day of summer holidays.

He spun her around, and how easy it was to carry her through the air! How good she felt to be lifted and spun!

They whirled like the dervishes of Turkey and Afghanistan, like the lovers in Manhattan, only now it was the real Lucy, the one now in Max's arms and who held him in her slender grip, the one who called him to begin this adventure.

Lucy thought of the heartbreak in Seattle, all of the setbacks and choices and little coincidences that had led her to this moment, and in other life spaces, of the loss of her old life and the acquisition of everything she wanted simply by being alive at this time in the universe's endless machinations.

And both remembered, and saw, all the possibilities, the lifetimes and life spaces, past, present, and future, reality and conjecture, all of which were real in and of themselves.

Around them, the world was solid, and yet both could sense, beyond their peripheral vision, all of the different possibilities extant, all of the other spaces and times intersecting, overlapping, melding into this single probability. The certainty and absolute rightness of this choice, above all outcomes.

Maxim Sinclair and Lucy Fitzgerald released, and the world was still there, though some distance away. Twin soul met the gaze of twin soul, and Max put his forehead on hers.

"Hi," he said, wiping tears from his face and Lucy's too.

Lucy laughed, cupped his face in her hands.

"Hi back."

The sun grew brighter.
Now.
All moments one.
Convergence
They kissed.

LABYRINTH

The wedding party cheered.

So did all the guests.

Lucy and Max released from their embrace under the gazebo, and Max had the most extraordinary expression on his face that, to Lucy, only added to his handsomeness on this important day.

Of course, he'd just married the love of his life, but that particular joy wasn't enough to sum up the expression on his face.

Lucy also felt it, and Max saw in her gorgeous, wedding day expression the same exquisite gaze in her eyes.

Throughout the cheers and whoops, Max and Lucy both pondered the same questions that all those emerging from peak experiences ask themselves, in different mental words, of course, but all based in the same underlying thoughts.

Max remembered a story about a psychiatrist who dreamed of the French Revolution, a dream that seemed to last for days, but really spawned when part of his bed head had fallen on his neck, simulating a guillotine. An epic drama, unfolding in the millisecond it takes for cold wood to touch human skin. And yet, that memory, too, seemed to manifest from their nuptial embrace.

Lucy remembered the minister pronouncing them husband and wife, remembered looking into his eyes, her heart full and light, feeling her lips touch the lips of the man she loved most in the world and the sweet dark that comes with the closing of her eyes and the surrender to kisses. It had only been a delicate instant ago, and somehow, the time between had spanned what felt like months.

The memories of what they had been through were now faded, and as in the case of all dreams and fantasies, the imagery, once sharp as real life, was a fuzzy evanescence of sounds and sights, feelings and thoughts.

Lucy and Max returned their attention to where they were, the sudden memories of a busy schedule for the day, the months of choosing centerpieces and invitation cards, all coming back into their memories. And yet, the otherworldly disorientation remained, like floating twelve feet off the ground. Then again, they had just gotten married. No earthly elation lifts you as high.

The newlyweds turned to wave at the guests. The wedding party — the Nates, Michael, Steven, Dominic, Max's close friends from college and work, along with Lucy's bridesmaids Alice, Daphne, and Ivy from the studio — stood beside them, all smiles. Their parents were there, sitting front and center on either side of the little white chairs brought here, to this garden. Mary and Jeffrey Sinclair, of course, had already seen their boy get married once, and Max remembered some skepticism at first when he'd told them his desire to wed a girl he'd only known for a few months. Then they'd met Lucy and understood.

"There's something about her that's different than Dinah," said Mary. "Like something in the air between you when you talk." One visit was all it had taken to convince Max's parents of what they'd known.

As for Lucy's mom and dad, there had been no controversy. They were just thrilled to see their daughter, who had worked so hard to get her life in order, to finally find this last piece of the puzzle.

But then Max saw Herb Weaver standing at the end of the aisle, classy and well groomed in a black pinstripe suit and looking every bit the old gentleman. Though he technically didn't have to attend once they'd gotten the plans approved and settled up all the fees, the park's events coordinator said that he always enjoyed dressing up. It was good to have him here in case anything went wrong. So far, nothing had. Weaver had managed everything smoothly.

Looking a few rows back on the bride's side, Lucy saw Kate Castillo and Richard, also very well dressed, Richard smiling broadly at them as he clapped. Though it hadn't been much of a drive for them, she hadn't seen them in years. And yet, it seemed like it was only an hour ago that they'd—

Wait, she thought. I have seen them. And then, another realization, the kind of epiphany that makes sense to you at the instant it enters your mind, and then the mind cuts it apart with reasoning and common sense.

Justin's not here, thought Lucy. No, wait, that's not...that's not possible...no...right, it was in my head. Right...

Max found himself looking for a little girl, eight years old, but very mature for her age, whose identity he only realized near the end of...now that was interesting, near the end of what? A dream from the night before maybe, but...no, only a few minutes ago. Only a few minutes...seconds.

The guests beyond them were people she recognized. There were at least a hundred people gathered here in the enclosure, the seating extending all the way to the twin column marquee, decorated in white carnations and ivy that marked the end of the rest of the garden and the beginning of this hallowed property. The green leafy hedges that formed the oval border of the enclosure, when seen from above, opened up into an "eye" with the open-air gazebo at the center, refolded to their oval shape on the other side.

"Congratulations," said the minister, as the applause dropped off. "If you'll just step this way, we're ready to sign the marriage certificate."

"Of course," said Max, who looked at his bride and allowed her to walk ahead of him. Lucy nodded at her husband — her husband! — and walked toward the table.

***

298

About an hour later, the ceremony concluded, pictures taken, Max and Lucy took a break from the mingling and walked the grounds of the park. The sun was bright, but it was cool, perfect for a summer wedding day walking around in heavy tuxes and dresses. They now had about ten minutes to kill before making their way back to the limo to take them to the reception.

"I forget how we found this place," said Lucy. "Wasn't it a recommendation?"

"Yeah, I think Dad had told us about it," replied Max.

"Yeah," said Lucy. "The hall's all set up. I don't know about you, but I'm really looking forward to those hors d'oeuvres. I'm starving."

Max nodded. "Oh God, yes! I wish I'd smuggled a burger or something under this jacket."

Lucy looked down at his chest. "It's double-breasted, probably would have fit. Should have given it a shot."

"Like hell," replied Max. "This ain't a rental that I can grease up."

"Why? You planning on wearing it again?" Max took one look at that cute smile and had to kiss her on the forehead.

"Not likely."

They walked, arm-in-arm like some Victorian couple, through the hedge labyrinth. Most labyrinths are circular, but this one was a giant square, snaking its way at right angles around the rounded eye of the central gazebo. Max liked the feeling he got: the feeling of getting lost, all the while knowing that all roads would lead you home.

"You sure we'll be able to find our way back in all this?" asked Lucy, noticing that the top of the hedge stood an impressive three feet taller than Max.

"Of course, we just go back the way we came. Or we just keep going until we come to one of the main paths. It's simple."

"Not so simple," said Lucy. "I'm feeling really disoriented."

She stopped in mid-step. "Tell me, during the ceremony, did you feel—"

"Yeah," said Max, cutting her off. "I did...I still do."

Birds chirped around them as they stood, hand-in-hand.

"Do you think it really happened?" asked Lucy.

"It...it feels like it did," replied Max, "but it's probably something more...conventional than that. I mean, we must have read the manuscript at least a dozen times before I sent it off."

"But then, why would I have felt anything? The story was your idea."

"Not completely. You helped me with it for most of it."

"I did? When?"

"You don't remember? It was back when—"

Max stopped...and smiled. "Huh..." he said.

"What?"

"Nothing."

Silence. A few more moments of sun and birds. Even so, they both felt it: the covert presence of ninety-two shared worlds. Thirty thousand stars behind a blue sky.

"What do you think it means?" asked Max, finally breaking the silence.

"I don't know," said Lucy. "Maybe..." She looked at her dress, then her new husband's shoes, both now blemished with the odd blade of cut grass, at the hedge maze where they were never more than a hundred feet away from the gazebo where their guests now mingled with champagne and finger foods.

"Maybe it's the wrong question."

"Then what's the right question?" asked Max.

Lucy paused, enjoying the feel of a cool wind that had just kicked up, feeling the air flow through her hair, on her skin.

"We're here now," she said after a moment. "It's our wedding day. Tonight we have a great reception planned, and then we're catching a plane to Ireland. And a month from now, we'll come home, and I'll be starting the renos on the studio, and you'll be starting your book tour."

Max nodded. "Everything's starting out, after today. Everything we ever wanted."

"Exactly," said Lucy. "So...we're here now. And this...thing that we both experienced, whatever it was that came before, is behind us. So it doesn't matter to me what it actually was, or what it actually means. What do you want it to mean?"

Max and Lucy watched the wheels turning behind the eyes of the other, and without saying another word, kissed each other. They continued to walk the hedge maze in reverent silence, experiencing each arm-in-arm step, until they turned around the corner. Moments later, they would find the main path back to the gazebo. Shortly thereafter, they'd get into the back of the white limousine and drive away, leaving the park behind.

About 150 feet southwest of the southwest corner of the now empty hedge maze, a seagull — a rare sight this far away from the ocean — landed on the ground. The pink and coral brick work was hot on his feet, and so he hop-hop-hopped his way toward his quarry: a single grub worm that lay dying. Nipping it in his beak in a split second, the seagull took flight over the compass rose, which showed him to be flying east-northeast. Not that any human eyes were there to note the bearing and distance.

GOOD TWIN

Tommy's mind was a house divided against itself. Now he had a chance to fix the foundation, but just one. A lot of pressure for one simple message.

He stood in the rain at the stop, waiting for the bus. In the pre-dawn mist and wet, he could already see the headlights three stops down along the narrow inner city road. The buildings were almost uniformly black, scorched, and falling apart. Tommy was surprised at how the damage seemed to be symmetrical, but then he remembered himself.

This lifespace is part economic collapse, part personal disaster. You helped make it this way, Tommy.

No other riders were waiting with him. It was just Tommy, his umbrella, and his briefcase. Tommy Thrones. Success story of the family, now wandering the back alleys of an alternate universe.

The bus finally arrived, and as the door opened, Tommy took a breath. In his thirty-four years, he'd learned that the only anxiety before a big event was the waiting for it. Once you started moving, it was all old territory, familiar and fast.

The driver was overweight and bearded, a Middle Easterner of some kind. The look of surprise on his face almost made Tommy laugh out loud, but he couldn't blame the driver for wondering. After all, how many tall, healthy men in a suit with a trench coat and briefcase ever graced his route?

Tommy took out the change he'd brought for the fare and dropped it into the machine with a clatter.

"Transfer?" asked the driver in a heavy accent. This time, Tommy did let out a chuckle.

"Uh, no thanks," replied Tommy. "I'll have my own way home at the end."

The driver nodded, shifted the bus into gear as Tommy looked toward the back.

There, the only other person sitting on the bus, was his mark.

Tommy made his way over, swaying with the movement of the bus and grabbing hold of the handlebars as he sat down on the seat across the aisle.

The kid himself looked like ten miles of bad road, with ripped jeans, running shoes whose white had long since faded away to yellow, and an drab olive green jacket that looked like it had once belonged to an actual soldier. The kid's face was lean, almost gaunt, though that wasn't necessarily beyond the norm for a fifteen year old, and the black circles under his eyes showed him to be less an insomniac and more a junkie. He carried a journal and pencil, of all things, and was busy scribbling.

"Poetry," said Tommy. The kid looked up. Tommy smiled to see the naked shock and confusion on the kid's face, the recognition. He really had taken him by surprise.

"How...wha...what's going on?" the kid stammered.

"You know me, then?" said Tommy. The kid said nothing. The bus swayed again as Tommy got up and extended his right hand. "I am real."

The kid took Tommy's hand. A strange feeling, like shaking your own left hand with your right. Tommy believed in strong handshakes. So did the kid.

"Where did you come from?" asked the kid. "Am I tripping?"

"No, you're not tripping," said Tommy.

"Am I dreaming?"

Tommy's smile dimmed. That was the same question he'd asked himself for years. Even though intellectually he would get his answer, the feelings would contradict his reason, always. He could feel them now, bubbling up. He had to act before they—

"No, you're not dreaming," said Tommy, "though I get why you'd wonder that."

The kid frowned, looked around the bus as if for an answer, but Tommy knew he wouldn't find any by looking.

"I get it," continued Tommy, and drawing the kid's gaze back toward him, "because for the past…three years now, I think, I've had to ask myself the same question. At least, three years in my time. I have no idea how long you've been here. For the past three years, I've seen this place in my dreams. What I didn't know then, but just found out now, was just how real it all was and is."

The kid had been facing him head on for some time now. Then he looked down at Tommy's hands. "Your pinky finger's still there," he said. Tommy glanced at is hands, not sure which pinky the kid was referring to.

"That's right," said Tommy.

"So you can't be from the future," said the kid.

"Why?"

"Because…" The kid held up his own left hand. The pinky finger was half missing from the tip. "If I lost my pinky finger, you should have lost yours, too."

Smart kid. "That's only true if I was from your future, bud," said Tommy. "It's not that simple."

"So…if you're not from the future, where are you from? Who are you, then?"

Bubble-bubble. The confusion was starting to haze inside Tommy's mind, that same red haze he would get whenever he'd wake up from those intense dreams and not remember what they were all about.

Keep talking. That's the key. You've done this before, Tommy. Push through it, and it'll pass.

304

"I'm from a different space," said Tommy, "further ahead, but just off to the right of this one. One where I got to keep my pinky finger."

"And...and what do you want with me?"

Here goes.

"I have a chance of a lifetime for you, Thomas," he said. The kid stared at him.

"A chance for what?"

"To make everything right," said Tommy. "To go forward, backward, and sideways in time and space. To undo your regrets. To create justice where you were mistreated."

The kid never broke his gaze, and Tommy could see the wheels turning behind his eyes, the little specks of hope mixed with cynicism, experience, trauma...

Keep it together...he's going to say yes...He has to say yes...you've got this...

"I'm offering you a chance to thread some gold into the tapestry of the world," said Tommy. "But if you choose this, you have to choose it with your whole heart, because I'm only offering this once."

Tommy felt the back of his own neck moisten, and the red haze return.

"One decision can't change the world," said the kid.

"This one did, in my world," replied Tommy.

Hurry up, kid! Decide!

The kid mulled as the bus came to a stop. Two passengers got on, and still the kid stared forward as the bus started up again. If he didn't decide soon, Tommy was going to seize. This was what the after effects of the Convergence did to him, and once that happened, he would slip back to his lifespace, and that would be that. But he couldn't leave without knowing the kid's answer.

"It sounds...it sounds like something I'd want to do," said the kid finally. "But what do I have to give up to get it?"

Tommy waited a beat before answering, doing his best to hide the relief as he exhaled.

"Everything," said Tommy. "Once you commit, you cut the threads that keep you here. Permanently."

The kid looked him in the eye — brown eyes on identical brown eyes — and grinned a dangerous smile. "Never much cared about this shithole world, anyway. What do I have to do first?"

Tommy didn't smile back. The violence he'd seen in his younger Alternate's eyes unsettled him, for that was a quality he still possessed in small increments. Little tyrants. All of us have little tyrants inside us. But this kid had given the little tyrant in his mind control of the wheel, and once that happens, there's no going back. As much as Tommy knew the role his younger Alternate would play to save them all, he himself was lost, and could never come back.

"Tonight, take the subway's last run before curfew," said Tommy, "the 5 line all the way to the northern terminus. A Mr. Weaver will be waiting for you. Here."

Tommy put the briefcase on his lap and opened it up. Inside was a yellow manila envelope. He took it out and handed it to the kid. "This will explain the rest."

The kid spent a few seconds looking over the envelope. Tommy knew why: in this lifespace, in this part of the world, he bet the kid hadn't seen paper that bright or clean in a long, long time.

The violent gleam in the kid's eye remained, and as much as it made the hairs rise on the back of Tommy's neck, he knew he had succeeded. The red haze in his mind had fully dissolved. The bubbling sensation was also gone.

Mission accomplished.

"This is my stop," said Tommy, as the bus drew to a halt once more. He extended his hand to his younger Alternate. "Thomas Thrones, it's been a pleasure. Good luck."

The kid took his hand, shook tightly.

"Same to you, Thomas," he said, with a smile that didn't reach his eyes. "My gut tells me you never took Mom's name."

"Your gut would be correct."

The kid's mannequin smile never left his face. Neither did the rage in his eyes, even as he released his grip. "Lucky bastard."

Without another word, Tommy walked down the aisle and disembarked, back into the rain, beside an apartment building that looked identical to the one he'd seen when he was boarding.

He watched the bus start to move, caught young Thomas Thrones' gaze as he drove off. The kid didn't wave, nor did he break his stare until the bus took him down the street, and out of sight.

"Good job," said a voice. Tommy smiled.

He turned to face Mr. Weaver, dressed in the same worker's hat and coat as when he had first met him. Typical of his appearances, his coat was dry, and only now getting wet from the rain.

The two men shook hands. "Good to see you again, sir."

Weaver scoffed. "Don't call me that, son. By definition, I work for a living." He looked down at the bus while Tommy spoke to him.

"You know this is a paradox, right? I remember meeting you here, only I never met you here. I remember Dad being both a great father and a complete asshole to me. I remember dying on that mountain, but also…well, you get the idea."

"That's how it works, Thomas," said Weaver. "All you gotta do is know that when you head back home, your mind will be healed. This is the last time that the ripple effects will catch you, and so for you and me, this is goodbye. And it will have to be a quick one. You've only a minute left here."

At those words, Tommy actually felt great sadness enter his heart. It came upon him so suddenly, he now wondered if he would choke up on his next words.

"What about us? What do we do now?"

Weaver smiled. "You live. And more than that…you thrive."

The Convergence worker waited a beat and finally extended his hand one last time. Doing his best to keep composure, Tommy shook it warmly.

"Goodbye, Mr. Weaver, and thank you!"

"Goodbye, Tommy, and good luck!"

Weaver's face, his hand, the rain, and the ravaged city all swirled and dissolved around him in fast-moving increments. Shafts of light began to pierce pinpricks into the sky, and warm, salty air seemed to blow in from the heavens…

***

Tommy Sinclair woke up on the beach, cramped from the canvas chair. He was burned, but the sun was now starting to set, and they were calling him. No time to be groggy. The ripple effect dreams always took it out of him, and it was usually a minute or two before he felt grounded in his own lifespace once again.

"C'mon, Thomas," he heard his father say. "We're starting our walk."

Tommy looked over. Beyond the dune, he could see his Dad gesturing over at him as if he was still a boy. He smiled, and got to his feet. They wouldn't wait for long, especially not the grandparents.

308

2064

Three of them ran, side-by-side, along the shores of that distant beach, less the graceful walk that Justin had envisioned, and more the last leg of a great race. A mad dash, on a bet, to see who could make it to the finish line first. And everyone ran. Everyone but the elders, who, despite their remarkable health, had left their running days far behind them. They were bringing up the rear, watching the younger ones do their thing.

And as Lucy watched those younger ones kicking up the sand, there was no sense of dislocation or displacement, no surrealism. Just the moment. That was enough for her.

Max, too, felt himself grounded in the present. This was a real beach in the real world, solid, compliant with the laws of traditional physics. Only the magnificence of the late afternoon — warming the back of Max's wrinkled neck, blinding his eyes as the sun caught the silver hair of his lover and set it ablaze as it tossed and waved like a banner behind her as they watched the younger ones dashing ahead of them — shook Max's certainty that this was not another dream like the one he'd had decades ago.

Though Justin and Annabelle were obviously out of breath, neither one of them stopped running. Neither Lucy nor Max was surprised. They knew their son and daughter-in-law inside and out, but especially their son. Even now, in his fifties, there was a bet on, and pride was on the line.

"You're slowing down, darling!" called Annabelle as she got ahead of her husband. Justin laughed and nearly tripped trying to speed back up

"I'm letting you win! You could use the self-esteem!" he shouted back between gasps.

"Sure, that's the reason!" said Mindy, catching up to her brother and sister-in-law, then passing both of them.

Lucy and Max looked at each other. They'd both acquired a reputation for being silent types over the past few years, always watching the younger ones at family parties and holidays, never letting go of the other's hand while in the same room. What Max and Lucy never told anyone was that they had reached a deep level of understanding, the deepest, that was something like telepathy. Such was the destiny of all true soul mates, and it had all started on their wedding day, when both caught a sense that something greater had been at play behind the scenes.

And especially at moments like these, as they watched their family and thought on what they had achieved, it was hard to deny destiny's handiwork.

Lucy and Max watched Mindy, their little girl and prodigy, now all grown up and in fantastic health, taking the lead in the race to the dune. She had never found her soul mate, never had any serious boyfriends, had never had children, and that was all right. It wasn't everyone's destiny, and there was so much time left for her.

Besides, running one whole branch of the Project was commitment enough for Mindy. Both Mom and Dad understood that perfectly.

"You're getting weak, old man!"

Tommy caught up with his father, clapped him on the shoulder. Justin muttered something that neither Max nor Lucy could hear at this distance. Annabelle laughed and covered her mouth with her hand in apparent shock.

"That's okay, Mom, that's just another new way of saying how much he loves me." Tommy reached over and kissed Justin's forehead, who swatted him out of the way and started a slow jog. Tommy and Annabelle followed suit as they tried to catch up with Mindy.

Max and Lucy looked at each other, feeling the energy. Real joy was contagious, magnetic, powerful in its lightness, and oddly quiet.

The two lovers noticed every detail: the sand under their bare soles. The sharp azure and cerulean dance of the summer sky washed out by the fierce glare. Familiar hands in each other's palms, familiar pressure of squeezing fingers. Flashes of smiling teeth catching the light.

Both wished they could still run. Real joy is also a powerful fuel. You can't sit still. You have to use it, have to let it carry you. Surrender's your only option. If you're able, it'll make you run, and keep running.

The finish line of this friendly race was a point along the shore where the sandy beach ended at some stone outcroppings. Mindy was just about there. Beyond it was a part of this stretch the family hadn't explored before. It felt like one of those dreams in which you're headed home, you know it's almost time, but you wake up before you can get to it. They would get there, though. Under the right circumstances, real life is better than any dream.

In their years as lovers and as parents, there had been moments, every now and then. Moments of déjà vu. Moments in which Max and Lucy stopped where they were, looked at their children — at Mindy's silent authority, at Justin's intellectual prowess — and wondered where they had seen it before. During those moments, they would find themselves irresistibly drawn to a memory of something that had lasted only milliseconds, that had begun and ended with the kiss on their wedding day.

Sometimes, Mom and Dad would share that moment together. Then, as now, they would look at their children, then look at each other, and for those seconds of silent gazes, they knew, as Shakespeare had written, the difference between a hawk and a handsaw. They knew what had been real.

Max knew it every time Mindy rubbed noses with him as a girl. Lucy knew it each time Justin had stood on his soapbox to explain something he'd learned in school. She knew that a phenomenon and an adventure that both thought had been at worst a reaction to the stress of getting married, at best a psychic connection between them, had indeed been real in the physical universe.

Then, as with any feeling of déjà vu, it would be over, and Mom and Dad would both wonder what it was that had stopped them in their tracks, so suddenly.

The Great Project they had created wouldn't have worked without Justin and Mindy being exactly as they were, and after all the good they had done in the world, it was only fitting that Tommy, still in his prime, took over the reins after this trip was done. Despite the ups and downs the planet had endured, it wasn't quite saved yet, and it deserved saving. The Sinclairs weren't alone in that crusade, but they were definitely in the lead, giving more fuel to Max and Lucy's subtle belief in the powers of destiny. This was the reason, in the grand scheme, why they had been brought together in this life.

"C'mon, guys! We're waiting for you!"

Mindy technically crossed the finish line first, but it didn't matter. By the time Max and Lucy joined the rest, they'd all forgotten about the bet altogether. Taking a look around at each of their faces, Max and Lucy took in the moment. They were an extraordinary family to the rest of the world, but they were family. They took in the moment as best they could, and then, before too long, it was time to go.

"All right," said Max. "Let's find out what's around the corner. You ready, sweetheart?"

Lucy leaned over and kissed him in the sun. "You know it, darling."

The Family Sinclair left the familiar part of the shore and wandered into unexplored territory, not for the first time in this life, and certainly not for the last.

THE END

312

ABOUT THE AUTHOR

Jody Aberdeen is a writer, actor, and coach in training living in the Greater Toronto Area.

Jody attended McMaster University where he earned a Combined Honors B.A. in History and English, and also served as President of the local chapter of Phi Delta Theta Fraternity. He was also a regular op/ed contributor to the *McMaster Silhouette* newspaper, and now blogs on *Peevish Penman*, Amy Sky's *Alive and Awake*, and other sites.

Jody helps to run the Toronto Wordslingers, a boutique guild of independent authors working towards turning their passion into a career. He is currently working on a new sci-fi adventure, *Overlife*, due to be completed and published in 2013.

In addition to writing, Jody is also an actor for film and TV, currently apprenticing for ACTRA, with credits in U.S and Canadian film, television, and Internet markets.

He is also training to be certified as a life coach and consultant with a special focus on helping amateur artists overcome the personal hurdles towards creating a career doing what they love most.

You can reach Jody via his website at jodyaberdeen.com or follow him on Wordpress, Twitter, and Facebook. Visit the Toronto Wordslingers at www.torontowordslingers.com to learn about our other authors.

(Photo Credit: Ryan Fisher, Rainyfresh Pictures)

Hillsview Active Living Centre